Romantic Suspense

Danger. Passion. Drama.

K-9 Ranch Protection
Darlene L. Turner

Guarded By The Marshal
Sharee Stover

MILLS & BOON

K-9 RANCH PROTECTION
© 2024 by Darlene L. Turner
Philippine Copyright 2024
Australian Copyright 2024
New Zealand Copyright 2024

First Published 2023
First Australian Paperback Edition 2023
ISBN 978 1 038 92174 1

GUARDED BY THE MARSHAL
© 2024 by Sharee Stover
Philippine Copyright 2024
Australian Copyright 2024
New Zealand Copyright 2024

First Published 2024
First Australian Paperback Edition 2024
ISBN 978 1 038 92174 1

MIX
Paper | Supporting
responsible forestry
FSC® C001695

Published by
Harlequin Mills & Boon
An imprint of Harlequin Enterprises (Australia) Pty Limited
(ABN 47 001 180 918), a subsidiary of HarperCollins
Publishers Australia Pty Limited
(ABN 36 009 913 517)
Level 19, 201 Elizabeth Street
SYDNEY NSW 2000 AUSTRALIA

Cover art used by arrangement with Harlequin Books S.A.. All rights reserved.

Printed and bound in Australia by McPherson's Printing Group

K-9 Ranch Protection

Darlene L. Turner

MILLS & BOON

Darlene L. Turner is an award-winning author who lives with her husband, Jeff, in Ontario, Canada. Her love of suspense began when she read her first Nancy Drew book. She's turned that passion into her writing and believes readers will be captured by her plots, inspired by her strong characters and moved by her inspirational message. Visit Darlene at www.darlenelturner.com, where there's suspense beyond borders.

Visit the Author Profile page
at millsandboon.com.au for more titles.

A man's heart deviseth his way:
but the Lord directeth his steps.
—*Proverbs* 16:9

DEDICATION

For Helen, Melanie and Sara
You have blessed my life.

ACKNOWLEDGMENTS

To my hubby: Jeff, thank you for putting up with my overactive writer imagination. I'm thankful that you get me. I love you.

To Valerie Beaman Miller: Thank you so much for letting me use Névé (and her name!) as the inspiration for my Alaskan malamute and for answering my questions. Anything I embellished for fiction is totally on me.

To my editor, Tina James, and my agent, Tamela Hancock Murray: You are both amazing and I'm thankful for your continual guidance.

To Sara Davison, Helen St. Martin and Melanie Stevenson: We've nicknamed ourselves the "Fab Four" as a joke, but I'm SO thankful God put us together. We fit perfectly.

Jesus: Thank You for always guiding my path. You've got me!

Chapter One

The computer screen flashed white and turned black. Constable Isabelle Tremblay's hand flew away from the keyboard and the hairs on her nape prickled. She glanced around the Harturn River Police Department's bullpen. All the monitors had gone dark. *Not good.* She shoved her office chair back and spun to her coworker. "What's happening?"

Before he could respond, menacing laughter exploded through their system, and a skull appeared on all screens. A message in bold red letters displayed beneath the frightening image.

IZZY, BACK OFF OR DIE.

A collective gasp filled the room.

Izzy bolted to her feet. She caught the meaning behind the message, and it confirmed her suspicions. Chief Constable Justin Tremblay's death wasn't from a heart attack.

Her father was murdered.

As quickly as the screens had flickered, they returned to normal. How had someone infiltrated HRPD's secure computer system? Their IT department was the best of the best. Plus she completed a double check recently of their firewalls. Her cyber knowledge verified they were impenetrable.

Or, at least, she thought so.

"Tremblay, my office. Now!" The voice of newly appointed Chief Constable Eric Halt boomed from the hallway.

"You're in trouble now," Constable Fisher said. "Did you click on something?"

She raised her hands. "No, I was just about to shut down for the day."

The older male constable clucked his tongue. "Well, I'm guessing from that message you're still secretly investigating your dad's death. You need to let sleeping dogs lie."

"I can't." Izzy shuffled through the hallway as her cell phone buzzed in her vest pocket. She ignored it and knocked on Chief Constable Halt's door.

"Enter."

Izzy inhaled and stepped into the office. "You wanted to see me?"

The chief lifted his index finger. "Thanks for the update. Make sure we're locked down. We can't let this happen again." He slammed the receiver back into the cradle and gestured toward the chair in front of his desk. "Sit."

Definitely not good. She obeyed.

Halt peeked over his reading glasses, eyes glaring. "Didn't I tell you to drop your investigation? This message tells me you didn't listen."

"Sir, I haven't used our department resources and have only investigated on my own time." She leaned forward. "Plus this message tells me I'm on the right track. Dad was murdered."

The man's eyes softened. "Listen, I'm really sorry about your father's death, but nothing suspicious materialized. He had a heart attack while driving and crashed. End of story."

Izzy was tired of hearing that lie. Even her own mother told her to back off, but Izzy couldn't. "He just had his annual physical and was in perfect health."

Halt drummed his fingers on his desktop.

"Well, he was under a lot of stress the past couple of months. That may have triggered the attack."

Izzy shook her head. "It didn't. I figured out from his journal notes he was investigating some sort of drug cartel. Do you know anything about that?"

The chief constable stopped drumming his fingers. "No. What else did you find?"

"The rest of his notes are in code. That's what I'm trying to ascertain."

"Odd." He pointed to his phone. "Well, IT informed me that someone clicked on a link included in a fake company email sent to all of us. Whoever sent it is good. The bogus link unleashed a virus. Did you?"

What? "No. That email came in just as I was shutting down to leave for the day."

He crossed his arms. "Well, IT narrowed it down to your computer. Are you absolutely sure? Don't lie to me."

She popped to her feet. "I. Did. Not. You know I have—"

"I know. I know. Your partner told me about your memory. Must be nice to never forget anything." He tapped his thumb on the desk. "I'll get IT to investigate further. We need to determine where the virus came from and if it has compromised our system." He placed his hand on the phone. "Dismissed."

Izzy left the office, his words lingering in her mind.

Must be nice to never forget anything.

Some days Izzy wanted to forget. However, her hyperthymesia prevented her wish from becoming a reality. Having a perfect memory had certainly given her an edge when solving cases in her hometown of Harturn River, British Columbia, but it had also been the brunt of continuous jokes throughout her life. To where she tried to keep her condition a secret. Until her ex-partner, Austin Murray, convinced her to use her detailed memories to their advantage.

Her cell phone buzzed again, thrusting her out of thoughts of the past—and Austin—the man she *had* tried hard to forget. Unsuccessfully.

She fished out her device and swiped the screen.

Sims. Her father's confidential informant.

Figured out the cipher.

Izzy sucked in a breath. Sims came through. Now she'd be able to read her father's final encoded entries in his journal. Perhaps his notes would lead her to his killer.

Good. Off shift. Where can we meet?

Three dots bounced on her screen as she waited for his answer.

1 hour behind Chuckie's Bar and Grill. Bring the journal.

Izzy tapped in her last message.

See you soon.

She hurried back to her desk, gathered her belongings and snatched her winter coat from the back of the chair before leaving the police station.

A brisk wind slapped her in the face, chilling her instantly. She wiggled into her coat and zipped it all the way to her neck before putting on her gloves. She underestimated the expected change in weather. The temperature fell, meeting the meteorologist's forecast of a cold snap in February in British Columbia.

She jogged to her vehicle and pressed her key fob to unlock the door. A piece of paper stuck under her windshield wiper caught her attention. A wind gust flipped the top half over, revealing a message.

We're watching.

She bristled and peered around the lit parking lot. Nothing suspicious materialized. Izzy lifted the wiper and removed the note. Only the simple two-word message appeared on the paper.

However, the underlying threat seeped off the page. Whoever hacked into their police system wanted to ensure she understood their order to stay away.

But *they* underestimated the Tremblay determination flowing through her veins. The threat only escalated her resolve to find her father's killer. Izzy suppressed the trepidation threatening to overpower her thoughts, shoved the note in her purse and climbed into her SUV. *I'll find your murderer, Dad, if it's the last thing I do.*

Forty minutes later at her house, Izzy finished scanning the last pages of her father's journal. She would not risk losing any valuable information if something happened to the book. Especially now that she was close to deciphering its contents. Her father must have suspected the threat on his life as he'd mailed the journal to her condo's address the day before his death. Because of this, she was positive it contained valuable information that would uncover his killer and what he'd been working on. Izzy yanked the thumb drive from her laptop as her eyes shifted to the brown journal sitting on her desk. A thought tumbled into her mind.

Keep the two separate.

But where should she hide the drive?

She spotted her father's box of items from the police station, and an idea formed. Izzy took out his favorite coin from its pouch and dropped in the drive. She wouldn't hide it inside her condo because that's the first place anyone would search. Izzy put on her jacket and placed the journal in her purse. She stuffed the thumb drive in one coat pocket and her bear spray in the other. Being off duty meant she had to leave her weapon behind, but the repellant would at least give her some type of protection. Izzy snatched her key fob and raced outside to hide the drive in her favorite spot in her backyard. Somewhere no one would think to look.

She turned into the darkened alleyway and parked her SUV beside a dumpster fifteen minutes later. Before exiting to meet Sims, she punched in her partner's personal cell phone number and waited.

"Hey, Izzy, what's up?" Constable Douglas Carver asked.

The man's experience had impressed her throughout the past few years, and she needed his advice. Plus his fatherly demeanor comforted her after her own father's death. "Doug, I have a lead on the cipher to decode Dad's notes. I'm about to meet with Sims but wanted to see if you could come too. I need your help."

"I'm in a meeting with Austin Murray going through pictures of his dogs. Halt tasked me with buying one for the K-9 unit. Where are you?" The concern in his voice filtered through the phone.

Izzy stiffened at the mention of her ex-partner's name. Austin Murray's failure to act at a crime scene had robbed their police station of Sergeant Clara Jenkins—Izzy's best friend and mentor. Clara died that night from a gunshot wound to the chest. Ten years had passed since Austin quit the force, and Izzy had stayed away from the man, even with Harturn River's small population of thirty-five thousand. Izzy had secretly fallen for her partner, but the pain of losing Clara caused Izzy to suppress her true feelings for the man.

She was aware of his K-9 ranch which also included horses, cattle, and other farm animals, but had purposely avoided going there. She bit her lip. "I'm behind Chuckie's Bar and Grill about to talk to Sims. How much longer will you be?"

"Izzy, what's going on? I can hear the concern in your voice."

She explained the events of the past hour, including the note on her windshield. "Sorry I didn't contact you earlier. There wasn't time. I could use your years of expertise. And backup, of course."

"Are you calling me old?" His teasing tone made her smile.

"Never."

"On my way. Don't do anything stupid." He clicked off.

A door slammed nearby, startling Izzy. She turned and spied Sims lighting a cigarette beside the bar's back entrance. She studied the surroundings before hustling to his side.

The informant puffed out a cloud of smoke. "'Bout time you got here. You bring the journal?"

She patted her purse. "Yup. Where's the cipher?"

He tapped his temple. "In here."

Izzy gritted her teeth. How had her father put up with this man? His cocky attitude had annoyed her over the last week. She found Sims's number hidden under the inside tab of the journal's cover. Her father had spoken of the man often and how he'd helped him put away many criminals, so she called Sims. Right away, he agreed with her suspicions of foul play in her father's death. "Sims, please tell me what you discovered."

He took one more drag of his cigarette before dropping the butt to the ground and stepping on any remaining embers. "It's really quite simple. Your dad always loved his books. He used the book cipher. Show me the journal."

Izzy withdrew the book and opened to a page containing her father's cryptic notes of numbers. "There's a number at the top that doesn't seem to follow the same sequence as the others."

"Interesting." Sims pointed. "I believe these numbers mean the page, line and word needed to decipher the message. You just have to figure out which book and edition he used."

Izzy palm-slapped her forehead. "Of course. Why hadn't I thought of that? How did you figure it out?"

"I remembered something he said to me the day before he died. He said he loved the way Sherlock used a book cipher in one of his novels."

"Right. *The Valley of Fear.* It was Dad's favorite." She latched on to Sims's arm. "Wait, do you think he used that book for the cipher?"

He shook his head. "Doubtful. Too easy. Since he sent the journal to you, it's a book only you would guess."

"Right." Izzy's memory pictured every book on her shelves, but nothing stood out.

"Don't limit it to your current bookshelf. Go way back, it could—"

A shot pierced the frosty night.

Sims dropped.

"No!" Izzy fell to her knees and placed two fingers on his neck. No pulse. She hung her head. The man was gone.

Movement rustled behind her.

She jumped upright and pulled out her bear spray, still clutching the journal.

"Don't even think about it," a sinister voice said. "I have a Glock pointed at you. Drop the can and turn around slowly."

Bear spray couldn't outrun a bullet. Izzy obeyed and turned to face her attacker.

The man stood away from the bar's back entrance light, concealing his identity. However, something about his voice triggered a memory. A meeting at HRPD's station behind closed doors six months ago. She had caught a portion of the conversation as she left the building. The angry words surfaced in her memory. Even though the speaker had lowered his tone, she didn't miss the whispered words.

He can't find out.

The sentence returned, but she couldn't assign the voice to a name. Had the person lowered their pitch tonight to disguise themselves?

"Toss the journal on the ground and kick it to me."

A phrase her father used to say came to mind.

Izzy always give an assailant what they ask for. Your life isn't worth it.

Besides, she had scanned the contents. She did as the attacker commanded.

"Now the drive."

She chewed on the inside of her mouth, contemplating how they acquired that information. "What drive?" She had to stall for time. *Doug, where are you?*

"Don't play coy. You're your father's daughter. Of course you made a copy."

"Did you kill my father?" She held her breath in anticipation of the man's answer.

"Give us the drive. Now!"

"Who's us?" she asked.

Rough hands grabbed her from behind and spun her around. "Me." He punched her in the face. "Tell us, or you'll get a worse beating."

She stumbled backward, her hand flying to her nose to ward off the sting. Blood oozed between her fingers. "I—I—don't know—"

Her father's words returned, but she ignored them. She couldn't lose the drive too.

The man raised his cell phone, showing her a picture of the texts Izzy and Sims had exchanged earlier. "We know you did as we've been watching." He raised his opposite fist to give her another blow.

This time, she blocked the punch.

His phone fell to the snowy pavement, but he stood his ground.

She stared into his face. A face her perfect memory would remember if she lived through the attack.

Pounding footsteps echoed in the alley.

She pivoted.

A blunt object came down hard on her head from behind. She spun and caught a reflection in the window of someone witnessing the exchange. Someone she didn't expect to see. *No!* Spots exploded and her knees buckled.

Her attackers fled into the shadows.

"Izzy!"

Her name registered, and she turned toward the voice as her vision faded.

A face passed under the light.

Austin?

Pain splintered in her head moments before her world went dark.

Austin Murray fell to his knees in front of his ex-partner, checking for a pulse. *Please, God. Help her be okay.* Steady. *Thank You.* "Doug, her vitals are strong."

Doug squatted in front of the man and drew in an audible breath. "This is Sims, her father's CI." He placed his fingers on the man's neck. "He's gone. Gunshot wound to the forehead." Doug withdrew his cell phone and stood. "I'll call it in." He stepped toward the bar's back door, requesting emergency services.

Austin examined Izzy's face. Blood dripped from her swollen nose, but a punch probably wouldn't have knocked her out. He gently turned her head and ran his fingers along her neck in search of a second wound. His fingers stopped at a bump forming at the back of her head. Austin fisted his hands, heat flushing his cheeks. Someone had beaten her up, but why?

You didn't make it here in time. He had failed her.

Again.

His mistake ten years ago had not only caused her to pull away, but was the reason he left the force to work on his father's ranch. He couldn't face the harm he'd inflicted. He'd frozen during a call that cost the life of Sergeant Clara Jenkins—Izzy's best friend.

An object to the right caught his attention, bringing him out of the past. He pushed himself upright and leaned down for a better look.

A cell phone lay face up with the cracked screen illuminated, revealing a conversation between Izzy and what Austin guessed was the CI named Sims.

Doug returned. "Paramedics and officers are on the way."

Austin pointed. "This must be Izzy's phone."

The older constable shook his head. "Nope. Hers has a bright pink cover on it."

Pink. Her favorite color.

"Sims, perhaps?" Austin asked.

Doug adjusted his winter gloves and moved to the CI's body. He patted the man's pocket, then took out a phone. "Nope. His is here."

"Odd. Maybe one of the attackers?" Austin reached for the cell phone, but snapped his hand back. *Don't contaminate the scene.* "Do you have an evidence bag on you?"

Doug extracted one from his winter jacket. "Of course. A cop's habit." He squatted in front of the phone, leaning closer. "Wait, these texts are between Izzy and Sims. How did the attacker get them?"

"Didn't you say someone hacked into HRPD's system earlier? Perhaps they got into Izzy's phone too."

Sirens blared nearby.

"Yes, and she also mentioned someone left her a note on her SUV's windshield stating they were watching." Doug read the screen before snapping a picture. He dropped the phone into a bag and placed it back on the ground. "Don't want it to get wet with the snow. The crime scene unit will want to see everything where it was. They'll then take it to our digital forensics team." He circled the area where Izzy had fallen, studying around her body.

"What are you looking for?" Austin asked.

"Did you see her father's journal? That's what Sims is referring to in the text. He was helping her with a cipher."

"I didn't see it when I arrived." Austin's gaze flicked back at Izzy, emotions bubbling inside. They had been partners for two years and had bonded to the point where he had strong feelings for her. Feelings he'd never acted upon since they worked together. Seeing her unconscious with a bloody nose heightened his desire to protect her. "Who could have done this? Who's watching her? Maybe her attackers took it. I realize I'm not a cop any longer, but can you give me a hint of what she was investigating?"

Doug placed his hands on his hips. "Can't you guess? Against Chief Constable Halt's advice, she's been looking into her father's death on her own time."

Austin had attended Chief Constable Justin Tremblay's funeral, but kept his distance as much as possible. He only offered Izzy and her family brief condolences before leaving the church. "But didn't he die in a crash caused by a heart attack?"

Doug nodded. "His wife, Rebecca, was in the car. She said he cried out before clutching his chest. The car veered toward the ditch and she failed to stop the crash. Fortunately, she only had minor injuries."

"So why was Izzy investigating his death?" Austin trusted Izzy's instincts and perfect memory, so she must have had a reason to doubt the findings.

Doug knelt beside his partner and shook her. "Come on, Izzy, wake up." He turned back to Austin. "She claims her father just received a perfect bill of health after his annual physical. She spieled off everything her father had told her about his doctor's visit. You know her memory."

Austin didn't miss the concern in the older man's eyes. "You're close to her, aren't you?"

Sirens intensified, and the flashing lights lit up the dark alley.

"Yes." Doug brushed a lock of Izzy's brown hair from her forehead. "I took her under my wing after—"

"After I screwed up."

The ambulance pulled into the alleyway, followed by a police cruiser and forensics van.

Doug stood. "I wouldn't put it like that. We all make mistakes, son."

"Well, mine cost Izzy's friend her life." Austin would never forget the look on Izzy's face from that night. Her pained expression revealed a mixture of anger and surprise, speaking volumes.

She had blamed him.

Doug grazed Austin's arm. "She eventually forgave you."

Austin highly doubted it. How could she when he still struggled with the guilt?

Voices jarred him from the past.

Two paramedics and multiple officers filled the area.

The bar's back door opened and screeching loud music filtered into the alleyway. A man emerged. "What's going on here?"

Doug approached. "Sir, stay back. Police need to cordon off the crime scene."

The burly man's eyes widened in the bar's back light. "Crime scene?"

"Didn't you hear the shot?" Austin asked.

He gestured through the open door. "With all the loud music? I saw the flashing lights from the front entrance."

One paramedic squatted in front of Izzy. The other checked Sims's pulse and shook his head.

"Get back inside, but don't leave the premises." Doug turned to an approaching officer. "Constable Fisher, can you escort this man back into the bar and question him?"

The constable eyed Izzy. "Is she gonna be okay?"

"Paramedics are checking her now," Doug said. "Go inside."

Austin relocated to Izzy's side. "She took a blow to the back of her head. I felt a goose egg."

The paramedic nodded. "Good to know. Doctors will check her for a concussion." He turned to his partner. "Vitals are strong. Let's get her to Harturn General."

"Can I come with you?" Austin suddenly felt the need to be by her side. Whoever had attacked her could still be watching.

"Are you related?"

Austin suppressed a sigh. "No, but—"

"I can vouch for him." Doug removed his cell phone. "I'll get her mother to meet you at the hospital. I have to finish up here. Let Austin go with her. I want someone she knows by her side in case she wakes up in the ambulance. I'll get Halt to send a constable to protect Izzy. Someone has obviously targeted her."

Thirty minutes later Austin paced outside the emergency room's doors. Since he wasn't family, they wouldn't let him inside, but her mother and sister arrived fifteen minutes ago. He had asked one of them to update him, but Rebecca

Tremblay's curt greeting didn't give him much hope of that happening.

But he couldn't leave without knowing Izzy was okay.

Austin plunked himself into a chair, leaning forward on his knees. *Lord, please help Izzy be okay and protect her from whoever is after her. I want to help. No, I need to help. I believe You've brought her back into my life for a reason. Show me what that is.*

Austin's cell phone buzzed. He dug it out from his pocket and checked the screen. His ranch foreman. Austin was supposed to call him an hour ago. "Sawyer, I'm so sorry I didn't call. I'm at the hospital."

"What? Are you okay?" he asked.

"It's not me. It's Izzy. She's been hurt, and I was with her partner when she called him." Austin recounted to his ranch foreman and best friend, Sawyer King, what happened. "I'm waiting to get an update on her condition. I'm worried, bud. Someone is targeting her. She needs protection."

"The police will help her. You're not part of the force any longer, bro."

A young boy and a woman shuffled into the

packed emergency waiting room. The boy held a washcloth over his nose.

Austin stood and pointed to his chair. "You can sit here."

The woman nodded and smiled. "Thanks."

The emergency room doors opened and Izzy's sister, Blaire, gestured for Austin to come.

"Sawyer, I gotta run. I'll be back as soon as I can. Can you feed the dogs?" Austin hated when he had to miss their feeding frenzy. It always made him smile.

"Of course. I'll pray for Izzy." He clicked off.

Austin shoved the phone back into his pocket and followed Blaire. "What's going on? Is your mother aware you're bringing me in?"

Izzy's younger sister turned. "Doesn't matter what she thinks. Izzy is awake and is asking for you."

Austin's jaw dropped. "She is?"

"Yes. She said she saw your face in a dream."

What? "A dream?"

"The constable outside the door said you were at the crime scene, so perhaps she saw you before she passed out?" Blaire stopped and turned. "Mom is quite upset, of course, with Dad just passing. Please be sensitive. She's in a foul mood."

"I understand."

She continued down the hallway.

A hooded man talking on a cell phone with his head down whisked by Austin, knocking into his shoulder. He glanced up. "Watch where you're going, man."

Austin raised his hands. "Perhaps you should listen to your own advice."

"Whatever." He cussed and continued down the hall. "Quit worrying. I took care of him. She's here and I'll get it out of her. I promise."

Austin didn't care for the man's menacing tone. Coincidence?

"You coming?" Blaire asked.

He shook off the thought and followed. *You're too jumpy*.

They walked into Izzy's room.

Blaire gestured toward him. "I found Austin."

Izzy's eyes widened. "Hey, you."

Austin hurried to her side and took her hand in his. "You okay? I was so worried when I found you unconscious in the alley."

"The alley?"

"You don't remember?" Odd. She never forgot anything.

"I. Don't. Know." Izzy rubbed her temples.

"Something's wrong with me. This has never happened before."

"What was the last thing you remember?" he asked.

She looked around the room. "A virus got into our system before my shift ended."

Austin checked his watch. He knew their shift times. "Izzy, that was three hours ago. You're telling me you don't remember going to meet Sims at the back of Chuckie's Bar and Grill?"

She bit her lip as tears trickled down her cheeks. "No."

Rebecca Tremblay caught hold of Austin's arm. "Please tell us what's going on. The constable wouldn't divulge anything, and now I can't find him."

"Wait, Doug said they would send someone to protect her." Austin rushed back through the doorway, glancing left, then right.

The corridor was empty.

I took care of him.

Was the man referring to the constable?

Izzy was still in danger.

And it was up to Austin to protect her.

Chapter Two

Izzy didn't miss Austin's right brow rise in bewilderment. She remembered that trait from when they were partners. He had left the room abruptly, then returned with a haunted expression. "What is it, Austin?"

He looked at Izzy's mother, then back. "You're in danger."

Her head pounded not only from the goose egg, but from the confusion rolling around her brain. "What makes you say that? You're scaring me."

"You really don't remember?"

Frustration tightened her chest. Missing a period of her memory had never happened to her before, and she didn't like it. It was as if a piece of her had vanished. "I don't. Tell me."

Austin moved closer to her bed. "You called Doug while I was meeting with him about my K-9 dogs. You asked him to meet you behind

Chuckie's Bar and Grill and said your CI found the cipher to your father's notes. Doug was concerned, and I went with him to help. When we arrived, we found Sims with a GSW to the forehead and you were unconscious."

Panic elevated her heartbeat, increasing the beeping coming from the monitor beside her. "I don't remember any of that."

Izzy's mother rubbed her arm. "Austin, you need to leave. You're raising her blood pressure."

"Mom, this proves to me that Dad didn't die by accident. Someone targeted him." Izzy focused on Austin. "What else do you know? Where's Doug? Is he okay?"

"He's fine and still at the scene. We found a phone beside you that displayed the texts between you and Sims. Somehow, your attacker hacked into your phone and got the information. They ambushed you and shot Sims." He pointed to her purse sitting on the rolling table. "Listen, is your father's journal in your bag?"

She reached her hand out. "Pass it to me."

"Sister, you need to rest," Blaire said. "This is too much. The doctor said you have a concussion."

"I need to know, Blaire."

Austin passed her the purse.

She opened it and rummaged through it. "It's not here. Neither is my phone."

Austin shifted his stance. "Doug removed your phone from the outside pocket since we're pretty sure someone hacked it. He was taking it to digital forensics."

"Makes sense." Izzy took out a piece of paper. "What's this?" She unfolded it and bold letters screamed at her.

We're watching.

"That's the note you told Doug was under your windshield wiper when you left the station." Austin turned to Izzy's mother. "Mrs. Tremblay, we need to get her somewhere safe."

Her mother placed her hands on her hips. "What makes you so sure she's not safe here?"

"Because I heard an odd conversation from a man in the hallway stating 'he'd get it out of her.'"

"That may mean nothing," Blaire said.

"Yes, it could, but he also said 'he took care of him.'" Austin air-quoted the words *took care of him*. "And now, I can't find the constable I'd seen come into the hospital. He rushed through the emergency doors after flashing his badge."

"I spoke to him earlier." Rebecca Tremblay tapped her manicured nails on her chin. "I thought he just went to the bathroom."

Izzy sat up and swung her legs over the edge of the bed, waiting for the sudden wave of dizziness to subside. "I have to get out of here."

Her mother darted to her side. "Izzy, you need to be in the hospital."

Izzy struggled to contain her emotions. "Mom, you don't get it. Whoever killed Dad is now after me. I need to leave."

Blaire snatched Izzy's bag of clothes from the chair. "Are you coming home with us?"

"I can't. That will only put you in more danger. I can't go to my condo either." She directed her attention to Austin. "Ideas?"

"You're asking him? Do you remember what happened ten years ago? We don't even know if the conversation he heard was about you." Her mother's angered questions blared in the small room.

"Mom. Stop. I trust his instincts." She stood but swayed.

Austin wrapped his arm around her waist. "Come to my ranch. These people don't know me. You'll be safe there."

His nearness brought back the feelings she had suppressed over the past ten years. Feelings she had never admitted to him—or even herself. She had cared deeply for Austin, but refused to act on her emotions because of their working relationship. She hadn't wanted to put anyone in jeopardy.

And now…her ex-boyfriend Dax's obsessiveness had deterred her from getting into any relationship with a man. Her heart couldn't take it.

However, Austin's solution would put him back into her life. Could she handle being so close to him again? Sure, she had forgiven him for Clara's death, but still didn't know why he froze that day. He had kept that piece of information to himself. Why?

She swallowed the thickening in her throat, yanking herself from the past. She had to concentrate on the here and now.

And finding her father's killer. For all of their sakes.

"Yes, that makes sense." Izzy took her bag of clothes from her sister. "Mom. Blaire. You can't tell anyone where I'm going. Got it?"

They nodded.

Izzy read the angst in their contorted expressions. "It will be okay. We'll get through this." She brought them both into a group embrace. "I'll keep in constant touch, but I need to figure out what happened in the past three hours. Something tells me my locked memories hold the answers to Dad's killer. I just have to un-lock them."

After picking up a new cell phone and clothes at a local store, Izzy massaged her temples as Austin drove through the log gate of Murray K-9 Ranch. Izzy had called Doug, requesting he meet them at Austin's home. She wanted to find out more of what happened at the crime scene. Austin had shared everything he saw, but Izzy's three-hour black hole remained closed.

The doctor hadn't liked her demand to leave the hospital, but once she explained the danger to herself and his staff, he relented. Her head scan revealed only a mild concussion, and her symptoms had lessened, so he gave her instruc-tions to stay awake for a few hours and have those around her monitor her before sleeping. Austin had reassured the doctor he had a former military medic on his grounds, and he'd have him ensure she was okay.

Izzy observed the log ranch house in the dis-tance as they drove down the long driveway. Even in late evening, the well-lit home revealed its beauty. She had visited the ranch many times before that devastating event ten years ago. She could rhyme off every detail in each building.

So, why couldn't she remember the missing three hours? The doctor had explained it may have been the blow to the head, or the trauma of the event, or a combination of both. Izzy guessed the latter.

Snow blanketed the grounds, generating a peaceful atmosphere. Ranch hands walked horses into the stable to the left of the main house. Another stable containing cattle and other animals was nestled on the north side of the property. A building to the right wasn't in her memory bank. "What's over there?"

"My K-9 kennels and training facility." Austin hit a button and the middle garage door opened. "That's right. I added to the buildings after I left the force."

"How many dogs do you have here?"

He parked and switched off the engine. "Right now, we have eleven, including my favorite dog, Névé. Her name means snow in Latin." Barking came from within the ranch house. "Speaking of her. She lives in the house and has a special place in my heart. I bonded with her after finding the pup abandoned on my property four years ago. We've been inseparable ever since. The rest are in the kennels. Are you okay with dogs?"

"Of course."

"Awesome. You'll fit in nicely then. Let's get you settled inside. Doug should be here any moment." Austin exited his F150 truck.

Izzy followed just as the door leading into the ranch house opened and a slender, muscular male stepped inside the garage.

A dog bounded around the man, then ran toward Austin, barking.

"Hey, baby girl." Austin squatted and the K-9 snuggled close, licking his face. "I missed you too." He pushed himself to his feet. "Izzy, meet Névé, pronounced 'nay vay.'"

Izzy held out her hand.

Névé sniffed before plowing into Izzy's legs. Izzy stumbled backward and giggled. "Whoa, girl."

"Névé, sit," Austin commanded.

The dog obeyed.

"Good girl." Austin reached into his pocket and tossed her a treat. "Sorry, she gets overzealous sometimes. She's not a great watch dog because she loves people, but she's strong and can rescue."

"She's beautiful. What type of dog is she?"

"Alaskan malamute." Austin gestured toward the man. "This is my ranch foreman and best friend, Sawyer King. Sawyer, meet Constable Isabelle Tremblay. Sawyer lives in the loft on the top level. He's an ex-medic, so he can make sure you're okay."

He approached and held out his hand. "Nice to meet you, Isabelle."

She returned the gesture. "Please call me Izzy. Sorry for intruding."

"Don't be silly. Happy to have you. Austin explained what's going on. I've alerted the ranch hands, and we're here to protect you too." Sawyer turned to Austin as a buzzer sounded. "That's probably Constable Carver. I'll let him in and then head to the loft. See you in the morning. Nice meeting you, Izzy."

"You too."

"Thanks, bud," Austin said. "I appreciate all your help."

Sawyer saluted and retreated into the house.

Austin walked to the back of his truck and lifted out Izzy's shopping bags. "Okay, let's head in and I'll show you to your room."

Izzy followed Austin and Névé into the large ranch home, stopping in the entrance. "Wow.

You've made extensive changes since I was here last." She studied the log beams and ceiling.

"A fire gutted the upper level five years ago, so I renovated." He gestured to the log stairs. "I'll put you upstairs. Follow me."

Izzy trudged up the steps with Névé at her heels. Seemed the dog wanted to be in their presence.

Austin stopped in front of a middle room and opened the door. "Here we are. Get settled." He set the bags on the log-framed bed.

Izzy entered the room.

A cowbell clanged, the sound resonating into the second level.

Izzy startled.

Austin caught her arm, pulling her into a strong hold. "Sorry, I forgot to warn you of my doorbell. You okay?"

His woodsy scent weakened her resolve to alienate herself from him. She broke their embrace. "It just startled me. My nerves are a bit on edge."

"You're safe here, Izzy."

Was she?

Maybe safe from her father's killers, but what about her heart?

★ ★ ★

Austin juggled three mugs of tea in his hands and set them on the dining room table. "Here you go. They're decaf."

Izzy and Doug huddled together, perusing the crime scene pictures the constable had brought with him. Izzy shifted her glance upward and smiled. "Thanks." She took the green mug and sipped.

Austin ignored the sudden hitch in his heartbeat. *Concentrate. She's here for protection, not you.* "How are you feeling?"

"The dizziness has subsided, but not the headache. I just took more pain meds." She addressed Doug. "Let's get started. I'm sure the pills will kick in soon, and I won't be able to concentrate any more than what my fuzzy brain can now."

Austin sat and checked on his dog.

Névé lay in the corner on her mat, snoozing. Content with no cares in the world.

The life of a dog. Austin sipped his chamomile tea. "You guys okay if I sit in on your discussion? I realize I'm not an officer any longer, but I can still offer my help."

"Well, since Dad's case isn't an official investigation, I don't see why not." Izzy placed her finger on a picture of the cracked cell phone.

"I don't remember this text conversation with Sims." She huffed and sat back in her chair.

Doug squeezed her shoulder. "Don't try so hard. It will come back to you." He picked up another picture. "Do you remember bringing bear spray with you to the alley?"

She shook her head. "I don't even remember going to the alley. Like I said, the last memory I have is of the virus shutting down our system." She fingered her tiny loop earring. "Wait, I remember evil laughter before a message appeared on every monitor."

"What did it say?" Austin asked.

"'Izzy, back off or die.'" She turned to Doug. "That's a start, right? I didn't remember that before. Perhaps by tomorrow, my memories will return."

Would that mean you don't need me any longer?

Wait, where had that thought come from? The Izzy that Austin remembered didn't need anyone for anything. Her independent nature and smarts stood out to him when they worked cases together. But they were also what made him secretly fall for her.

Don't go there. He needed to shift his thoughts. "Doug, did you find the constable that was supposed to be guarding Izzy at the hospital?"

"Yes. We found him unconscious in a utility closet. He didn't see who knocked him out."

"Not good." Austin pointed to the cell phone picture. "Have they been able to get prints off the phone?"

"Still working on it." Doug faced Izzy. "Here's what we pieced together. Sims told you he found a cipher and asked you to bring your dad's journal to the alley behind Chuckie's Bar and Grill. You called me when you arrived and told me about the meeting, requesting my help. That's when Austin and I left for the bar." He took another sip of tea as if gathering his next thoughts carefully. "Sims was shot, and you were attacked before the suspects took off with the journal."

"And that's when we arrived," Austin added. "We didn't see anyone else at the scene."

"Constables canvassed the area but found no leads. Fisher spoke with the bar owner. The man missed the entire exchange. Claims his loud music drowned out the shot that killed Sims." Doug tapped his thumb on a picture of the bar's back entrance. "I wonder why Sims chose this location. Do you have any idea, Izzy?"

She placed her hands on the table and pushed herself upright, then paced around the room.

Austin remembered the habit well. It was her way of picturing details from her memory.

She stopped beside Névé and squatted, petting the dog.

Woof! Névé lifted her head and licked Izzy's face.

Austin's heart warmed at the exchange. He could get used to the two girls bonding. *Stop.* He stared into his cup of tea while he waited for her response.

"I remember Sims told me he used to meet regularly with Dad there. Why, I'm not sure." Izzy returned to the table. "Does Halt know yet how HRPD's system was hacked?"

"No. IT and digital forensics are working together on it." Doug gathered all the pictures and stuffed them into a file folder. "It's getting late and you need your rest, Cinderella."

"Funny. Stop calling me that. You know I hate it." She finished her tea and pushed it aside. "And yes, I remember that detail."

Doug stood. "Okay, I'll reconnect with you tomorrow."

Izzy's azure blue eyes brightened. "Maybe if I go home and look through my condo, it will bring back some memories. I must have returned there before going to see Sims, as I wasn't dressed in my uniform."

Doug shook his head. "That's not wise. If they hacked your phone, they probably also have your address."

Izzy crossed her arms. "But I have to know, Doug. Something there might unlock those three hours."

He reached out and grasped both of her arms. "I need you to be safe. Stay here." He shifted his eyes to Austin. "Please make sure she listens."

Did the man *know* his partner? When Izzy made her mind up on something, no one could stop her.

Especially when it came to her father. They'd had a close relationship. If Justin Tremblay had been murdered, Izzy would rearrange the universe to find the culprits.

Of that, Austin was certain.

And he'd help her.

Austin chuckled. "I'll do my best, but you know her stubborn nature."

"Yeah, that's what I'm afraid of." Doug tapped the folder on the table. "I'll leave this here, as the pictures may spark your memory." His cell phone buzzed, and he unclipped it from his belt, swiping the screen. "Good news. Got a hit off the print on the phone. Ex-con named Ned Bolton. Izzy, that ring a bell?"

She gasped. "Yes. That's Sims's former prison mate. That can't be a coincidence."

"Nope. Fisher is getting a warrant for his arrest."

"I want in on the interrogation." Izzy raised her hands. "And don't say no. We can figure out a way to get me to the station incognito."

Doug pursed his lips. "I realize I can't convince you otherwise, but get some rest tonight." His phone buzzed again, and he swiped the screen. "No!"

Névé hopped to her feet and barked.

Austin tensed.

Izzy latched on to Doug's arm. "What is it?"

"They got to me, too." He raised his phone to show them the screen.

Tell Izzy, we WILL find her.

Austin's pulse thrashed in his ears.

No one was safe. Would the suspect discover his ranch, too?

Chapter Three

Austin nursed a cup of strong coffee the next morning as he waited for Izzy to get up. The text from the suspect took them all by surprise and she couldn't wind down, but paced the living room. She finally went to bed after midnight. He prayed she at least got a few hours of rest. He barely slept. Having her back in his life after ten years kept him awake, thinking about her safety. Thankfully, Sawyer helped Austin ensure the ranch was locked up tight.

Névé hovered at Austin's feet, staying by her master. She had obviously sensed the tension radiating from both him and Izzy.

Austin reached and stroked her ears. "You're a good girl."

Woof! She snuggled closer before lying down.

Austin opened the police folder Doug had left and examined the pictures one by one, hoping to gain some insight into what had happened to

Izzy. After five minutes, the only thing Austin gained was fury toward whoever had attacked his ex-partner. He slammed the folder shut and squared his shoulders, determination setting in to help Izzy find the suspects and protect her.

"What did that folder do to you, bud?" Sawyer entered the dining room, holding a steaming cup of coffee.

Austin leaned back in his chair and folded his arms. "Sorry. I'm just angry over whoever did this to Izzy."

"No need to apologize. I understand. I remember you telling me what she meant to you." Sawyer's eyes remained on Austin. "Your expression reveals that she still does."

Austin drank from his mug to subdue the feelings obviously showing on his face. He had to keep them in check. Izzy probably still blamed him for Clara's death, even though Doug had said differently. How could she not? Austin did.

He blew out a breath. "Seeing her unconscious last night hit me hard, bro."

"I get it, but please be careful. I remember what you went through back then."

Sawyer had just started working for Austin's father when the incident that ended Austin's policing career happened. The two became best friends quickly and Sawyer was now Austin's right-hand man in both friendship and Austin's K-9 training business. He also oversaw the ranch. "I will. I just need her to be safe."

"Well, she is here. The ranch hands have all agreed to keep their eyes open and protect her." Sawyer stood. "Speaking of them, I must get our daily chores going. You feed the dogs?"

"Done. Depending on how the day goes, I may give them a break from training." Austin finished his coffee and rose, heading toward the kitchen, but stopped at the window. "Looks like twenty centimeters fell overnight. Did the contractor plow the laneway?"

"Yes, they came in the early hours. I'm about to help the guys with the entrances. Just needed some fuel." Sawyer chuckled and took another drink.

"Good, thanks."

Névé barked and hopped up, darting toward the entrance.

Izzy appeared in the doorway, rubbing her eyes. "Morning." She squatted and kissed Névé's forehead. "Hey, girl. Happy to see you, too."

Did Izzy realize how cute she looked in her sleepy state?

Austin's eyes shifted to Sawyer.

His friend gave a slight head shake. His meaning coming loud and clear.

Keep your distance.

Austin cleared his throat. "Izzy, how are you feeling?"

She gave the dog another kiss and rose to her feet. "A little better. I fell asleep finally."

"Good. How about some coffee and breakfast?"

"I'm heading to the stable to help the guys shovel." Sawyer stood. "Morning, Izzy."

"Morning. Sorry, I didn't mean to interrupt."

"You didn't." Sawyer slapped Austin's back. "Remember what I said. Text me if there's anything you need, bro."

"Got it." Austin turned to Izzy. "Bacon and eggs?"

"Sounds delightful, but you don't need to go to all that trouble for me." She wrapped her sweater tighter around her waist.

"No trouble. I have a fire going in the living room if you want to warm up while I make breakfast."

Her cell phone buzzed. She removed it from her sweater pocket and swiped the screen, reading. "It's Doug. They found Ned and are bringing him in." She tapped in a message before dropping the phone into her pocket and cementing her stance. "Austin, I need to be there. Ned may have information about my father's death."

So much for a hearty breakfast. "Do you think that's wise? You'll put yourself back in their sights if the suspects are watching the station, which they most likely are."

"I know, but I need to question him."

"Can't they conference you in?" How could he make her understand the danger she was about to put herself in? "Would your chief constable even allow it? You're too close to it and wouldn't be able to remain objective."

Her eyes flashed. "Don't tell me I can't remain objective after what happened with Clara."

Névé whimpered.

Austin winced and raised his hands. "Sorry. You're right. None of my business. I just don't want to see you get hurt."

Her shoulders slumped forward, tears pooling. "Sorry, Austin. I didn't mean that. I just need to find out what happened to my father. And to me in those three hours. Maybe Ned knows something."

Austin could never resist this woman. Plus he guessed she'd probably sneak out on him, and go anyway. Best help her do it safely.

He eyed his dog, and a plan emerged. "Okay, I have an idea. Doug wanted me to bring some of my K-9s into the station. How about I take Névé here and some others? I can give you some rancher clothes and a hat to disguise you as one of my workers. You up for some spy work?"

Her eyes brightened, and she lunged forward, throwing herself into his arms. "Thank you!"

He stumbled backward at her sudden movement, but caught his footing, holding her tight. His stomach fluttered at her closeness. *Step away.* He jerked back, staring into her face. "But we'll need Doug's approval first."

"Of course. I'll call and convince him right now."

"You will. No doubt in my mind." He chuckled. "Okay, there's some yogurt and fruit in the fridge. You eat and I'll be back with your disguise."

Fifty minutes later, after loading three dogs in the back of his K-9 vehicle and driving to the HRPD police station, Austin parked in the building's rear lot.

The door opened and Doug appeared, gesturing them inside.

Austin shut off the engine and turned to Izzy. "Since Névé has bonded quickly with you, I'll let you take her by the leash. Keep your head down. If these people hacked into your system, they may have eyes inside. We need to keep your identity hidden. Got it?"

She yanked her tuque down farther on her head, then tucked her hair inside before putting on wide-rimmed reading glasses. "Got it."

Sawyer had helped gather her disguise of a bulky plaid flannel shirt, jeans, work boots, and a man's winter jacket and hat. Hopefully, it would help with their ruse.

"Let me get the dogs out. I'll bring them to your side." He didn't wait for an answer, but hopped out and around to the back. He opened the cages and secured the leashes for Névé, Goose and Thor. "Come."

The dogs jumped down and trotted behind him as Austin moved to the passenger side.

Izzy climbed from the vehicle.

Austin handed her Névé's leash. "Let's go."

The duo rushed forward with the dogs and entered through the door Doug held open.

"Thanks, Constable Carver, for agreeing to meet my dogs." Austin raised his voice in case anyone was watching or listening. He gestured toward Izzy. "This is Bud. My ranch hand."

"Your dogs are beautiful." Doug held out his

hand to Izzy. "Good to meet you, Bud. Come with me."

They advanced farther into the station, and Doug leaned closer to Izzy. "Halt isn't happy about this, but approved it. Let me do the talking, though. It was the only way he'd let you in the room."

"Understood."

"No one else knows you're coming. I've put Ned in the farthest interrogation room." Doug turned to Austin. "Take the dogs into the observation room next to it. Can you keep them quiet?"

Austin didn't like leaving Izzy, but had no choice. At least he'd be able to hear and see everything going on. "Absolutely, unless they alert to danger. That's how they're trained."

A man dressed in a suit opened a door at the other end of the corridor, gesturing a woman inside. Chatter escaped into the hall from those already gathered. She turned her head and Austin recognized Harturn River's mayor before she entered HRPD's boardroom.

Doug pointed. "There's an early morning board meeting at the other end, so we have to tread carefully. They're always watching."

Austin, Doug, Izzy and the dogs proceeded through the area, passing a couple of constables.

The pair nodded a greeting to Austin and Doug, but didn't even look twice at Izzy.

Clearly, her disguise was working.

But would she be able to stay quiet and fool the man who had attacked her?

Izzy tugged at her hat, ensuring any hairs at the back of her neck were hidden before she slouched and shuffled into the interrogation room behind Doug. She had to conceal everything about her identity, including her body language, if they were going to trick Ned Bolton.

The man was slumped forward, his wrists handcuffed to the metal bar attached to the table. He rested his head on his hands as he snored.

How could he sleep at a time like this? Irritation exploded in her chest, and she struggled to keep her anger from lashing out at the suspect.

Doug slammed his police folder on the table, jarring the convict from his snooze. "Sorry for waking you, Ned." Doug's sarcastic tone blared in the small room. He wiggled the handcuffs. They clanged on the metal bar. "We need your undivided attention."

"Huh?" Ned yawned and sat upright. "Why am I under arrest?"

Doug gestured for Izzy to sit as he dropped into one of the two chairs across the table from Ned. "This is Detective Bud. He's interested in your case."

Izzy took the chair to the right, turned it around and straddled it. Maybe a bit dramatic, but she had to think like a man. She nodded.

"You going somewhere?" Ned gestured toward her winter coat.

"He's getting ready for an early takedown." Doug took out an evidence bag from his pocket and shoved it in front of Ned. "Recognize this?"

The man's eyes bulged. "You found my phone. Thought I lost it in a bar."

Gotcha. Obviously this thug wasn't firing on all cylinders and definitely not the leader of the supposed drug cartel Izzy's father had been investigating. A leader would know better than to identify property held in police custody. Perhaps this would be easier than they thought.

Izzy analyzed Ned Bolton's face, hoping to jar any memories of what happened last night. The only evidence that remained for her was the bruise on the left side of her nose and a lump at the back of her head. Thankfully, she concealed the black and blue with makeup.

The scrawny man tapped his thumb on the table, jiggling the cuffs. He leaned forward, and a long wiry red curl sprang out from under his baseball cap. His wrinkled plaid flannel shirt gaped open because of a missing top button, revealing a soiled white T-shirt underneath.

Clearly, not a criminal mastermind, but what connection did he have to the crime scene?

"So you claim this is your phone?" Doug asked.

"Yup."

"You admit you were at a crime scene where we found this?"

Once again, his eyes widened. "Wait, what? No. I lost it."

Likely story.

Doug flicked his eyes to Izzy, then scowled.

He wasn't buying it either.

Doug continued to address Ned. "Do you know Constable Isabelle Tremblay?"

The man looked left and shifted his gaze to the floor. "No. Should I?"

Izzy cleared her throat, signaling her partner to probe further.

Doug bolted out of his seat.

His sudden action startled even Izzy. Seemed her frayed nerves were still on edge from the man's attack.

Doug walked to the mirror where Austin watched from behind, then turned. "You're lying. Were you hired to beat her up?"

"I ain't sayin' nothin'."

Doug approached the table. "Let me see your hands."

Ned cowered, attempting to hide them.

Doug pointed at the man's reddened knuckles. "You get that from punching her in the face? You're going down for assault—and murder."

He straightened. "What? She's dead? She wasn't when I—"

Izzy chuckled. *Gotcha. Again.*

The man gave her the once-over. "Why ain't you talkin'?"

Oops.

"He's only observing today." Doug smirked and placed his hands on the table, leaning into Ned's personal space. "So you were there? Come on. We don't want you. We want your leader."

Good diversion, partner. Izzy had almost blown it by not concealing her girlish chuckle.

Ned bit his lip.

Doug inched closer. "Who killed the man we found shot to death? Was it you?"

Ned's jaw dropped and he recoiled, distancing himself from Doug's forceful question. "No! It was him."

"Him who?"

Ned blew out a ragged breath. "Don't know his real name, but…" He looked around the room and then leaned forward. "He could be watching. He has spies everywhere."

Doug's eyes snapped to Izzy's.

Not good.

Doug placed a notebook and pen in front of Ned before uncuffing him. "Write what you know."

Ned took the pen in his left hand and scribbled on the page.

The action propelled a scene into Izzy's head.

A left hand flying toward her face in the dark.

A memory from last night?

Izzy massaged the left side of her nose. More than likely, Ned Bolton had been her attacker.

"Tell me who this is?" Doug turned the notebook in Izzy's direction, and she caught the name on the page.

Padilla.

"The one who hired me to beat up the cop," Ned whispered.

"Beat her up, but not kill her?" Doug asked.

"So, she's not dead. Good. You can't charge me with murder then." He rubbed his throat. "I'm thirsty. Give me a drink and I'll tell you everything."

"Tell us what you know first. Then I'll get you a drink and something to eat." Doug tapped the name Padilla written on the page. "Okay, tell us exactly what this person hired you to do."

"Be his muscle and help get information out of her."

"His muscle?"

How could this small man beat anyone up? Izzy fingered her nose. Then again, he had a good left hook.

"Don't let my size fool ya." Ned flexed his biceps. "I might be small, but I'm mighty. Friends called me Scrapper for a reason." He coughed before wiping perspiration from his forehead.

Were they making him nervous?

Doug tucked the notebook back in his vest pocket. "Alrighty then. Tell us what information he was looking for."

"He took her journal but wanted a thumb

drive." He raised his hands. "That's everything. Are you going to release me——"

One of Austin's dogs barked from the other room.

It was alerting, but to what?

Ned's jaw dropped. "You have a dog in here?"

Doug stood. "Bud, let's check out what's going on." He turned to Ned. "We'll be back."

They entered the corridor, and Izzy opened the observation room door, sticking her head inside. "Is one of your dogs alerting to something?"

Austin stiffened. "I trained Goose in tracking. Névé in search and rescue. Thor in…" His eyes widened.

Izzy grabbed his arm. "What?"

"Explosives." He turned to Doug. "You need to evacuate the building and notify the bomb unit."

Doug nodded. "I'll gather our prisoner and get everyone out." He spoke into his radio as he ran back into the interrogation room.

Austin nudged Izzy. "You need to get out. Thor can find the bomb." He engaged his dogs. "Come!" He unleashed the German shepherd. "Thor, seek!"

The K-9 barreled down the hallway and

stopped in front of the boardroom, barking. He raised his snout, circled and took off running again.

Were the police board members still in there? Izzy had to warn them. She thrust open the door. "Everyone, evacuate the building. Possible bomb."

Mayor Fox sprang to her feet at the same time as Izzy's Uncle Ford.

Vincent Jackson—her father's best friend—rose. "How did someone get a bomb in here?" His tone demanded an answer.

Izzy didn't have time to explain. "Not sure, sir. Please evacuate."

The rest of the members screamed and scampered from the room.

Austin released the other two dogs. "They're not trained in explosives, but can certainly help. Seek!"

Goose dashed in the same direction.

Névé stayed by Izzy's side.

Izzy observed the malamute. "She's not a protection dog, right?"

"No, but she senses danger from the other two and likes you. I need to follow the dogs. Evacuate." Austin ran toward the station's front office where Goose and Thor had headed.

"Not a chance." Izzy followed with Névé at her heels.

Constables and HRPD's civilian staff hustled to the exit. Their tortured expressions revealed everyone's horror. Izzy couldn't remember a time when their station had been attacked in this magnitude.

Was it all her fault?

Thor's heightened bark cut off her thoughts.

Izzy hurried to catch up to the K-9s and Austin. She stepped inside the bullpen.

Thor sat a few feet away from a desk. *Her* desk.

"Thor, Goose, retreat!" Austin's forceful commands stopped Izzy in her tracks.

It was then she noticed a backpack under her chair. A beeping filled the room, then intensified.

Izzy's heartbeat slammed in her chest. The bomb was about to blow.

The K-9s bolted toward the entrance where Austin stood. He turned. "Get out!"

Beside her, Névé growled and latched on to her coat, tugging her back into the hallway. The group scrambled to get away from the ticking time bomb.

They reached the exit and Austin thrust open the door, hauling her with him.

Seconds later a thunderous explosion rocked the building, sending debris pelting through the station and out the shattered front glass doors.

The impact shoved Izzy to her knees on the snowy walkway. The attack revealed one thing.

None of them were safe from Padilla.

Chapter Four

"Good job, guys. You saved lives today." Austin ruffled Névé's fur with one hand and Thor's with the other as he waited for the paramedics to examine Izzy. If Thor hadn't alerted to the bomb, things may not have turned out well at HRPD's station. Goose snuggled closer and Austin chuckled. "You too, boy." *Thank You, Lord, for my dogs.*

Everyone had evacuated in time, and the explosion had been isolated to the front of the building. Austin and Izzy had a few minor cuts, and the dogs appeared to be fine. However, Austin had arranged for his vet to meet him back at the Murray K-9 Ranch. Austin would not take any chances with his dogs.

Firefighters had arrived and extinguished the flames. The bomb unit had also determined there were no more explosives on the property. Austin concurred as he had commanded Thor to seek, but the German shepherd hadn't alerted to any further dangers.

A crowd now gathered in the parking lot. The board members had remained at the scene along with constables and civilian workers. Even the cold February temperature didn't deter the multitudes from checking out the explosion.

Izzy shook the paramedic's hand and then approached Austin. "I'm good to go."

Austin noted the bandage over her right brow. "You sure about that, especially after what happened yesterday?"

Névé left Austin's side and nestled next to Izzy—her new favorite spot.

And that warmed Austin's heart.

Izzy bent down and petted the malamute's head. "Hey, girl. Thanks for saving my life."

Thor barked.

Izzy chuckled. "You too, Thor." She turned to Austin. "I'm impressed by your training. These dogs are so smart."

"Thank you. Speaking of them, we need to get back to the ranch, as I want the vet to examine them."

Izzy took off her hat and scratched her head. "Did they get hurt?"

"I think they're fine, but I don't take any risks with my K-9 family. So, let's—"

"Izzy!" A slender man jogged across the parking lot.

A balding man and a woman followed.

"Uncle Ford, I'm glad you're okay." Izzy wrapped her arms around the man.

He gestured toward the others. "You remember your dad's friend Vincent and our town's mayor, Georgia Fox?"

"Of course." Izzy shook their hands before gesturing to Austin. "This is Austin Murray and his K-9s, Névé, Thor and Goose."

Izzy's uncle pointed to her clothing. "What's up with the odd getup?"

"Just doing some role playing for an undercover mission." Izzy stuffed the hat into her coat pocket.

Good save, Izzy. She was still quick on her feet. Not only did she have a perfect memory, but her street smarts once again impressed Austin.

Georgia kneeled in front of the K-9s. "You saved the day." She looked up at Austin. "Good work."

Austin dipped his head. "Thanks, ma'am."

"I thought I'd heard a dog bark earlier." Vincent held out his hand. "Good you were here at the station. Odd coincidence."

Austin didn't miss Izzy's flattened lips and slight shake of her head. Even though they'd been apart for ten years, he still could read her like a proverbial book. Her expression held an obvious message.

Stay silent.

"Austin!" Doug practically skidded across to the group. "Thanks again for showing me your dogs. I'll give the chief constable an update, and we'll get back to you. These three sure proved their worth today."

Izzy's partner had perfect timing and was also keeping up with the ruse. Austin stuck out his hand. "Pleasure doing business with you, Constable Carver."

Doug shook his hand, then pulled back and snapped his fingers. "Wait. I need to talk to you about one more thing. Can you meet me around back at your K-9 vehicle? I want to discuss a visit to your training facility, but first, I have to consult with Constable Tremblay about her undercover ops."

Austin didn't miss the slight tilt of Izzy's head. These two were good at playing the game. It was clear they didn't trust anyone.

Doug turned to the board members. "Will you excuse us?"

"Of course." Ford grazed his niece's arm. "Stay safe, Izzy."

She nodded. "Glad to see you're all okay."

The mayor once again bent down beside the dogs. "We owe our lives to these fine animals."

All three barked as if agreeing to her statement.

The group laughed before trudging off toward the ambulance.

Doug inched closer to Austin and Izzy. "Sorry for the charade, but I didn't want them thinking you came here together."

"Good cover," Izzy whispered. "What do you have to report?"

"Let's head to Austin's vehicle." Doug looked around. "You never know who's listening or watching. Today's attack proves to me your father was on to something, Izzy. We need to take all precautions."

Izzy hissed in a breath and put the tuque back on.

Austin bristled, shivers snaking down his spine. He observed the onlookers. Was the culprit among them?

Urgency propelled him forward. He had to

get Izzy back to his ranch. He tugged on his K-9s' leashes. "Come."

The group relocated to the side of the building, sidestepping any remaining debris. Thankfully, the blast hadn't reached the area where Austin had parked.

He clicked his key fob and released the hatch. "Up," he commanded his dogs. The trio hopped into their cages and Austin closed the doors. "Okay, what information do you have?"

Doug once again glanced around before responding. "Forensics reported the explosion took out the hallway and our bullpen. Seemed whoever did this only wanted to destroy part of the building."

Izzy latched on to Doug's arm. "How did someone get into the station so easily to set explosives?"

"Not sure. The only individuals I saw were our staff, constables and the board members. Do you remember seeing anything odd when you came in earlier?"

Izzy tapped her gloved finger on her chin. "I saw the mayor and Vincent go into the boardroom. Constables Fisher and Reynolds passed us in the corridor, but it's highly unlikely they'd do it."

"Well, we'll be questioning everyone in attendance at the station today." Doug stuffed his notebook into his pocket. "We'll also check video footage of anyone coming and going. If it wasn't destroyed."

Austin read the angst on her face. "We need to get you back to the ranch. And out of harm's way."

"Agreed. One more thing. Did Ned's interrogation spark any memory of that three-hour window?"

Her eyes brightened. "Yes, Doug. Thanks for the reminder. I remembered a left fist coming out of nowhere in the dark and punching me in the face. I noticed Ned wrote with his left hand. It had to have been him who attacked me."

"I'm going to consult with Halt to get him to check your father's reports on recent investigations. That might help figure out this case, and also lead us to this Padilla."

Austin shifted his stance. "Izzy, you don't know what case your dad was working on?"

"No. He wouldn't tell me. Normally, he would have assigned it to someone at the station, but he said this one was for 'his eyes only.' Not sure why." She bit her lip. "His notes revealed something about a drug cartel, though."

Doug's radio crackled. "Carver, Halt here. We've had reports of a suspicious hooded figure seen nearby. Officers are in pursuit. If Izzy is still here, get her to safety. Now!"

Their leader's voice sent chills throughout Austin's body. Chills not from the cold weather but the continued danger following his ex-partner.

"Iz, we have to go." Austin hurried to the passenger side and opened the door. "Get in." He raced to the driver's side.

She climbed into the vehicle. "Doug, send me regular updates. I want to monitor the case from Austin's ranch."

"You know Halt won't allow that." He sighed. "But I know you and your clever computer skills will get information. I'll see what I can do. I need to get Bolton in lockup. Stay safe." Doug closed the door and tapped on the hood.

Austin started the engine and sped from the station's parking lot with one thought stuck in his mind.

He had to protect the woman in the passenger seat with his life.

After cleaning up and changing from her annoying disguise, Izzy sat sipping a coffee in

Austin's rustic living room. Névé had taken up residence at Izzy's side. Literally lying on top of her feet as if pinning Izzy down, preventing her from going anywhere. Did the malamute sense Izzy's desire to escape and dive headfirst into her father's case? Izzy hated that her hands were tied. She was good at what she did, and her sharp memory could help the team, but she also knew Chief Constable Halt wouldn't let her investigate.

But what was stopping her from doing her own sleuthing? On her own time? She popped forward, disturbing Névé's hold on her. *That's it. I'll request a vacay.* It wasn't like she didn't have banked time she could use.

Woof!

"Sorry, girl. I know what you're thinking. Stay out of it." Izzy rubbed the dog's fur. "But, I can't."

Névé tilted her head to the side, as if questioning her motives.

"Don't judge me, okay? I need to solve this case. Protect my family. If they came after Dad, what's stopping them from getting to my mom, Uncle Ford and Blaire?"

Woof!

Izzy pushed herself upright and walked to the

window overlooking the extensive property. "I know. I know. I'll be careful." She examined Austin's ranch grounds. Snow had covered every inch and glistened in the sun's rays. *Beautiful. I could live here.*

Where had that thought come from? Being around Austin again had warmed her heart. The kindness and gentleness she remembered from when they were partners resurfaced, bringing with it the feelings she had once. *He didn't feel the same as you, remember?* He had cut off all ties after he left the force. If he felt the same way as she had, wouldn't he have tried to stay in touch?

Then again, your anger at Clara's death pushed him away.

Izzy had struggled with how that horrifying call played out. Izzy, Austin, and Clara had responded and Austin entered the apartment first. An abusive man held his bruised and battered wife at gunpoint. The events turned ugly when he pointed the gun at them, and Austin had froze for some odd reason. His hesitation allowed the man to get a shot off. A shot that killed Izzy's best friend and mentor.

Izzy had blamed him. At first. But after long talks with her father, she realized Clara's death wasn't Austin's fault. It was the angry man's fault.

But it had cost Clara her life. Izzy had forgiven Austin years ago, but that night still haunted her. Every detail. The abused wife's injuries. The man's red, angered expression. Clara's blood.

Izzy shut her eyes to block out the scene.

Why had she forgotten memories she wanted desperately to remember but she couldn't forget that horrible night?

Having a perfect memory had not only brought praise from her childhood schoolmates and friends, but ridicule. Because of that, Izzy had tried to hide her abilities, but soon realized she had a gift.

We don't hide our gifts. God gave them to us for a reason. Use it, Izzy.

Her father's words had encouraged her to take advantage of her sharp memory, so she did. But she also tried hard not to brag, as she'd seen jealousy over the years from friends, colleagues and even her sister, Blaire.

A ranch hand riding a horse appeared down the driveway, jolting Izzy from the past. *Concentrate.*

She fished out her cell phone, chose her leader from her list of contacts and waited for him to pick up.

"Tremblay, what's wrong? You okay?" Halt's tone conveyed his worry.

"I'm fine." She bit her lip and pushed away her trepidation at the question she was about to ask.

"You lying low?"

Her leader gave her the perfect segue. "Yes. That's why I'm calling, sir. I have vacation banked from last year and would like to take it now. Sorry for the short notice. Is that okay?"

Tapping filtered through the phone.

He was drumming his fingers on his desk. A habit she'd coined as his thinking pose.

She waited, knowing better than to interrupt him.

He puffed out a breath. "Fine. But Tremblay. Don't go investigating your father's death. It's too dangerous."

Seemed her boss was good at reading her thoughts.

"But if you do, be sure to give me updates."

Was he silently giving her permission?

She smiled. "Thank you, sir."

"Your dad would want me to protect you, Izzy. Please stay put." He paused. "And don't trust anyone, and I mean anyone." He clicked off.

Izzy froze. A shudder zigzagged up her spine.

Chief Constable Halt had never called her Izzy, only Tremblay. *That* she remembered.

Did he know something she didn't?

"Did I hear you talking to someone?"

She pivoted, her hand flying to her chest. "Austin, you scared me."

He held out a plate of cookies. "Sorry. I brought you some homemade chocolate chip cookies. Your fave."

He remembered.

She snatched one and stuffed it into her mouth. "Mmm...so...good," she mumbled.

"Now, who were you talking to?" He set the plate on the log coffee table before sitting in a rocking chair.

"Well, first, Névé then Halt." She plunked down on the plaid couch.

Névé hopped up beside her.

Izzy ruffled her ears. "Are you allowed up here?"

Woof!

"She likes you, and yes, she's allowed." He snagged a cookie. "What did Halt say?"

"I asked him if I could take some time off. He said yes, but then warned me to stay away from the case."

"So, he knows you well, then."

"Yes, already. But then he gave me his permission without giving me his permission."

Austin tilted his head. "Come again."

She told him about her conversation with Halt, including his warning and the use of her given name. "Do you think he knows something about the case Dad was working on?"

"Possibly." He leaned forward, elbows to knees. "Iz, I know you and I'm positive you'll investigate the case. I'm not sure you should. You're too close to it."

She blasted to her feet. "How can you say that? I need to find out the truth, Austin. My father was murdered, and this person may come after my family next." She hated the tear that had just escaped without warning. She normally wasn't an emotional person.

He stood and brought her into a hug. "I'm sorry. I'm just scared for you."

Izzy melted in Austin's arms, and she wanted to stay sheltered there.

Don't trust anyone.

Halt's words returned, but surely he hadn't meant Austin.

Did he?

Her cell phone dinged, and she retreated from

his embrace. She removed the device, swiping the screen.

Izzy, don't think you or your family are safe. Don't investigate or Blaire is next.

Izzy's legs buckled, and she crumpled to the floor.

Névé barked, circling her as if in protection mode.

No! Lord, don't let them take my family.

Chapter Five

Austin squatted beside her. "What is it, Iz?" He petted the malamute before commanding the dog to sit. She sensed Izzy's distress and wanted to help.

Izzy raised her phone.

Austin read the menacing message. He balled his hands into fists, curbing his anger from bubbling to the surface. *Lord, protect the Tremblay family from this evil man.*

"Padilla is threatening Blaire. I have to get to Mom's. They need me." She tried to push herself up, but fell back onto the floor.

Once again, Austin brought her into his arms. "You do that and you might provoke whoever this is even more."

Her heart hammered in rhythm with his. "Iz. Breathe. In. Out."

She repeated the breathing technique multiple times before pulling away and standing. "I have to call Blaire."

"Understood. How can I help?"

She chewed on her bottom lip. "Can you call Doug? Get him to ask Halt to send patrols near Mom's place?"

"I will."

Névé brushed around Izzy's legs.

"I didn't think she was a protection dog." Izzy bent down and kissed Névé's head.

"She's not, but she senses your anxiety. Plus she likes you." He took out his cell phone. "I'll call Doug and also get Sawyer to ensure the property is secure."

"Thanks." She headed toward the kitchen but turned at the living room entrance. "Oh, I would like to set up a makeshift office where I can go over everything I remember of the case. I'm hoping maybe it will jog my memory. Where can I do that?"

Austin suppressed the urge to argue, but he knew it wouldn't do any good. "You can use my office. There's lots of room and two desks. Can I help? I know I'm not an officer any longer, but maybe a second set of eyes would help."

"Absolutely. I'd like that."

"There are lots of supplies in my office you can use to make up an evidence board if you want."

"Awesome, thanks." Izzy continued into the kitchen.

Austin turned to Névé and pointed at Izzy. "Heel." He didn't want Izzy to be alone. Even if the malamute wasn't a protection dog, she could provide company for Izzy.

He grabbed his two-way and hit the button. "Sawyer, come in."

Seconds later the radio squawked. "What's up?"

"Can you do another perimeter check? Izzy just got a threatening text." Austin walked to the window and peered out into his front yard. All seemed quiet, but he wasn't taking any chances when it came to Izzy's safety.

"Will do. She okay?"

Austin raked his fingers through his dark brown hair. "Shaken up. I'm worried about her."

"Understand. I'll report back in fifteen minutes. Taking Bucky out for a ride."

Sawyer had named the rescue horse a month ago, when Austin had brought the black beauty to the ranch. They'd been inseparable since.

"Appreciate it. I'll fill you in later."

"Copy."

Austin punched in Doug's number and waited.

He answered after the first ring. "Everything okay, Austin?"

"Not entirely sure." He explained the situation to Izzy's partner. "Can you send someone to Rebecca's home to double-check on her and Blaire? Izzy wanted to go, but I told her no."

"Let's hope she doesn't sneak out."

"I have my best spy at her heels. Literally." Austin pictured Névé not letting Izzy out of her sight. It impressed him that the two had bonded so quickly.

"Good. She needs to stay put. I have Halt breathing down my neck." He paused. "Listen, she's probably getting ready to dive deeper into the case."

Doug knew his partner well.

"Yup. She's already asked for office space." Austin chuckled. "Don't worry. I'm watching, and I have informed my ranch hands of the situation."

"Good. Thanks for the update. I'll contact you when I have more information about her family."

"Appreciate it. Talk later." Austin clicked off the call and entered his office.

He found Izzy sitting at his desk with Névé

lying in her doggie bed. The sight warmed his heart. *I could get used to this.*

Stop. Focus. Remember your vow.

After Clara's death, Izzy and Austin's friendship had fizzled. Austin guessed she blamed him for his mistake that night. He spent long hours talking to his adoptive parents and decided being a police officer wasn't for him. He agreed to stay at the ranch and learn the ropes, so he tendered his resignation to Chief Constable Tremblay. Izzy's father had tried to talk him out of it, but Austin had made his decision. There was no going back.

He couldn't take the silence with Izzy. He was about to tell her his true feelings for her, but after that night, he clammed up. They'd never have a relationship because of what he did. After a year had passed, he tried to get into the dating game but no one measured up to his Izzy. Every girl he dated broke it off within weeks, claiming his lack of attention to them was evidence that he had baggage. They weren't wrong.

He was unworthy of love. His biological parents had proven that to him when they gave him up for adoption. They didn't want him.

And neither did any woman.

So he'd vowed to himself to focus on the

ranch, and talked his father into starting a K-9 training facility. Two years into his K-9 training business, his parents had died in a horrible car accident along the Rocky Mountains. Austin had been heartbroken and thrust himself further into ranching and training dogs.

And never gave another thought to policing. Until now.

He wanted to keep Izzy safe and help her solve this case. Even if that meant putting himself in danger.

Could he stay objective and not allow his rising feelings for this woman overpower him?

You've got this, Austin.

He mustered strength and approached his desk. "You look good sitting here."

Wait, did he just really say that?

He cleared his throat. "I mean, you look comfy." He was a bumbling fool. *Get it together, Murray.*

She smiled and picked up a picture of Austin with his father. "I've always loved this picture of you two. This was taken when you first joined HRPD, right?"

"Excellent memory."

She huffed and placed the photo back down. "Apparently, not always."

"It will come. We just need to help it along." Austin opened a closet and brought out his rolling whiteboard. "Add your pictures to this. I use it for planning training routines for the dogs." He pushed it in between the two desks.

"Perfect." Izzy spread out the pictures from the file folder Doug had left on the opposite desk. "Let's start by adding these to the board."

"Are Rebecca and Blaire okay?" Austin lifted the tape out from his desk drawer and handed it to her.

"They are. Blaire yelled at me for putting them in a state of panic, but I had to warn them."

"Sorry. Doug is sending a patrol car." Austin eyed the photos. "Okay, where do you want to start?"

"Don't you have work to do?"

"Sawyer and the ranch hands can handle it." He picked up a picture. "How well did you know your father's CI?"

"I barely knew Sims. Dad referred to him often, but never by name. Said he was reliable. I found his name and number on the inside cover of Dad's journal." She broke off a piece of tape and added the pictures one by one.

Austin picked up a black marker and wrote the name Padilla at the top of the board, then a question mark below it. "Did your father ever mention this name?"

"No. I remember everything before the cyberattack at the station." She picked up a red marker and wrote *Drug Lord* beneath his name, then *bath salts*. "We know he—or she—is selling this form of drugs."

"How do you know that?"

"That information was in Dad's journal, just not the name Padilla." She tapped the marker on her chin. "Maybe he didn't know."

She drew a line beneath Padilla and wrote Ned Bolton's name beside it, connecting the two.

"Or didn't want to record the name. Do you think Ned was just a thug or a dealer under Padilla?"

"Good question. I got the impression he was only an enforcer."

"Yeah, he didn't seem the salesman type." Austin wrote *thumb drive* to the right of the pictures. "Okay, we know from your interview with him that Ned said you had a thumb drive. Any ideas of where you would have hidden it?"

Izzy paced the spacious office.

Her thinking mode.

She stopped at the window and turned. "I'm drawing a blank."

"Be patient. It will come. I just know it." Austin's radio squawked, and he unhooked it from his belt. "Go ahead."

"Perimeter is secure."

"Thanks, Sawyer." Austin checked his watch. "It's getting late and we haven't eaten all day. Time to start supper?"

"On it. Heading to the kitchen now."

Austin set the radio on his desk. "Anything else you want to add before we break for supper?"

Izzy set the marker on the board's ledge. "I hate not being able to remember. It's so unusual—and hard."

"Welcome to my world." Austin plunked into his desk chair. "You're trying too—"

Izzy snapped her fingers. "Wait. I want to go to my condo. I must have hidden the drive somewhere there."

"That's not wise, Iz. Your place is probably being closely watched by Padilla and his men." How could Austin convince her it wasn't safe?

"I have to, Austin. I have to try to help jog my memory."

Austin pushed himself upright. "If Chief Constable Halt finds out, he won't be happy."

"I don't care." Her raised voice caused Névé to hop up on all fours and bark.

"Névé, silence," Austin commanded.

The dog whimpered but obeyed.

"I'm sorry, Austin, but I need to find out the truth. With or without your help." She flew out of the room.

Austin squatted in front of his malamute. "Sorry, girl. She's just on edge."

How could Austin keep his ex-partner safe when she wouldn't listen to reason?

Izzy was tired of people telling her what to do and what not to do. First Blaire, then Austin. *Get it together, Iz. It's not their fault. They're only trying to protect you.*

Well, with Blaire, she wasn't so sure. She and her sister had been at odds for a while now. Why, Izzy didn't know. She had confronted her younger sister, but Blaire wouldn't give her a reason. Only that she was tired of having to live in her sister's shadow.

What exactly did that mean? Blaire was smart, beautiful and everyone loved her. Izzy, on the other hand, had butted heads with some. Could it be because of Izzy's perfect memory? Was her sister still jealous of that after all these years?

Sometimes Izzy wished it was her sister who had hyperthymesia and not her. It had been both a blessing and a curse all these years. Right now, it was creating havoc not being able to remember.

Lord, if You're listening, please show me what happened in those three hours. I feel it's vital to Dad's case. Protect my family. Help soften Blaire's heart toward me. I want my sister back.

Her cell phone trilled, and she swiped the screen. Doug. She hit answer and entered the country-style dining room. Table and chairs, along with furnishings made from logs, adorned the spacious area. "Hey, partner. You have good news?"

"Not much. Nothing on the cell phone, and the video footage from the station was wiped clean. We determined where the hack came from, though."

"Where?" Izzy plunked down at the table.

"Fisher confessed to clicking the link, but they spoofed the IP address to mimic yours. However, digital forensics traced it to a company called King & Sons." Tapping on a keyboard could be heard through the phone. "We can't find much on it and are wondering if it's a shell corporation."

Izzy ran her fingers along the smooth wood plank table, admiring the finishing. "Let me look into it from here."

"The digital team can handle it, Izzy."

"Doug, you know my hacking skills, and it's driving me nuts to not do anything."

Doug harrumphed. "I know I can't stop you, but please be careful."

She stood and sauntered to the large bay window, peering out into the backyard.

Sawyer entered the barn, leading his horse into the stable.

Wait. Izzy froze.

Sawyer's last name was King. Was there a connection? Probably a stretch, but how well did Austin know his ranch foreman? "I'm doing this, Doug. I need to know who King & Sons are."

If not for the case's sake, but for Austin's.

He could have a wolf among his dogs.

"I know your skills and I'm not stopping you." Doug was silent for a moment. "Izzy, Austin told me about your plans to go to your condo. Stay away."

Izzy banged her palm on the wall beside the

window. *Tattletale.* "I may have hidden the drive there, Doug. I have to go."

"When are you going?"

"In the morning." *And I need to convince Austin to take me.*

"I'll have someone patrol the area overnight. Just to be on the safe side."

"Good, thanks, bud. You're the best. What would I do without you?"

He chuckled. "You'd be lost. Have a good evening and stay safe. I'll touch base in the morning. Don't leave the ranch until you hear from me. Got it?"

She saluted, even though he couldn't see her. "Yes, boss. Night." She ended the call.

A crash resonated from the kitchen area.

Woof!

"Hey, girl, let's go find Austin. He has some explaining to do." Izzy marched across the hall to the kitchen with Névé at her heels, then halted at a full stop.

Austin was drenched in white powder.

A broken bag of flour lay on the floor.

"Stay back. I need to sweep up the mess." Austin puffed a cloud of white from his mouth.

How could she stay mad at the handsome rancher when his face was covered with flour?

Her hand flew to her mouth to conceal the laughter wanting to escape.

"Go ahead. Laugh. I'm sure I look a fright."

She giggled. "What were you planning on making with the flour?"

He wiped his face with a dish towel. "Biscuits."

Izzy walked to the narrow door. "If memory serves me correctly, the broom is in here." She opened the door and brought it out.

"Thanks. Be careful not to slip."

Izzy tiptoed to where the mess lay and swept. "Austin, why did you tell Doug about me wanting to go to the condo?"

"Thought he should know." He snatched the dish cloth and wiped the counter. "Besides, he asked me to keep him informed."

Her neck muscles corded. "I was going to tell him. I can take care of myself, you know. Or did you forget that?"

"Of course not, Iz. But you're under my roof, and it's my responsibility to keep you safe."

Cool your jets, Izzy. He's not the enemy. "I'm sorry. I know you're only trying to help."

"God brought you back into my life for a reason."

"God? I think He forgot about me." She finished sweeping and grabbed the dustpan.

"Why would you say that? I thought you believed."

"I do—well, I did. Until He stopped showing me His plan for my life."

Austin took the dustpan from her hand. "I understand. It's hard to see God's journey for us when we can't even see around the bend in front of us. He knows the big picture." Austin placed the pan near a pile of flour.

She stopped sweeping. "When did you get so profound in your thinking?"

"Let's just say I've been digging into God's word more during the past ten years."

"I'm impressed." She swept the rest of the flour into the dustpan.

"So, you're not upset with me anymore?"

"Hard to stay mad at you, especially with flour on your face." She reached up and wiped a spot from his cheek, lingering a little longer than she should.

Their gazes held, silence booming in the spacious kitchen. Emotions wrestled inside Izzy, and she struggled to contain them.

What are you thinking, Austin?

Questions flooded Izzy's mind. How could

her feelings from ten years ago return in such a short period? Did he feel the same? Why did he freeze that day?

The front door slammed.

Austin cleared his throat and stepped away, breaking the awkward moment. "That's Sawyer. He's making supper for us after he cleans up."

"Austin, how well do you know Sawyer? Do you trust him?"

"Completely." He emptied the flour into the garbage can. "Why would you ask that?"

How much should she tell him? "Doug mentioned the team traced the station's hack to a company called King & Sons."

"Come on, Iz. King is a popular last name."

Doubts crawled over Izzy's arms like an inchworm, sending chills exploding throughout her body as a question rose.

Could Austin be unbiased when it came to his best friend?

Chapter Six

While sipping coffee, Austin studied Izzy's evidence board the next morning to piece together what happened during her attack. Frustration corded his muscles over the fact that she could have died. Thankfully, he and Doug had arrived when they did. Their presence had scared off the suspects.

Izzy had added *King & Sons* to the whiteboard under Padilla's name with a question mark. Austin clenched his jaw. Did she really think Sawyer could be part of this illegal drug ring? There were many King families across the province. When Izzy had asked Sawyer at the supper table how many were in his family, Sawyer said he was an only child.

"Morning, bud." Sawyer moved beside him, coffee in hand. "What's all this?"

"Izzy's evidence board. We're trying to piece

together what happened during that three hours she can't remember."

Sawyer sipped his coffee. "I wanted to mention something. Had a rough day yesterday with the ranch hands."

Austin's neck muscles tensed. "Do I need to intervene? Be the bad guy? I can."

Sawyer chuckled. "Oh, I know. I've seen that streak. No, just some issues with the new younger guy, but I've got it under control. Laid down the law of the land, so to speak."

"How's Maverick doing?"

They had hired Maverick quickly after they lost an employee to another ranch on the other side of Harturn River. Austin had presumed the man was fitting in perfectly. Perhaps that had been an incorrect assumption.

"Just a few incidents with two other hands. I nipped it in the bud yesterday. I hope." Sawyer approached the board and tapped on Ned Bolton's picture. "Wait, Ned and I went to school together. Why's he on here?"

"He attacked me." Izzy entered the room with Névé at her heels. She massaged the bruise on her face. "Did this to me."

Sawyer winced. "Ned did that to you? So sorry."

"Sure did. How well did you know him?"

Sawyer rubbed his temple. "We hung out together for a bit, then he got in with the wrong crowd. Was suspended from school for fighting. Never saw him again after that."

"I guess he got his nickname of Scrapper honestly." Izzy walked to the board and wrote *Scrapper* beside Ned's name.

Sawyer turned to Austin. "Time to round up the dogs. You in?"

"Austin, before you answer that, Doug just called. He gave my condo the all-clear, so I wanted to go over there now." Her eyes shifted to Sawyer. "If I can steal him away for a few hours."

Sawyer shrugged. "Fine by me. I'll grab Maverick. I want to introduce him to the dog training aspect of the ranch. Izzy, are you sure you should be leaving? It's not safe."

Austin finished his coffee. "I'll be with her, and I'll take a couple of dogs with us."

Névé barked.

Austin leaned over and ruffled the dog's ears. "Of course you can come."

"Be careful you two." Sawyer walked to the entranceway and turned. "Take your own personal SUV, Austin. We don't want to advertise the ranch if you take the K-9 vehicle. They may be watching her condo." He left the room.

Austin bristled. "He's right, but first you need breakfast, Iz." He touched the small of her back, nudging her toward the door. "Go."

Fifty minutes later Austin parked along the side of Izzy's street a few houses down from her condo. Turning off the engine, he shifted in his seat to face her. "Okay, we'll walk from here and pretend we're out for a stroll with our dogs. You take Névé and I'll take Goose."

"Got it." She climbed from the SUV.

Austin shook his head. "But wait for me to leave first. Iz, you haven't changed." He pursed his lips and got out of his vehicle, hustling around to the rear. He opened the back and let the dogs out.

He passed Névé's leash to Izzy. "Remember, easy stroll."

"Got it, Austin. Let's go, girl." Izzy and the malamute trudged through the snowbank and onto the sidewalk.

Austin and Goose followed. "Beautiful day for a walk, right?"

"Sure is, hon." Izzy winked.

He loved that she played along with their charade and he wasn't wrong. The sun provided not only warmth but added to their cover. Perfect day for a romantic stroll.

If only that was the truth.

As they approached Izzy's condo, Austin tugged at her arm. "Wait here with Névé. Goose and I will check things out before you go any farther. I realize Doug said it was clear, but that was earlier this morning. I'll whistle when it's safe. You remember the signal I used to give while we were on calls?"

"Of course. One long whistle means it's safe. Two short equals danger. Got it." She positioned herself beside a tree. "Girl, wanna play in the snow?"

Névé barked.

"Of course you do." Izzy scooped snow and tossed it to the malamute.

She launched into the air and caught it in her mouth.

Austin longed to stay and play with the duo. Perhaps start a snowball fight, but he and Goose had a job to do. He'd trained the German shepherd not only in scents but in protection. "Let's go, bud."

After walking around the block of Izzy's condo, Goose and Austin perused the property.

The shepherd hadn't alerted to anything, so Austin let out one long whistle.

A couple moments later Izzy appeared with Névé at her heels and smothered in snow.

Austin chuckled. "Did you dunk my dog in the snow?"

"Nope. Just wrestled with her. She's a good girl."

"That she is." He gestured toward her detached condo's door. "Wanna go in the front or back?"

"Back. Some of my neighbors are nosy."

"That's why I love the country."

The group slogged through the snow and Austin turned as they rounded the corner, checking for any spying eyes. However, the neighborhood was silent.

Good.

He followed Izzy up the back steps.

She inserted her key and pushed open the door. "Let's get in quickly before Ezra sees us."

"I remember him. He still lives behind you?"

"Yup." They stepped into the back entryway.

Goose growled.

Névé barked.

Austin stiffened. Not good.

His dogs were alerting to something or someone inside the house.

★ ★ ★

Izzy's pulse skyrocketed, sending her adrenaline racing through her body and into a panicked state. *Breathe, Izzy. Remember, you're a cop and should be used to danger.* But it was different when that danger was in her own home. She reached for her sidearm, only to realize it wasn't on her hip. She was off duty. Izzy hurried to her deacon's bench and took out a tactical flashlight she kept there for emergencies. She lifted it as a weapon.

Névé nudged her legs as if guarding her from harm.

Austin lowered Izzy's arm. "Iz, let Goose go first. He's also trained in protection."

"I am too."

"I know that. Just let Goose do his job. We don't even know if there is anyone inside." Austin unleashed the shepherd. "Seek!"

The dog bounded down the hallway into the front of the house. His nails clicked on the floors as Izzy pictured him moving from room to room.

After what seemed like an hour, Goose returned to their location, barked, then glanced backward.

"What does that mean?" Izzy once again raised the flashlight.

"He's found something, but isn't alerting to danger." Austin snatched the flashlight from her hand. "Let me go first."

"Wait, who's the cop here?" She smirked. "Trying to be the hero?"

"Nope, just a gentleman." Austin addressed his dog. "What did you find, boy?"

Goose barked, trotted down the hall and turned from the living room entryway.

"He's telling us to follow. Névé, heel." Austin moved toward Goose.

Izzy followed with the malamute at her side and stepped into her living room.

And halted in her tracks.

Her furniture, bookshelf and end table drawers were all overturned. Books lay everywhere. The perp had cut open her couch cushions.

Not good.

Someone had invaded her home.

Izzy balled her fists as anger replaced the panic consuming her earlier. "Ugh! Someone was looking for the flash drive, and I don't know if they would have found it because I don't remember where I put it." Her heightened tone boomed in the room.

Névé barked at Izzy's tempered statement.

"Sorry, girl." Izzy rubbed the dog's ears.

Once again, Goose barked and trotted toward Izzy's office.

"There's more." Austin took out his cell phone and followed Goose, peeking into the room. "It's a mess too. I'm calling Doug. Izzy, we need to get out of the house and not touch anything." He punched buttons and positioned his phone to his ear.

Izzy realized they had to vacate the premises, but she wanted to see her favorite spot in the condo—her office and reading room.

Austin's conversation with Doug morphed into the background in a tunnellike effect as Izzy marched to her office but remained in the doorway. They had pulled out her desk drawers, and their contents littered the floor. Slashed paintings lay ruined. Every one of them.

Izzy's hand flew to her mouth. *How could someone do this?* Now she understood how it felt to be on the other end of that proverbial stick. A tear rolled down her right cheek, followed by another.

Hands grasped her shoulders from behind, and she jumped.

"Sorry, Iz. Just didn't want you to go any farther into the room. Doug is on his way with forensics."

Austin turned her around before she could rid herself of the tears streaming down her face.

He wiped them away with his thumbs. "I'm sorry. I know this is your favorite room, and it violates your privacy."

"My dad gave most of these paintings to me. Now they're ruined. Every one of them." She fell into his arms and sobbed.

Austin's hold tightened around her body.

Névé whimpered from the hallway.

"She wants to console you too, but we need to get out of the house." He took her hand and led her toward the rear entrance. "Once forensics is done, we'll go back in and try to figure things out. Okay?"

She nodded and let him guide her outside. The cold stung her face, bringing her out of the stupor holding her captive. Izzy yanked her hand away and plunked down on the bottom step. "Whoever did this won't get away with it. Mark my words, I *will* find those responsible. They will pay."

Sirens filtered through the streets.

"Howdy, neighbor!" Ezra's head popped up over the fence, peering into her backyard.

Great, he was all she needed right now. "Hey, Ezra."

"What's going on and who are these dogs? I hate dogs. Theys ain't goin' to bark constantly, are they?"

Izzy pushed herself up. "Don't worry, Ezra. They're not staying."

Clouds moved in, blocking the sun and darkening the region along with Izzy's mood.

The sirens screamed louder, indicating Doug and his team were almost there.

"Them coppers coming here?" Ezra clucked his tongue. "This neighborhood is goin' to the dogs."

Izzy ignored his obvious intentional pun. She might as well tell him, as he'd find out anyway. "Had a break-in, Ezra. Don't worry. Your house is fine."

"Did you see anything suspicious, sir?" Austin approached the sixtysomething man.

"Did not and if there were burglars, I would have seen them." He tapped his temple. "Nothing gets by these eyes."

Well, apparently they did. Izzy zipped her coat up farther, attempting to ward off the chill and her foul mood.

A car door slammed.

"Officers will probably ask you questions, Ezra. Catch ya later." Izzy waved before turning to Austin. "Doug's here. Let's go."

After Izzy had a walk with Austin and the dogs and visited a coffee shop, Doug allowed them to enter the condo. Snow had changed the previous sunny sky into a darkened, ominous one, and blanketed the area once again and created havoc.

Izzy stomped snow from her boots as she walked up the steps and entered her trashed home. "It's coming down hard."

"Already have accident reports coming in." Doug turned from her living room fireplace. "I started the gas fireplace to take the chill off."

Izzy whipped off her hat, gloves and coat, throwing them into her closet. She positioned herself with her hands out in front of the fire. "Thanks. So much for a beautiful day."

Austin joined her, followed by the dogs. He pointed to a corner not touched by vandalism. "Lay down."

The K-9s obeyed.

"Now that forensics is finished, I want you to give me your statement." Doug brought out his notebook. "Tell me what happened. Was anything stolen?"

"I don't think so." Izzy recounted their steps in explicit detail from the time they arrived to when they backed out of her condo. She itemized every trashed object as she pictured the scene in her head. "Now, we didn't go upstairs or check the other rooms. I assume they struck there too?"

"I'm afraid so. Do you think they were looking for this supposed flash drive you hid?"

"Don't you, Doug? Did any officers canvass the area for other B and Es?"

"Yes, and nothing surfaced. Apparently, one neighbor behind you had lots to say about our police force helping the area go to the dogs."

"Ezra. He's quite the handful." Izzy rubbed her hands together, hoping to speed up the warming process. "I want to look through the house now. See if it sparks any memories of where I hid that drive."

"Yeah, I'm guessing from the trail of carnage the burglars left, they didn't find it." Doug rubbed his brow. "Sorry, Izzy. When I patrolled earlier, there were no indications someone had broken in. No footprints. Nothing."

Austin picked up a ripped cushion. "So, they must have just been here. Do you think they're watching the house? I did a sweep and saw nothing suspicious. I thought the footprints were yours checking out the place."

"I have units patrolling again now." He

tucked his notebook away. "I have to go do the paperwork."

"Where are you working from since the station is under repair?" Izzy squatted by a drawer and lifted it, replacing the coasters back inside.

"For now, in the library. Not the ideal spot, and Halt is antsy to get back into our building. However, it won't be for a few weeks." Doug walked to the front door. "You okay here by yourself?"

Were they? Izzy prayed they would be. "We'll be fine. Can you send a unit to Mom's and check on them?"

"Will do. I'll give you an update later. Tell me if you find the drive." Doug left the condo.

"Where do you want to start?" Austin righted an overturned chair.

Izzy stood and tapped her chin. "I'll do a cursory look through the rooms and then decide."

She spent the next few minutes moving from room to room with Névé at her heels. Seemed the malamute wasn't leaving her side. Not that Izzy minded. She had fallen in love with the sweet animal.

Izzy approached her office. "Should I start here, girl?"

Névé barked.

"She agrees." Austin entered the room and picked up a painting. "I remember this one."

Tears threatened to spill, but Izzy willed them back. "Dad painted that one of his old homestead. Lots of memories there. Blaire and I used to pretend we were princesses on a quest. We made swords out of branches and ran through the fields."

"How's she doing?"

Izzy let out a long sigh. "She hasn't been herself lately."

"Guy problems?"

She raised her hands, palms up. "Not sure. She hasn't dated since the last one broke her heart." Izzy didn't want to talk about dating.

Sitting at her desk, she scanned the room slowly, looking for any signs of possible stolen items.

But nothing came to mind.

"Anything missing?"

She shook her head.

"Do you think you would have hidden it in here?" Austin propped the painting against the wall.

"Wish I could remember, but nothing is coming to me." She drummed her nails on the desk.

Izzy, if you were to hide a thumb drive, where would you put it?

An open box caught her attention. She had packed up her father's things from his office at HRPD and brought them here, intending to take them to her mother, but hadn't.

The lid leaned on its side against the cardboard box. The perp had looked inside.

Her breath caught. Something about the box drew her like a butterfly to its favorite flower. She pushed herself up and brought it to her desk.

She rummaged through the contents. Her father's books, nameplate, pen set, spring jacket, and…

Her fingers stopped when she grazed a metal object—his challenge coin. Why wasn't it in its velvet pouch? She lifted it from the box and examined the engraving.

Izzy's grandfather had given it to his son when he first became a police officer.

Stay safe, son. Always come home to your family.

It was what Hezekiah Tremblay said to his son and then later to his granddaughter when Izzy joined the force.

Chief Constable Justin Tremblay always carried it in his pocket. Or at least Izzy thought that. She had found it in his desk drawer the day after he died. *Why didn't you have it in your pocket?*

Not that she believed the coin held a secret to staying safe, but her father always had it on him, rolling it between his knuckles. Just like that famous pirate from the movies.

She sat straighter as a memory flashed.

Her removing the coin from the green pouch before heading out her back door.

She sprang to her feet.

Austin turned from picking up her books. "What is it?"

She held up the coin. "I think I put the flash drive in my dad's challenge coin pouch before going outside."

"What does that mean?"

She winced. "I believe I hid it in the back-yard."

The recent snowfall may have buried the pouch. How would they ever find it?

"Do you have any idea where you think you would have hidden it? A special spot in your yard?" Austin took the coin from her fingers and examined the object. A roaring lion was etched on one side. He flipped it over. *Be strong and of a good courage. Joshua 1:9.* "I love this verse."

"So did Dad." Her face twisted in confusion. "No, I don't know where I put it." She fisted her palms and banged on her desk.

Névé and Goose hopped to their feet, ready for action.

"Is this memory lapse what most people have to deal with?" Izzy raked her hand through her shoulder-length brown waves. "I'm not used to feeling this frustrated over memories."

Austin chuckled. "Welcome to everyone else's life." When she didn't respond, Austin rubbed her arm. "Sorry, not trying to make light of your situation. I know this is frustrating."

"It's just the unknown and I hate the unknown." She chewed on her lip. "It's why I'm struggling with God right now. He seems to have hidden His path for me."

There was a story behind her words. What was it? "What's made you feel that way?"

Not that Austin didn't question God and His direction for Austin's life.

"Never mind." She eyed the malamute. "Wait, isn't Névé a search and rescue dog?"

"Yes, but for *humans*, Iz. Too bad we don't have a human scent we could try." Austin handed the coin back to her. "It's okay, Iz. It will come."

Her eyes brightened. She pointed to a jacket. "That's my father's. His scent would probably still be on it and the pouch, right? The box has remained closed over the last two weeks."

Austin lifted it out of the box. "It's a long shot, but worth trying. Are you sure it's probably in the backyard?"

"My flash of memory revealed me pulling the strings to close the pouch and grabbing my jacket. I went out the back door. Not sure what it means and that's all I remember."

"Well, let's go then." Austin turned to the dogs. "Come."

Once Austin and Izzy put on their coats, the group exited through the back door.

The wind bit Austin's face, and he drew in a breath. The sun had disappeared behind dark clouds, bringing an ominous feeling seeping into his bones.

"Let's get my girl working before the wind picks up even more." Austin turned to Goose. "Goose, guard."

The shepherd lifted his nose in the air and advanced to the edge of the condo.

"Wait, isn't Goose a scent dog? Couldn't he help too?" Izzy stuffed on her hat.

"He is, but Névé is better, and I want Goose

protecting us in case those assailants are watching." Austin squatted in front of his malamute and raised the jacket to her nose.

She sniffed the clothing.

"Névé, track!"

She lifted her snout and sniffed the air before moving throughout the backyard, stopping to stick her nose in the snow. She sniffed along a two-foot tree stump holding a birdhouse, then over to the fence, then back to the stump.

"Is she confused?"

"No, she's making sure she has the scent correct." Austin observed his dog as she circled the stump, then sat. "She's found something."

They trudged through the snow toward the birdhouse.

Austin removed a treat from his cargo pants pocket. "Good girl." He ruffled her ears and tossed her the treat.

"So, she's alerted to something in either the stump or the birdhouse." Izzy ran her gloved hand along the stump, squatting to get into the low area.

Austin did the same to the birdhouse. "Is there something special about this feeder?"

"Only that my dad made it for me." She sprang up. "Wait, it's weathered throughout the years and I noticed a hole starting near the bottom."

Austin moved beside her.

She took off her gloves and threw them on the ground before sticking her index finger in the hole, then drew in a sharp breath.

"What is it?"

She edged her middle finger in the opening and pulled out a green velvet pouch. "Yes! Good job, Névé."

The malamute barked.

Izzy opened the pouch and dropped the contents into her palm.

A tiny flash drive.

Behind them, Goose barked.

Austin froze.

His other dog was alerting to danger.

Névé also growled.

Pfft. Pfft.

Bullets hit the stump.

Snow sprayed at their feet.

Goose barked again and barreled toward the shots.

Névé pounced on top of Izzy, knocking her to the ground.

"Get behind the stump!" Austin dropped beside Izzy and Névé, nudging them around their only means of cover. His gaze darted back and forth in search of the shooter.

They were right. The suspects had been watching from a distance and were just waiting for the right time to strike.

And he had no weapon to protect them.

Chapter Seven

Izzy's heartbeat jackhammered like a rabbit when cornered by an enemy with nowhere to run. *Lord, protect us. We're defenseless.* She stuffed the drive and pouch into her coat pocket, then wrapped a protective arm around Névé and waited for more shots, praying they wouldn't reach them.

But no further gunfire erupted.

The dog snuggled into Izzy as they ducked behind the thick stump. She eased her head around the side. "Can you see anyone?"

Barking sounded in the distance.

"No, stay back. Goose is searching."

Approaching sirens returned to the neighborhood.

"Good, I'm guessing Ezra called it in. For once, I appreciate his nosiness." Izzy hauled out her cell phone and hit her partner's number. "Calling Doug."

"Izzy, we're out front now. What's going on?"

She put him on speaker. "Doug, shots fired. We're pinned behind the stump in the backyard. I think the shooter is gone."

Goose continued to bark.

Austin inched closer to the phone. "Doug, follow Goose's barking. He's alerted to something."

"Copy. I'm sending Fisher around back to you." A car door slammed.

Movement sounded, and Izzy peeked out.

Fisher stood in a protective stance with his weapon raised. "Stay put. I don't want you guys catching stray bullets. Carver will give the all-clear once the others have secured the area."

"Got it." Izzy wanted to join her colleagues but couldn't. If she tried, she knew Fisher would probably report her to Halt. Izzy respected Fisher's great police work, but they didn't always see eye to eye on some aspects of a situation.

Austin leaned closer. "You still have the drive?"

"In my pocket."

"Good, I was scared you dropped it in the snow when Névé tackled you." He rubbed the dog's back. "Good girl for protecting Izzy."

Woof!

Fisher's radio crackled, and Doug's voice sailed over the airwaves. "Get Austin here. Suspects are gone, but his dog is alerting to something and won't move."

Izzy and Austin rose to their feet.

"On my way." Austin plodded through the snow toward Goose's barking.

Izzy scooped up her gloves and put them back on, then followed with Névé by her side. "Fisher, stay here in case they circle back."

"Tremblay, this isn't my first rodeo."

Oops. Izzy, stay out of it. You're not on duty. "Sorry, I know." She patted his shoulder and continued after Austin.

Moments later they arrived at the edge of the tree line at the end of Izzy's street. Goose paced, barking into the woods.

"Goose, out!" Austin commanded.

The dog obeyed and sat.

Izzy approached Doug. "Thanks for getting here so quickly."

"You okay?" Doug kept his eyes trained on the forest with his gun raised.

"Yes. Any sign of the shooter?"

"None, but I'm wondering if they're hiding in the woods. Austin, thoughts on what your dog is alerting to?"

"He's definitely agitated about something." Austin looked down the street. "You have any other officers that could join me? I'll get Goose to track into the woods, but I don't want to go in unarmed."

"We're down a few men right now." Doug's radio crackled.

"Carver, movement spotted near Tremblay's condo." Fisher's breathless voice revealed he was running.

Once again, Goose growled.

Névé joined him.

Something or someone was agitating the dogs.

"Doug, I know you have permission to carry a secondary weapon. Can I have it?" Izzy stuck out her hand. "I'll go with Austin. You join Fisher."

"Are you trying to get me into trouble? You're off duty."

"I know, but what choice do we have?" She tilted her head. "It's not like you're giving a gun to a civilian."

He shook his head and took out his secondary gun from his ankle holster. "Don't make me regret this decision." He handed it to her.

"I've got this. Go." Izzy pointed back toward her condo.

Doug jogged down the street.

"How do you want to do this, Iz?"

She checked the gun before raising it. "I'll go first. Then we'll let the dogs do their thing." Izzy didn't wait for a response but advanced as quickly through the snow as she could, entering the woods. She stopped and surveyed her surroundings, listening for movement. The darkened clouds and snowstorm reduced the visibility, making it difficult to see anything in the dense forest.

A chickadee trilled from its perch above their heads. A jay squawked in return as if warning their friends of predators who've entered their forest.

"Slow down, Iz." Austin caught up to her. "Remember your partners."

"You're not my—"

Goose growled.

A shadow passed in between trees in front of them deeper into the forest.

Izzy raised her weapon. "Police, show yourself!"

The figure darted behind a Douglas fir.

"Goose, track!" Austin commanded.

The shepherd bounded through the snow toward the lurking suspect.

If it was a suspect. But who else would be in the forest hiding in the dead of winter and not answer her command?

"Give it up. You're surrounded." Izzy inched closer to where she'd last seen the person with Névé by her side. Seemed the malamute wasn't letting her go anywhere by herself.

Goose dashed toward a cluster of firs, then sat and barked ferociously.

"He's got something." Austin quickened his pace.

Izzy rushed by him. "Let me go first. I'm armed."

"Yes, but I also have a German shepherd ready to attack at my command." He moved a branch from her path. "We do it together."

She couldn't argue. Goose had already proven his worth. However, Austin's hesitation from years ago crept into her memory. Would he freeze like he had back then?

Trust, Izzy. Trust.

Her father's simple mantra played in her head like a skipping record. Why had it come to mind now?

Because the chief constable had believed in Austin's instincts even after he knew about what had happened that night. He had always given Austin the benefit of the doubt.

She didn't like it, but her father was right. Izzy nodded.

They proceeded toward the barking German shepherd.

Moments later they came upon the object of the dog's angered growl.

A man wearing a balaclava, waving a knife. "Get him away from me!"

"I trained this dog to attack to protect those around him." Austin stepped beside Goose.

"Drop your weapon." Izzy inched closer.

"You think I'm dumb? I do that and I'm a dead man."

Izzy searched her memory bank for voice recognition, but none came. She did not know this person. "We can protect you. Tell us why you ransacked my house."

"He'll kill me and my family. And yours." He lifted the knife higher.

"Who are you talking about?"

"Padilla."

"Who is this Padilla?" Wait, if this man only had a knife. Who shot at them? "Is Padilla nearby?"

Silence.

Austin gestured toward Goose. "Tell us or I'll command him to attack."

The man's cell phone rang. "That's him. If I don't answer, he'll kill us all."

"Why would you say that?" Izzy took another step closer.

"Because he's watching." He lifted his chin at something behind them.

Izzy whirled around, looking in the direction they had just come.

Névé growled. She had also seen what Izzy did.

A figure dressed in black from head to toe stood pointing a rifle at them.

A memory flashed.

The same shadowy figure lurking in the dark alleyway.

"Who are you?" Izzy yelled.

The phone continued to ring.

The man pointed to his ear.

Izzy turned back around and spoke to the suspect. "Put it on speaker."

He hit the button. "We're here, boss."

"Constable Tremblay, nice to see you again." The menacing, distorted voice sailed through the speaker.

"Who are you and what do you want?" Izzy

turned back toward the figure standing in the distance.

"I think you know. Lower your weapon." He paused. "The flash drive for your sister's life."

"What makes you think I have this supposed drive?" Would he call her bluff?

She had to contact Doug to get reinforcements here, but had no radio. Could she somehow get her fingers to tap her SOS feature on her cell phone?

"I saw you pull it out from the birdhouse." He tapped the scope on his rifle, then shifted the weapon toward Austin. "Do it or he dies."

The perp in front of them held out his hand. "He's gonna kill us all, man. Hand it over."

Izzy sucked in a ragged breath.

"Don't do it, Iz." Austin looked at Goose, then Névé, then back to Izzy.

She knew him well enough to know he had a plan. A plan obviously involving his dogs. Could she trust him with her sister's life?

Trust, Izzy. Trust.

The mantra played again in her mind, and she dipped her chin in acknowledgment.

"Goose, Névé, get 'em!" Austin's whispered command spoke volumes as he gestured one arm toward the man with the knife and the other toward Padilla.

Goose leaped and seized the man's arm. The assailant cried out and dropped the knife.

Névé barreled through the snow in a zigzag fashion toward Padilla.

The combined effort was enough to distract the man in black.

Izzy lifted her weapon and squeezed the trigger, providing covering fire for Névé.

She wouldn't let Padilla shoot the dog she now loved.

Austin lunged at the man in front of them. "Goose, out!"

The German shepherd released his grip on the suspect's arm. Austin shoved the man's hands behind him, pinned him down and placed his knee on his back. With his right hand, Austin removed his cell and hit Doug's number.

"Austin, you guys okay? I just heard a shot."

"Got one suspect in custody. Izzy is in pursuit of Padilla. Send backup. Now!" Austin prayed they'd arrive before the drug lord got off more shots.

Névé barked.

Austin turned to check Izzy's bearings.

The man in black snaked through the trees, but stopped behind a large Douglas fir, taking aim once again.

Névé and Izzy needed help. Now. "Goose, protect and cover!"

The German shepherd rocketed through the snow toward Padilla in the same zigzag pattern the malamute had taken. It was how Austin trained his dogs when in a dangerous pursuit.

Thankfully Austin had trained the Alaskan malamute in the same fashion as he had his protection dogs—just in case.

Lord, keep them safe and bring help quickly.

"Izzy, he's taking aim. Névé, cover!" Austin prayed the command would also tell Izzy what to do.

She ducked behind a cluster of trees.

Another shot rang out, but the bullet flew wide, spraying the snow near Goose. The dog compensated and changed directions.

The suspect squirmed beneath Austin's hold.

Austin struggled with letting the man go, but Izzy needed help. *Trust.* The word came to him in a flash, and he knew the source. He had to trust in Izzy's abilities—and his dogs. God was in control. Wasn't He? Doubts still tended to seep into Austin's thoughts, especially lately.

He shoved his knee harder into the middle of his captive's spine. "You're not going anywhere, bud."

Loud voices entered the woods.

Good, help had arrived.

"Let me go or I'm a dead man."

"The police can protect you."

"You don't understand. Padilla's connections go deep. He has eyes everywhere." Once again, he squirmed.

"Tell me who he is and we can stop this."

The man cursed. "You can't."

Movement along the path caught Austin's attention. Doug and the others had appeared with their weapons raised. "Status report."

"Shooter passed that way," Izzy yelled, pointing north. "Austin has the other pinned down."

"You stay here in case he circles back. Get the suspect to Fisher. He's still at your condo watching." Doug and the additional constables pursued, trudging through the snow.

Izzy and his dogs returned to Austin's side. She stuffed the gun into the waistband at the small of her back and squatted in front of the suspect. "Has he said anything?"

"Only that no one can stop Padilla."

Goose and Névé flanked Izzy.

Izzy gestured toward them. "Have you met my friends here? I will stop Padilla."

"Your father couldn't."

Austin didn't miss Izzy's tortured expression. "Iz, let's get this guy to Fisher. You need to check on Blaire." He hauled the suspect to his feet, keeping a firm grip on him.

Her eyes widened, and she bolted upright. Izzy extracted her phone from her coat pocket, tapping on it before putting it up to her ear. "Pick up, Blaire."

Austin waited, holding his breath that Izzy's sister was okay and Padilla had only been bluffing. *Please make it so, Lord.*

"No answer." Izzy tapped her phone again. "Calling Mom as Blaire lives at Mom's place for now. She's a criminal profiler and has been working from home."

Seconds later Izzy brought the phone back down. "Austin, we need to get to Mom's. She's not answering either. Something isn't right."

"Let's go." Austin nudged his prisoner forward, addressing his dogs. "Come."

After getting an update from Doug that Padilla had disappeared, Austin drove to Rebecca Tremblay's house on a cul-de-sac near Harturn River's town limits. Izzy had returned the gun to Doug to do all the necessary paperwork involved in discharging a weapon. He promised to keep her updated once they interrogated the suspect. However, Austin doubted they'd get much more out of him than what they had. The thirtysomething had clammed up, stating he knew better than to rat out Padilla or his organization. Austin sensed the man really didn't know Padilla's identity anyway.

Izzy jumped out of the vehicle before Austin could cut the engine. "Wait for us, Iz. Ugh!" He exited the driver's side and jogged to the back to open the cages. "She's stubborn, isn't she? Névé, heel."

The malamute scampered to Izzy's side.

Austin attached Goose's leash. "Come, boy."

Izzy punched a code into the box on the wall and took out a key. She inserted it into the lock and thrust open the front door. "Mom! Blaire!"

So much for entering quietly. Seemed Izzy's concern for her family had trumped her protective police mode. "Izzy, wait up a second." Austin unleashed his German shepherd. "Goose, protect!"

The dog trotted in front of Izzy and Névé.

Austin yanked on Izzy's arm. "Are you trying to get yourself killed? Let Goose lead the way."

She clenched her hands into fists and pounded on her hips. "You're right. I let my emotions take over. I lost Dad. I can't lose Mom and Blaire, too."

Goose growled and whirled around, facing the front entrance, barking and baring his teeth.

"Izzy, what—"

Austin and Izzy pivoted.

Izzy's uncle stood in the doorway with his hands raised.

"Uncle Ford! What are you doing here?" Izzy thrust herself into his arms.

"Goose, out. Sit." Austin gave Névé a silent command to do the same.

The K-9s obeyed.

"What's going on? I got an SOS from your sister." Ford closed the door behind him. "She has me as a contact on her smartwatch."

Izzy clasped her uncle's arm. "I think the same people who got to Dad are after Mom and Blaire."

"You still think Justin was murdered?" Ford tilted his head, folding his arms across his chest. "I thought we settled this after his funeral. You need to let it rest."

"Sir, with everything that's happened in the past couple of days, Izzy was right about her father's death." Austin hated to get in the middle of family matters, but he didn't care for Ford's attitude.

The man inched closer and waggled his finger into Austin's face. "You stay out of it. This doesn't concern you."

Izzy lowered her uncle's arm. "Not true. He's given me refuge and saved me more than once. Tell me when Blaire sent the SOS."

He checked his phone. "About fifteen minutes ago. I got caught in traffic trying to get here and when I called, she didn't pick up." Ford raced down the corridor. "Rebecca, where are you?"

Pounding resonated upstairs.

"Mom?" Izzy took the steps two at a time.

Not again. "Goose, Névé, heel!" Austin flicked his hand toward Izzy.

The dogs bounded after her, along with Ford. Austin followed.

Ford reached the top. "Rebecca, where are you? Blaire?"

The pounding increased along with muffled yells to the left.

"It's coming from Mom's room." Izzy dashed down the hallway.

The group entered the room.

A dresser blocked the walk-in closet door.

Someone had trapped Izzy's mom and sister inside.

Austin turned to Ford. "Help me move this."

They shoved the dresser to the right, and Izzy opened the door.

Her mother and sister scrambled to their feet. Their hands were bound behind them. They turned and stumbled from the room.

Izzy removed Rebecca's gag and untied her before bringing her into an embrace. "Are you okay?"

Ford approached Blaire and did the same. "Tell us what happened."

"The doorbell rang and when I opened the door, a masked man burst inside holding a gun. Then he—" Rebecca's sobs ended her account of the intrusion.

"I had my phone in my hand behind my back, so I quickly pressed the SOS button, hoping I could at least get Uncle Ford here." Blaire hurried to her mother's side and rubbed her arm.

"You did, but it must have only gone out to me as there are no police here." Ford brought his sister-in-law into his arms and caressed her back. "Shhhh…it's gonna be okay, Becky."

Austin noted the way Ford used Rebecca's

nickname and how cozy he appeared to be with his brother's wife. Austin observed Izzy.

Her contorted expression told him she also noticed her uncle's intimate action. She took her mother's hand and guided her to a chair in the room's corner, breaking her uncle's hold. "Tell us what happened next."

"He took away our phones, then tied our hands and gagged us. Made us go upstairs and pushed us into the closet. We heard him moving the dresser in front of the door, so we realized we wouldn't be able to escape." Rebecca bit her lip. "Then everything silenced. It was like he just wanted to hide us."

Izzy spoke to Austin. "Padilla's way of telling me he's in control. We need to get Mom and Blaire into protective custody."

Austin's thoughts exactly, and he knew the perfect place for them to find refuge.

Murray K-9 Ranch.

He just had to beef up security first. Austin wouldn't let anything happen to the rest of Izzy's family.

Not on his watch.

Chapter Eight

Izzy adjusted the number of copies to two and hit the print button. She wasn't taking any chances this time around with her father's journal. She downloaded all the scanned pages from the drive and wanted a physical printout to add to her board. Visualizing every detail was how she worked and did her best thinking. She took an extra copy for safekeeping.

Névé slept on her mat placed in the room's corner. The dog's presence comforted her, but left her with a question. How would she say goodbye to this amazing animal when she solved her father's case and put those responsible behind bars?

And she *would* do that.

Austin had convinced Izzy's mother and Blaire to take refuge at his ranch. They had balked at the idea and Uncle Ford did too, but in the end, Izzy sold the idea as family time for bonding. Uncle Ford warned them he'd be checking in on them often. He didn't want his "girls" to be stressed by not being in their own place. He knew his sister-in-law well. Izzy's mother did not like change and losing her husband was huge. She had struggled ever since his death.

Izzy's father had done everything for her mother, even though she was highly capable. Spoiled by her husband, Rebecca Tremblay had gotten used to his pampering.

An image of Uncle Ford rubbing her mother's back popped into her mind. Izzy dug her fingernails into her palms. Why did his intimate touch bother her so much?

Because it's too soon.

Her father just passed. However, maybe the gesture was nothing. Uncle Ford was a kind, caring person and wanted to console his sister-in-law.

Concentrate. You have enough problems to deal with right now. Namely…getting those three hours back.

Izzy sighed and took the first printout from the tray, taping it to her evidence board. She placed the second copy in an envelope. She'd hide it in her room later.

Her cell phone buzzed in her back jeans

pocket. She took it out and hit answer. "Tremblay here."

"Got something for you." Doug's voice filtered through the phone.

She put him on speaker and set her cell on the desk she'd commandeered. "I hope it's good news. I sure could use some."

"Everything okay?"

"Just tired and want the three-hour black hole to disappear." And she'd been struggling with having Austin so close. Not that she would admit that to Doug, but her past feelings resurfaced, and she had fought hard to stuff them away. Forever.

"It will come. So, we examined your mother's home, but didn't find any prints that weren't hers or Blaire's. The suspect most likely wore gloves." Rustling papers sounded through the speaker. "The perp you caught is Conroy Phillips. Has a past record of misdemeanors. Disturbing the peace, drunk driving, petty thefts. Nothing substantial. Until now."

Izzy wrote the name on a piece of paper. "Did you get anything from him?"

"Fisher and I cross-examined him hard. He's pretty tight-lipped, but he let two things slip. One was that Padilla's organization is far-reaching. Across Canada and even into Washington State."

"That makes sense, as it's right on the British Columbia border. Did he say anything about the drugs they're selling?"

"He only mentioned the bath salts, but we already knew about that."

"We need to find where they're producing the drugs and shut it down." Izzy sat on the corner of the desk and studied the board. "What was the other thing you discovered?"

"He let it slip that Padilla is close to finding where you're hidden."

Izzy's muscles locked, and she dropped her pen. It hit the desk and rolled onto the floor. "How? We've been so careful."

"But you haven't stayed put, Izzy. You need to stop leaving the safety of the ranch."

She hated being confined to one spot. The Tremblay blood in her prevented that from happening. "But I have to find the truth and get justice for Dad."

"I realize that, but stop putting yourself at risk. Let Fisher and I do the investigating."

How could she make him understand her need to bring her father's killer to justice? She had sensed her father's troubled mood before his death, but had failed to find out the cause. She'd been too busy with her own cases that she'd hadn't taken time to sit down with him and have a heart-to-heart.

And now it was too late.

Tears threatened to fall. She breathed in and out to stop them. *I miss you, Dad. Miss our chats. Why didn't I spend more time with you lately?*

"Izzy? You hear me?"

Doug's question ended her pity party.

"I did, and I'll be careful. I promise." However, she wouldn't promise not to leave the ranch again if her investigation warranted her to.

"Keep me apprised of your progress, as I know you will not stop." He chuckled. "Take care."

"You too." She clicked off the call.

She returned to printing the pages of her father's journal and adding them to the board.

"You're gonna need another board soon." Austin set a cup of coffee on her desk. "Here's some fuel for your afternoon."

"Thanks." She took a sip. "This is good. You still roast your own beans?"

"Of course. You know how much of a coffee snob I am." He scooped up the fallen pen from the floor and set it beside her notebook, turning the page in his direction. "Who's Conroy Phillips?"

"The guy you caught in the woods." Izzy explained what information Doug had provided.

"Well, Sawyer and I have increased the ranch hands' awareness after your mom and Blaire arrived." He removed his cell phone from his back pocket. "Sawyer just texted me a schedule for their regular patrols of the property. We've got you covered."

"That means a lot to me, especially with Mom and Blaire here too." She organized the copies of her father's journal and tucked them into the folder. "I made extras just in case."

"Don't blame you. Perhaps lock the drive in the desk drawer. Keys are in the pencil holder."

She did as he suggested. "Where are Mom and Blaire?"

"I set up a table in Blaire's room so she can work in there. Your mom is—"

"Right here." Rebecca Tremblay rubbed her eyes and stepped into the office. "I had a little snooze, then heard voices and wanted to see what you're doing."

"Sorry, did we wake you?"

"It's okay, Izzy. I didn't want to sleep long anyway." She pointed to the board. "What's all this?"

Izzy grimaced. She didn't want her mother to

see all of her dad's journal pages. "My evidence board for the case Dad was working on."

Her mother's eyes flashed. "Why are you still investigating? Your father died from a heart attack."

"Mom, how can you say that after everything that's happened?"

"Coincidence."

"I don't believe in those. Dad was in perfect health. He showed me his test results and I remember everything vividly." She took a breath. "And someone stuck you and Blaire in a closet, Mom. That's not a coincidence, and you know it!"

Névé lifted her head at Izzy's raised voice.

She cleared her throat. "Sorry. I'm just tired of people not trusting my intuition. And these attacks prove it's more than that. Dad was investigating something that got him killed."

Her mother's lip quivered. "I just don't want to lose anyone else."

Izzy rubbed her mother's arm. "I'm not going anywhere."

"Mrs. Tremblay, my employees are rotating their patrols of the ranch property. They'll be watching the place around the clock. The front gate is locked. No one in or out without our approval."

"I appreciate that. I realize I said earlier I didn't want your protection, but I was wrong. You're a good man, Austin."

Névé barked.

Izzy's mom giggled. "Yes, you're good too, girl." She pointed to the journal page printouts. "That's Justin's handwriting. What do these numbers mean?"

"It's a code. A message for me, but I don't know what cipher Dad used." Izzy bit her fingernails. "That's the piece of information his CI had given me before he died." She tapped her temple. "But it's within those missing three hours locked in my memory somewhere."

Her mother turned. "Well, remember what your dad always said when he couldn't figure something out?"

"'Walking is where I do my best thinking.'" Izzy lowered her voice to mimic her father's, then focused on Névé. "What do you say, girl? Wanna go for a stroll?"

The dog perked her ears up and leaped up on all fours.

Austin chuckled. "You had her at stroll. How about I take you around the property and then to my K-9 training area? I would like to show it to you."

"Sure. Mom, you wanna come?"

"No. I'm going to grab something to read from Austin's huge bookshelf and curl up by the fireplace."

"Mom, don't tell anyone about the journal, okay?"

"But why?"

How much should she tell her mother? She didn't want to scare her, but she must protect her family. "I don't trust anyone else but us."

"Fine. I'll catch you later." She left the room.

Austin unclipped the two-way radio from his belt. "First, I need to tell Sawyer we're going outside and to be on the lookout for us. I don't want anything catching us off guard."

Conroy's warning that Padilla was close to figuring out Izzy's location barreled into her head. A wave of angst slammed her body.

Was it true and if so, how?

An arctic breeze snaked down Austin's neck, and he tightened his blue-and-green-plaid scarf. He led a bundled Izzy around the property to help give her both exercise and some thinking time. Névé bounded ahead of them, playing in the snow. With all of his men on guard, Austin felt it safe to release Névé from her duties so she could enjoy their time together.

Izzy giggled, then hurried ahead and plopped herself beside the dog.

Lord, I would love this to be the norm. Me and Izzy walking on the ranch with Névé.

The idea warmed his chilled body, but then the hurt after the night of Clara's death slammed into his chest, stealing his breath and icing his veins.

Izzy's silence after the call had nearly killed Austin. He had planned to tell her his true feelings for her after their shift, but his hesitation cost more than her friend's life. It cost him Izzy's respect.

It took him months to move on from the woman in front of him. Right now his ranch kept him busy, and he didn't have time for anyone in his life.

At least, that's how he justified his single status. Truth be told, he longed for a wife and kids to share this special place with him. His adoptive parents had worked hard to build the ranch, and now Austin continued their legacy.

Sometimes Austin wondered who his biological mother and father were, but he always pushed the thoughts aside. They had abandoned him as a baby, and that was hard to come back from.

Austin had vowed that if he ever had children, he would hold them close. Love them with his entire being and never let them feel unwanted.

Like his biological parents had made him feel.

Tom and Mandy Murray took him in after he'd been in and out of foster homes, loved him, and adopted him when Austin was ten years old. He was the child they could never have. "A gift from God," they often said.

The couple raised him to respect people and treat everyone with kindness. However, when he was bullied at grade school for being adopted, Austin's insecurities over his biological parents' rejection of him had multiplied. He began acting out and was suspended at one point. When questioned about his sudden change in demeanor, Austin had shared with his parents how the kids were making fun of him for being adopted, stating he wasn't loved.

Austin never forgot his father's actions and words. He pulled him into an embrace and said, "Son, being adopted is a gift. It means God loved you enough to send you into our lives for safekeeping. Until one day, when you grow up and have kids, you can show them how love works. It's not about the bloodline. It's about love—pure and simple."

Austin smiled as the memory of his father's words brought both happiness and sadness all rolled into one. *I miss you, Mom and Dad.*

Izzy's laughter brought him back to his ranch. *God, what's my path? Will I find someone to love?*

Love was Austin's deepest desire. He wanted to show love because Tom and Mandy Murray had shown him what true love meant. Both in terms of their marriage and their affection for their son. Austin.

But for now, Austin would put his love toward his dogs. He eyed Izzy. *Maybe, just maybe.* "Iz, you want to come now and see how I train the dogs?"

"Sure." She stood from making snow angels and brushed her jeans off. "Lead the way."

Moments later they entered the Murray K-9 Ranch's kennels. The large building housed all his dogs comfortably, minus Névé, and was also where he trained during the winter months. Dogs were always Austin's passion, so when he left the police department, he threw himself into learning how to train dogs. His father helped him get the ranch set up, and it soon blossomed into the lucrative business he had today—raising dogs to get them ready for K-9 units across the country.

Izzy whistled as she gazed around the building. "You have a state-of-the-art business going on here."

"Thanks. I provide dogs to police departments across Canada. Even have had interest from some in the States." Austin opened a golden retriever's cage. "This beauty is almost ready to go to the Yukon. I've been training her to become an avalanche dog. This is Penny."

Izzy squatted in front of the retriever. "Hello, Penny. You're beautiful."

Behind them, Névé whimpered.

Izzy stood. "What's wrong with her?"

"Sometimes malamutes don't play well with other dogs, especially of the same gender. And she's jealous you're giving Penny attention. Névé can be territorial." Austin picked up a nearby shovel. "Want to see how Penny can find someone in the snow?"

"Sure. How do you train them for that?"

He snickered. "You'll see. You up for a game of hide and seek?"

She tilted her head to the right, crossing her

arms. "Something tells me you're using me for bait."

"Yup. First, I need to put Névé back in the house. I don't want her interfering with Penny's training."

After taking the malamute into the house and burying Izzy safely in the snow, Austin brought the golden outside and squatted in front of her. "Penny, search!"

The dog bounced through the snow, zigzagging across the yard. She stopped in various spots, sniffing the snow, then veered to a new area and back again. Seconds later she bolted directly toward where Austin had buried Izzy and dug ferociously as her tail wagged in a helicopter spiral. She'd found the avalanche victim.

Penny buried her head into the hole she dug and tugged on the rope training tool Austin had given Izzy. Moments later Izzy's snow-covered head appeared.

Austin approached the fort-like pile of snow he had constructed to train. "Good girl, Penny." He helped Izzy to her feet. "And that's how it's done."

"Impressive." Izzy rubbed Penny's head. "She's so smart. When is she going to the Yukon?"

Too soon for Austin's liking. "In a couple of

weeks, her handler will return to complete her final training. He's been coming every month for a week at a time. They've bonded well. I insist on that before I let my dogs go. It's part of the contract."

"It must be hard to give up the dogs after training them."

Was Izzy reading his mind again? "It is, but I want all different agencies to benefit from what these animals can do. They simply amaze me more and more every day."

Snowflakes floated in front of them before multiplying. The wind picked up and rattled his flagpole nearby.

"You ready to head in? Looks like the storm is intensifying." Austin swept snow off the golden.

"Yes. Being buried chilled me to the bone. Think I'll join Mom in front of that fire." She rubbed her gloved hands together.

"Let me get Penny back into her home and I'll—"

A gunshot echoed throughout the property, sending more than weather chills down Austin's back.

Had Padilla breached the Murray K-9 Ranch?

Chapter Nine

Izzy dropped into the snow and yanked Penny down with her, protecting the dog from harm. "Austin, where did the shot come from?" Had Padilla and his men found them? Rapid-fire heartbeats constricted her chest, sending her pulse throbbing in her head.

"Sawyer! Who's shooting?" Austin yelled into his radio.

Multiple dogs barked from the kennels, and Penny squirmed beneath Izzy's hold. "It's okay, girl. I've got you."

When no response came, Austin pressed the button again. "Sawyer, report!"

Shouts filled the air moments before Sawyer and a few ranch hands raced around the corner of the K-9 building, each carrying rifles.

Izzy pushed herself into a crouched position, staying low in case of more gunfire.

Sawyer approached. "Movement spotted at

the property edge. Izzy, I suggest you get inside. We're going to inspect the grounds."

Austin clipped his radio back on his belt. "Who fired?"

A blond man in his late twenties raised his hand. "I did, Austin. I was the one who spotted someone suspicious on the south side."

Austin frowned. "Well, did they fire first, Maverick? I only heard the one shot."

Maverick—the new guy.

Izzy read Austin's wrenched face. He was upset. Why the harsh tone? Had Maverick given them issues since his arrival?

The man switched his hold on the rifle to his left hand. "I saw a gun."

"Are you sure? You're too trigger happy." Austin took the rifle from him. "Please go clean out the north stable."

Maverick's expression morphed into something else before it vanished and he stomped away, but Izzy caught it.

Deceit? Contempt?

Did Austin see it too?

Maverick's attitude didn't sit well with Izzy. Her police intuition's warning bells screamed deceit.

Sawyer shifted his stance. "Don't be so hard on him, Austin. He's—"

"New." Austin threw his hands in the air. "You keep defending him, Sawyer. Why?"

The ranch foreman's gaze lowered to the ground. "Something about him reminds me of myself at his age."

"You vetted him, so I'm trusting our lives with your instincts." Austin addressed the other men. "Do another perimeter sweep. Find whoever was lurking. I need to ensure Izzy and her family are safe."

Izzy withdrew her cell phone. "I'll get Doug to have an officer patrol the area." She reached her partner and explained the situation. He agreed to have someone drive around Austin's ranch. Izzy clicked off the call.

Sawyer barked orders at the men, and they scattered in different directions.

"Iz, let's get Penny in her kennel and you back inside." Austin placed his hand on her lower back and nudged her toward the K-9 building.

"How long has Maverick been working here?" Izzy reached the door first, opening it for him and Penny.

"A month now." Austin ran his hands over the golden's body before opening her kennel. "You're good, Penny." He tossed her a treat. "Your reward for finding Iz in the snow."

Penny woofed before catching the bone-shaped snack.

Izzy chuckled at their interaction. She was impressed at how well Austin was doing with his K-9 training. Her father would say God turned ashes into beauty as He knew Austin's path would lead him here—where he was meant to be.

Was that true? Did God know what lay beyond the path's bend?

Because right now, Izzy couldn't see through the fog.

Austin poured water into Penny's dish and closed the kennel door. "I didn't mean to be so abrupt with Maverick. He's just been making too many mistakes and he could have gotten himself—or you—killed by his recklessness."

"Can I be honest?"

"Of course." Austin opened the door for her.

"I get the sense something is off about Maverick. You know, that cop intuition thing." Izzy strode outside.

The snowflakes now blanketed the property with a white wall. Izzy readjusted her scarf and followed Austin back to the ranch house. The fire was calling her name, and she couldn't wait to send its warmth into her chilled body.

Once inside, Austin stomped the snow from his boots and took off his coat. "I agree, Iz. I can't put my finger on it, but lately Maverick has been—what's the word I'm looking for—almost sneaky. Sawyer assures me he came with positive recommendations from the last ranch where he worked."

"Why did he leave there?" Izzy wiggled out of her coat and hung it on the wall hook.

Névé bounded into the hallway and snuggled into her.

Austin chuckled. "She doesn't always warm up to people so quickly."

Or maybe she sensed Izzy's emerging feelings toward her handler. Izzy squatted in front of the dog and kissed her forehead, suppressing her emotion. "Shall we go get warmed up, girl?"

Névé barked.

Izzy moved into the living room and noted an opened book turned upside down on the rocker. However, her mother was nowhere in sight. Once her mother got her nose in a novel, nothing could distract her. Perhaps she went to the kitchen for a snack.

Izzy walked to the fireplace and held her

hands out in front of the flames. "You didn't answer my question."

"Maverick claims he wants experience training dogs and found out about my ranch through my website." Austin removed the poker from its hook, jabbed the coals, then threw another log on the fire. "But I'm not ready to train him. Is that mean of me?" He positioned himself beside her, holding out his hands.

His powerful presence gave her a sense of protection, renewed friendship, and—

Dare she hope for more?

"There's nothing wrong with being cautious, Austin. I realize you still have that cop intuition, so trust your gut." Izzy swept a stray curl off his forehead.

Their eyes locked, holding in place.

Austin looked away, breaking the connection. "I need to check with Sawyer on the perimeter. Névé, stay." He unclipped his radio and spoke into it as he exited the room.

Izzy's shoulders slumped. *Remember, he never felt the same as you. Don't forget about Dax.*

Between the two heartaches, she couldn't—and wouldn't—love again.

The pain went too deep.

And that's something she'll never forget.

Névé trotted over to her and licked her hand.

At least someone loved her.

Thumping footfalls tensed her already tightened muscles.

Austin reappeared. "Your uncle is at the front gate, demanding to talk to you. Says he may be able to help you with your father's coded journal pages."

Izzy's jaw dropped. "But how did Uncle Ford find out about those?"

"I told him." Her mother entered the room, carrying a glass of water.

Why couldn't her mother trust Izzy's instincts and leave things alone? "Mom, I told you not to tell anyone."

"Your uncle is not just anyone. He's family and feels he can help." She picked up her book from the rocking chair and sat. "Blaire is finishing up work and coming too."

Izzy cemented her hands at her side.

Austin held up his cell phone. "Iz, do I let him in?"

She nodded.

Perhaps her mother was right. After all, Uncle Ford knew his brother well.

And right now, she'd welcome any help in solving this case.

Before more people were targeted.

Austin placed a tray of warm muffins in the middle of his dining room table. Izzy had pulled him aside and suggested they meet here instead of his office. She didn't want to compromise the case by having anyone else seeing the evidence board. The pictures and her notes were police business. He agreed and helped her spread the copies of her father's journal pages in the middle of the table. Austin made a fresh pot of coffee and poured everyone a cup.

Sawyer had informed Austin that his men secured the property. No sign of the person Maverick had supposedly seen. Sawyer reported fresh footprints near the fence, confirming Maverick's claim. Izzy had shared that the officer cruising the area had seen nothing suspicious.

But that didn't mean someone wasn't out there.

Izzy put a muffin on her plate. "Uncle Ford, what makes you think you can crack this code?"

The man fingered his mustache. "Because I knew Justin longer than any of you. We weren't born twins, but sure had the same tendencies. I understand how he used to think."

Blaire broke a muffin in two. "And remember, Uncle Ford almost became a cop, too. He has the street smarts."

Austin didn't miss the praise in Blaire's tone. Or Izzy's contorted expression.

Why such a drastic difference between sisters? What had warranted the friction between the two?

And why had Izzy distanced herself from her uncle? Austin had seen it the moment he entered the ranch. Ford had hugged her, but Izzy's rigid body screamed with annoyance.

Was it because of his attention to her mother?

Ford patted Blaire's hand. "You're too kind."

Izzy coughed, then stuffed a bite of her muffin into her mouth.

Austin had been away from his ex-partner for years, but still could read her expressions. He placed his hand on hers and mouthed, *You okay?*

She dipped her chin in response before turning to the group. "Let's begin. What I know is, Dad used a code and right before his CI was killed, Sims shared the cipher with me." She tapped her temple. "But it's locked in that three-hour window I can't remember."

"Odd that Miss Perfect Memory can't remember something," Blaire huffed, then sipped her coffee.

Austin read the jealousy on Blaire's face and the pain on Izzy's. Clearly, the Tremblay sisters were at odds.

He remembered Izzy telling him they were close. Inseparable was the word she used.

He caught Izzy's expression before she pointed to the printouts on the table. "You'll see that Dad used a series of numbers. Everyone grab a printout and see if anything jumps out at you."

The group did as Izzy instructed. Silence filled the room as each observed the numbers.

"I've looked into different ciphers, but honestly, I don't know which one Dad would have used." Izzy slammed the paper she held on to the table and stood.

Névé jumped up from her position in the corner, alert to Izzy's sudden moves.

"I think we need to pray about this." Ford returned the printout he'd been holding to the table and reached for Rebecca and Blaire's hands.

Izzy whirled around, her eyes flashing venom.

Not good. Austin needed to intervene before the situation got messy. He raised his hand to stop any words he guessed she was about to say.

"I think prayer is a good idea." He patted Izzy's seat. "Come sit, Iz."

She exhaled. "Fine, but can you pray, Austin?"

"Sure." Austin stole a peek at Ford.

The man's countenance transformed from lovable into an unreadable emotion. Frustration? Anger?

Ignoring the question of why the animosity between uncle and niece existed, Austin bowed his head. "Father, we come to You today requesting Your help. Izzy needs to remember what Sims told her regarding her father's cipher. Please give us all direction in helping solve the mystery. We also pray for protection from whoever is trying to do this family harm." Should he also pray for family unity? *Son, always listen to God's still, small voice.* Something his father said and right now, that voice nudged Austin. "Also, can you bring this family closer? They need each other during these rough patches. We pray this in Your precious name. Amen."

He stole a glimpse at Ford.

The man stared at Izzy's bowed head. Even though his earlier expression had been unreadable, the one on his face now revealed an emotion that spiked Austin's guard.

Contempt.

Why did the man hold anger toward his niece?

Blaire snagged her cell phone. "I'm going to search on ciphers. I realize you did, Izzy, but maybe talking about them among us will spark something."

"Great idea, Blaire." Ford snatched a muffin and took a bite.

"Okay, here's what comes up for ciphers. Transposition, concealment." Blaire continued to read from the list of common ciphers.

Rebecca slammed her hand on the table. "Wait, isn't there one about using books? At least, I've seen that in the movies. Justin loved to read." She turned to Izzy. "Remember how he used to read to you?"

"Yeah, his favorite." Blaire tossed her phone back onto the table.

"Not true, Blaire. He just knew you didn't like to read. When he tried, you always hid under the covers and hummed to yourself. I'm hardly his—" Izzy shot to her feet, then paced around the table.

"What is it, Iz?" Austin stood and placed his hand on her shoulder, stopping her meandering.

"I think Sims may have told me that Dad used

the book cipher and that I just have to figure out the reference book."

Blaire leaned back in her chair, crossing her arms. "Hmm. Well, that's like finding a needle in a haystack. You have a ton of books, sister. Use that memory of yours to figure it out."

"I wish it was that easy." Izzy plunked onto her chair and held her head in her hands.

"What do you mean?" Rebecca shifted a paper toward her. "How does it work? What do the numbers signify?"

Austin ignored Blaire's poor attitude and pointed to the printout. "Each number refers to a page, line and word on that line. However, the key is to use the correct book and edition or the code is useless."

Izzy hissed out a breath. "I have no idea what book he would have used. I can picture each on my bookshelf, but none that stand out."

Ford's phone dinged and he swiped the screen. "I gotta get to a special police board meeting."

Izzy tilted her head. "I thought they were the last Wednesday of each month."

"They are, but the mayor called this one. Something about urgent business." Ford placed his hand on Rebecca's arm. "Call if you need anything."

She nodded.

Ford gestured toward the printouts. "I hope you understand my brother's cryptic notes, Izzy. Catch you all later."

"I'll walk you out." Austin led him out of the dining room and into the hallway. He lifted Ford's coat from the hook and handed it to him. "Have a good evening."

Ford poked Austin's chest. "You stay out of Izzy's life. You almost ruined her ten years ago. Don't do it again."

Wait—what? Heat singed Austin's face, and he fought to suppress his anger. "I'm only offering a place of refuge for her and her family. That's all." *Liar.* Austin hated that the man had obviously read the emotions Austin battled to keep under wraps.

"I don't like that you've conveniently come back into her life. I don't trust you, dog man." He stomped out of the house, leaving a menacing tone lingering in the air.

And Austin wondering who they could trust.

Chapter Ten

Izzy stepped outside later that evening with Névé on one side and Austin on the other. Lingering snowflakes floated to the ground, and Izzy tipped her face toward the sky. She opened her mouth and let the frozen white droplets fall on her tongue. Something she and Blaire used to do as kids. The thought of Izzy's strained relationship with her sister made her clamp her mouth shut, blocking out the memories. After supper, Izzy had invited her family to go on a walk around the property. Sawyer claimed the ranch was secure, and no one lurked in the shadows. However, both Blaire and their mother said they were retiring after a long, stressful day. Seemed all the talk about ciphers and her father's case had tuckered her family out.

Probably for the best. Izzy had had enough of her family for one day. Austin had mentioned Uncle Ford's hostility toward him as he left.

Right now, she only wanted a peaceful evening. After all, what more could she ask for—a handsome man, a sweet dog and stillness in the fresh air? Izzy breathed in.

I could get used to this.

"What are you thinking?" Austin's baritone voice added to her romantic dreams.

If only you could read my mind. Then again, that probably wouldn't be a good thing. "Just how peaceful it is here." Best leave it at that. Anything more may expose the feelings she struggled to contain. She had to slam the box shut and throw away the key if her heart was going to survive being so close to Austin Murray. "You sure it's safe for a walk?"

"The ranch hand on duty just reported everything was quiet, so we're good." Austin scooped up some snow and chucked it. "Névé, catch."

The dog barked and bounded across the field, jumping to catch the snowball.

"I'm sorry about Uncle Ford's harsh treatment. He had no right to do that."

"What's his story, anyway? I never met him when we were partners, and you didn't talk about him much. Was your dad younger or older than Ford?"

"Older. Uncle Ford grew up in the shadow

of my father and always wanted to be like Justin Tremblay. He followed him into the police academy but didn't make it. Uncle Ford was devastated but happy with how well Dad did." Izzy kicked at a mound of snow. "He went on to further his career in science and works for a pharmaceutical company. He's done really well for himself."

"I get the impression he favors Blaire over you, or is that just my imagination?" Austin pointed left. "Let's go this way."

Izzy turned in the direction he suggested and rounded the corner of the ranch. The horse stable was well lit with a powerful floodlight over the top of the large red barn doors. "It's not your imagination. Blaire has always been Uncle Ford's favorite. Not exactly sure why. Maybe because she's the younger sibling, like him."

"Can I ask you a question?"

Izzy hesitated. How personal did she want to get with this man? Could she go there again? Their friendship had been deep, and she missed their talks. She breathed in and took the plunge. "Sure."

"What happened between you and Blaire? You used to be so close when we were partners."

Not the question she was expecting. She'd

figured he'd ask about her love life as he used to tease her relentlessly about the lack of men in her life. How much could she reveal when she didn't really understand Blaire's secrecy herself? She let out an audible breath.

"That bad? Sorry if I'm interfering where I shouldn't. I realize we haven't seen each other in a while."

"To be honest I'm not sure myself. A couple of years ago, I discovered something question-able about the man she was dating." Izzy pic-tured the case that had come across her desk vividly. "I was working on a missing children's case, and when the father's picture came on my screen, I was shocked. It was Blaire's boyfriend, Luca. He was married with two children and a suspect in his daughter's disappearance." Once again, Izzy lifted her face toward the sky and let the snowflakes fall like feathers onto her skin. Something about the snow felt like cleansing to Izzy. Winter was her favorite season. "We ques-tioned Luca, but he had a solid alibi."

They walked to the edge of the ranch prop-erty, near the tree line. Thankfully, the fence kept intruders from breaching the premises—at least that's what Sawyer claimed.

Austin whistled. "Wow. How did Blaire take it?"

"Not good. She wouldn't believe me, so I invited both Blaire and Luca over to my condo, then confronted him." She'd never forget Luca's anger or the hurt in Blaire's saddened eyes. However, her hurt was directed more toward Izzy than her married boyfriend. "He told Blaire he and his wife were in the middle of a messy divorce. I didn't believe him. Blaire did."

"You mean she kept seeing him?"

"Yup. Even after Mom and Dad's insistence that she break up with him." Izzy puffed out a breath and watched it linger in the frosty night air. "They finally broke up a year ago, but she wouldn't tell me why. Ever since I told her Luca was married, our relationship changed and Uncle Ford took her side in everything. Yelled at me for interfering."

"I'm sorry. You were only trying to help. She should have known you were doing it out of love."

A coyote howled, interrupting the serenity on the ranch property.

Névé growled, positioning herself in front of Izzy and Austin.

Seconds later another coyote answered from the opposite direction—and louder. The animal was close.

Were they marking their territory?

A shudder prickled Izzy's spine, and she clutched Austin's arm. "That was too close. Do coyotes often come on your property?"

"Sometimes. Normally, the barking dogs keep them away." Austin guided her toward the ranch house. "Let's head back."

"Good idea. I've had enough excitement for one day. I don't want to add a coyote confrontation to the list."

"Névé, come," Austin commanded.

The malamute obeyed, trotting beside Izzy.

"She's well-trained." Izzy was impressed with Austin's skills. "You've done well for yourself here."

"Thanks. Training dogs is my passion and even though the path to get here was rough, I feel it's what God called me to do."

She knew Austin spoke about the night Clara was killed. Was he finally ready to talk about it? "Austin, what—" Her cell phone buzzed, interrupting her question. She fished it out from her coat pocket and checked the screen.

Doug. She hit the answer button. "Hey, partner, what's up?"

"Sorry, I realize it's late, but I had to give you a quick call. Two things. We've connected the King & Sons shell corp to a known drug ring funding the community with those bath salts. Plus the coroner has linked a recent drug overdose death to the same drug, but says whoever is making the salts has modified them to be more deadly."

Izzy stopped in front of the ranch house steps. "No! We need to stop Padilla. That was the drug Dad was investigating."

"Anything more on the journal?"

"Getting closer, but no. What's the second thing you called for?"

Névé bounded up the stairs, with Austin close behind.

"A warning. The chief constable will call you. Something about a board meeting."

Did it have to do with the impromptu meeting her uncle had dashed off to? "Great. That's all I need." Her phone buzzed. She checked the screen. "That's him now. Thanks for the update." She followed Austin and his dog into the ranch foyer.

"Stay safe."

"You too." Izzy clicked off Doug's call and turned to Austin. "Halt is calling. I gotta take this."

He nodded. "I'll get us some lavender tea."

Izzy smiled. He always knew what made her relax. That was her favorite tea to settle her nerves.

She stomped the snow from her boots and kicked them off before moving into the living room, hitting the speaker icon. "Tremblay here."

"Sorry for calling so late, Isabelle."

Isabelle? First Izzy and now Isabelle. Something was definitely wrong. "No worries. What's going on?"

A sigh sailed through the speaker. "I told you to stay at the ranch, but the police board has called an important meeting tomorrow that you need to go to."

"Did something happen at the meeting tonight?"

"How did you find out? It was called at the last minute."

Izzy placed the phone on the coffee table and wiggled out of her coat. "Uncle Ford was here and left quickly to attend. He's on the executive board. Why do I have to go?"

"The mayor received an anonymous tip about

you, and now I'm under review for allowing you to help with Ned Bolton's interview. I tried to explain the situation, but Georgia—Mayor Fox—wouldn't listen. She's convinced you acted inappropriately. I disagree with her claims, but you need to come in and defend yourself."

Izzy plunked herself into a plush plaid chair. "And you."

Névé whined and nestled her snout on Izzy's lap.

The dog had obviously sensed Izzy's shift in emotions.

She stroked Névé's head. "Did she give you details?"

"She said she'd present everything at the meeting."

"When and where is it, sir?"

"Harturn River Library at eight thirty tomorrow morning."

Austin appeared holding two mugs, but hesitated at the entranceway.

She waved him in. She needed his support right now. "Okay, sir. I'll be there."

"Isabelle, please be careful. Can you get Austin and his dog to protect you? You know how short-staffed we are here. We assigned all the constables to cases at the moment."

Izzy's gaze shifted to Austin. She raised a brow in a silent question.

He dipped his head, confirming his help.

"He's in, but what are you thinking?"

"I don't like the timing of these allegations. Something is off to me, and it might only be a ploy to get you to come out of hiding."

Izzy leaned forward, disturbing Névé.

Could her chief be right and she was walking into a trap?

Austin tossed and turned on his king-size bed as nightmares held him in their haunting grip, plunging him back to a seven-year-old cowering behind a hay bale. He shivered—not from the cold—but from the wrath of the man who threatened to whip him. Again. All because Austin had eaten the last cookie.

"You can't hide, Austin." His foster father's voice boomed in the large barn. "You have to pay for disobeying me."

Why did you leave me, Mom and Dad? The recurring question had followed him to every foster care home he'd been sent to. Tears flowed down his cheeks as he hugged his knees to his chest, attempting to make himself as small as possible.

Maybe then *he* wouldn't find him.

Austin's battered body couldn't take much more of the man's fury.

Scratching sounded nearby. What was his foster father doing?

Whoosh!

A glow appeared over the hay bale. Seconds later smoke filled the barn and Austin sneezed, giving away his location.

The man sneered as he towered over Austin, holding his whip. "There you are."

More scratching followed by dogs barking.

Austin raised his hands. "Please don't hurt me. I'm sorry I ate the last cookie. I was so hungry. I'll never do it again. I promise."

"It's too late for your sorry excuses." The man cracked the whip. "Time for your punishment."

The scene morphed and a different man stood behind a whimpering woman, holding a gun to her temple. "Stay back or my wife dies."

The woman's bruised and battered face confirmed the man's capabilities. Clearly, if he'd done that to her already, he'd follow through on his threat to kill his wife.

Austin tensed as something in the man's expression reminded him of his foster father from when he was seven. The multiple blows he'd inflicted returned tenfold, sending Austin into a stupor. His mind and body suspended in time, eliminating any takedown scenarios from emerging.

Clara and Izzy yelled, but their cries were muffled in his trancelike state.

A shot rang out and Clara dropped, blood appearing on her chest.

"No!" Austin jerked upright in his bed, jolting himself awake. His pulse pounded in his head. Two horrifying scenes from his past thrust together into one jumbled nightmare. Again? What had prompted the dream to return after years of silence?

Névé barked and scratched at Austin's door, dragging him back to reality.

Smoke seeped through the opened window. Even in the dead of winter, Austin left it cracked open for ventilation. Where was it coming from? It had also invaded his dream.

A glow flickered behind the slats in his blinds. *What is that?*

Austin thrust his comforter aside, vaulting out of bed. He flew to the window and raised the blinds. The sight before him seized his breath and locked his muscles.

Flames crawled up the sides of his K-9 training building like a monster reaching for its innocent victim. "No!"

His dogs were in danger, and he had to save them.

Chapter Eleven

Austin nabbed his cell phone and radio before yanking open the door, nearly colliding with his malamute. "Névé, come!" Austin had started training the dog in search and rescue when she was about twelve weeks old, but how would she handle a fire? Austin raced through the house, yelling, "Fire!" He reached Izzy's room and pounded on her door. "Izzy, get up! Fire!"

Névé barked.

The door swung open and a wide-eyed Izzy appeared. "What's going on?"

"K-9 building's on fire. Get your mom and sister out of the house in case it spreads. Now!" He didn't wait for an answer but veered into the hall and pressed an alarm button he had installed for occasions such as this. It would alert everyone on the premises.

The siren pierced through the ranch house and across the property.

Pounding footfalls above him revealed Sawyer was leaving his room in the loft.

Austin didn't wait, but snatched his coat from the hook and fled into the night as he hit 911 on his phone, requesting emergency services. After disconnecting, Austin called the on-call vet for his region. He hated to phone so late, but guessed his dogs would need Dr. Sarah Gardner's services. She agreed to come to his ranch immediately. *Lord, please save the dogs.*

Despite the growing heat from the fire, the freezing winter air stung his exposed skin, and Austin put on his coat and gloves quickly.

Sawyer bounded down the steps. "The guys are getting every hose and bucket that will reach the building."

They could barely hear muffled barks above Austin's siren. "Good. You've confirmed they're out of their cabins?"

"Yes."

Austin hit a button before pocketing his phone. The alert silenced, and the barking grew louder. "Let's go. We need to get to the dogs."

"We're coming too!" Izzy yelled from the doorway. Rebecca and Blaire followed her down the steps.

Austin pointed to the stable. "Sawyer, get the

horses out. Just in case. Send someone to guard the north stable and the cattle. I'll work with the others on the flames."

Sawyer nodded and ran to the large red stable doors, yelling for another ranch hand to help.

Austin beelined toward the K-9 building, the women close behind. Maverick had hooked up the long hose and sprayed the door. How had he gotten there so quickly? Austin ignored his question, thankful for his help, and instructed the others to form a line to the faucet on the side of the stable. They obeyed and quickly filled bucket after bucket, dousing the flames enough to clear a path to the entrance.

Austin pointed to the group. "Izzy, I'm going in. I need to get the dogs out. You help with the bucket brigade. We need to get the flames out as much as we can. Firefighters are about ten minutes away."

She latched on to his coat sleeve. "It's too dangerous. You can't go in."

"I have to." Austin placed a mask over his mouth and wrenched the door open.

Heat assaulted him as if he'd stepped into a large oven. He stumbled backward. The flames had reached inside the building.

Dogs barked. Some whimpered.

Lord, please help me. I need to save them.

Névé bolted around Austin's legs and darted through the entranceway.

"No! Retreat, Névé!"

She continued inside. The malamute rarely ignored Austin's commands, but this time she was on a mission.

Save her friends.

Austin inched through the doors and made his way to each of the dog's cages. He unlocked them and opened each one. "Cover!" he commanded, pointing toward the entrance.

Penny, Thor, Hunter and five others fled their smoky prisons into the night.

Névé whimpered.

Austin turned at his dog's cry.

And gasped.

Névé tugged an unconscious Goose by the collar, dragging the shepherd around the wall of flames, intent on one thing.

Getting Goose to safety.

Thankfully, his malamute had the strength to haul heavy objects.

One dog left.

Austin hustled to the end of the row and unlocked Wolf's door. The Belgian Malinois lay silent on the floor. "No!" Austin scooped the dog into his arms and staggered through the building.

Flames erupted in front of Austin, blocking his path. *No! Lord, help.*

A blurred image of Maverick appeared in the doorway overtop of the blaze. "I've got you!" He aimed the hose at the flames and sprayed.

They sizzled and additional smoke rose higher.

Austin coughed through his mask while he waited for Maverick to unblock the path to the door.

Finally, after what seemed like an eternity, the flames dissipated. The sixty-five-pound dog slowed him down, but Austin ignored the weight depleting the strength in his arms and continued toward the entrance.

Sirens pierced the night as the flashing lights from the fire trucks, police cruiser and an ambulance lit up the ranch property.

Seconds later the vet's vehicle sped down the driveway.

Help had arrived.

Relief relaxed Austin's grip, and he dropped to his knees to set Wolf on the ground. He whipped off his mask and gulped in the cold winter air. "Come on, boy. Come back to me."

He checked for a pulse and found a steady one. *Thank you.*

Izzy raced to his side. "Is he okay?"

"Not sure. The vet just arrived. Can you get her here right away?"

She nodded and dashed back toward the ranch house.

Austin searched for his dogs while rubbing Wolf's body. He found them in the distance with Névé barking commands. She had rounded them up like a perfect search and rescue dog.

Good girl.

Also, Goose had regained consciousness. *Thank You, Lord.* Austin turned back to Wolf. He was the only one still in jeopardy.

Firefighters had joined Austin's crew and soon had their hoses aimed on the K-9 building. Thankfully, they had prevented the flames from spreading to the stables, cabins and his ranch house. Constable Fisher spoke to the fire chief.

Rushed movements caught his attention. Dr. Sarah Gardner stumbled through the snow with Izzy by her side. The vet's mobile backpack jostled as she ran.

Austin waved. "Over here!"

Sarah reached Wolf and dropped to the ground. "Hey, Austin. How is he?" She wiggled out of the backpack's hold and unzipped the bag, withdrawing a stethoscope.

Izzy waited nearby.

"Still unconscious, but breathing." Austin's fingers grazed Sarah's arm. "Please save him."

"You know I'll do my best." She glanced back at the other dogs. "I see Névé is keeping her friends away from the blaze."

"She actually hauled an unconscious Goose from the building." Austin bit the inside of his mouth. "They will all need to be checked out."

A horse whinnied nearby.

"And the horses," Sarah added.

"Sawyer got them out and the flames never reached the stable, but to be on the safe side, yes, they should be. Do you need to call in help?"

"Figured I'd need it after you explained the situation, so I already did. The vet from a couple of towns over is on his way." She listened to Wolf's heart. "It's strong. He'll be—"

"Austin!" Sawyer hurried toward them. "You need to see this." He held his tablet in the air.

Austin flew to his feet. "What is it?"

"One ranch hand took this on the east side of the property." Sawyer clicked the screen and handed the tablet to Austin.

A photo of a hole cut in his electrified barbed wire fence.

Austin froze.

Someone had breached the premises, leading Austin to one conclusion.

The fire wasn't an accident.

Izzy noted the alarm on Austin's face after looking at Sawyer's tablet. She darted to his side. "What is it?"

Austin turned the tablet in her direction. "Someone cut the fence. Sawyer, how did they do it without being electrocuted?"

Izzy's hand flew to cover her mouth, but not in time to stifle her quick intake of breath.

The two men peered at her.

"What are you thinking, Iz?" Austin handed the tablet back to Sawyer.

Dare she give them her thoughts? She caught Austin's gaze. "You won't like it."

"You feel it was an inside job?" Austin fisted his hands.

"Someone had to have turned off the power to the fence, so the suspect could cut the barbed wire." Izzy waved at Fisher, gesturing him to come over. "We need to get forensics here."

Fisher raised his index finger, indicating he'd be there momentarily.

Sawyer crossed his arms, hugging his tablet. "But if it was an inside job, why wouldn't the person just open the front gate? It would have been easier."

Austin let out a heavy sigh. "Because there's no camera on that side of the property. Remember, I spoke about adding one as it's a blind spot." He pounded on his leg. "I should have done that."

"But we've vetted all our ranch hands, Austin." Sawyer shook his head. "No, I don't think one of them did it. You know we can turn the fence on and off remotely with our new technology. Why couldn't someone else hack into our system and do the same thing?"

Austin stared at Maverick as the ranch hand watched the firefighters.

Did Austin suspect the newest member of his crew?

"Sawyer's right. Someone could have done that. I'm probably wrong." Izzy read the frustration on his face. She understood how he thought. He blamed himself for this attack.

Fisher approached. "What's going on?"

Izzy pointed to the tablet. "Sawyer, show him the picture."

The ranch foreman held it up and Fisher viewed the screen, then whistled. "Someone got through your fence." He turned to Izzy. "You think whoever did that started the fire?"

"I do, but we don't know for sure the fire was arson." Izzy noticed her mother and sister petting the dogs. Anger burned inside Izzy, and she bit the inside of her mouth to stop it from rising. However, the thought of someone purposely setting fire to the K-9 building tore at her heart.

"I'm going to check on the horses." Sawyer hurried toward the side paddock containing the animals. Thankfully a ranch hand reported that the cattle and other animals were safe in the stable at the side of the property.

"Austin, Wolf is awake and Randall is here to help," Sarah yelled from her position, pointing to a lone male figure approaching across the yard.

"Thank You, God. I need to get all the dogs into the stable." Austin left the group to meet the second vet.

Emotions attacked Izzy as she watched Austin speak with Randall before pointing to Névé and the other dogs. She could tell by his angered expression that Austin was concerned about his animals. Izzy turned back to Fisher. "We need to treat this as arson, as that's what my gut is telling me."

"And a Tremblay gut is always right, is that it?"

She didn't miss his sarcasm. "Fisher, let's work together on this, okay? We're a team."

He scowled. "Well, you certainly don't act that way with all of your secret investigations."

Excited voices rose from the charred K-9 building, interrupting their conversation. Izzy pivoted to study the scene.

The lights from the property revealed a firefighter raising what appeared to be a jerrican.

"Looks like your suspicions are correct, Tremblay. Since you're officially on vacation, I'll handle this." Fisher trudged in the snow over to the firefighters.

Austin approached, with Névé by his side. "What's going on?"

She gestured toward Fisher and the firefighter. "My guess is they found the cause of the fire and it wasn't an accident." Izzy cupped his gloved hand with hers. "I'm so sorry. I feel like this is all my fault."

"It's not yours, it's mine. I've been procrastinating on getting a camera on that area of the ranch."

"Stop. You always blame yourself when you shouldn't." Izzy released his hand and bent to pet Névé. "You're a brave girl."

"She is. Névé saved not only Goose but all the dogs. She alerted me by scratching on my door." He rubbed the malamute's head.

"Can I look at your security system? You know I'm good with computers, plus we can check your video footage."

"Tremblay, I need to talk to you and Austin." Fisher approached with the chief in tow.

Austin leaned closer. "That doesn't sound good."

"Nope." Izzy waited for the duo to reach them. "What's going on?"

Fisher gestured toward the chief. "You know Chief Hammond, right?"

"Yes," Izzy and Austin said simultaneously.

"Tell them what you told me, Chief."

"Blaze is out now. Thanks for your good work in slowing it down." Chief Hammond slapped Austin on the back.

"Thank you and your firefighters, Chief. Is it safe to move the horses and dogs into the stable?"

"Yes, the stable is far enough away, but we'll continue to monitor everything for a bit."

Austin removed his two-way radio from his coat pocket. "Sawyer, move the animals into the stable. Dogs too. We'll have to figure out later where we'll house them. I just want them out of the cold now."

"On it, bro." Sawyer's voice crackled through the speaker.

"Bad news though. Definitely arson." Chief Hammond paused. "We found the jerrican, but it appears the fire's only point of origin was the entrance."

"So what does that mean, Chief?" Austin once again pocketed his radio.

"Not entirely sure, but I'm guessing whoever set the fire didn't want to do lots of damage."

"Tremblay, I believe the fire was some type of distraction." Fisher shifted his stance. "The question is why?"

Izzy's jaw dropped. "To get us out of the ranch house."

Fisher tilted his head. "Why?"

Izzy addressed Austin, ignoring Fisher's question. "We need to get back inside. Now!" She stumbled through the deep snow with one thing on her mind.

The flash drive and prints containing her father's notes.

Behind her, Fisher yelled at her to wait up, but she didn't have time to respond. She looked over her shoulder, noting both Névé and Austin had followed. Izzy reached the ranch house and bounded up the steps, stopping only to remove her boots. She sprinted into Austin's office and searched the desk where she'd left the flash drive.

Gone.

She eyed the evidence board.

Printouts of her father's journal.

Gone.

"No!" She fled the room and almost collided with Austin. "Stolen." Not that she couldn't recall the number sequences, but right now she didn't trust her supposedly perfect memory. Those missing three hours from the night of her attack still hadn't returned.

"What about your second set?"

"That's where I'm headed. Please pray." Not that it would probably help. She ran to her bedroom and checked where she hid the copies. In an envelope taped behind a wall picture.

She gently eased the picture's bottom edge away from the wall and reached under. Her fingers grazed the envelope. Relief washed over her tense body, thankful she had listened to her gut and hid the prints. "Thank you." Maybe God was listening after all.

"They there?"

Izzy turned at Austin's question. "Yes."

"Awesome. Let's put them in the safe. Sawyer and I are the only ones who know the combination."

Izzy wrenched the envelope from the hiding spot. "Good idea." She bit her lip. "I can't believe someone set your K-9 building on fire to get the thumb drive. If they could bypass your security, why not just kill us?"

Austin took off his gloves. "Because it *was* an inside job. Perhaps someone paid one of my ranch hands to get the drive, knowing they wouldn't also murder someone."

Izzy pictured his long look at Maverick earlier. "You're thinking Maverick?"

"Unfortunately, yes. He's the newest hand here on the ranch."

If Padilla could get to one of Austin's staff, that meant—

He knew where she was hiding.

Chapter Twelve

Austin waited for Fisher and the forensic team to complete their search for evidence in his house. Anger rose, and he refrained from pounding the stable's wall. The group had gathered there while the team dusted for prints and searched for signs of the perp. Had it been Maverick who'd helped Padilla breach the Murray K-9 Ranch? Austin prayed that wasn't the case.

It was now three thirty in the morning, but it seemed no one would go to bed. The excitement had given them all a caffeine-like shot. However, the question remained...how long before they crashed?

Sawyer and the men constructed makeshift kennels at the back of the heated stable, so the dogs could stay there until the K-9 building was repaired. The vets had examined and treated all the dogs. The horses were unaffected by the fire. Austin praised God for saving all his animals. He didn't know what he'd do if any of them had died. He stabbed his pitchfork into the hay repeatedly.

"That hay giving you problems?" Izzy chuckled and picked up another pitchfork. "Let me help."

Austin clenched his jaw. "I'm so angry that one of my men may have helped the perp."

"We don't know that for sure. Remember, I want to check your system as soon as Fisher gives us permission to go back inside."

"Shouldn't your digital forensics do that? You don't want to get in trouble."

"Hmm. Seems I already am. I have to go in front of the police board in a few hours, remember?"

"Right." Austin jabbed another fork full and threw the hay into his favorite horse's stall. Austin had bought Jasper five years ago, and they'd been a team ever since. They enjoyed long rides across the area.

"Did you talk to your men?"

"Yes, Sawyer and I spoke to everyone. They all deny aiding the perp or starting the fire."

"And Maverick?"

Austin stopped working and leaned on the pitchfork. "I think I'm rusty after ten years of no police work. I can't get a read on him, but something bothers me. Just can't put my finger on it yet."

"Want me to do a deep dive on him? Give you peace of mind?"

Austin blew out a long breath. "Not sure. Sawyer does all the hiring and I trust him. I'm concerned if you do that, then that will undermine our relationship."

"Let me know when—"

"Tremblay, you in here?" Fisher's loud voice boomed in the stable.

"Over here." Izzy set her pitchfork aside and waved. "What's going on?"

Fisher kicked at a stack of loose hay. "House is clear to enter now. Forensics just left." He acknowledged Austin. "We'll inform you of what we find."

"Thank you."

"I'd like to check your video footage. Do we have your permission to do that?"

Austin stole a peek at Izzy and raised his eyebrow, waiting to see if she'd respond.

She caught his gesture and cleared her throat. "Fisher, you okay if I do that?"

He placed his hands on his hips. "You think that's wise?"

She smirked. "No, but I know the ranch better than the rest of the force. Or, we could look at it together."

"Well, from what I understand, the mayor is out for your head. You need to be cautious on getting involved." Fisher shifted his glance to Austin. "You good if we look at it together? As much as I give Tremblay a hard time, I'd hate for her to get in trouble."

"Appreciate you looking after her." He hung the pitchforks on their wall hooks. "Let's go to my office."

"I'll tell Mom and Blaire that they can go back to bed." Izzy tucked her hat back on. "I'll meet you there."

Five minutes later the trio hovered around Austin's computer screen. Névé lay on her mat in the office's corner, snoozing. Seemed saving the day had worn his dog out. He thanked God again for keeping them all safe.

Austin adjusted the footage's time to a few minutes before midnight and hit play. "I'm guessing whoever cut the fence did it shortly after midnight because it was around 1:00 a.m. when Névé woke me." Austin pointed to the monitor on the right. "Fisher, you watch this screen. We have six cameras on the property, so three will show here and three on the other. Izzy, keep your eyes peeled on the left monitor."

They studied the video in split screen mode, revealing all angles of the ranch. Except for the blind spot.

"Look here." Izzy pointed to the video covering the property's south side next to the K-9 building.

A blurred image in black splashed gasoline on the walls of the building, scratched a match to life, and then tossed it against one wall, keeping his head concealed. Immediately, flames ignited.

Fisher leaned closer. "Rewind for a few seconds."

Austin obeyed.

"Stop there." Fisher tapped the screen. "See how he looks down? He knows a camera is watching."

Austin pounded the desk. "So, it was an inside job."

"Do you recognize anything about the perp's body language?" Fisher rubbed his chin.

Austin once again rewound the tape and hit play, studying the person closely. He let it play out until the suspect disappeared from the frame. "It could be any of my crew."

"Or someone else entirely." Izzy pulled up a chair. "Let's check out the rest of the footage."

The group examined the videos, even after Maverick, Sawyer and the crew arrived on the scene.

"Do you think it's odd Maverick got there first?" Izzy tapped his desk. "You and Sawyer knew about the fire first, and then you sounded your alarm."

Austin cracked his knuckles before massaging his palms. "Well, his cabin is the closest to the kennels and when I questioned him, he said he smelled the smoke and immediately took action."

Fisher put his hat on. "Looks like a dead end. Gotta get back to work." He waved on his way out of the office.

Izzy nudged Austin. "Okay, let me sit. I want to do a deep dive in your security system to see if someone hacked in."

Austin stood and let her sit in his chair, observing how quickly her fingers flew across his keyboard before the code appeared on his screen. "Wow, that was fast. I forgot how good you are with computers."

"I've loved to push buttons ever since I was a little girl, so I guess it comes naturally." She waved toward the door. "Can you get me a coffee? There's no going back to bed for me now."

"You got it." Austin left and threw a pod into the coffee maker. After fixing it the way Izzy liked it, he entered his office and set it in front of her. "Here you go."

She took a sip. "Aww, that's better. Thanks." She set the cup down and continued clicking on keys.

Seconds later she straightened in her seat, her hand hovering over her mug. "Whoa. This guy is good."

"What do you see?"

She tapped her index finger on a branch of codes. "Hacker's signature."

"What does that mean?"

"Someone got into your system. Most hackers are narcissistic and love to leave a bit of code to mark that they've been in someone's system."

Austin plunked into his chair. "So, maybe not a member of my crew."

If the hacker breached his security system, what else did they do?

Constable Isabelle Tremblay tugged on her police uniform, took a huge breath and walked into the Harturn River Library's conference room. Time to face her accusers and help defend her leader. She placed her hand on her chest, willing her rapid heartbeat to subside. *Stay calm. You've got this.*

Austin had driven her into town along with Névé and planned on taking his dog for a walk in a nearby park while Izzy met with the board. He prayed for her before she went inside. While thankful for his support, Izzy still wondered about God's path for her life. She had made a commitment to Him in her teenage years after getting in trouble with her father when she'd made bad friend choices, but lately God seemed to have hidden His plan for her life. Wasn't He listening anymore?

Izzy set aside the question and advanced farther into the room.

Chief Constable Halt approached. "Morning. You okay? I heard from Fisher what happened overnight. You must be exhausted."

"I'll be fine. Thankfully, the four cups of coffee have given me some energy. Plus, knowing I have to defend myself here has kicked in my adrenaline. Trust me, I'm wide awake."

Doug hurried to join them. "Izzy, don't worry. We've got your back. And yours too, Chief Constable Halt."

"Thank you. He's right. We'll defend your actions. I've already met with the board regarding mine. Have you remembered anything more about those missing three hours?"

Izzy pinched the bridge of her nose. "Not really, but we now know Dad used the book cipher for his code, but I haven't figured out the reference book yet. Too many other happenings have interrupted my thoughts."

"Understood. It will come." Halt gestured toward a chair facing the group gathered. "The mayor wants you front and center."

She gritted her teeth. "Let's get this over with."

Before she could sit, her uncle grazed her arm. "Izzy, just be honest, and the group will understand." He leaned closer. "Well, most of them. I don't trust these characters." He rushed to take his seat.

What did that mean? Her mysterious uncle continued to baffle Izzy. She shook her head, sat in her appointed chair and waited for the mayhem to begin.

Mayor Georgia Fox stood and cleared her throat. "Looks like we're all here, so let's get started." She walked to the front of the group. "Thank you for coming on such short notice, but as you know, I received an anonymous tip that needs to be handled immediately."

Izzy gazed at the crowd, noting the board members present, her partner, chief constable, and other coworkers.

Mayor Fox brought out her tablet from her bag and swiped the screen. "Constable Tremblay, here's what your accuser said and I quote, 'Constable Tremblay has been secretly investigating her father's supposed murder on company time, using police resources, and even disguised herself to come to the station when she was told to stay away. It's her fault the station was bombed. And... Chief Constable Halt sanctioned it all. I'm calling for his resignation or I will go public with this knowledge. Then see what Harturn River residents say. Your choice.'"

Izzy's muscles tightened. While she was investigating her father's death, she had not used police resources or done it on duty. Who had accused her? She noted each board member carefully. Was it one of them or perhaps a coworker? She and Fisher didn't always get along, but would he do this? Probably not. The rest of the constables had always been nice to her, so no, it couldn't be them. And why attack their leader? He was always fair to everyone.

Georgia slid the tablet back into her briefcase. "I realize our meeting here may be unorthodox, but after discussing it with the executive board last night, we wanted all of you to hear this at once." She circled Izzy. "What do you have to say for yourself, Constable Tremblay?"

Doug shot to his feet and raised his right hand. "Mayor Fox, sorry for interrupting, but can I say something?"

Georgia flattened her lips, clearly not impressed by his interruption. "Go ahead."

He walked to the front of the room and stood beside Izzy, smiling, before turning to face the group. "Mayor Fox and board members, you will find no finer officer than Constable Isabelle Tremblay. Yes, she may irritate some by her forthwith attitude and determination."

The group laughed.

Doug raised his index finger. "But she gets the job done and crosses no lines she shouldn't. I stand behind and beside my partner. I was the one who agreed to let her come in disguise to the station. Chief Constable Halt and I required her presence in the interview, hoping it would jog her missing three hours of memory."

Board member Vincent Jackson rose to his feet. "Wait, wait. Your father told me about your impeccable memory and that it has helped solve many cases. You're missing three hours?"

Izzy changed her position. "Yes, I was attacked two nights ago, and I believe details in those missing memories will help solve Dad's murder."

Her uncle Ford stood. "My brother died of a heart attack, and I'm tired of you thinking otherwise."

Once again, Izzy stiffened.

Halt stood. "With all due respect, Ford, while we can't comment on an ongoing investigation, we now agree with Constable Tremblay. There's something suspicious about her father's—your brother's—death. She did not use company resources or investigate while on shift. I also stand by my decision to allow her to come to the station. The bomb was not her fault, and I want to know exactly who this accuser is, Mayor Fox."

She raised both hands. "I honestly don't know. Someone delivered the letter to my office by courier and signed it 'concerned citizen.' But even if I knew, I wouldn't reveal a source." She paused. "Unless, of course, you had a warrant."

Izzy adjusted the tight bun at the back of her head and stood. Time to address the group. She had to choose her words wisely, as this board was known for its stern consequences for those they deem rule breakers. Her leader's reputation was at stake. "Good morning, Mayor Fox and board members. First, I want to thank Chief Constable Halt and Constable Carver for their support. I'm not sure who would accuse me of not abiding by the rules, but I promise you, I didn't break any while on duty." She flexed her hands, attempting to curb the anger rising toward her accuser. "But yes, this person is correct about a couple of things. I looked into my dad's death because it wasn't an accident." She took a second and stared at her uncle.

His stoic expression conveyed his thoughts. He was not happy with her.

She ignored him and continued. "As you know, I have hyperthymesia and what that means is I can recall things in detail. My father showed me his blood work from his annual physical and told me everything the doctor said. We had a very close relationship." She pushed back the tears threatening to rise. "I remember the conversation vividly. He was in perfect health. Somehow someone got to him and caused his accident." Once again, she paused for effect. "Wouldn't you each want to know if *your* loved one was murdered?"

Murmurs filled the room as the attendees whispered to each other.

Mayor Fox banged her palm on a nearby table. "Order!"

The group silenced.

"We already know I disguised myself to be present in the interrogation room while a suspect was being interviewed." She walked to the right side of the room and turned. "My father's CI had contacted me about a key component of whatever case Dad had been working on. For some reason, it was top secret. Not sure why. I agreed to meet with the CI, but someone attacked us. He was killed, and they hit me on the back of my head. That's what caused me to block out three hours of my memory, so I had to find out what happened during that window. It's vital to solving my father's murder."

Vincent raised his hand. "Did it help you remember?"

"Only a bit. Still lots missing, unfortunately."

The man leaned back in his chair, folding his arms. "Well, I, for one, understand why you did what you did."

Others nodded.

Mayor Fox cleared her throat. "Okay, do you

have anything else to add before the board convenes to make a decision, Constable Tremblay?"

Izzy stared at her leader. What more could she say to protect the man from whatever penalty the board would dish out? "Only that I beg you not to punish Chief Constable Halt for my actions. If you want to suspend me, go ahead, but he did nothing wrong. He was just placing his trust in one of his officers." She scanned each of the board members' faces. "Most of you knew my father. He had an impeccable track record and was a man of integrity. Don't tarnish that reputation now by punishing someone he trained from the ground up. Plus don't you want his killer to be found? I know I do." She smiled and sat.

Mayor Fox spoke to the group. "This meeting is adjourned. Since I have another pressing matter to attend to, the board will meet tomorrow morning to make our decision. Dismissed."

Izzy quickly texted "done" to Austin. All she wanted to do now was get back to the ranch and once again study her father's codes. Maybe being away from the pages for a few hours had helped clear her mind.

"Good job, partner." Doug squeezed her shoulder.

Halt approached. "I want you to know that

whatever happens is not your fault." He waggled his finger at her. "Got it?"

She saluted. "Yes, sir." Her cell phone dinged. Text from Austin.

Névé and I are in the car, ready to take you home.

Wait, did he just say home?

She reread his message and drew in a sharp breath.

He did.

"What is it?"

"Nothing, Chief Constable." She tucked her phone away. "I'm sorry about all this."

"You best get going." He glanced right, then left, before leaning closer. "I want you back safe at the ranch."

"Heading there now." She turned to Doug. "Call with updates, okay?"

Her partner nodded. "Stay off the grid."

She knew what that meant. Disconnect from any computers.

But how could she do that when a killer was still on the loose?

Austin turned right onto the secondary road, leading away from Harturn River. He'd chosen the less traveled route. Drivers used the divided highway, but Austin preferred the countryside drive. "How did it go? You've been quiet ever since we left the library."

"Sorry, I'm just upset about the whole thing. I get why Mayor Fox has to investigate the claim. It's part of her job, but this is a man's reputation at stake."

"Yours too. Surely the board will side with you."

"I tried to appeal to their emotions, but my uncle is still mad at me and he has a loud voice, so to speak." She huffed. "The others will listen to him."

"Let's pray that doesn't happen."

"I want to know who sent the allegations to the mayor. Apparently, the anonymous note was delivered to her office by courier." She yawned. "I want to get back to the ranch and focus on Dad's message. Plus I'm growing used to the serenity there."

Névé barked from her kennel in the back.

Austin chuckled. "She enjoys having you." And so did he, but he wouldn't voice that thought.

The malamute barked again, then growled.

Austin's pulse elevated. He trusted his K-9's instincts. Something else had caught her attention.

"What is it, girl?" He checked the rearview mirror. It was then he noticed a delivery truck approaching at full speed. "Not good."

"What?" Izzy turned and cried out. "He's coming fast!"

"Hang on." Austin gripped the wheel of his SUV and stepped on the accelerator.

The vehicle swerved on the icy road, and he fought to maintain control.

Izzy pounded on the dash. "He's gonna ram us!"

Seconds later the truck smashed into their bumper, shoving the SUV forward over the double-line road.

The wheels hit a patch of ice and spun the vehicle.

Izzy screamed.

Névé barked.

Austin prayed.

He compensated and yanked the wheel, righting the vehicle once again.

But the driver didn't stop. The truck hit them again, sending them toward the embankment at full speed.

Lord, save us!

The SUV launched over the ditch, plowed into a mound of snow and crashed into a tree.

The airbags deployed as Austin's head whacked against the cushioned steering wheel.

Pain registered as the impact sent an explosion of spots flickering in his vision moments before the darkness sucked him under.

Chapter Thirteen

Izzy jerked awake, pain piercing her right arm as confusion plagued her mind. Where was she? How long had she been unconscious? A barking dog registered, and she turned, noting Austin's face buried in the airbag. She unfastened her seat belt and inched closer, wincing from the pain in her arm. She pulled his head away from the wheel, using her left hand. "Austin!" She checked his pulse. Steady.

He was alive but out cold.

Once again, Névé barked while she scratched at her cage, as if she knew her master was in trouble.

Izzy withdrew her cell phone from her coat pocket and hit 911, praying her signal was at least strong enough to call for help. "Come on. Work for me." *Please, Lord.*

The operator answered and inquired about her emergency.

She identified herself as a police officer, naming her badge. "Car accident. Possible suspect still in the area. Male in his early thirties is unconscious. Need an ambulance and backup at my location." She named the road, mile marker and the delivery truck's license plate number. She included the model and color.

"You positive about that information?"

Izzy had read it moments before the truck hit them. "Absolutely."

"Can you get out of the vehicle?"

She had to. Austin's life was on the line. "I'm going to try. Get help here fast."

"They're on their way."

Izzy punched off the call and took in her surroundings. The darkened interior obstructed her view out the front windshield. She looked right, then left. The entire front of the vehicle was buried in snow.

Mounds of snow.

Their only escape route was through the back. But how could she get Austin to safety? Her wounded arm prevented her from being able to get him out quickly. A vision of Névé hauling Goose from the burning building formed in her mind.

Névé could do it. Malamutes could haul lots

of weight, but first Izzy had to get to her and clear a path out through the back. She turned in her seat. Another stab of pain stopped her in her tracks. She grasped her arm, sucking in a ragged breath. Her pulse elevated at her sudden action. *Slow movements, Iz. You can do this. You have to do this.*

Izzy didn't know if the vehicle would blow. She had to get them all out now. She couldn't lose Austin. Again.

And Névé too.

She breathed in. Out. In. Out. Her heartbeat slowed. "Okay, girl. I'm coming to you. We have to get Austin out."

Névé barked.

First, Izzy reached over Austin and hit the button to release the Expedition's tailgate. It popped open and cold air snaked into the vehicle. She ignored the chill, put her seat down and gingerly crawled into the back. Pulling on the passenger side right lever, she flattened the seat. Then did the same to the left. She wiggled over to the driver's side and reached around to bring Austin's seat as far back as it would go. Once again, she winced from the pain throbbing in her arm.

"Time to get you out of your kennel." Izzy

inched into the back and pushed the tailgate open the rest of the way, then unfastened Névé's kennel door. There was just enough room on the crate's other side for the dog to bring Austin through the back. "Okay, girl, we need to do this together. I'm counting on your strength."

Woof! The dog nestled close.

Izzy kissed Névé's forehead. "Okay, what's the command for you to tug Austin out?" Izzy searched her mind looking for the answer, but Austin never gave the malamute such a command. She'd have to wing it. "I'm going back up front to help."

Izzy crawled toward Austin's driver's seat and unfastened his seat belt. "Austin, this would be easier if you just woke up! Please."

The only sound came from Névé's panting.

Izzy patted the console. "Névé, come."

The dog obeyed, crawling in between the two front seats.

With her left arm, Izzy hauled Austin to the right toward his dog. She drew his zipper down from his neck, then lifted his hood. "Névé, mush!" She took a hunch on the command since she knew malamutes pulled sleds.

Instantly, the dog latched on to Austin's hood and tugged backward.

Using her left hand, Izzy helped ease Austin from his position enough so his dog could pull him out through the Expedition's back. She crawled alongside the dog, interjecting to ensure Austin wouldn't hit his head. "You've got this, Névé. Keep pulling."

Finally, the malamute hauled Austin to the edge of the tailgate. "Névé, stop!"

Izzy couldn't have her dropping Austin out of the vehicle. She had to protect his head, but it would be a challenge for her to get over the crate and Austin.

She held her breath, anticipating the throbbing pain in her arm would increase, then pushed the crate to a different angle. She shimmied her way through and hopped out the back.

"Okay, Névé, down." Izzy tucked her arms beneath Austin's shoulders. *This is gonna hurt, Iz.* But she couldn't risk Austin bumping his head, and she needed to get him out of the vehicle.

Névé leaped from the tailgate.

Izzy gently brought Austin out, ignoring the fire burning in her arm. She set him in the snow. "Névé, mush!" She pointed toward a tree.

Once again, the malamute clamped on to Austin's hood and dragged him over to where Izzy had indicated.

Izzy followed and ruffled the dog's head. "You're such a smart dog."

Névé snuggled next to Austin, licking his face. Her form of CPR?

Izzy smiled and plunked herself beside him, glancing back at his Expedition. They had plowed into a mound of snow before hitting the tree. The snow from the enormous birch tree must have fallen on top, completing the burial. Thankfully, the back end had escaped the white grave. *Thank You, Lord, for helping us get out.*

She focused on Austin and nudged him. "Austin, can you hear me? Wake up!"

Nothing.

She caressed his face. "Come back to me." Izzy leaned down and kissed his forehead, letting her lips linger for a second. "I miss you," she whispered. All she wanted to do right now was bring him into her arms and hold tight. He had always confessed to being her protector, but now the tables were turned.

Time for Constable Tremblay to protect her long-lost friend. She harrumphed. Who was she kidding? The emotions resurfacing were for more than a friend. Dare she open her heart again? Or would he reject her like he had after Clara's death, abandoning their friendship?

No, she couldn't risk the pain, especially after dating Dax. The man's obsessiveness forced her to end things, breaking her heart just after opening it again. Their relationship had ended with her taking out a restraining order against him.

Even though Izzy knew Austin wasn't Dax, he had deserted her in her hour of need.

Névé growled, pulling her from past regrets.

Izzy froze.

Movement from the road caught her attention, and she flew to her feet, whirling around.

A flash of a figure dressed in white appeared in her peripheral vision moments before a shotgun blast boomed.

Izzy threw herself on top of Austin and Névé, shielding them with her body.

Pain exploded in her arm.

Sirens sounded in the distance. Help was coming.

But would it arrive too late?

Austin struggled to wake up and move his body as tightness seized his chest. He fought to clear his dazed brain. Sirens blared in the background, followed by a dog barking. Why did his head hurt so much? Something shifted on top of him and the pressure eased. Névé licked his face. The crash! *Austin, wake up. Izzy could be hurt.* He willed himself to rise, but his body wouldn't listen.

"Austin! Wake up. We need to take shelter."

Izzy's panicked voice cut through Austin's fog, jolting him awake. He opened his eyes.

Névé's face appeared inches away from him. Obviously, the dog wanted her handler to wake up too.

"Izzy, are you okay?" Austin's question came out in a squeak. He cleared his throat and eased upward. "Where are we?"

"Stay down for a moment." Izzy pushed on his shoulders. "We're under attack. One shot fired. Help is on the way."

Austin rubbed his head. "I must have whacked my head good."

"Can you move? We have to get behind the tree."

"Yes, but I need help to get up." He grabbed her right arm.

She cried out.

He hesitated. "Sorry. Are you hurt?"

"Slammed into the armrest upon impact, but I believe it's only sprained."

A chill snaked down the back of his neck not only from the rush of cold air, but the thought of Izzy getting hurt. He observed the vehicle. "How did you get me out?"

She pointed to Névé. "With help from a furry friend."

Austin braced himself and pushed upward. "Good girl." He patted her head.

The malamute barked and hopped up on all fours.

Angst bombarded Austin, and he changed his position to protect Névé. "Is the shooter still out there, Iz?"

"I don't think so. Probably heard the approaching sirens and fled." She brushed the snow from her uniform. "Let's get behind the tree, just in case."

Austin pushed himself up and scrambled to hide with Izzy and Névé. He glanced around the tree and once again studied his Ford buried in the snow. He guessed the front end was probably demolished from the impact. *Thank You, Father, for saving us.* "Iz, did you catch the truck's license plate number with your sharp memory?"

"Sure did and gave it to the 911 operator." She brought out her phone. "Going to call Doug." She hit a button and put the call on speakerphone.

"Izzy, you okay? We're almost at your location." Doug's frantic voice crackled in the limited cell reception.

"Minor injuries. I gave the truck's license plate number to the 911 operator, but I'll text it to you, too."

The loud sirens announced the arrival of emergency services. An ambulance, fire truck and police cruiser pulled to the side of the road.

"I'm here now, but yes, text it to me. We'll get on it. Another cruiser is searching the area for the truck." A car door slamming came through Doug's phone as the connection severed.

Izzy tapped on her screen before pocketing her phone and turning to Austin. "I need to tell you something. The delivery truck had King & Sons on the side. I failed to mention that to the operator as I was in a bit of a hurry to get help, but wanted you to know."

"Them again." He sighed. "You still think Sawyer is involved?"

Doug's head appeared over the embankment. "Izzy, Austin, where are you?"

"I'm not sure who to trust anymore, but Sawyer seems to be on the up-and-up. I don't think the King in the name is any relation to him." Izzy stood and waved. "Over here."

Austin brought himself upright and leaned

against the tree for support. His shaky legs told him he required rest. The previous adrenaline from a night of chaos had left his body after the crash.

Doug maneuvered down the embankment, gun in hand. "Did you see the shooter?"

"Only quickly." Izzy pointed to the right. "I saw the suspect run that way, dressed in white. I'm guessing to camouflage in the snow."

Austin massaged the growing bump on his forehead. "They must have followed us from the library, but I took alternative routes and didn't catch a tail. I made sure of it. The truck came out of nowhere."

Izzy's jaw dropped. "Doug, do you think this whole accusation was a ruse to get me out of hiding? Whoever it was understood police business and also knew we'd be there."

"What do you mean?" A gust of icy wind sent chills down Austin's neck. He zipped his coat.

"That if they implicated Chief Constable Halt's decision in my conduct, I would come to defend him."

Doug tapped his temple. "Smart thinking."

Austin noticed the paramedics trudging through the snow. "They knew where the meeting was being held. The suspect has to be someone you know well, or maybe someone on the force, or who attended the meeting."

"It's not one of us." Doug's radio crackled, but the caller's words were broken. "Come again."

"No. Sign. Of. Suspect."

"Copy that. Keep looking. They couldn't have gotten too far on foot." Doug holstered his weapon. "Listen, you guys get checked out and then if the paramedics clear you, I'll take you back to the ranch." He focused on Izzy. "In the meantime, I'll get started on checking into the truck and I'll take your statements at Austin's place."

Izzy cradled her right arm, using her left hand. "Have the team dig deeper into King & Sons as it was their delivery truck that rammed us. I want to know who they are and what they deliver. Unfortunately, I haven't had time to look into them."

Austin noted the tension in her voice.

Whoever had steamrolled them off the road was about to face the wrath of Constable Isabelle Tremblay.

Not that Austin blamed her. This had to end before anyone else got hurt—or killed.

Chapter Fourteen

Later that afternoon, after getting cleared by the paramedics and resting, Izzy arranged the second set of prints on her evidence board after she made copies. She didn't trust that whoever was trying to kill them wouldn't find out about her secret copy. She fingered the sling, protecting her right arm. Her sprain would heal in time. *Guess I won't be going back to work anytime soon.* Although, her father had taught her to shoot using both hands.

The paramedics had taken Austin to the hospital to be examined by a doctor. Thankfully, he only had a mild concussion, and the doctor sent him home with instructions. When they had arrived back at the ranch, Sawyer hovered around his friend to make sure Austin obeyed the doctor's orders.

Dr. Gardner had checked Névé over and gave

her a clean bill of health, so Austin gave his dog multiple treats for hauling him from the vehicle.

Izzy gazed at the malamute sleeping in the corner. Tears formed as she thought about having to leave once this case was solved. She squeezed the bridge of her nose, willing her emotions to remain at bay. *I'll miss you, sweet girl.*

She tucked regrets away and picked up the tape to add the last page to the board.

"Why aren't you resting?" Blaire shuffled into the room.

Izzy startled from her sister's stealth-like approach. "You scared me. Blaire, I need to get answers and they're here in Dad's secret code."

"Weren't you just at a meeting because you're involved in a case you shouldn't be?"

Izzy didn't miss the hostile tone in her question. "I'm on vacation and not using company resources. Don't you *want* to find out what really happened to Dad?"

"How many times do we have to tell you? It was an accident. Uncle Ford says—"

"What's with you and Uncle Ford lately? It's like you're two peas in a pod."

Blaire's eyes clouded. "He was there when I needed him. He listened and didn't judge me."

Izzy dropped the tape. "What are you referring to? Have I offended you? You haven't seemed to be yourself lately."

Blaire took two long strides forward and waggled her finger in Izzy's face. "You know exactly. Luca and I were in love, and you wrecked everything."

Izzy's jaw dropped. "He was married and a suspect in a child's abduction! I only wanted to protect you."

"No, you and your holier-than-thou attitude judged me. Luca and his wife were getting a divorce."

"Do you really believe that? If that's the case, why were they still together?" Izzy crossed her arms. "When we went to the house the day of his child's abduction, he and his wife certainly didn't look like they were on the outs. In fact, Luca said he'd been on the phone planning a ceremony to renew their vows when his daughter was taken."

"You're lying!" Blaire's voice raised a notch.

Névé hopped up on all fours.

"Be quiet. Austin is resting down the hall." Izzy caressed her sister's arm. "I'm sorry for everything you've been through with Luca, but I never judged you. I've made my own mistakes with Dax."

She jerked her arm away. "Well, Luca told me you're the reason he broke up with me."

Izzy stumbled backward. "What? That's absurd. Why would he say that?"

"He said he couldn't date someone whose sister thought he was guilty." A tear fell down her cheek. "That's why he's still with his wife."

Izzy blew out a breath. When would her sister acknowledge Luca's lies? He probably never loved her. However, Izzy would keep that thought to herself. Her relationship with Blaire was already on shaky ground. "I realize it's hard, but it's time to move on. Please trust me when I say I never meant to hurt you. I'm sorry that I obviously did, and hope one day you can forgive me." Once again, she grazed Blaire's arm. "I miss you. We used to tell each other our deepest secrets and fears. We haven't done that in a long time."

Blaire jerked away from Izzy's touch. "Well, I'm not ready to forgive and forget." She stomped out of the room.

Izzy plopped into the desk chair, burying her head in her hands. *Lord, I'm not sure if You're listening, but can You bring my sister back to me? We need each other.*

"You okay, Iz?" Austin's softened voice revealed his concern.

She popped her head up. "Sorry if Blaire's yelling woke you. I'm frustrated. My sister seems to hate me and claims I interfered with her and Luca's relationship." She leaned back, folding her arms. "I just wish she could see his lies."

"I'm sorry she feels that way. I'm here if you want to talk."

"Appreciate that." Izzy always loved their conversations and missed his friendship. "How are you feeling?"

"Still have a bit of a headache, but not bad." He pointed to the evidence board. "I see you have the copies back up. Any headway?"

"I'm afraid not."

Austin advanced farther into his office and bent to pet Névé on his way to the board. "Good girl, keeping Iz company."

The dog snuggled into Austin and licked his face.

"Aw, I love that she loves you so much." Izzy stood and walked to the board, studying each number. "I wish I could figure out Dad's reference book. I have so many, and I'm not sure which one he would have picked."

Austin positioned himself beside Izzy, his woodsy scent wafting into her space.

Don't do that to me.

It was getting harder and harder to keep herself from falling for this man a second time.

Who was she kidding? It only took seeing him again for those emotions to return.

He tapped one sheet. "Wait, these numbers in the top corner kind of resemble a date."

Izzy abandoned thoughts of Austin and peered closer. "You're right. It does. How did I miss that?"

"Well, it's squished together. Perhaps your dad tried to disguise it from prying eyes. So what happened on October 3, 2000? Wait, October 3 is your birthday. Did you get something special that day?"

Izzy searched her memory bank and inhaled audibly. "Yes, it was the birthday he gave me my first Nancy Drew book. *The Hidden Staircase.* That's it! That has to be the reference book."

"Do you have that book at your condo?"

"Yes. I need to go get it."

Her mother shuffled into the room. "You're not going anywhere. When will you realize someone is trying to kill you?"

Izzy pivoted and faced her mother. "Well, I need a book from my condo."

Her mother swiped the screen on her cell phone. "I'll get Ford to pick it up and bring it."

Izzy's gaze snapped to Austin's. She raised a brow, silently pleading for help.

She didn't want her uncle involved. Something irritated her about his actions lately. She only wished she understood why.

Austin gave her a slight nod and placed his hand over top of Izzy's mother's. "Rebecca, Sawyer is heading out for a run of dog food anyway. I'll get him to swing by." He turned to Izzy. "That okay with you?"

"Of course. I'll give you my key."

"Fine. Don't accept my help. Again." Her mother marched out of the room.

How many times would a family member leave the room angry with Izzy today?

Izzy withdrew her keys from her purse and handed them to Austin. "Sorry about that. Not sure why my family seems to have it in for me right now. I'm just trying to find out the truth."

"No need to apologize. I'll get Sawyer on it right away, so you can get started on decoding the message." He took a step, but turned. "Wait, where would the book be?"

"In my office. However, he'll have to search through them because the perp tossed all my books on the floor and I haven't been back to clean them up." She raised her finger. "But I'll get Doug to meet him there. I don't want Sawyer to go in unprotected. Padilla or his men may still stake out my condo. Plus I need to see if he has any updates."

"Good plan." Austin left the room.

Izzy sat back at her desk and punched in her partner's number.

He answered on the second ring. "Hey, you. Was just gonna call you. I have news."

"Good, and I have a favor to ask." She explained the situation.

"No problem. I can do that." The rustling of papers sounded through the phone. "So, no prints found on the jerrican."

"No surprise there. It's winter, and the perp would have worn gloves anyway. What else?"

"We did a thorough analysis into King & Sons. We know it's a shell corporation, but the team discovered something very interesting."

Izzy sat straighter in her chair, anticipating some good news. The cheerful tone in her partner's voice was a dead giveaway. She hoped. "What did they find?"

"Sawyer is on his way to your condo," Austin said, stepping into the room. He halted. "Sorry for interrupting."

"No worries." Izzy picked up a pen and tapped the desk. "Doug was sharing what he found out about King & Sons. I'll put you on speaker, Doug."

"Hey, Austin. I'm heading to Izzy's condo as soon as I'm off the phone." A chair scraping sounded through the phone.

"Appreciate your protection for Sawyer." Austin sat at his desk.

"No problem," Doug said. "Izzy, to answer your question, King & Sons delivers kitchen equipment and specializes in fixing burners."

Izzy sprang to her feet. "As in burners that could be used for cooking drugs?"

"Possibly. That's our guess too. Here's the interesting part. We linked the company to none other than our honorable mayor."

"What? Oh, that just takes the cake." Was Georgia responsible for the supposed accusations against them?

"Well, let's not jump to conclusions. Could be someone trying to implicate her. She's ruffled feathers to get into office. We're still looking into it."

Izzy sat back down. "Thanks for the update."

"Sorry it's not more."

"Well, it's better than nothing. I'm hoping once I decode Dad's message, I'll have information for you."

A squawking radio sailed through the speakerphone. "Just a sec, Izzy. I'm getting an update."

Izzy tensed, waiting to hear if it had to do with her father's case.

Muffled voices sounded in the background.

"Izzy, I just learned that someone killed Bolton and Phillips in jail," Doug's voice blared.

"What?" A realization dawned on Izzy.

They would never be safe from Padilla if they didn't soon find answers to the missing pieces of her perfect memory. Somehow, they held the key.

Austin returned to his office forty minutes after ensuring the ranch's perimeter was still secure.

Izzy stood motionless in front of her evidence board.

Exactly where he'd left her. *Lord, show her the hidden message.*

Austin inched into the room, stopping to pet

Névé, who continued to stay with Izzy. "You're a good girl."

Izzy spun around. "Sorry, didn't hear you come in."

Austin handed her a cup of coffee. "Sawyer back yet?"

"No. I've been studying the numbers and other pages of the journal, trying to make sense of it all." She pointed to two pages on the board. "These numbers are different and follow the same format as my birth date clue."

Austin got up and positioned himself beside her. "So, more dates, but dates of what?"

"I'm thinking drug deals, perhaps? These two pages came before the coded ones. Not sure if that's significant or not."

He breathed in, soaking up his closeness to her as he realized it would end soon and she'd be out of his life forever.

And that thought scared him to the core.

Since she'd been thrust back into his life, he realized he didn't want to let her go again.

Did she feel the same?

Austin's gaze locked with hers. He caressed her cheek. "Iz, I—"

"I'm back!" Sawyer's booming voice sounded from the hallway.

Austin cleared his throat and stepped backward moments before his friend entered the room.

Sawyer raised the book. "Got it." He handed it to Izzy.

"Thanks." She cradled the book as if it were a child. "Did you have any issues at the condo?"

"No, your partner cleared the house before I went in." He whistled. "Quite the mess in your office."

"I know. I hate not being able to go clean it up, but I can't take the risk of Padilla's men following me there again." Izzy opened the book and sat at her desk.

"Alrighty then. I'm off to fix the fence." Sawyer spoke to Austin. "I hope you're okay with this, but I picked up surveillance equipment for the blind spot while I was out. Maverick and I are going to hook it up now before supper."

Austin locked his arms at his sides. "Do you trust him, Sawyer? I know you did a reference check on him, but he acts suspiciously around me."

"He doesn't with me. Perhaps your police spidey senses are misfiring."

"Maybe. Just monitor him. Thanks for installing the camera."

"No prob." Sawyer left the room.

"Iz, I changed my mind." Austin rolled his desk chair over beside her. "Can you get Doug to look into Maverick? I need to know he's okay, especially with everything that's been happening."

"Sure. I'll text him right now." Izzy keyed on her cell phone. "Okay, done. Time to work on decoding Dad's hidden message. Wanna help?"

"Absolutely."

"You read out the numbers and I'll check the book. Let's hope this is the correct edition." Izzy hopped up and yanked the printout from the board. She handed it to Austin before sitting. "Okay, ready."

Thirty minutes later, after false and frustrating leads, Izzy slammed her hand on the desk. "That's it! The first set of numbers is longitude and latitude."

Austin rolled his chair over to his desk and grabbed his laptop. "We can see it on the map better using my laptop. Give me the numbers."

She spieled them off.

Austin typed them in and immediately a map appeared on his screen. He enlarged it.

And drew in a sharp breath.

"What is it?" Izzy shot out of her chair and peered over Austin's shoulder.

He pointed. "That location isn't far from here, but it's a secluded wilderness. What would we be looking for?"

Izzy picked up the printout. "Wait, there's more numbers on the bottom. Maybe a second clue?"

She snatched the book and relocated to the evidence board. "Read them out to me."

He said each one slowly, allowing time for her to look up the words.

She wrote them on the board one at a time, then stood back.

Austin studied her father's additional message. Tall, Behind, Secret, Trees, Entrance, Cellar.

"That's a jumbled mess." Austin tilted his head, observing each word separately. "What does it mean?"

"Dad and I liked to play this game. Figure out the message in the scrambled words." Izzy chewed on the end of the marker.

Seconds later her eyes widened, and she frantically wrote the secret message below the words:

Secret cellar entrance behind tall trees.

"That's it! Dad found something in the forest. A building." She snagged her cell phone from the desk. "We need to go look. Now!"

"Shouldn't you call Doug?" Austin didn't

like that she'd put herself at risk so quickly after being run off the road.

"Good point." She punched in his number and waited. "No answer. I'll leave a message." She gave Doug the details before hanging up. "Are you okay to go?" She snatched the eraser from the ledge and removed the clues from the board. Just in case.

He clamped his lips shut. Knowing he wouldn't be able to contain her excitement at the thought of perhaps finding a missing piece to the mystery, he willed strength into his body. "I'm good. Let me grab my hunting rifle and a flashlight. If it's a cellar, we'll need the light." He addressed Névé. "Come."

His malamute trotted behind him as a question rose in Austin's mind.

He guessed something sinister lay hidden, or why else would Chief Constable Tremblay go to the trouble of hiding the message?

No, Austin wouldn't go into the wilderness unarmed.

Chapter Fifteen

Izzy skulked behind a snowcapped fir tree, peering in all directions for any potential suspects. However, the forest remained silent in the late afternoon hour on the frigid winter day. The only sound interrupting the surrounding solitude was Névé's breathing. Both she and Austin stood close, guarding Izzy. Not that she couldn't protect herself, but Austin's rifle gave her peace of mind. She remembered his impeccable aim and took solace in his close presence. She knew he was unhappy with her for not waiting for her partner, but she needed evidence. After all, maybe they had decoded the message incorrectly. Even though she might put her career on the line if the board found out, lives were at stake. The sooner they stopped Padilla, the sooner the community would be safe from both him and his deadly drugs.

Izzy spotted a cluster of tall trees along with

two sets of footprints. She pointed. "That could be where Dad found the secret entrance."

Austin raised his rifle. "Let me go first, since you're not armed. Névé, stay." He trudged through the snow, stopping at trees to hide his approach. He reached the group of trees and circled them, searching in various spots. Suddenly he stopped and bent down, brushing off snow from something beneath the bushes. He waved her over.

Izzy and Névé advanced as Austin had. She searched the woods for signs of life and any spying eyes, but found none. She hurried to where Austin stood. "What did you find?"

He pointed to a secret door hidden by a group of bushes. "Exactly where your dad said it would be. You open it. I'll cover you."

Izzy squatted and grasped the handle with her left hand, peering back at Austin. "Just a sec. Why isn't this door locked?"

Austin shrugged. "Perhaps they guessed nobody would find it?" He pushed another branch away. "Wait. There's the chain and lock. Someone obviously forgot to lock up. Careless." He gestured toward multiple tracks around the bushes. "Looks like someone was here recently.

Maybe we should get out of here and give Doug the details about the opening."

No way. Izzy's inquisitive mind had to know more before bringing in the team. "I want to check it out quickly first."

He pursed his lips.

"I know what you're thinking. We'll take it slow and if we hear anyone inside, we'll leave. Ready?" She kept her voice low in case there were people behind the door.

He nodded and turned to Névé. "Silence," he whispered.

The malamute raised her nose in the air, standing tall on all fours. Ready for action, but remained quiet.

Izzy tugged the heavy door open. The hinges creaked in annoyance and she winced, holding her breath.

But only a dark stone staircase appeared, leading downward.

Izzy flicked on the flashlight and shone it through the entrance, then turned to Austin. "Let's go together. Slowly."

He dipped his chin in acknowledgment and moved to her side, turning to Névé. "Come."

Izzy guided their way, using the flashlight's beam as they descended. Once at the bottom, she peered left down the only hallway in the hidden cellar.

"Let's see where this leads," she whispered.

They inched their way along the damp corridor walls. Izzy listened for any type of movement, but the cellar remained silent. After a few minutes, they reached a door. She eased it open. "More stairs but going up. Odd."

Another door appeared at the top.

"Let me go first." Austin raised his weapon and advanced through the entry.

Izzy and Névé followed, stepping into a dark room.

"What is this place? We're no longer underground." Izzy shone the flashlight, the beam revealing stone walls of a boarded-up house. "Where are we?"

"This has to be the old Montgomery place. The family moved Mrs. Montgomery to a nursing home years ago, but they never sold the property. Their daughter lives on the other end of the town."

Izzy moved the beam around the room. Rows of tables lined the area. Burners sat on top of each, along with chemicals and gas masks. This had to be where Padilla's men cooked the drugs.

Austin paced the room, feeling around the

obscured windows and one door. "Sealed tight. The only way in is the secret cellar entrance."

"No one is here. Let's get a closer look." She shone the flashlight as she approached the nearest table.

A burner marked with King & Sons on the side was placed at one end. A row of small bags on the other. She pointed to the company's logo. "Interesting." She inched closer. Heat radiated from one burner. "Someone was just here. This one is still warm."

"We gotta hurry." Austin pointed to a bag. "I'm guessing this is the bath salts you mentioned." He turned from his position beside her. "Check this out, Iz."

Boxes stacked in the corner reached up to the ceiling. She whistled. "I'm guessing they're getting ready to transport these." She shone the light upward. "Wow, they have an advanced ventilation system. Padilla thought of everything." Izzy handed him the flashlight. "I'm going to take pictures to send to Doug."

"Do it quickly because we can't stay in here long unprotected."

She took out her phone and snapped pictures of everything in the room. Tables full of drugs, burners, various chemicals, glass beakers and multiple boxes. She pocketed her phone. "Okay, let's go."

They retreated out of the room, back down the stairs and up toward the cellar entrance.

Austin moved ahead of her. "Let me go first." He raised his rifle and inched up the stone steps, then through the opening.

Seconds later his face appeared. "It's all clear."

As Izzy stepped into the fresh air, she breathed deeply before studying the forest. All remained quiet. She followed Austin to the clearing.

Névé growled.

Both Izzy and Austin stopped at his dog's warning.

A branch cracked behind them. Someone had entered the forest to the right of their location.

Austin shoved her behind a cluster of trees.

"Bro, check out these footprints," a snarly voice said. "Should we call the boss?"

"Naw. Look at the paw prints. Probably just someone out for a walk in the snowy woods with their dog." The other male voice boomed in the forest. "We don't want him getting mad at us. You remember what happened the last time we were wrong about something? Almost lost our lives. Padilla doesn't play nice, even with his staff."

So this *was* Padilla's cooking lab. Izzy couldn't wait to update Doug.

"Yeah, I remember. Still have the bruise on my face to prove it." He paused. "Let's inspect the area and ensure we're alone. I see prints this way."

Izzy bit the inside of her mouth, waiting for the men to proceed farther into the forest.

"Man, it's snowing again. I don't see anyone. Whoever it was, is gone. Let's get back to work. I don't want to get stuck here again. It's too creepy in that dark house."

"We need to remain hidden. That female cop is getting too close. Our spy is setting it up so she'll be out of the picture soon. Just like her old man."

Izzy bit down hard to keep herself from crying out. *Spy?* She glanced at Austin.

His widened eyes told her he had caught the reference.

Padilla had indeed sent an enemy into their camp.

The question was…who?

Austin entered his office and handed Izzy a cup of orange hot chocolate. He had added whipped cream and dropped miniature marsh-mallows on top. "Your fave."

She smiled and took a sip. "So good. You remembered."

"Yup, you're not the only one with an excellent memory." He sipped his mug of hot chocolate, the orange flavor lingering on his lips. "Anything from Doug yet?"

She shook her head. "I'm waiting for his call." She plunked herself down behind her desk, placing her cup in front of her. "I miss my dad. He'd know what to do about this case."

Austin set his mug aside and brought her upright into his arms. "I know. I'm sorry. It's hard losing a parent. I lost both of mine at once in a tragic car accident."

"I remember it happened after Clara died. That must have been so hard for you to deal with on top of everything."

She didn't know the half of it. He had longed to reach out to her, but their strained relationship had prevented him from calling. He had caused her too much pain. He released her from his embrace. "Thankfully, Sawyer was working here by then and he was a huge help to me. His faith in God was an inspiration and after long talks, I resurrendered my life to Him."

"Well, God doesn't seem to show me His path for me anymore or be listening to my prayers."

"Sometimes God shows us, but our blinders prevent us from seeing His plan." He paused. "At least, that's what Sawyer said to me."

"My dad used to say something similar, but sometimes life's just too hard." Izzy moved behind her desk and drank more hot chocolate as if wanting to silence their God conversation.

Whipped cream lingered on her top lip, distracting Austin. What would it be like to kiss her? He had wanted to for years, but of course, their working relationship prevented him from disclosing his true feelings for her.

What about now? *Tell her, Austin. Tell her how you really feel.*

Would she abandon him like everyone else had in his life? His biological parents didn't love him enough to keep him. His adoptive parents technically hadn't abandoned him, but their absence in his life was a deep loss. *Why take everyone from me, God?* Every woman he'd dated in the past ten years had left him, stating he couldn't commit.

They weren't wrong. He kept comparing each to Izzy, and even though he tried his hardest to have feelings for them, he just couldn't.

Plus she probably wouldn't forgive him for not saving Clara that night.

No, Austin. Lock away your feelings and throw away the key. She doesn't feel the same.

Time to move on. "You have whipped cream on your lip." He leaned closer and rubbed it away with his thumb, allowing his touch to linger.

A soft gasp escaped her lips, and her eyes locked with his.

Even though his earlier determination to stay away was fresh in his mind, he couldn't help but caress her cheek. "Iz—"

"Don't, Austin." She pulled away.

See, she doesn't feel the same.

Her cell phone rang. "It's Doug." She hit the speakerphone button. "Hey, partner. I'm with Austin."

"Good, I need to talk to you both. Sorry to bother you so late."

Izzy dropped into her chair. "What's going on?"

Doug cleared his throat. "First of all, Izzy, next time you get a lead, wait for me."

She fingered the sling on her right arm. "Doug, I realize I should have waited, but I didn't want you coming all the way out there if the uncoded message was nothing."

"I get it, but you're already in hot water. Anyway. I gave Halt the information, and he's getting a search warrant based on the evidence you provided." He inhaled. "The team will be raiding the cookhouse soon, but you can't be involved."

She slouched. "I get it."

"We've had another teen overdose from the bath salts, so the chief is eager to stop Padilla."

Izzy's hand flew to her mouth. "How old?"

"Fourteen."

"That's three in the last month linked to the drug." Izzy massaged her neck. "No wonder Dad was trying to get to the bottom of the drug ring. I just don't understand why he kept his investigation a secret."

"My guess is because someone higher up the chain is linked to or *is* Padilla." Doug's whispered voice came through the speaker.

Austin guessed the man was struggling to hold his emotions in check.

"You think it may be Mayor Fox?" Izzy rose and walked to the window, peering into the darkness.

"Not saying that and Halt is looking into her connection with King & Sons, but something made your dad write his notes in code."

"Whomever it is, is now targeting Izzy. They silenced her father and now want to do the same to her." Austin noted Izzy's location. "Please get away from the window."

"Another good reason for her to lie low," Doug said. "One more thing. You asked me to look into Maverick. It took some digging, but I found out he was born near Kelowna to a Joyce Shaw and Owen Maynard. Worked on—"

Austin bolted upright. "What?"

Izzy pivoted. "You recognize those names?"

"Yes, they're my biological parents." Realization set in and he stumbled backward. "Maverick is my brother?"

A crash echoed throughout the top level of the ranch house, followed by Blaire's bloodcurdling scream.

Chapter Sixteen

"Blaire!" Izzy sprang to her feet. "Doug, intruder at Austin's."

"Sending units now." Doug clicked off the call.

Izzy stuffed her phone into her pocket. "Austin, get me one of your rifles and ammo. Blaire's in trouble."

He crouch-walked to his rifle cabinet, punched in a code and removed two, stuffing additional ammo into his pocket. He handed a rifle to Izzy and turned to his dog. "Névé, come."

Izzy checked the chamber before raising her weapon. "Stay behind me and keep low. We don't know what we're dealing with."

"You forget I was your partner once." He tapped his temple. "My police training isn't totally gone from here." He lifted the rifle toward the stairs. "Let's go."

She didn't miss the annoyance in his tone. Was he thinking about their last call together that ended in tragedy? Something told Izzy that Austin wouldn't make the same mistake twice.

At least, she prayed that was the case.

She ignored the trepidation locking her shoulders and crept up the stairs, staying low on the right side of the steps. Even though it hurt to cradle her left hand with her injured right, she continued upward. She wouldn't let her injury cripple her ability to protect her family.

They reached the top of the stairs.

Izzy raced to her sister's room and stopped in front of the closed door, waiting for her ex-partner and his dog.

"Sissy, help!" Her sister's cry turned to muffled screams, as if someone had their hand over her mouth.

Izzy's pulse magnified, sending her into action. She mouthed to Austin, *Ready?*

Austin pressed his back against the wall to the right of the door, flanking her with Névé by his side, and nodded.

Izzy pointed her weapon and pushed the door open. "Police! Stand down."

She moved into the room and stopped in her tracks.

A masked man held a Glock to her sister's temple and grasped his other hand over her mouth.

Tears welled in Blaire's widened eyes.

Anger bubbled inside of Izzy at the idea of this man hurting her only sister. She raised her gun higher, ignoring the pain shooting in her right arm. "Let. Her. Go."

"Can't. Padilla wants you all dead."

Izzy didn't recognize the man's raspy voice.

"Blaire!" Izzy's mother yelled from down the hall.

"Keep her away or your dear mother will die just like your father."

Izzy's breath hitched. "Mom, go back to your room and lock the door!" She focused on the man. "Did you kill my father?"

"I didn't, but I know who did." He sneered. "Let's just say it's someone you'd never guess."

What did that mean? "Tell me more."

Austin edged to the right, keeping his rifle trained on the masked suspect.

The perp angled his gun at Austin. "Stay there." He thrust the gun back into Blaire's temple. "Or she dies."

Névé's low growl rumbled nearby.

The situation had escalated fast. Izzy had to contain the problem or it would end badly.

And she wouldn't let that happen. *Think, Izzy, think. What would you do, Dad?*

A thought entered her mind.

Reason with the man. Talk him down.

"Listen, we're not after you. We want Padilla. Tell us what you can and it will go a long way." Izzy took a baby step forward.

"Right. I don't have a death wish. Not happening. We're here to do a job and get our reward." He pressed the gun harder into Blaire's temple. "Lower your weapons now!"

Blaire whimpered.

Lord, if I do that, my sister is dead. How can I protect her?

Névé let out another deep growl and inched toward Izzy.

Was the K-9 the answer? Izzy shot a glance at Austin and shifted her eyes back to Névé. Then back to him.

She didn't miss his slight dip in his chin.

Izzy lowered her weapon. "Okay, okay. Take me instead. Isn't it really me Padilla wants?"

"You're only part of the deal."

"You said 'we're here.' Who else is on the grounds?" She took another tiny step.

"Padilla has lots of spies. Everywhere." He cocked his head. "Haven't you found that out yet?"

Austin lowered his rifle. "How did you get by my security?"

The masked man gestured toward the opposite side of the room. "First, toss your weapons over there out of reach."

They complied.

Izzy caught Austin's slight flick of his wrist.

Névé changed to a crouching position as if she was about to take a nap, but Izzy knew better. Austin had just given her a special command.

Izzy had to distract the man. "Okay, we did as you said. Answer Austin's question. How did you breach the property and how many are in your party?"

"And did one of my men help you?" Austin added.

"Not one of your men, but someone closely connected." He chuckled. "Padilla has a black hat hacker working for him. He could bypass all your security. You should have learned that the first time it happened."

"I have an armed man patrolling the front gate. Did you hurt him?" Austin's voice raised a notch, the anger evident in his tone.

"Knocked him out. We're not here for your men." He waved the gun toward Izzy. "We're here for the Tremblay family. There's a price on all of your heads. Your father got too close and now you have too. For that, the rest of your family must pay."

Izzy studied her sister. The terror on Blaire's contorted face punched Izzy in the gut. She had to save her. Izzy wouldn't let anything happen to her, not with their broken relationship lurking in the background.

Izzy steeled her jaw and squared her shoulders, mustering courage. She raised her hands. "Let Blaire go. Take me instead."

Blaire shook her head and muffled sounds seeped from beneath the man's hand.

Izzy snuck a peek at Austin.

He gestured toward Névé.

Time to act.

An idea formed. "Blaire, it's going to be okay. Just like that time the boy in high school cornered you. Remember?" Izzy massaged her jaw and stuck out her hip, signaling to her sister what to do. The same actions she did years ago.

Blaire's eyes once again widened, but she blinked twice. Their secret code for yes.

Izzy caught Austin's attention and dipped her head, praying he understood her gesture.

She turned back to her sister and nodded.

Blaire thrust her head upward, catching the man's chin.

He cried out from her sudden movement, releasing his tight hold.

Blaire bit his hand and shoved her hip into him, knocking him away. His weapon fell to the floor.

"Névé, get 'em!" Austin clamped his hand over his opposite arm, signaling a hold tactic.

The dog leaped from her crouched position and barreled toward the masked man. She latched on to his right arm and held.

Once again, the man cried out. "Get this dog off me. I hate dogs!"

Izzy snatched the rifle again and trained it on him. "Okay, Austin."

"Névé, out!" Austin commanded.

The K-9 released her grip.

Izzy moved in front of the man and whipped off his mask, studying his face. "Wait, I remember you. You're the courier who delivers to our station. Tell me who Padilla is."

The twentysomething blond's twisted expression revealed a switch from his earlier sneer to terror. "His clutches reach into prison. I know nothing." He clamped his mouth shut.

Austin yanked the man's arms behind his back, holding him tight.

Izzy set down the rifle. "Blaire, you okay?"

Blaire thrust her arms around Izzy. "Thank you for saving me, sissy."

Austin shoved the assailant toward the door. "Let's go downstairs and wait for the police."

Izzy released Blaire and grabbed the suspect's gun, stuffing it into the back of her waistband.

The man turned from the entrance. "I will tell you that Padilla is coming for you, so beware." He gestured toward Névé and eyed each person slowly. "Not even that mutt can save you from him. All of you are in danger."

Izzy sucked in a breath.

She had to solve this case in order to save everyone she loved.

Austin closed the doors connecting the living room to the hall entrance to give Izzy and Blaire privacy. He left Névé to keep them company and give them an added sense of security. His K-9 had saved the day. Even though she wasn't a guard dog, Austin had trained her on how to subdue and hold. It had taken some time to get

Névé to listen and watch his commands, but finally the high-spirited malamute had gotten the tactic correct. This was the first time he had to use it, so Austin was grateful it worked. God was protecting them all.

After Doug and Fisher arrived, they escorted the assailant from the ranch.

The sisters wept and told each other how sorry they were. It seemed the escalated situation had been the catalyst to pave the road to mending their relationship. *Thank You, Lord. Please bring Izzy back to You.*

The constables had failed to catch the other perps, but promised Austin they'd keep an eye on the property for the rest of the evening and overnight.

Sawyer had found the wounded ranch hand and taken him to the hospital to get checked out. Before leaving, he'd ensured the grounds were once again safe.

Austin stepped into the kitchen and stopped short.

Maverick sat nursing a coffee.

Austin's face flushed at the sight of his supposed brother. He quelled the anger burning inside and sat across from him. "Tell me who you really are. No more lying."

"I never lied to you." Maverick studied the coffee steaming in his cup. "I just never said who I really was."

Austin folded his arms and tapped his index finger on his biceps. "Tell me now and leave nothing out. I'm not in the mood."

Maverick sipped his coffee, then set it down. "I'm your brother."

"I don't have a brother." Austin wasn't ready to believe Maverick. Not yet. He required proof.

"Yes, you do. I *am* your brother. Dad died from cancer five years ago. However, a year ago, my—our—mother died in an accident. A tornado whipped through the area and destroyed her home, killing Mom." His voice hitched. "I was working at a nearby ranch when it happened. We were left unscathed."

Austin noted the sorrow in Maverick's voice. He had cared deeply for the mother and father Austin had never known. "I'm sorry for your loss. My parents died in an accident, so I understand how it feels to lose both."

"I know. I searched for your name, but couldn't find you. Then I guessed your adoptive parents must have changed your last name, so I put in your birth date as Mom told me what it was in her letter to me. I'm good with computers and did an extensive search on everything I knew about you. That's how I eventually found you and the Murray K-9 Ranch."

Austin unfolded his arms. "Wait. If I'm your brother, why haven't you contacted me before now?"

"Because Mom and Dad kept you a secret."

Austin bit the inside of his mouth. Was he that much of a disappointment that they'd remained silent? "Why wouldn't they tell you?"

"No idea. The answer to that question died with them."

"Then how did you find out about me?"

He removed a paper from his shirt pocket and shoved it across the table. "I found your original birth certificate. It was tucked into a letter written to me among my mother's belongings."

Austin unfolded the document and noticed the name.

Austin Jacob Shaw.

His adoptive parents had changed his name to Austin Timothy Murray—after his new father.

He observed Maverick's features. Even though the younger blond didn't match Austin's dark hair, Austin stared into the same blue eyes as his own.

I have a brother!

Doubt once again rose its ugly head as questions filled Austin's mind. "Why didn't you tell me exactly who you were when you arrived at the ranch a month ago? And how did you find me?"

Maverick picked up his mug and finished his coffee before settling his gaze on Austin. "I confess. I was skeptical when I found out I had an older brother. Once I discovered where you were, I applied to be a ranch hand." He huffed. "I guess that part of our bloodline is the same. I really worked on a ranch. Anyway, when I got here, I expected you to be harsh as my employer back at the old ranch."

"And you thought all ranch owners operated the same?"

"Yes."

"My adoptive parents—Tom and Mandy Murray—taught me to respect people. However, it didn't come easy for me." He paused, gathering his thoughts. "I went from foster home to foster home. The last one before I came here was a horrifying experience. My foster dad abused me when I was seven." Austin rubbed the scar above his brow. "That's where this came from. He pushed me down the stairs and I hit my head. Among other beatings."

"I'm so sorry you went through that, and I'm sorry I didn't trust you at first. I quickly realized you're a man of integrity. Your men speak highly of you. I'm proud to call you my big brother."

Austin drew in a sharp breath. "I'm a big brother."

"You are. Can you forgive me for not telling you earlier?"

Words Tom Murray said to Austin many times filtered into his mind.

Son, don't go through life holding back forgiveness. If you do, it will turn into bitterness and God doesn't want that. Forgive as He has forgiven us.

His father had been referring to his birth parents abandoning him and the foster father who had abused him. However, the statement now applied to Maverick. Could he forgive the brother he never knew about?

He searched Maverick's expression for any further deception.

But found none.

Austin stood.

Maverick did the same.

Austin embraced his little brother. "Yes." A tear rolled down Austin's cheek. *Thank You, God, for this unexpected gift.*

Maverick withdrew from the hug and took an envelope from a pocket. "One more thing. I also found this among Mom's things." He handed it to him. "I'm heading to bed, but I think you may want to read it. She explained some things to me in my letter and probably did the same in yours."

Austin examined his mother's handwriting.

Austin Jacob Shaw was written on the outside of the envelope.

"Thanks, Maverick. Good night. See you in the morning." He hugged his brother once more. "Thanks for sharing everything with me."

Maverick nodded and exited the room.

Seconds later the front door slammed shut.

Austin plunked down in his chair, disbelief still lingering. He traced his mother's handwriting. Dare he open the envelope? Did he want to put himself through the agony of what was inside on such a stressful day?

Who was he kidding? He had to know.

He ripped open the envelope and removed the letter, unfolding the small page.

Dearest Austin Jacob,

You must have a million questions. I'm sorry for giving you up. I never forgave myself for that and if you're reading this letter, it's because God has taken me home. Let me explain.

I became pregnant at fifteen. I made choices I wasn't proud of and your father—Owen—was older and left for college before I knew I was pregnant. He had broken up with me and cut off all communication. My parents made me put you up for adoption. We were poor, and they said they couldn't feed another mouth. I regretted that decision every day.

Owen returned after college and we rekindled our romance. I told him about you and we tried desperately to find you, but couldn't. We married, and a few years later, Maverick was born. Yes, we should have told him about you, but we didn't want to get his hopes up that he had a brother. We tried searching your date of birth, but it didn't help us narrow down our search at all. I gave up and figured God knew you were happy. I couldn't interrupt that.

Anyway, I just wanted to tell you there wasn't a day that went by where I didn't think of you and wonder about the man you've become, but I'm trusting God worked it all out.

I hope to be reunited with you one day in heaven. I pray every day that you're a believer too.

Son, I love you with all my heart.

Until we meet again,

Mom xo

Tears flowed down Austin's cheeks as he folded the letter and tucked it into the envelope. Emotions flooded him. Years of feeling abandoned dissipated after reading his mother's words. He now knew the truth—

His mother loved him enough to give him up, so he could have a better life.

"Mom, I *will* meet you one day because I know the One you worship," he whispered.

He held his mother's letter to his chest and replayed the conversation he'd just had with his only brother.

Austin straightened as a thought rose.

They had to find Padilla—and fast.

Austin wouldn't lose the last member of his family.

Izzy gripped Blaire's hand as tears clouded Izzy's vision. She blinked them away and breathed in, mustering courage to apologize. She had to take the first step in mending their relationship. Time to swallow her pride and admit any wrongdoing on her part. "I'm sorry I wasn't there for you when Luca broke off your relationship. I failed you. Can you forgive me, sissy?"

Blaire averted her gaze, staring out the window.

The roaring fire crackled, interrupting the sudden silence. Would Blaire forgive her?

Névé nestled herself at Izzy's feet as if anchoring her in place. Izzy loved this dog and didn't know what she'd do when the case was solved. How could she leave Névé when she'd grown attached to the dog—and her handler? The thought brought another wave of tears. *Izzy, Austin isn't interested. Move on.*

Doug had promised to keep Izzy updated on the suspect's interrogation. It frustrated her not to be there, but knew she had to stay away. The board was watching her every move, and she wouldn't put Chief Constable Halt's career in jeopardy again.

After what seemed like an eternity, Blaire cupped Izzy's hand in hers. "Only if you can forgive me. You risked your life to save me tonight, and it made me realize how selfish I've been. None of this was your fault, sissy. Luca deceived me and I put blinders on." A tear slipped down her cheek.

Izzy wiped it away with her free hand. "Love can do that to us. I understand. I didn't mean to get in the way of you coming to that realization yourself."

"You were only trying to help, but I continued to believe his lies." Her eyes hardened. "I won't let any man do that to me again. Ever."

"Blaire, don't close your heart totally."

"Someone needs to listen to her own advice." Blaire tapped her fingers on Izzy's hand. "I can see how you feel about Austin. It's written all over your face when he's in the room."

Izzy puffed out a sigh. "I'm a cop. I should be able to hide my emotions."

"It's hard when it comes to love."

Love? Did she love Austin? She did once. "He doesn't feel the same. He's only ever wanted to be friends."

"Not true. What I see on your face, I see on his when you're around. He worships the ground you walk on." Blaire stroked Izzy's face. "Don't let true love slip away."

Was that what Izzy felt? True love?

Woof!

Névé chose that moment to snuggle closer.

Blaire chuckled. "And clearly this beautiful animal feels the same way."

Was it that simple? Hardly.

"Dad would tell us both to trust God. God knows what's around the corner and has it all planned out for us." Blaire bit her lip. "I'm learning that now. Mom, too, even though it's taken her a bit of time to realize it."

"You're right. He would say that. It's just hard to do. Trusting in Someone you can't see isn't easy." Izzy broke away from her sister's hold and stood, disturbing Névé.

Izzy moved to the window facing the other side of the property and peered into the darkness. Snow sparkled in the ranch's spotlights. Izzy loved the winter's fresh blankets of snow. Its beauty on the mountaintops never failed to make her pause and ponder the greatness of their Creator.

So how could she doubt God when she saw evidence of Him all around her? *He's got you, daughter.*

Words her father told her recently on one of their father-daughter dates.

I'm trying to believe that, Dad.

She turned back to her sister. "Sissy, let's not grow apart again, okay? I've missed you."

Blaire popped upright and embraced Izzy. "Ditto." She broke their hug. "Except I have to tell you my recent news and you won't like it."

"That doesn't sound good."

"You know how I've been growing my skills as a profiler?"

"Yes, and I'm so proud of you. Dad would be too."

"Well, I put in for an opening in the White-horse headquarters and I got it. It's a promotion and great for my career." Her lips quivered. "I'm moving, sissy."

No! Just when God gave her back her sister, He snatched her away. Izzy studied the dancing coals in the fireplace, avoiding her sister's eyes as she knew her emotions would be out in the open.

"Say something."

Izzy turned back to Blaire and forced a smile. "I am happy for you. You've been working hard and you deserve it. I'm not sure I can say good-bye. When do you leave?"

"In a month. Mom knows, but I made her promise not to tell you until I could. Uncle Ford knows too."

"Wait, you told Uncle Ford before me?" Izzy failed to subdue the anger in her voice.

"I'm sorry. You and I weren't on the best terms, and Uncle Ford has been there for me."

Izzy dug her nails into her left palm, diverting her frustration. "You're right. I'm sorry." She pulled her sister back into her arms. "I am proud of you. I'm just going to miss you."

"You'll have to visit me. The Yukon is beautiful."

Izzy broke their embrace, and once again sat. "You know how I love the snow, so you won't be able to keep me away. I remember how you took some college trips there. Wait, isn't that where you met the hottie?"

"You mean Dekker Hoyt? Funny. My sergeant suggested I post for the opening and gave me a raving recommendation." Blaire yawned. "I have an important video call with my new sergeant tomorrow morning, so I'm heading to bed. I love you, sissy."

"Love you more."

Blaire opened the double doors and turned from the entrance, smiling. "No, you don't." She blew Izzy a kiss.

"Night." Izzy's shoulders relaxed for the first

time all day. She finally had her sister back. For a month.

Moments later Austin appeared in the doorway. "I'm heading to my room and just wanted to say good night. Is Blaire okay?"

Izzy pushed herself upright. "Yes. We had a friendly talk."

"I'm glad. I just had an interesting conversation with Maverick. He is my brother." He waved an envelope in his hand. "I have a letter from my birth mother."

"What? That's outstanding, right?"

"Yes, it's all good. I'll tell you more tomorrow. You need rest. Doesn't the board make their decision in the morning?"

"Don't remind me. Not looking forward to that." She hated that the board held her and her chief constable's careers in their hands.

And she hated that Padilla still walked free. *Lord, if You're listening, show me what I'm missing from those three hours.*

Izzy still had a nagging feeling it was something of vital importance.

Chapter Seventeen

After a celebratory breakfast with all his ranch hands and Izzy's family, where Austin introduced Maverick as his brother, Austin carried two fresh coffees into the dining room where Izzy sat. Rebecca and Blaire had gone to their rooms, but earlier talk at the table had been light after such a taxing few days. Even Névé sensed the change in atmosphere. She pranced around the room.

Having Izzy in his home had brought joy back into Austin's life. Joy he hadn't realized he was missing. Even if it was from terrible circumstances, and he knew she'd soon leave after Padilla was caught. Sadness jabbed his heart at the idea of her waltzing back out of his life. *Stay, Iz. I can't bear the idea of life without you.*

However, she didn't feel the same. Her rigid body language whenever he got close proved his theory.

No, Austin had to put a future with Izzy out of his mind. At least, he now had a brother in his life.

Austin set her coffee down. "More caffeine to fuel your day."

"Appreciate it. Keep them coming." Izzy tapped her temple. "There's still something locked in here, and I'm determined to find it." She stood quickly. "Hold on. I just remembered there's one other message we didn't decode. While I wait for the board's decision and for Doug's report on the cookhouse bust, I'm going to take another crack at it." She glanced at her phone. "The temperature is better. You know I think best outdoors, so I'll bundle up and head to your gazebo. It's my favorite spot on your property."

"I'll go with you. I don't want you out there alone. Not with all these break-ins."

Ten minutes later Austin set a thermos in front of Izzy at the picnic table in the middle of the gazebo. She had her father's notes and the Nancy Drew book out.

He leaned his rifle against the gazebo's railing, sat across from her and took a sip from his thermos. "Nothing better than coffee made from freshly roasted beans, especially on a winter day."

She untwisted the lid and inhaled. "Sure smells delightful."

Névé barked.

Austin fished a ball from his winter coat pocket and chucked it across the yard. "She loves running in the snow."

The malamute bounced through the deep snow, chasing the ball. After scooping it up, she barreled toward them.

"I can see that." Izzy's phone rang, and she swiped the screen. "Halt calling with the board's decision, I presume."

Austin shifted to get up. "I'll give you privacy."

She placed her gloved hand on top of his. "No, stay. Please."

He nodded and sat back down.

She hit the speakerphone. "Morning, Chief. What's the verdict?"

"First a quick update on the takedown. We served the warrant to the daughter. She had no idea someone had taken over the old place. Claimed she hated the dilapidated building and never wanted to see it again, so she'd put it out of her mind. Odd. We'll look into her claims and verify her story. Carver reported they breached the premises in the middle of the night and are still investigating the scene. That's all I know at this point."

Izzy tapped her finger on the table. "Okay, and the board meeting?"

"They were lenient on both of us."

Izzy exhaled, her breath vapors rising in the cool air. "Thank God. Did they give a reason for their decision?"

Austin squeezed Izzy's hand.

"Well, the fact that the toxicology report revealed your father was drugged had an enormous influence on their decision. It—"

Izzy blasted upright. "Wait. You finally received the report? When?"

"Moments before the meeting. Sorry, didn't have a minute to call and let you know. You were right all this time, Izzy. The drug caused your dad to have a heart attack, which led to his car accident, according to the coroner." A long sigh sailed through the speakerphone. "I'm just sorry we didn't listen to you from the very beginning."

Izzy plunked down on the bench. "Me too."

"The board did caution us both about not following rules in the future, though, Izzy. They're watching. Mayor Fox still isn't happy."

"Sir, have we found out anything more about her involvement with King & Sons?"

"After the meeting, I confronted her, but she denies everything. I'm not sure, but I think someone may be setting her up to get her out of office."

Austin examined Izzy's scrunched face. He knew that expression well. Her wrinkled forehead revealed her reservations.

She still had doubts about the mayor.

A gust of wind lifted a page from Justin Tremblay's journal.

Izzy slammed her hand on top of the paper to stop it from flying away. "I'm still not convinced, but hopefully, Doug will find out more with the raid. Let me—" She righted the page and leaned closer. "Chief, I gotta go." She ended the call without saying goodbye.

"What is it, Iz?" Austin inched forward. "What do you see?"

She tapped a sequence of numbers. "This is the message I couldn't figure out, but the wind shifted the page in a different direction, giving me a new angle. A new perspective, so to speak."

"I love how God does that."

"I suppose." Izzy bit her lip. "I'm beginning to see God's handiwork, but it's hard."

"It is, but He's there, Iz. You just need to know where to look." Time to change the subject. "What did you find?"

"There are more numbers in this message. Not sure why I didn't notice it before."

"Too much on your mind. What do you think the extra numbers mean?"

"Well, Dad used the book cipher, so I want to follow it again." She opened the book and flipped to the corresponding page, line and word. "The number left is 4."

"What if the 4 represents the letter of the word?"

She snapped her fingers and pointed at him. "You might be on to something there. So the fourth letter is *F*."

Austin tore off a corner of a page and wrote the letter down.

Névé barked and sped off toward the property line.

"What's gotten into her?" Izzy flipped to another page in *The Hidden Staircase* and searched for the next word.

"Probably an animal. She gets distracted easily sometimes."

"Are all your dogs still okay in the barn? When will the new kennels be ready?"

"Next week. Sawyer and Maverick are with the dogs now. Maverick wants to learn about becoming a K-9 handler and I'm excited to train him." The idea of getting to know his new-found brother sent goose bumps traveling over his entire body. They had talked for an hour earlier this morning, and Maverick revealed his love for dogs.

"That's awesome. I'm so happy for you." She whipped off her plaid flannel scarf. "Wow, it's warmer out than I thought." She stuffed it in her pocket.

"What's the next letter?"

She ran her finger down the page. *"O."*

Austin jotted it beside the *F*.

Izzy turned the pages quickly. "Next is *R*."

Austin scribbled it onto the page. He stood and observed where Névé had gone, but failed to locate his dog.

Odd.

"Névé, come," he yelled.

Nothing.

Izzy positioned herself beside Austin. "Where did she go? You can go look for her. I'll be okay here."

"I don't want to leave you."

"I'm fine. What can happen?" She gestured toward the rifle. "Besides, I have Beulah here beside me."

"You remembered my rifle's nickname?"

"You forget my perfect—well, almost perfect—memory?"

He chuckled. "Right. Okay, I'm just going to the edge of the property and then back. If I can't find her in five minutes, I'll radio Sawyer." He handed her the pen. "You finish decoding."

"Got it."

Austin prayed for safety and trudged as quickly as he could through the deep snow to the fence line, calling his dog's name.

Névé still didn't answer.

Austin's gut told him to go back to Izzy, but before he could turn around, movement to his right flashed in his peripheral line of sight.

But it was too late.

Someone whacked him from behind.

Stars flickered in his vision as he fell on his back. Snow intermingled with spots moments before he plummeted into the murky darkness.

Izzy eyed the rifle to her right before returning to the last number in her father's code. She riffled through the Nancy Drew book's pages until she found the last letter corresponding with the number. *D*. She wrote it next to the other three and leaned back, studying the word.

FORD

She stood too quickly. Spots twinkled as a memory flashed. The missing piece to the three-hour puzzle.

Her uncle's reflection in the bar's window. He'd been watching that night.

No! Padilla couldn't be her sweet, loving uncle. Sure, they'd been at odds lately, but over-all, Uncle Ford had always been kind. Izzy's dad and uncle were inseparable.

She looked at the decoded message once more. FORD. Her father had discovered his brother's betrayal and knew his connection to the police board, so he coded the message to Izzy in his notes.

Izzy plunked back onto the bench and bur-ied her head in her hands, remorse filling her as she thought about how her father must have felt when he learned of his brother's betrayal. *Dad, I wish you would have told me sooner. I could have helped.*

But her father knew he'd be putting his

daughter in danger if he brought her in on the case. She lifted her head and snatched her phone. She had to call the chief.

Footsteps crunching on the snow sounded to her right. She stilled and looked up.

Her uncle and an armed man appeared out of nowhere.

"Put the phone down." Her uncle's voice was menacing.

She dropped the phone on top of the paper containing her uncle's name, sprang to her feet and reached for the rifle.

"Don't even think about it." Ford stepped forward. "It's time for you to pay for interfering. Theo, grab the rifle for me."

"Austin!" Izzy had to get his attention. "Help!"

"He can't hear you. He's incapacitated at the moment."

"What did you do to him?" Izzy lunged for her uncle, but he was too quick.

He yanked her injured arm backward.

Pain shot across her shoulders, immobilizing Izzy. *Lord, help me save Austin and Névé! You know how I feel about them. I can't lose them too.*

He sneered. "And his pesky malamute is asleep. I lured her to the fence with food. Don't worry, the drug in the meat was just enough to put her to sleep for a bit. I would never hurt a dog."

Snow mixed with freezing rain pelted Izzy's face. The dark clouds had rolled in while she concentrated on her father's secret message. A message that came too late. "But you killed your own brother?" Fury fueled inside Izzy's body and she fought to contain it.

Izzy, remain calm when your anger wants to guide your actions. Remember your training.

Her father's words bull-rushed her right at the time she needed them most. He had often guided her in her police career.

Theo passed the rifle to her uncle.

"Technically, yes, but Padilla was the one who ordered his execution."

"Wait, you're not Padilla?" She observed the thug standing to the right of her uncle. "Is it you?"

"Pfft! Hardly. Theo does all our dirty work, but now that your team has raided the cook-house, we'll need to find another spot." He tapped his temple. "I have a new one in mind."

"How did you kill Dad and why, Uncle Ford?"

"Easy. I slipped something into his coffee

when he went to the men's room while we were out for our weekly morning breakfast."

Once again, Izzy fought the urge to pounce on her uncle, but she knew he and Theo would overpower her. "So the drug caused him to have a heart attack and crash after he picked up Mom."

"That wasn't supposed to happen. Thankfully, Rebecca wasn't hurt badly." He raised the rifle, waving it at her head. "But you? Your persistent interfering has to stop. I should shoot you right now, but Padilla still wants to talk to you."

"Is Padilla Mayor Fox?" Izzy had to keep him talking. She stole a peek at the barn, but it seemed no one had heard what was happening outside.

"That's not for me to say, and if you're thinking the others will help you, don't. Theo and I piped sleeping gas through Austin's air filtering system in the barn where all his ranch hands were working and in the house. Everyone is out cold. Don't worry, Blaire and Rebecca are fine. I have plans for them."

"What do you mean?"

"I've convinced Padilla they're not a threat. I love your mother and want to marry her. She's another thing my brother stole from me. I saw her first, but he wormed his way into her heart."

Izzy raised her chin, pursing her lips. "She will never marry you."

"Don't be so sure. I'll *save* her from Padilla's men." He air-quoted around the word *save*. "Then she will say yes when I propose. I am a decent human being, though. I will wait a month or two after your funeral."

"You're sick." Izzy's breakfast turned to lead in her stomach, bringing a wave of nausea at the thought of her uncle's actions. "Why? Tell me why you're doing this. Revenge?"

"Partly, but there's something I've kept from the family. Even my dear older brother. I have a love for the slots, but that love has consumed my life. I had to fund my gambling habit somehow, so when Padilla approached me to be the cooker, I jumped at the chance." His cell phone chimed, and he fished it from his pocket. "Time to go."

"I'm not going anywhere with you."

"You will if you want me to leave your boyfriend alive."

"Don't you hurt Austin."

"Then do as I say." He motioned for Theo. "Use your zip ties and secure her."

Think fast, Izzy. Could she leave something

behind that would give Austin and Névé a breadcrumb? She remembered the scarf in her pocket. She had to distract them first. "Wait, tell me how long you've been helping this drug ring." She shoved her hands into her pockets.

"Padilla approached me eighteen months ago. Said the current cooker betrayed the organization by skimming money off the top. Had to get rid of him. Padilla found out about my gambling habit."

"How?"

"Padilla has ties everywhere and knows everything. Okay, enough stalling. Let's go."

Izzy made an exaggerated look over her uncle's shoulder, hoping it would distract them.

"What do you see?" Uncle Ford pivoted.

Theo did the same.

Izzy pulled the scarf from her pocket and tossed it on the picnic table's bench.

"Ain't anything there, boss." Theo approached Izzy and fastened her arms behind her, nudging her forward. "Go."

Izzy's pulse thundered in her head as tension corded her neck muscles. "Uncle Ford, where are we going?"

"Not too far. Padilla wants to meet you."

Lord, help!

Theo pushed Izzy toward the property's edge.

Her cell phone rang from its position on the picnic table and faded into the distance as her captors led her through an opening cut into the fence.

The ice pellets turned to heavy snow as the temperature plummeted and a snowstorm threatened the area. Something else to add to the trepidation building inside Izzy.

She set her fears aside and memorized the path in order to retrace her steps.

Izzy prayed Austin could follow their tracks before it was too late.

Chapter Eighteen

Pressure weighted Austin's chest. Whines and wet kisses smothered his face as he struggled to clear his foggy brain. Finally registering that Névé was trying to wake him, Austin sat up. He rubbed his eyes and face with the back of his hand. "Girl, you're okay. Where were you?"

She barked, her breath reeking of foul meat. Had someone lured his dog away with treats?

"Izzy!" Austin brushed off the snow covering his coat, pushed himself to his feet and looked toward the gazebo, which appeared to be empty.

Where was she? He had to find her, but first he had to examine his dog. He squatted and removed his gloves, running his hand along her entire body. "You okay, baby girl?"

Névé barked.

Thank You, Lord.

Austin rubbed the back of his head where someone had knocked him out, and stood. He ignored his anger at himself for allowing the person to get so close undetected and hurried toward the gazebo, removing his two-way radio. "Névé, come."

Austin pressed the button. "Sawyer, Maverick. You there?"

No answer.

He reached the picnic table and noted Izzy's phone. Something was wrong. She wouldn't have left it behind. The piece of paper containing the decoded message flapped in the wind under the phone. Austin read what Izzy had uncovered.

FORD

He gasped. Ford Tremblay was Padilla?
No!

Austin once again hit the radio button. "Sawyer! Maverick! Where are you? Izzy is gone."

The airwaves remained silent.

Austin dug out his cell phone and called Blaire. It went to voice mail.

He hit Doug's number and waited, praying that the team had vacated the cookhouse bunker.

"Carver here."

"Thank God. Doug, Izzy is missing!" Austin failed to contain the panic in his voice.

"Austin, calm down. What happened?"

"Someone lured Névé away, and when I went to look for the dog, I got hit in the head from behind. When I came to, Izzy was gone but her phone is still here in the gazebo. I believe it was her uncle. She decoded the final message and it said FORD."

"What?"

"And I can't get in touch with my ranch hands or Blaire. Can you get here quick?"

An engine came to life, filtering through the phone's speaker. "Yes. Fisher and the team are finishing up at the cookhouse. Everyone was taken to lockup. I'll update Halt. You wait for me before going anywhere. You hear?"

Could Austin promise that? Izzy's life was at stake.

"Austin."

"Fine. I'm heading to the stable to see what's going on. Get EMS here. I believe we'll need them."

"Will do. Be there in ten. Hopefully. The storm is picking up and making the roads slippery. Stay put." Doug clicked off.

At the mention of the weather, a gust of wind

picked up an object and swirled it into the air. Austin took a step and snatched it.

Izzy's scarf.

Austin stuffed it into his pocket, then searched around the gazebo. He noted faint tracks heading toward the fence line. He almost missed them, as the snow had mostly filled them in. Austin counted three sets. One smaller-sized prints and two larger. Austin followed them until he reached the fence. A gaping opening revealed their escape route. Austin banged his hand against his leg. Someone had once again breached his property.

He suppressed his anger and peered through the hole. The tracks headed toward the woods, but stopped. The snow had mostly filled them in. Why hadn't Izzy's abductors taken her to the road and fled by vehicle? He racked his brain, thinking about where these woods led and what buildings were hidden in the forest.

But nothing came to mind.

His radio crackled.

"Austin. You there?" Sawyer's words came through faintly.

Austin pressed the button. "Sawyer! Where are you? What happened?"

"Stable. We were all knocked out by some sort of gas in the air filtration system."

"You okay? What about Maverick and the others?"

"All here and we're sleepy. Just coming to. What's going on?"

"Izzy's been abducted."

Sirens sounded in the distance.

"Help is coming. I'm going to check on Blaire and Rebecca. Meet me there."

"Copy."

Fifteen minutes later, after paramedics and police arrived, Austin ensured his men and Izzy's family were okay. Rebecca and Blaire were presently getting checked by the paramedics. They had refused to acknowledge Ford's involvement. However, Doug and his team would go on that assumption. They hadn't been able to get much out of the men they'd arrested yet, but revealed both the cooker and Padilla weren't present at the raid.

Ford Tremblay fit the bill as a cooker with his chemist's occupation, but the identity of Padilla remained a mystery. Seemed everyone was too scared to snitch on the drug lord.

"Sawyer, can you think of a reason the suspects would take Izzy toward the north forest?

I'm trying to rack my foggy brain. There's nothing in those woods, is there?" Austin rubbed the back of his head where he'd been hit. "I've lived here for years, and the only place I can think of is a dilapidated cabin. Surely they wouldn't take her there. It's too obvious."

"I can't think of any other structures, either." Sawyer turned to the men. "Any of you?"

They all shook their heads.

"I also want to know how these men have continually evaded my security." Austin circled the room, studying each face for deception. He stopped in front of Maverick. Surely his brother wouldn't help criminals.

Would he? After all, Austin barely knew him.

Maverick raised his hands. "Wasn't me."

A man to the right of Austin's brother inhaled sharply. "Wait. I remember something. The other day, when Ford was here, he asked me about your ranch and Névé's favorite food. I thought nothing of it because he just seemed interested in your K-9 facility."

"He was obviously plotting then to get the malamute away from you, Austin." Doug addressed the other two officers in the room. "Do another perimeter sweep."

"We already did."

"Do it again!" Doug glanced around the living room. "Where's Fisher?"

One constable shifted his stance. "Said he was called out to do a special task by the chief."

Doug punched his cell phone. "Chief, what do you have Fisher working on?" A pause. The constable's eyes widened. "You didn't?"

Austin stiffened. Not good.

"Let me know if you hear from him. He's MIA." Another pause. "Copy." Doug stuffed his cell phone in his uniform pouch. "Seems Fisher was lying. We'll figure that out later." He pointed to the constables present. "You two split up and search the property."

They nodded and left.

"What did your chief say?" Austin shoved his hands in his coat pocket.

"That he never sent Fisher anywhere. I don't like it, but the man has taken breaks before without telling anyone."

Austin remembered Izzy saying she didn't always get along with Fisher, but that he was a good cop. Odd that he'd show insubordination now in the heat of a major situation and with Izzy missing.

Austin slumped in his chair. *Where are you, Iz?*

Névé positioned her head in Austin's lap as if sensing her handler's sorrow.

Austin fingered her scarf and bolted upright, pulling the flannel cloth out. "We can find her with this and Névé's skills."

"Are you sure you're up to it?"

Izzy was more important than Austin's aching head. "I'm fine. I've got to find her."

"You care for her, don't you?"

"Of course I do. She was my partner."

"It's more than that." Doug tilted his head. "In fact, I've seen the two of you together these past few days, and you're both too stubborn to admit your own feelings. She's not your partner any longer. Take the step. I'm pretty sure you both want to."

Austin sighed. Was the man correct? "I'll sort that out later. First, we need to find her." He turned to Sawyer and Maverick. "You both watch the place and contact me if she returns, okay?"

They nodded.

Austin held the scarf in one hand and snatched his rifle with the other before eyeing his dog. "Névé, come. Time to find Iz."

He prayed the snowstorm hadn't covered her scent.

Austin couldn't lose the woman he loved. Again.

Izzy huddled in the corner of the chilly log cabin, praying that Austin had found her scarf and was on his way with Doug and Névé. Her uncle and Theo had taken her to a new structure hidden by a wall of Douglas firs behind the old logger's cabin. The scent of fresh lumber told Izzy the building had recently been constructed.

Uncle Ford sat across from her, sipping from a thermos.

She studied his handsome face. How could he have deceived them all, including his own brother? "You deserve an award for your performance all these years. How long have you hated your brother?"

He blew on his nails before rubbing them on his sweater. "I'm good, aren't I?" His eyes darkened. "Growing up, Justin succeeded in everything he did. Sports, school, girls. I was always the second runner-up, but it was after he stole my Becky out from under me that my anger escalated. I took to the casinos and drowned my sorrow at the slots and poker table."

Izzy shifted in the wooden chair and winced from the pressure of her bound hands. She felt around the back of the seat and stubbed her finger on a tiny protruding nail. She cringed, but relief washed through her. *I can use this to help free my hands.* First, she had to stall her uncle. "You're a coward. I can't believe you'd betray and kill your own brother."

"My brother died years ago to me."

How could one child turn out so differently from the other? Even though Izzy and Blaire had their differences, they still worked them out—one by one.

Izzy focused on her surroundings, searching for a way out of the small cabin. She had memorized each step and figured they were approximately two kilometers from Austin's property. "Why did Padilla build the cabin in this part of the woods?" She slowly rubbed the zip tie against the nail, praying her uncle wouldn't notice.

"The town owns this chunk of the forest, so it was an easy spot to sneak into and hide. Plus no one comes here any longer, so we're going to build an addition and use it for a new cookhouse since you found the one on the Montgomery property." Her uncle chuckled. "Besides, Padilla has an in with the town."

"Are you referring to Mayor Fox?"

"Maybe."

"Who's Padilla?"

Her uncle harrumphed. "You mean, you haven't figured it all out, Miss Perfect Memory?"

"You were present the night Sims was killed. I now remember seeing your reflection in the window."

"I'm shocked it took you that long."

"Boss, Padilla's here." Theo's voice sounded through the radio. Uncle Ford had tasked Theo with guarding the entrance.

Her uncle stood. "Well, now you get to meet our leader and mastermind before you die."

Pounding footfalls stormed the small porch.

The door burst open, bringing a gust of snowy wind.

And someone resembling the abominable snowman.

Padilla shook off the snow and removed a fedora, revealing his balding head.

Izzy's jaw dropped. "You."

No wonder the drug ring could keep one step ahead.

Austin trudged through the deep snow as quick as possible, following Névé into the forest north of his property. The tracks had disappeared under an inch of fresh-fallen snow, so Austin and Doug were trusting the malamute's keen nose and search and rescue skills. After all, Austin had trained Névé hard to make her one of the best SAR dogs in the area. She had found countless lost hikers, especially during the winter months. Malamutes loved this time of year, so Austin had been called upon many times to use Névé's talents.

But right now, his dog was leading them toward the abandoned cabin at the base of a mountain. "This can't be right. She's taking us toward the old logger cabin the town deemed unfit recently and is planning on demolishing in the spring."

Doug ducked under a snow-ridden, low-lying branch. "This area is owned by the town, right?"

"Yes." Austin gripped his rifle tighter. "But I trust Névé. She hasn't failed me yet."

At the mention of her name, Névé stopped, looked back at them and sniffed the air before bounding up the mountain's incline.

Doug's radio squawked a broken message. "King—Son—owned—"

"That's Halt." Doug clicked the button. "Come again."

"Carver! Found—Fisher—Padilla—" The chief's words cut off.

"Ugh!" Doug tried again. "Didn't get that. Repeat."

Static followed by a pop sailed through the radio.

"Normally radios work here." Austin checked his phone. No signal. "Must be because we're deep into the forest, heading up a mountain. Plus the severe weather isn't helping. Do you think he said Fisher was Padilla?"

"I refuse to believe that." Doug adjusted his tuque. "Fisher can be a pain, but he's good at what he does. He wouldn't betray his oath to serve the community."

"Well, money can be a huge temptation to some." Austin searched the woods for his dog. "Where did Névé go?" The radio had distracted him, but he didn't want to call out for the dog for fear of any suspects in the area.

A flash of white and black bounded between trees a few feet ahead of them.

Doug pointed. "There!"

Austin advanced toward Névé and stopped short.

The K-9 had positioned herself beside a tree, growling at something ahead of her.

Austin followed the dog's line of sight.

A figure sat against the decrepit cabin's railing, his gun sitting on his lap.

Austin lifted his right fist in a stop command, then gestured in Névé's direction.

Doug withdrew his gun and nodded, pointing to the left.

Even though Austin hadn't been on the force for ten years, he recognized Doug's intent. He would go left.

Austin raised his rifle and moved right, toward his dog, quickly but in stealth mode—as much as possible in deep snow.

Doug leaned against a tree, raising his gun. "Police! Stand down."

The perp jolted, his gun dropping in the snow.

"Névé, get 'em!" Austin whispered command revealed his intent.

The dog barreled toward the man and latched on to his sleeve.

The suspect cursed. "Get this creature off me!"

Doug sprinted to the man, scooping up his gun. He stuck it in his pocket.

"Névé, out!"

The malamute released her hold.

Doug unhooked his cuffs and secured the

thug to the railing. "This will have to do until we can radio for help."

Austin lowered his rifle. "Where's Izzy? Where are they holding her?"

Behind him, Névé growled and took off, running through a wall of Douglas firs.

"She's caught Izzy's scent again. We have to follow." Austin raised his weapon.

"Wait, Austin." Doug yanked on the man's collar. "What's behind those trees?"

"Trouble." He pressed his lips into a flat line, his intent clear.

He was done talking.

"I'm following Névé," Austin said. "You coming?"

Doug searched the suspect. He found a cell phone and a radio. Doug shoved them into his own pockets before pushing on the railing. It held. "It's secure." He poked him in the chest. "Don't try anything."

Austin removed his scarf. "Put this over his mouth. We don't want him giving up our presence."

"Open up." Doug shoved it across the gunman's mouth, fastening it at the back of his head. "There. Let's go."

It was now up to Doug, Austin and Névé to save Izzy.

★ ★ ★

Terror twisted Izzy's stomach at the sight of the drug lord who had also been her father's best friend.

Vincent Jackson—executive member of HRPD's police board.

No wonder he'd been able to stay ahead of the team. Had her father suspected him and that's why he investigated the drug ring in secret? And had Vincent set the mayor up to make it look like she was guilty?

"I fooled even you, Izzy. That crack on your head by Ned sealed the deal and interrupted your perfect memory. I used that to buy time and get to you." He clucked his tongue as he waved his gun back and forth. "However, you proved hard to kill. That stupid handler and his K-9 kept getting in the way. I can't believe I'd been so close to you all this time. I constructed this hideaway to do all my planning, including secret team meetings. Next to Austin's ranch. Who would have thought?"

Izzy gritted her teeth as fury coursed through her, turning her veins to ice. Even though warmth flooded her body from the portable heater, a chill coiled around her spine. A chill permeating from the two evil men in the room. "Seems you weren't as smart as you thought." She continued to saw through her plastic binds with slow, concealed movements. "How could you betray your best friend?"

"Justin? I only got close to him to stay connected at HRPD. Well, that and his recommendation for me to get on the police board." He gestured toward his partner. "That's where I met Ford. I did a deep dive on him and discovered his dirty secret. He loved to gamble, and I knew he was a chemist, so I approached him about becoming my cooker. I guessed the temptation would be too great for him to resist."

Izzy wiggled her fingers, rubbing her wrists together to test the strength of the zip ties. She had made little progress in cutting through. *Keep them talking.* "Why, Vincent? Why bring these bath salts into our community? You're killing teenagers. For money? Is that it?"

A moment of sadness flashed over the man's face, removing his earlier menacing expression. Seconds later it vanished.

"Since you're going to die, I'll tell you *my* dirty little secret. I had an affair with Georgia years ago."

Izzy drew in a sharp breath. That was the connection to the mayor.

"This all happened before she took office. She broke it off with me when she found out she was pregnant, stating she wanted to work things out with her husband." Once again, his eyes softened. "I was in love with her and she broke my heart."

"But what has all that got to do with your drug ring?"

"When Georgia delivered the baby, she knew right away our child had special needs. She was planning on running for mayor, so she contacted me to let me know she wanted to put our baby up for adoption." The man's face reddened as the vein in his neck popped.

Izzy read Vincent's expression. "And that made you angry."

"Yes! She was going to abandon our baby all for her stupid candidacy. I told her right away I would take our baby girl. I put her in a special needs home and kept our secret." He hissed out a breath. "I soon found out I needed more money than my job would give, so I hatched a plan to make more. Took me a while to put it into motion. You know the rest."

His child's needs made Izzy feel bad, but that

didn't give him the right to kill. "I'm sorry about your child, but you've taken lives. Do you think your daughter would really want you to do that?"

"You know what they say—the end justifies the means." His eyes once again hardened. "And Georgia will pay for her part in this."

"You set her up to take the fall? Let me guess, you put the ownership of King & Sons in her name?"

"Smart girl. But your father got too close, and we had to eliminate him." He gestured toward Izzy's uncle. "Ford didn't flinch when I ordered him to do it."

Her uncle smirked.

"You're lucky my hands are tied right now." Izzy turned back to Vincent. "How did you infiltrate HRPD's systems and Austin's?"

"I have a black hat hacker on speed dial. He's the best in the region." Vincent checked his watch before addressing her uncle. "They should be here soon."

Her uncle moved to the front window. "Good guess. I see a couple of shadows out there and a dog."

Izzy stilled. "What are you talking about?"

Her uncle turned, a smug smile appearing

on his face. "You didn't think we only wanted you, did you?"

Lord, no!

Chapter Nineteen

Austin stepped through the trees, following Névé with Doug at his side. Austin's elevated heartbeat ratcheted up with the sight before them.

A newly constructed cabin lay hidden among more trees.

Even though it was midmorning, the storm had darkened the forest, preventing them from seeing clearly, but a glow coming from the cabin revealed it was occupied.

A shadow skulked by the window holding a gun.

This had to be Padilla's hideout.

"What's the plan?" Austin kept his voice low.

Doug hit his radio button and requested backup, giving them their location. However, only a crackle answered. He tried again, but no one acknowledged his call for help. "Ugh!"

Austin tried his two-way again, but it was

useless. They were too deep into the woods. Plus the mountains were impeding the signal. "We have to help Izzy."

Doug gestured toward the cabin. "You check around back for another entrance and whistle when you find one. I'll whistle back in acknowledgment." He pointed to the door. "I'll position myself there." He gestured toward the K-9. "Can she bark on command?"

"Of course."

"Get her to bark when you're ready. I'll breach first, then you enter. I realize you're trained, but it's been a few years." He paused. "If there's no other entrance, return here and we'll go in together. We can't wait for backup since my radio isn't cooperating. Let me lead, okay?"

Austin nodded. "Névé, come." He crouch-walked to a tree on the right with his dog at his heels. *Lord, protect us all!*

Austin and Névé moved to the rear, and he spotted another door. He whistled, praying no one inside heard.

Doug returned the whistle, sending his signal.

Austin reached the entrance and positioned himself to the right, raising his rifle. Before giving the command, Austin prayed. *Lord, I'm sorry I sometimes doubt Your plans. Please forgive me. You know I love Izzy. Even if You don't bring her back into my life, please save her. Don't let her die. Give me strength not to hesitate this time. I choose to trust You fully. No matter what.*

Austin inhaled and turned to his dog. "Névé, speak!"

The K-9 barked.

He waited until he heard Doug breach the front and yell, "Police! Stand down."

Austin kicked in the door, pointing his weapon.

"Well, it's about time you arrived." A voice snickered. "We've been waiting."

What?

Austin scanned the tiny one-room cabin. A couch sat at one end with a rocker next to it. A table and chairs formed the small kitchen area.

Ford stood over Izzy with a gun pointed at her temple.

Vincent Jackson tilted his head, raising his weapon higher. "Welcome to the party."

"You're Padilla?" Austin advanced farther into the cabin.

"I am and my spy here was right." His eyes shifted to Ford. "He said you'd come because you're in love with his niece."

Austin's gaze locked with Izzy's.

Her lips quivered, and she looked up at Vincent. "Leave them out of this! It's me you want."

"Give it up, man. Our team is on the way." Doug took a step forward.

Vincent waved his gun toward the sofa. "Drop your weapons, gentlemen, and have a seat, or the beautiful Isabelle Tremblay will die."

Her uncle thrust his Glock into Izzy's temple.

"You'd hurt your niece? You're sick." The scene with Clara and Izzy flashed through Austin's mind. He would not hesitate. *You've got this.*

Beside him, his K-9 continued her low menacing growl. Clearly, she sensed the danger of the situation.

Doug remained planted in place. "How about you two lower *your* weapons first? Let's talk this through. Tell us what you want."

The constable was stalling for time, but for what? Their cry for help went unanswered. No one was coming.

Austin returned his attention to Izzy.

She turned her head slightly and lowered her eyes, looking behind her.

It was then he noticed her slight movements. She was trying to free her hands.

And he had to buy her time.

"How did you get onto my ranch so easily?"

Austin kept his grip on his rifle tight, ready to fire at a moment's notice. "Did you buy off one of my men?"

"I can answer that." Ford shifted his stance. "I hinted at it with one of your men, but he proved loyal to you. But I got out of him what treat your dog likes and good information regarding your ranch."

"Did you set fire to my kennel?"

"Of course, but only to get you out of the ranch house. I trusted you'd stop the fire. I wouldn't purposely kill a dog. I just had to buy time to steal my brother's journal notes and the drive."

"Unbelievable." Austin subdued the anger boiling inside and stole another glimpse of Izzy.

She gave him a slight nod, showing she was ready.

But how could they overpower two armed men? Plus warn Doug?

A thought rose. He lifted his rifle higher. "Well, seems we have a standoff here. Reminds me of the case we worked on eleven years ago, two towns over." His eyes caught Izzy's.

She dipped her chin in acknowledgment.

He knew her perfect memory wouldn't let her forget her actions that day.

Austin caught Doug's attention and tapped his index finger on his rifle toward Izzy, praying the man would catch his drift.

Doug turned to Izzy, giving his head a slight nod.

Time to strike.

Austin said a quick prayer and braced himself with what he knew she was about to do. "Now!"

Izzy leaped from her chair and plowed into her uncle, taking him off guard.

Ford's gun discharged before it clattered to the floor.

Doug dropped.

"No!" Izzy pushed her uncle hard to the right.

Vincent—aka Padilla—aimed his gun at Izzy. "Time to die, little girl."

"Névé, get 'em!" Austin gestured toward Ford.

The dog catapulted through the air, taking Ford off guard.

Austin aimed his rifle at Vincent. "Stand down or I'll shoot."

Padilla turned his gun on Austin.

This time, Austin didn't hesitate. He fired at the same time as Padilla, hitting him in his forehead.

The man collapsed, his lifeless eyes staring at the ceiling.

Pain burned Austin's leg, registering Padilla's aim had also met its target.

Austin dropped his rifle before sinking to the floor.

"No!" Izzy fell by Austin's side. "Don't leave me." Tears clouded her vision.

Austin clutched his leg. "I'm okay. Get weapons. Check Doug." His forced, broken words revealed his pain.

Izzy scrambled to Doug and turned her unconscious partner over. Blood seeped from his right shoulder. She applied pressure. "He's bleeding badly. When is help arriving?"

"They're not. We bluffed." Austin winced. "No reception."

"What?"

Her uncle snickered. "They'll both bleed out before anyone finds us."

Névé growled and seized the man's sleeve, holding him tight.

"Get this dog off me!"

"Let him suffer, Austin." Right now, Izzy didn't care about her uncle. She pressed harder on Doug's wound. "What are we going to do?"

"I can go for help." Austin crawled to the

couch and tried to push himself upward, but fell back down, yelling in pain.

Izzy spotted the trail of blood he left on his way to the couch. "You're not going anywhere. I'll go."

"But do you even know where you are?"

"I memorized the path we took to get here." She noted Doug's paling complexion. "He's losing too much blood. If I can get to the edge of the clearing, I can call for help."

A contorted expression flashed on Austin's face.

Izzy remembered he had shared his fear of abandonment because his biological parents had given him up as a baby. "I'm coming back, Austin. I won't abandon you or Doug."

His shoulders slumped. "I know." He pointed to Névé. "Take her with you. She'll listen to your commands."

"But what about my dear old uncle?"

"Tie his hands and feet to a chair. Hand me Ford's Glock and I'll keep guard." He maneuvered his way to Izzy's side. "I'll apply pressure on his wound."

Izzy released her hold.

Austin pressed on the injury with his left hand.

She rummaged through Doug's pockets. "Where are his cuffs?"

"Securing one of Padilla's men by the old logger's cabin."

Izzy snatched her uncle's gun from the floor, handing it to Austin. She hurried to the tiny kitchen and searched the drawers. Finding rope, she examined the other wooden chair for protruding nails. "Good, this one doesn't have a nail. I guess you should have thought to look before pushing me into a chair that had a means of escape." She hauled it over to where Névé had her uncle subdued. "Névé, out!"

The dog released him.

She pointed to the chair. "Sit."

Her uncle glared at her, defying her command.

Izzy kicked behind his knees, and his legs buckled. She shoved him into the seat, yanking both arms behind his back with all the force she could muster.

She ignored his audible wince and secured his hands with the rope, looping it through the chair. She did the same to his feet before positioning herself in front of him. "You will pay for killing my father. I will make sure the judge comes down hard on you. My mother will never marry you now."

He spat in her face.

Izzy resisted the urge to punch the man, but wiped her face with the back of her hand. She wouldn't do anything to jeopardize putting her uncle behind bars. "I won't stoop to your level."

She approached Austin and squatted to face him. "You sure you'll be okay?"

"God's got me and you. Believe, Iz." His lips turned upward into the smile she'd always found hard to resist.

"Austin, I—"

"Go, Iz. Doug needs you. We can talk later."

Izzy traced his lips with her fingers. "I will be back for you." She pocketed Doug's radio before snatching up his gun and moving to the door. "Névé, come."

The dog ignored her command and trotted to Austin's side, licking his face.

"I love you too, baby girl. I'll be fine." He pointed to Izzy. "Névé, heel."

The malamute whined but raced toward Izzy, obeying her handler.

Izzy put on her gloves and opened the door. A gust of wind blew icy snow into her face, but she pressed forward with Névé at her side. Izzy ran as fast as she could through the deep snow, retracing her steps. *Memory, don't fail me now.*

God's got you. Believe, Iz.

Austin's words returned to her like a beacon from a lighthouse on a stormy night.

Was he right? Was it time to believe?

God, I've questioned Your path for my life. I'm stubborn and thought I could do it all on my own. Thought I knew better than You. I've taken the wrong roads, haven't I? I'm sorry.

She wiped a tear away. *I surrender my life back to You. Take it and do what You will with me, but please help me to get out of the forest quickly. Doug and Austin need medical attention.*

After ten minutes of slogging through the snow, they came to a fork in the woods. She searched her memory. *Right, Izzy.* She stepped forward, but Névé barked and tugged on the bottom of her coat.

"What is it, girl? This is the way I came."

The dog barked again and bounded to the left.

What was Névé telling her? Should she trust in her own memories or the SAR dog? *Show me, Lord. I'm bad at trusting.*

Névé stopped and glanced over her shoulder, barking ferociously as if saying, "Follow."

"Okay, girl. You lead the way."

Ten minutes later Izzy and Névé reached the edge of the woods. "You knew a shortcut, didn't you?"

Névé barked and bounded into the clearing.

Thank You, God, for this amazing dog.

Izzy followed the malamute and once they cleared the forest, she pulled out her partner's radio. "Dispatch, this is Constable Isabelle Tremblay." She stated her badge number and waited, praying for good reception.

"Tremblay, go ahead," Dispatch said.

"Officer down and civilian wounded. Need emergency medical assistance and evac." She gave Dispatch her location.

"Izzy, you're okay?" Chief Constable Halt's voice blared through the speaker.

"Yes, sir. They shot Doug and Austin. Padilla is down and my uncle, Padilla's cooker, is secured."

"Fisher is at the ranch. I'll send him to your location and get paramedics to you stat. Hold tight."

"Get here fast! Doug has lost a lot of blood."

"On our way."

Névé whimpered.

Izzy tucked the radio into her pocket and squatted in front of the dog. "Austin will be okay, girl. I promise." She hugged the malamute tightly and prayed for the Lord to save the man she loved.

Thirty minutes later Izzy reached the cabin with Constables Fisher and Reynolds, and two paramedics. She'd taken them there via Névé's shortcut.

Izzy dropped at Austin's side, her shoulder slumping in relief that he was still conscious.

"You're back faster than I thought you'd be." Austin smiled.

However, his pale complexion told Izzy his condition had worsened. She rubbed his arm. "Névé got me out through a shortcut. She's one smart dog."

Névé responded by licking her handler's face.

While the paramedics attended to Doug, Fisher had explained his earlier absence to Izzy and Austin. He had gotten a tip from an informant and had to respond in secret. The information had led him to the mayor's office, where she confessed that she had lied. Her anonymous tip about Izzy's actions had come from Vincent.

"That doesn't surprise me knowing what I know now." Izzy gestured toward her uncle. "Can you get him out of my sight?"

"With pleasure." Fisher left their side.

Izzy sat beside Austin. "I have to talk to you before the paramedics check your wound." She shifted herself closer to him. "I wanted you to know I don't blame you for Clara's death. I did—at first—but my dad helped me see it was only the assailant's fault. Not yours." She rubbed the stubble on his chin. "It's time for you to forgive yourself."

"Iz, I do now. God has shown me I need to put the past where it belongs. In the past. I only froze because the situation took me back to a beating my foster father gave me. It was a night I almost died." He paused, as if gathering his thoughts. "I was also going to tell you something the night Clara died, but never got the chance. Then we drifted apart, and it's taken God ten years to bring you back into my life." Tears welled before he continued. "I don't understand why God chooses some circumstances to take longer than others, but what I do know is, He knows best and I trust His timing. I trust in His journey for me. For us." Austin took her hands in his. "I want you in my life, but as more than friends."

Névé barked as if agreeing with Austin's statement.

Izzy chuckled. "That's funny, because I was going to tell you the same thing that night. I was done fighting my feelings for you and planned to ask for a transfer."

"Well, I guess God had something else in mind."

Something better. "I'm sorry for pulling back the past few days. I dated a man who became obsessed with me and I vowed not to get involved with anyone else, but then you stole my heart. Again."

"Sorry. Not sorry." He chuckled as his gaze dropped to her mouth. "Will you go out on a date with me, Iz?"

"Yes." Izzy didn't hesitate, but tilted her face upward and leaned forward, meeting his lips with hers in a tender kiss.

Beside them, Névé barked.

Izzy chuckled, but kept her lips firmly on his. She had waited ten years for this kiss, and she wanted to relish the moment.

After all, God had not only given her the man

of her dreams and a dog she loved, but planted her firmly on His path for her life.

And she planned to trust Him with everything.

Epilogue

Sixteen months later

Austin climbed the steps of the stage on the Murray K-9 Ranch's backyard. He stepped into the middle of an archway adorned with pink and red roses. Maverick positioned himself on one side of Austin. Sawyer on the other. His two best men. Austin wouldn't have it any other way on his wedding day.

Névé bounded up the stairs and planted herself in front of Austin, turning to face the crowd sitting in chairs lining the back lawn.

"Névé, speak," Maverick commanded.

She barked, signaling her approval to let the ceremony begin.

The small gathering consisting of family and close friends laughed.

Austin smiled. Everything was perfect for their wedding, even the clear blue June day sky.

He thought back over the past sixteen months and marveled at God's handiwork. Not only had Doug survived his injuries, but the constables were able to round up all of Padilla's men after Ford confessed everything. He was convicted of killing his brother after police found the drug used in his condo and Vincent's text telling him to murder Chief Constable Justin Tremblay. They had also discovered ingredients in his garage, linking him to the drug cookhouse. His fate was sealed.

Izzy grieved the loss of her uncle, but became closer to her mother and Blaire. The family's bond was now unbreakable, even after saying goodbye to Blaire as she relocated to the Yukon.

Austin and Sawyer had trained Maverick hard with the dogs, teaching him everything they knew. He excelled quickly and agreed to stay on the ranch. After Austin had proposed to Izzy, the two men, along with the ranch hands, built a cabin at the other end of the extensive property for Sawyer and Maverick to share. Austin had teased them, stating it was a temporary living arrangement until they found the women God had planned for their lives.

Both had said it wouldn't happen. They were happy being single.

But Austin guessed God probably had other journeys in store for them.

The guitarist strummed on the fretboard, declaring the start of the ceremony, before playing a soft tune.

Blaire Tremblay emerged from around the two large trees in the backyard, holding her flowers that matched the archway Austin stood under. She had made the trip back to British Columbia from the Yukon to witness her sister's—and best friend—wedding. She slowly made her way to the front.

The pianist joined in with the guitarist, announcing the bride's entrance.

The crowd rose to its feet.

Izzy appeared with her mother by her side, smiling from ear to ear.

Austin couldn't contain his soft gasp. Her beauty mesmerized him. Dressed in a flowing, strapless white gown, she took his breath away. Her hair was swept into a crown of curls with a tiny tiara tucked inside, sparkling in the sunlight.

Izzy stopped at the row of constables dressed in their uniforms. She kissed Doug's and the chief's cheeks before continuing to the front. She stopped at the base of the stairs.

"Who gives this woman to this man?" The pastor's voice boomed through the microphone.

"Her father and I." Rebecca Tremblay kissed her daughter's cheek and placed Chief Constable Justin Tremblay's badge into the center of Izzy's bouquet.

The perfect way to honor her fallen father.

Austin moved to the front and walked down the steps, holding out his hand.

Izzy kissed her mother's cheek before taking Austin's hand and walking up the stairs.

They stood under the arch, facing each other, with Névé sitting in front of them.

"You're beautiful," Austin whispered.

She chuckled. "Well, you clean up nicely, my handsome rancher. I love you with all my heart."

"Love you too." Austin smiled, taking in his surroundings and the moment.

God had answered all his prayers. He gave Austin a woman he adored, and a family he had longed for all his life.

Austin only needed to wait for God's perfect timing because He really did know best.

★ ★ ★ ★ ★

Guarded By The Marshal

Sharee Stover

MILLS & BOON

Colorado native **Sharee Stover** lives in the Midwest with her real-life-hero husband, youngest child and her obnoxiously lovable German shepherd. A self-proclaimed word nerd, she loves the power of words to transform, ignite and restore. She writes Christian romantic suspense combining heart-racing, nail-biting suspense and the delight of falling in love all in one. Connect with her at www.shareestover.com.

And ye are complete in him,
which is the head of all principality and power.
—*Colossians* 2:10

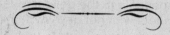

DEDICATION

This book is dedicated to those enduring a season of change and transition. With God, you're never alone!

Chapter One

"I'm confused how evidence in an ongoing investigation disappears." Heartland Fugitive Task Force commander Beckham Walsh restrained his irritation while staring at the woman he'd avoided for nearly three decades. "What process did your department neglect?"

Grand Island police chief Danielle Fontaine squared her shoulders from behind her desk. Long, chestnut layers framed her oval face. Her defensive posture, complete with narrowed brown eyes, shadowed by thick lashes, and pursed full lips, reminded Walsh of her as a young recruit. Stubborn, determined, and gorgeous. All the traits that had attracted him in the beginning of their relationship three decades prior still applied.

"I assure you, we will figure out what's going on."

"Dani," Walsh said, using her nickname, "that's a placating comment."

She sighed. "I wasn't in command when your team secured the evidence here. I'm unaware of the particulars of this specific case. Please bring me up to speed."

"The munitions are part of a multi-jurisdictional illegal weapons operation. Enrique Prachank, the trafficking leader, is a fugitive and about as slippery as an oiled catfish. He's eluded capture for over a year."

Dani sucked in a breath. "Your case is connected to Prachank?"

"Yeah." Walsh paused. "You're aware of him?"

"Isn't everyone in law enforcement?" Worry replaced the calm she'd exuded. "I'm not defending or minimizing the situation, but only one of those guns is unaccounted for." Still, that missing firearm was tied to Prachank's many crimes, including arms and drugs dealing. The evidence could help bring Prachank down. Now they needed to determine how it'd disappeared from the Grand Island PD.

"It reflects a compromise in the chain of custody, jeopardizing the entire case," Walsh concluded, conveying the seriousness of the implication.

Glancing at his watch, he winced: 2030. The late hour wasn't helping his attitude at all. Thirty years of combined experience between the military and law enforcement, and the never-ending war on incompetence persisted. Still, grace overrode accusations and his goal was resolution, not blame.

"I'm certain at worst it's a labeling issue," Dani said.

"If you believed that, you wouldn't have called me here," Walsh contended.

"I didn't." She lifted her chin, challenging him. "As a courtesy, I notified you of the anonymous text advising the case number and missing item."

Recollections of the intense takedown that HFTF had diligently pursued bounced to the forefront of his mind. Months of hard work, sacrifices, and stress to keep the cache of illegal weapons off the streets was now threatened.

"I'll get to the bottom of it when I speak with Jayne Bardot, my evidence technician."

"Why haven't you done that already?" The words came out harsher than he'd intended.

Dani quirked an aggravated brow. "She's unavailable. Jayne's a trusted employee, and

I have confidence she'll clear this matter to your satisfaction."

Walsh huffed out a breath. It was like they'd traveled back in time and replayed their original roles.

Him the accuser, Dani the defender.

The repeat of their past, resulting in the subsequent rupture of their relationship, wasn't an event he wanted to revisit. Yet, here they were, circling the same mountain nearly thirty years later.

"Send the security footage to my team." He gestured at her computer monitor. "We'll scan for intruders." And anything else that revealed the truth.

"I've reviewed the videos and found nothing suspicious," Dani argued.

"Great." Walsh forced a smile. "Then it won't hurt for us to do it again." *The right way.*

They held their silent standoff.

Only the sleek black dog splayed at her feet moved, stretching his legs and squeaking out a yawn. Walsh glanced down, a grin tugging at his lips, and addressed Dani, "May I pet him?"

"Sure, his name is Knox."

The moment lightened the tension as Walsh knelt to stroke the dog's short coal-colored fur.

"He's a purebred mutt."

"Those are the best, right?" Walsh spoke to Knox. "He has a lot of Doberman features."

The dog shifted into a regal sphinx position, offering a better view of his narrow brown-and-black snout.

"He's got Great Dane blood mixed in, too." She offered him a dog biscuit from a box in her desk.

Walsh passed it to Knox, who happily munched on the treat.

Dani's disposition softened with the canine deflection. Walsh shifted into investigator mode, aiming to gain her trust with the common interest. "What're his specialties?"

"Evidence recovery and explosives detection."

Ironic, considering Dani's department lost the evidence which was their current topic of discussion. The thought lingered on his lips. He withheld it thanks to the throw-no-stones reminder nudging his conscience. He considered his failures, which left his heart and ego forever scarred. Walsh's career centered around protecting others, and he'd botched that job with the most important person in his life. A flash of his deceased wife, Gwen, flitted to mind unbidden. Walsh shoved it away. That was a long time ago. He couldn't change her outcome, nor did he fear a recurrence. Living as a bachelor ensured he'd never face that pain again. A ring erupted from Dani's pocket, jolting Walsh to the present. He perched on her desk, leaning closer to eavesdrop.

Dani frowned, pushing back in her chair to create distance. "It's Jayne. I'll answer on speakerphone."

Walsh nodded but didn't move. Speaking to the evidence tech was of utmost importance.

She swiped the screen. "Hey, I've been—"

"I must talk to you. Now. It's urgent!" the woman screeched into the line. "Not on the phone, only in person."

"Jayne, what's wrong?" Compassion overrode Dani's question.

"Please hurry!"

"Okay. Where are you?" She spoke calmly, though Walsh didn't miss the concern in her expression.

"Meet me at the abandoned Mills Warehouse off County Road 436 in Broken Bow."

"Jayne?" Dani glanced at the device, as if expecting it to explain. "She hung up. Did you get all that?"

"Yes, let's go." He jumped to his feet.

"It's unnecessary for you to accompany me."

"Negative." Walsh set his jaw. "Nonnegotiable."

"Fine." Dani dragged the word for several syllables. "You drive," she said, resuming control of the situation.

Walsh grinned at the ploy.

Knox barked, quickly standing on all fours.

"Sorry, you wait here until I return," Dani said.

"He's welcome to join us." If he wasn't mistaken, Dani's hardened expression softened.

She holstered her duty weapon and snagged a leash from the hook by the door. "In that case, come on, Knox."

The Dobie mix trotted to her side.

Walsh led the way to his black SUV and settled Knox in the kennel behind the front seats. "We equip our SUVs with canine kennels and supplies." The sudden realization that he'd said that to impress her had his neck warming.

"Wow, that's very cool." Dani was seat-belted and waiting when he slid behind the wheel. Her purse rested as a barrier between them. "Knox and I are always together since Lincoln PD partnered us eight years ago."

That captured Walsh's interest. "I wasn't aware you were a handler." He didn't know anything about the woman he'd avoided at all costs after their clash.

"I retired Knox when I took the GIPD promotion. He's still adjusting."

With the impact of a swift kick to the gut, Walsh struggled not to react to her words, contemplating his own impending mandatory retirement. A poisonous snake threatening to strike and take him out of the game.

Shoving aside the dread, he reverted to his best defense—avoidance and denial. "Dogs are an intricate part of HFTF. We owe them several team successes."

"HFTF's reputation is unsurpassed." Dani surprised him with the compliment, and the short reprieve from their heated discussion lessened Walsh's tension. "Thanks. I didn't realize you'd taken the job at GIPD."

She nodded. "Recently, and I'm sorry for this mess. There is no excuse for the evidence issue. You have my word that I will rectify and ensure this doesn't happen again."

"How well do you know Jayne?"

"She's a sweet young woman and a responsible single mother."

Walsh noticed Dani's stiffened posture. Fabulous. He'd put her back on the defensive. "Does she normally call panicked and demanding your attention like this on a Friday night?"

Dani hesitated, conveying more than her words. "No," she replied. "She's high-strung. Most likely, whatever is happening isn't as bad as she made it sound."

"Trying to convince me or you?"

"Both, I guess." She shrugged and looked out her window. "We met at a women's ministry lunch about a year ago. We've become close friends. She's a great asset to the department."

"Aha, you went into rescue mode," Walsh surmised, then clamped his mouth shut, fearing he'd offended Dani again.

"Probably." Her gentle response relieved him. "Most cops possess the rescuer mentality. It's why we pursue law enforcement careers."

"No shame in that," he added, hoping to maintain the cordial conversation.

Dani quieted, and he traversed his thoughts. Why, after three decades, had their paths intersected? Should he broach the topic, or would that erect bitter walls?

They drove for a half hour in silence before Walsh said, "I'm not familiar with Broken Bow, so you'll have to guide me."

"Broken Bow is a town northwest of Grand

Island, boasting a population of a little over three thousand."

"Impressive."

The corner of Dani's lip quirked. "That's one of the few benefits of growing up in this area." She provided directions through the country landscape.

At last, the warehouse loomed ahead.

"Take the frontage road instead." She gestured to a lane that paralleled the building.

"Perimeter check," Walsh deduced.

"Right."

"There are binoculars in the console."

Dani withdrew them, surveying their surroundings.

Walsh turned off the headlights and carefully navigated the dirt grooves. Thanks to Nebraska's summer drought, the road mimicked desert conditions. It also eliminated proof of whether the tracks were recent. They drove around the perimeter, then moved toward the building.

"Clear." Dani replaced the binoculars. "That's Jayne's maroon sedan under that oak tree."

He parked beside the vehicle and shut off the engine. Dani exited the SUV, then released Knox, snapping on his leash. Walsh checked his magazine and with his gun in hand, the trio approached the warehouse.

He gripped the door handle and tugged. "It's locked."

"Maybe she went through the side entrance."

They reached the east entrance and stepped in, allowing the door to close softly. A glow at the far corner provided the only light in the expanse.

"Jayne?" Dani's voice echoed in the eerie darkness.

Walsh touched her arm, lifting his Glock slightly in reminder. He'd activated his weapon-mounted flashlight and swept the beam around the room. Dani looped Knox's leash over her wrist and withdrew her gun, mimicking Walsh's moves. They proceeded cautiously.

Boxes wrapped in plastic and set on pallets consumed the area.

Decaying grain and something pungent assailed his senses. Their boots padded on the cement floor as they surveilled the warehouse. A figure emerged, looming in the shadows in an alcove between two large stacks of pallets.

"Dani!" A willowy woman burst forward, arms outstretched. "Thank you for coming!"

Her long, dark hair fluttered like a cape as she rushed toward them.

Dani holstered her weapon. "What's going—"

"I don't think he followed me." Jayne's wide blue eyes bounced around the room, landing on Walsh for a second before scanning the warehouse.

"Who?" Walsh kept his gun at the ready, surveying the dim space.

Jayne shook her head. "It's important you find—"

Rapid shots cut off her sentence.

Instinctively, Walsh and Dani tackled Jayne and Knox to the floor in a synchronized effort. She and Walsh pushed them into the safety of the corridor and returned fire.

The hollow room amplified the deafening sounds as though a hundred guns shot back.

"Dani." Jayne's voice was soft behind them.

She lifted a hand, silencing her friend without turning to address her. They needed to focus on the return assault.

Then, as quickly as it began, the gunfire ceased.

Dani and Walsh held their positions, not daring to move.

A thud preceded an explosion. A flash-bang grenade erupted, blinding and deafening them.

Walsh ducked, blinking hard. "Stay here." He shifted ahead of Dani, eyes stinging, and bolted after the shooter.

Dani maintained cover for Walsh through her blurred vision, then turned to check on Jayne.

Eyes closed, her friend's head lolled to the side.

"No, no." Dani scurried closer, brushing her knee against Jayne's outstretched arm.

A brass key rested in her open palm.

Dani's attention shifted to the spreading crimson stain seeping through Jayne's pale-yellow T-shirt. "Walsh!"

When he didn't immediately respond, Dani hollered louder. "Walsh!"

A slamming door and heavy footfalls drew closer. "Dani!"

"I'm here! Call 9-1-1!" Her gun, weapon light still activated, lay on the ground.

He skidded to a halt, his six-foot-four-inch frame towering in front of her. "Were you hit?" He withdrew his cell phone and dialed on speakerphone.

"No. Jayne's hurt." Dani held her in an awkward embrace. "I can't see where."

"Is she—"

"No." Dani pressed her fingers to Jayne's neck. "She's got a faint pulse."

The line rang twice before a woman answered. "Nine-one-one, what's your—"

"This is deputy US marshal, Commander Walsh," he barked. "I need an ambulance at the abandoned Mills Warehouse. Patient is female, mid-thirties, GSW to the chest. Pulse is slight and erratic."

"EMTs are en route," the operator responded.

Walsh disconnected. "Let's get her into the recovery position."

She nodded.

They positioned Jayne on her right side, her top leg bent to brace her knee on the ground, then straightened her right leg. Walsh adjusted Jayne's arms, sliding one straight above her head and tucking the other under her cheek.

He dug into his pockets, then tugged off his T-shirt, exposing the black compression shirt underneath. "Use this to absorb the blood."

Dani held the tan fabric against the wound, soaking it within seconds. They had to get Jayne to the hospital before she bled to death.

Knox paced, whining softly.

"Did you check him over for injuries, too?"

She blinked, processing Walsh's question.

"Dani?" He placed a beefy hand on her shoulder. Like an electric shock, his touch jolted her to the present.

"Come here, Knox," she cooed, snapping out of her daze and shrugging off Walsh. She detested the quiver in her voice as she groped the dog's short fur. "He's okay."

"Good."

"I was certain I'd moved fast enough to protect her." She stroked Jayne's dark hair away from her face. "I'm so sorry. Lord, we need You. Please help her," she prayed aloud.

"Help's on the way," Walsh assured her.

"I don't understand what happened here."

Knox sat beside her and nudged her arm with his cold nose.

"I'm glad you're okay," she whispered before returning her focus to Jayne. "How? Why?"

"I'll secure the scene while you ride in the rig with her." Walsh's steady response reminded Dani of her responsibilities.

She was a cop first, and she'd not fall apart. Especially not in front of Walsh.

"No. I'm needed here." Dani stood, shoulders back. "Were you able to trace the shooter's escape? See what he drove?" She assumed her command composure, emotionally distancing herself from the situation.

"I walked the perimeter and saw no tracks, though it's hard to tell with the hardened earth." Walsh gripped his cell phone. "Pretty sure he exited through the south door."

Dani shook her head. "There were no other cars besides Jayne's."

"He could've driven a UTV and hidden it in the tree line." He hesitated. "Unless he was waiting to ambush us." Suspicion hovered in his tone.

"What're you saying?"

"Jayne lured you here."

"She did not!"

Walsh frowned but didn't respond.

"Maybe he broke the window to escape after tossing the flash-bang?"

"Negative, the glass is on the inside."

Dani glanced at Jayne. The implications slammed into her with the force of a hurricane.

She'd failed to protect her friend. Jayne worked hard, balancing her role as a single mother with her job at the PD. An impossible task in divided devotions in Dani's opinion. She should know—her mother's daily struggle to be enough was proof.

Dani had surrendered everything for her career, believing her ex-husband Mark's promises that their marriage was all he'd needed. Instead, he'd abandoned her for a younger woman with whom he'd built a beautiful family. The same obligations he'd sworn he hadn't wanted from Dani. Just as her father had done to her mother, trading them in for something better.

Bitterness welled within her at history's cruel propensity to repeat. Never again would she succumb to that pain.

Dani swallowed the emotions rising like bile in her throat.

Why hadn't she protected Jayne? She'd take her place this instant! Dani's sole existence, other than her job, affected no one else. "She tried to warn me," Dani whispered.

Dani was expendable. Jayne was young and had so much life to live. She had an infant daughter who relied on her, especially after Tessa's drug-addict father had overdosed. Tessa would be an orphan if Jayne died.

"Tessa!" Dani blurted.

Walsh faced her.

"We have to check on Jayne's baby as soon as we get out of here." The six-month-old had no one else. No wonder Jayne had made Dani promise to care for Tessa if anything happened to her. Had Jayne feared she was in danger? Where was Tessa now?

"Okay. Rescue is coming. We'll take care of Tessa once Jayne is transported." Walsh pocketed his phone. "Locals will process the crime scene."

"No!" She whipped her head to look at him. "I'm handling the investigation."

"Dani." Walsh's annoyingly calm composure teetered on placating. "We need objectivity."

He was right, and she hated admitting that. They were outside her jurisdiction. She studied her ex-boyfriend, and the idea bloomed.

"Fine. Then let your team do it." Dani checked Jayne's wound again. HFTF's success rate was unsurpassed among neighboring task forces. Walsh couldn't argue that. She knew of the interagency task force's cooperative efforts with the FBI, ATF, US Marshals, and other local agencies in Nebraska, Iowa, and South Dakota. They'd sort this out.

"She deserves the best. Please." She'd never spoken more honest words. Loath to admit her desperation, her concern for Jayne overrode her intentional standoffishness with Beckham Walsh. Regardless of their past, Jayne needed their help.

He sighed. Not infuriation, rather resignation. "Okay."

"I'd like to be included in the case."

He seemed to study her before dialing and selecting speakerphone. Dani appreciated his willingness to let her participate in the discussion.

"Heartland Fugitive Task Force," a woman answered.

"Eliana, please initiate a team conference call," Walsh said.

"I'll patch them in," she responded. Within a few seconds, several clicks confirmed the joining members.

"Grand Island police chief Danielle Fontaine is here with me. She'll work this case with us." Walsh provided a succinct recap of the events for his team. "EMS is on the way. HFTF will take the investigation lead, starting with the crime scene examination. Any evidence collected will go to the Iowa state lab to avoid conflict of interest, since Jayne is the GIPD evidence technician. Additionally, Skyler, manage all ballistics processing."

Dani bristled, then silently acquiesced to his judgment call.

Sirens screamed in the distance.

"Finally," Dani softly addressed Jayne, "Help's almost here."

"Please state your name when you speak for Chief Fontaine," Walsh directed.

"Eliana Kastell, tech specialist," the woman who'd answered said. "Elijah and Graham are the closest to your location."

"Eliana's system provides real-time GPS for the members," Walsh explained to Dani.

"ETA 10 minutes," a man said. "Sorry, DEA agent Graham Kenyon."

Knox whined, his gaze flitting between the back of the warehouse and Dani.

Walsh jerked his chin, getting her attention.

"What's up?" Dani whispered, stroking the dog's ears.

"Good," Walsh said. "Kenyon twins, take the lead on the evidence handling, especially recording the chain of custody, and secure the transfer to the Iowa state lab."

"Officer Elijah Kenyon," another man replied. "Won't Nebraska have a problem with that?"

"I'll notify them of the conflict of interest within this internal investigation," Walsh answered.

"ATF agent Skyler Rios," a woman said. "You've confirmed the missing weapon?"

"Yes," Walsh responded.

Skyler added, "I'll send all ballistics to my NIBIN contact and advise it's an urgent request."

Dani recognized the reference to the National Integrated Ballistic Information Network. An inside connection expedited processing.

Knox nudged Dani's arm. "Shh." She stroked his scruff.

"The rest of you assemble at the Rock by midnight," Walsh ordered.

A chorus of "Roger that" and "Affirmative" bounced over the line before he disconnected.

"What's the Rock?" Dani asked.

"Our Omaha headquarters." He glanced at Knox. "Is something wrong with him?"

The K-9 whined, again nudging Dani's arm. "Oh, sorry, sweetie, I didn't realize I still had your leash attached to me." She wriggled free of the lead and the dog scurried off, nose to the ground.

Walsh and Dani exchanged confused glances, then followed Knox to the far side of the building, where he disappeared into a hallway.

Dani ran to catch up and spotted a tall stack of boxes concealing a door.

Was the shooter still there?

Based on the increased siren decibels, reinforcements were closer. Walsh withdrew his
weapon again. They shoved aside the boxes, revealing the sign that read Janitor's Closet.

A strange mewing, comparable to a cat's late-
night cries, rose from the gap beneath the door.
Knox scratched at the entry and the howls intensified, competing with the sirens outside.

"What's making that noise?" Dani tried the
handle. "It's locked."

"May I?" Walsh's hulking size and muscular
frame hadn't diminished over the years. If anyone could break down the door, it'd be him.

She stepped aside, and he rushed forward,
shoulder-first.

It didn't budge, and he winced.

Dani peered closer. Steel. No wonder.

Remembering the key in Jayne's palm, Dani
said, "Wait here." She spun on her heel and
sprinted to the main warehouse, retrieved the
key, then hurried back to Walsh.

They flanked the entrance, guns at the ready,
and Dani unlocked the door, then nudged it
open.

Dani gasped, dropping to her knees. "Oh,
no." She lifted Jayne's distraught six-month-old
daughter from the carrier. "Tessa." Cradling

her, she asked, "What's a fugitive and a missing weapon got to do with Jayne and Tessa?"

"Apparently," Walsh replied, "everything."

Chapter Two

Dani paced the Rock several hours later as HFTF worked the case. The infant's feathery hair tickled her cheek as she cradled and patted Tessa's back. The baby hadn't enjoyed the extended ride to Omaha. To Walsh's credit, he'd not complained, and Knox had done his best to comfort Tessa. She'd found his fur intriguing, making the last forty minutes of the commute bearable.

HFTF's K-9s sprawled around the room, peering up as she passed by them. Walsh had introduced her to his team, whom he was clearly proud of, and they'd all been welcoming.

"You should be in bed," Dani whispered against Tessa's tiny ear.

Walsh held her gaze with an I-told-you-so look. She'd pleaded with him to delay the transfer to Child Protective Services the entire drive. He'd agreed only because it wasn't a violation of protocol since Jayne was injured, not deceased. Her heart refused to transfer the baby into a stranger's care. She'd promised Jayne that she'd look after Tessa. She intended to keep that promise. Whatever it took. And guilt for not protecting Jayne weighed on Dani. Until they received confirmation Jayne would recover, she wanted Tessa close.

"Need help?" Eliana Kastell, HFTF's computer technician, asked from her seated position at the kidney-shaped table. Auburn strands had escaped her messy bun, and even at the late hour her green eyes were bright.

Dani had instantly taken to the woman. "Is she asleep?" She turned slowly, allowing Eliana to see the baby's face.

"Yep, she's out." Eliana leaned back, revealing her pregnant belly.

"Eliana, go home and rest." ATF agent Skyler Rios slid into the chair beside her. Walsh had told Dani on the ride over of his plan to train Skyler to be his successor.

She assessed the agent, who oozed strength and professionalism. Her dark hair was pulled in a severe ponytail, accentuating the narrow lines of her face. Her intense gaze and no-nonsense manner testified to Skyler's capability.

Deputy US marshal Riker Kastell leaned toward Eliana and kissed his wife's cheek. "That's what I told her."

The group's easy communication style and kindness impressed Dani.

"No way, I'm in my second trimester and feeling great." Eliana shifted her computer, giving Skyler elbow room.

Dani slid into a chair.

"We're grateful for your help." Walsh stood before the evidence board, which was covered in pictures, maps, and information.

"Dani, any update on Jayne?" FBI agent Tiandra Daugherty asked.

"She's out of surgery, but still in critical condition." Dani's throat constricted.

"We're praying for her," Deputy US marshal Chance Tavalla replied.

Two men entered the room carrying large boxes that they placed on the table. Dani did a double-take. Except for their clothing, the men were identical. One wore jeans and a black pullover. The other, dark cargo pants and a light T-shirt with the HFTF logo on the right pocket.

The team distributed coffee and sandwiches.

"Figured you needed fuel." The man in the

dark cargo pants extended his hand to Dani. "Officer Elijah Kenyon."

She shook his proffered hand. "Chief Dani Fontaine."

"Pleased to meet you, ma'am."

The second man pushed Elijah aside good-naturedly, shaking Dani's hand. "DEA agent Graham Kenyon. And, no, you're not seeing double. I'm the better-looking one."

"I wondered if I was hallucinating," she teased.

"Do I get combat pay for riding with him?" Elijah pointed at his twin.

"Graham's driving is horrendous," Tiandra said, revealing a slight southern accent filled with playfulness. The FBI agent jerked a chin toward Graham.

"Right?" Elijah consumed a section of the wall with his massive six-foot-one-inch muscular frame. "He gives me heartburn."

"I'm a trained professional," Graham replied, narrowing his gray-blue eyes at his twin.

Dani appreciated their light chitchat, but her raw emotions contrasted with the aromas, upsetting her stomach. "I'll take a coffee, please."

Tiandra passed her a cup.

"Thanks," Dani said. "Whatever Jayne intended to share tonight was important enough to warrant privacy."

Tiandra extended her long legs out and crossed her ankles. "Why endanger Tessa?"

"She put her in the closet to protect her," Dani countered defensively, knowing her friend wouldn't have let Tessa come to harm.

Riker shook his head. "Wouldn't a sitter be a smarter choice?" He addressed Dani, pinning her with his blue eyes.

"Tessa is in full-time day care. Jayne picks her up right after her shift ends. She hates being away from her baby."

Compassion filled Eliana's emerald irises. "GIPD's video footage confirmed Jayne left work at 1700."

"That's a considerable unaccounted window between then and our arrival at the warehouse," Walsh noted.

Skyler leaned forward. "Any progress finding a relative to care for Tessa?"

"None," Eliana said. "Jayne's mother passed two years ago, and her personnel documents list Dani as her emergency contact."

Her friend's trust in Dani left her speechless.

"What about Tessa's father?" Walsh asked.

"He died after Jayne learned she was pregnant." Tessa nestled against Dani and the scent of baby lotion wafted to her.

Her developing friendship with Jayne apparently lacked details. They'd discussed their present or future dreams, not their histories.

"There's gotta be someone," Dani protested.

"We'll keep searching," Eliana assured her.

Dani thoughtfully contemplated her next words. "I promised Jayne that I would take care of Tessa should anything happen to her."

Understanding quietly passed through the group.

"Broken Bow PD is unhappy with us for taking over the shooting investigation at the warehouse." Walsh sighed, redirecting the discussion. "I smoothed things over, but tread lightly."

"Can't blame them," Riker responded. "We rolled into their jurisdictional wheelhouse and took over."

"We don't want to open Pandora's worms." Walsh confused the two clichés. "Don't release details of the intersecting investigations."

"Knowledge is power. Only NSP could usurp us," Elijah replied, referencing the Nebraska State Patrol.

"I pulled a lot of strings, favors, and basically

promised my ranch for their permission to work this case," Walsh reminded the group.

The man she remembered would've never gone through all that trouble to help her. Dani's gaze lingered on Walsh. Flickers of gray added to the attractiveness of his sandy brown hair. His brown eyes were soft and inviting, and his muscular physique hadn't diminished over the years either. Walsh's strong demeanor exceeded his handsomeness. Humbled, she said, "I appreciate all you're doing."

"Crime scene processing was minimal except for the casings," Graham advised. "It's all bagged and logged into the Iowa crime lab."

"Let's address the obvious elephant we're avoiding." Walsh sat opposite Dani.

She'd noticed his distancing all evening. Not that it surprised her, considering their decades-long estrangement. Had he told his team about their falling out? No, when would he? They'd been together since the warehouse shooting.

Memories of their past flittered to mind. Walsh's investigation into Cortez PD Chief Varmose, then Dani's boss, had destroyed she and Walsh's relationship. If he'd told her what he was doing, instead of hiding the case and his role, they might've had a chance. Or not.

Yes, she'd missed Chief Varmose's corruption until it was too late. But in her defense, she'd also been a rookie cop, brand new to Cortez PD. Wasn't loyalty to the brotherhood part of the job? She'd stuck to her guns, believing the best about Varmose, and proved herself committed to her agency and her commander. Until Walsh had presented the undisputable evidence against the chief, simultaneously making her the scapegoat to the rest of her co-workers. Their disdain and assumption that Dani was involved in the sting had almost cost her everything.

Tonight, Walsh had striven to help her. She appreciated his efforts, while reasoning he owed her that much after nearly destroying her career years prior. She was at Beckham Walsh's mercy, but they weren't friends. Detachment from him was fine.

"The GIPD-compromised evidence—specifically the Smith & Wesson 9 mm pistol directly linked to the multi-jurisdictional weapons trafficking takedown involving Enrique Prachank—" Walsh began "—is crucial. We're all aware of the critical need to recover that ASAP."

Dani averted her eyes, staring at the tabletop.

"I have concerns regarding any other evidence we stored at GIPD," Walsh said.

Like salt in a painful wound, Dani winced at the implication.

"That being said," he continued, "Dani will work with us to determine the item and system breakdown."

Expecting condemnation and judgment in their eyes, Dani forced herself to look up. Not one person offered a harsh glance. Inhaling a fortifying breath, she said, "I'm confident there's a logical explanation. Since Jayne cannot assist us, we're on our own to discover those details."

"We'll conduct this investigation with no special treatment, shortcuts, or favoritism. Jayne's participation and/or responsibility is obviously a tremendous concern."

Dani stiffened. His comment reiterated her view of the real Beckham Walsh.

She'd never leave Jayne's future in the hands of this über-focused egomaniac. Walsh ignored allegiances, satisfying his ambitions, regardless of the fallout. He'd proved himself in that respect, and he'd never blindside her again.

"Dani, are you familiar with the case Walsh referenced?" Tiandra asked.

"The bare bones."

"Mastermind criminal Enrique Prachank established and controlled an underground arms and drug dealing network spanning South Dakota, Nebraska, and Iowa. He trafficked weapons of both legal and illegal varieties," Tiandra said. "We tied one of his guns to multiple murders. It's the key evidence we have against him."

"Like taking down Capone with tax evasion instead of his other crimes," Dani postulated.

"Right. You take what you can get," Skyler replied. "The murder charges will earn him life in prison."

Elijah leaned forward. "We have to sever the head of the snake, or they'll just resume their activities."

"He's a fugitive, correct?" Dani asked.

"Yes. Prachank's been on the run for over a year. He's also our priority case." Chance stroked his German shepherd, Destiny. "Grand Island PD is one of the contracted off-sight evidence storage locations."

"It's all negotiated in our multi-agency memorandums of understanding," Walsh inserted.

Dani was aware of the agreements, but she didn't interrupt.

Chance nodded. "Prachank's gotta have the missing weapon."

"Find that and you'll find him," Dani concluded.

"Jayne asked us to meet her at the location." Walsh redirected.

"Technically, she called me," Dani argued. "Obviously, she assumed the warehouse was safe."

Walsh's frigid stare corrected her. She wasn't mulling the facts with the perspective of an investigator.

"I'm sorry, go on."

"She might've lured you there." Graham munched on a sandwich.

"Assuming that's true. What's Jayne's motive?" Riker addressed Dani, "Did you have an argument? Any reason she'd want revenge or retribution?"

The group pinned Riker with shaking heads. "What?" He lifted his hands in surrender. "It's a valid question."

"Riker battled his own brother's vengeance," Tiandra explained. "His thoughts start with that intention."

The details sparked hope in Dani. If they'd each faced personal challenges, surely, they'd have compassion on Jayne's. "I saw Jayne three weeks ago at church. We always meet for breakfast after service. Kind of a tradition. We had a pleasant conversation about nothing in particular," Dani said. "She doesn't report directly to me. Additionally, I've been out of town at a conference for over a week. Just got back today."

"Did she seem distraught?" Chance asked.

Dani shook her head. She and Jayne's single relationship status had bonded their friendship.

"Is she dating?" Skyler questioned.

"No, she's focused on her daughter." Dani considered the way Jayne doted on Tessa.

"She's balancing a full-time job with parenting," Eliana surmised.

"An impossible task. Something takes a backseat." Dani regretted the words immediately.

"Might explain the evidence issues," Elijah agreed.

Great, she'd added fuel to the fire.

"Monday, we'll interview her coworkers," Graham advised.

"It's late." Walsh stacked his files. "Recoup over the weekend."

"Technically, it is Saturday," Eliana said goodnaturedly.

Walsh nodded. "Right. Take the rest of today and Sunday off. Then tackle your assignments, and we'll reconvene on Monday. Dani, HFTF has a small condo here in Omaha. You're welcome to stay there."

"Thank you." She'd dreaded making the two-hour return trip to Grand Island.

The group stood and huddled, offering prayers for wisdom, for protection over Tessa, and for Jayne's healing. Dani's chest tightened with humility and appreciation as their collective amens filled the room.

She glanced at the baby. "I have nothing for Tessa except her carrier and what's in the diaper bag."

"Brilliant thinking to grab the carrier's car seat base. That's essential. You can borrow the playpen we have," Eliana offered, glancing at Riker. "Our little one won't need it for a few more months." She stroked her belly in a nurturing and protective manner.

"Thank you." Overwhelmed with gratitude, Dani blinked away tears. What was wrong with her? The late hour and chain of events were playing on her emotions.

"I'll bring it over," Riker offered.

"Oh, and I'll add in some other must-haves for you," Eliana added.

"You all are amazing." Dani forced down the lump in her throat.

"It's what family does." Tiandra gave her shoulder a squeeze.

The group dispersed along with their dogs, leaving her alone with Walsh.

"I'll give you a ride to the condo," he said.

"I hate to move her." Dani brushed her cheek against Tessa's soft skin. "But we both need sleep."

"Agreed…" Walsh hesitated.

Dani tilted her head. "What's up?"

"You won't want to hear this, but—"

"Jayne wasn't involved in anything underhanded," Dani cut him off. "Tessa was her life. She'd never willfully endanger her."

"Reconsider Child Protective Services assuming temporary custody. They'll keep Tessa safe and allow you to focus on the case."

Dani glared at him. "I promised Jayne I would ensure Tessa was protected and cared for. I can't just hand her over to strangers, regardless of their qualifications." Especially not after almost getting her mother killed.

Whatever it took, Dani would keep her promise to Jayne and be Tessa's caregiver until she recovered. And, she had to prove Jayne's innocence and arrest the shooter. The one question she couldn't answer was what Jayne had tried to tell her before the incident. That information could've cost their lives.

Worse, Dani had a feeling the danger wasn't gone.

Walsh led the way to his SUV, helping Knox into the kennel while Dani settled Tessa's carrier into the car seat base they'd retrieved from Jayne's car at the warehouse. Her movements spoke of experience. He wondered about her personal life since their breakup all those years ago. She'd apparently done all right for herself after leaving Cortez PD. Regret for how he'd handled the investigation into her then chief, Varmose, and the man's subsequent conviction still stung. Walsh had never meant to hurt Dani, yet he'd done exactly that. As one of the investigators, he couldn't risk his career by warning her ahead of time. She'd never forgiven him for blindsiding her.

He'd only been doing his job.

His ambition preceded all. That was what a good cop did. Wasn't that the excuse he'd given when he'd failed to protect those he'd cared for? First Dani, then his deceased wife, Gwen.

Recently, Walsh wondered whether he'd misplaced his loyalties. Once he retired, the marshals would replace him without a second thought. His commitment had cost him everything, and he'd have nothing to show for it in the end.

Not even his law enforcement identity.

What did he have besides his job?

All the could've been's lingered in his mind. His and Dani's relationship had started out wonderfully, but it never got beyond the new stage, thanks to Walsh's career pursuits.

Dani's fierce loyalties were unwavering. Regardless of the evidence against Varmose, she'd exploded at Walsh, touting her boyfriend had used her to get information on the captain while blindsiding her to the aftermath. She'd ended their relationship. Rightly so.

His career had soared after that, permitting him to deliberately evade any close connection with her. He focused on cases geographically distanced from central Nebraska, only recently learning about Dani's promotion to GIPD.

She faced him. "Why are you looking at me like that?"

Walsh blinked, searching for an explanation to divert the conversation, and blurted, "You're a natural." He swallowed. "With the baby."

"I've spent time with Tessa, so I'm familiar with what works to calm her down."

She offered nothing more and Walsh took the hint. Right. Better to sustain a professional relationship. Asking her personal questions led to the reverse. A vulnerability he'd not return if the conversation focused on him.

His failures had morphed Walsh into a loner with too many regrets. That was nobody's business. He glanced at Tessa before closing the door. All his dreams of a happily-ever-after family had died with his wife, Gwen. He'd missed the opportunity for a normal life, devoting himself to law enforcement. Soon, that would mean nothing. The fear of his uncharted future pricked at him. Only four years remained before his mandatory retirement from the marshals.

Dani shut her passenger door and he slid in behind the wheel, starting the engine.

Their conversation dwindled on the drive to the condo—a recent acquisition for housing HFTF witnesses.

Once they reached the property, Walsh parked, and they exited the vehicle.

Approaching lights demanded their attention. Dani set the carrier down, then drew her gun. Walsh stepped closer, exhaling relief at the sight of the familiar pickup. "It's Riker. Go ahead, and I'll help him carry in stuff."

"Come on, Knox." Dani and the Dobie mix ascended the exterior staircase to the second-level unit.

Walsh maintained a visual on them while walking to Riker.

"Sorry, would've been here sooner, but Eliana kept adding things for Dani." Riker chuckled, opening the back door.

They withdrew several bags and a strange rectangular object.

"It's a Pack 'n Play," Riker explained.

Walsh grunted. His military and law enforcement experience had instilled skills and training to handle dangerous equipment and situations. But the unfamiliar baby contraptions Riker hauled to the apartment baffled him.

Dani held open the door while they carried in the load. Riker set up the Pack 'n Play and Walsh helped Dani unpack the bags. "Eliana also threw in some extra clothes and supplies for you as well."

Dani blinked. "Thank you."

"You've got enough for twenty babies." Walsh handed her a package of diapers.

"Unfortunately, we'll go through those fast,"

Dani replied. "Bless Eliana! She thought of everything." She held up two large bottles. "Baby wash and lotion."

Tessa grunted from her carrier. Dani changed the infant into strange pajamas with no leg holes and mittens over her hands, then transferred her to the playpen.

"Doesn't she need blankets and a pillow?" Walsh asked.

Based upon Riker and Dani's dumfounded expressions, the answer was no.

"Alrighty." Walsh withdrew his keys. The universal sign for *I'm leaving*. "Take tomorrow, er, the remainder of today and Sunday. I'll pick you up at 0900 Monday."

"Thanks," Dani replied. "I should've driven my vehicle. I'm sorry to impose on you."

"No problem," Walsh assured.

"Please extend my appreciation to Eliana for everything." Dani accompanied them to the door.

"Will do. Night." Riker turned and jogged down the steps to the parking lot.

"Walsh," Dani said.

He faced her. "Yeah."

"I won't deny my friendship with Jayne affects me." She glanced over her shoulder at the playpen. "Based on the team meeting, it sounds as if you've fought personal battles without compromising your integrity. I'm no exception."

He'd witnessed Dani's unrelenting loyalty that blinded her to reality once before with her old chief, Varmose. Though she'd come around to accepting the truth about the man's corrupt involvement after Walsh had provided evidence. Yet that stubborn streak returned, and it appeared they were on the same opposing sides again.

"Jayne was in trouble or had found something significant. She'd never endanger Tessa." Dani wrapped herself in a hug.

Walsh shoved his hands into his pockets, torn between wanting to comfort her and wanting to scream at her delusional reasoning. Jayne was guilty and involved. He just didn't have the evidence. Yet.

"She hasn't always made the best choices, from the little of her past she shared," Dani justified. "However, she lives for Tessa. Give me time to learn why this happened."

Walsh glimpsed at the baby resting in the playpen. His heart extended to the innocent caught in this mess, but it changed nothing. If Jayne was guilty, he'd arrest her.

"Get some sleep. We'll talk more later." He turned without another look at Dani, inhaling the humid summer night air.

The door closed softly, and he sighed. Their brief reunion rekindled familiar and unwanted emotions. Losing Dani had devastated him, but it had never diminished his feelings for her, professionally and personally.

That was his job as a commander, and he felt the same for her as he did all the HFTF staff.

Liar. The thought assailed him, and he flinched.

Dani was different. She'd invaded his heart in ways he'd never imagined possible. She was like no other woman he'd ever known. Dani had strength and intelligence that had skyrocketed her in their academy days. Her slender, lean build masked the physical capabilities she possessed. They'd competed without issue, becoming fast friends before their budding romance. But when Dani looked at Walsh, he felt his knees grow weak and his pulse race. She still took his breath away. And, truthfully, he feared his inability to remain impartial to her.

He descended the steps to the ground level. Dani might be right about Jayne, but his instincts said otherwise. He intended to uncover the truth about the woman. Nobody endangered those he cared for and got away with it. He'd put whoever had attacked them at the warehouse behind bars and expose Jayne's involvement.

A flicker in the distance grabbed his attention.

Walsh surveyed the landscape. Had he imagined it? He stepped back, looking up at Dani's apartment door. No light glowed from her unit's windows.

Had the shooter followed them to this location?

For a moment, Walsh considered moving Dani and Tessa.

Another visual of the area and he spotted only cars parked in the lot and the slight breeze fluttering the leaves of the trees.

They'd spent hours at the Rock before driving here. He was hypervigilant. Besides, if she'd gotten Tessa to sleep, he didn't want to wake them over nothing.

Resolved, he returned to the SUV. Sliding into the driver's seat, he withdrew his binoculars and scanned the surroundings.

His breath hitched at the motion of a person shifting between parked cars in the neighboring housing development. Homing in on a black-clad figure drawing closer, he shut off the SUV's overhead light, snagged his gun and exited the vehicle.

He started for the intruder, keeping to the

shadows, and moved to the main apartment building. As he neared the first-floor window of a unit, a dog barked, then pawed at the glass.

Walsh ducked behind a bush, spying the figure bolting in the opposite direction.

"Stop!" Walsh disregarded his surreptitious approach and gave chase.

He lost sight of the person after he dodged between two trucks parked beside a fence. Was it a car thief or burglar? Or had he come for Dani?

Furious, Walsh spun on his heel and stormed to his SUV, resolved to stay and provide protection detail. With too many unanswered questions, he couldn't risk leaving Dani and Tessa unattended. He considered notifying Dani, but knew he'd only wake her if necessary. However, he'd involve Chance and Graham. They'd take shifts in the hope the intruder returned.

If he did, Walsh vowed he'd not escape again.

Chapter Three

Monday morning arrived too soon. Even with Sunday to rest, minus a trip to the ER to ensure Tessa was all right after the warehouse incident, Dani hadn't fully recuperated from the shooting late on Friday. She had spent the morning checking in at GIPD, ensuring she was only a phone call away should her staff need to reach her. Walsh's SUV pulled into the parking lot. His attempt at surreptitious security detail hadn't worked. She'd seen him, Chance, and Graham performing shifts outside the condo over the weekend. Her heart warmed at their concern for her and Tessa.

Tessa's bags sat by the door. Walsh hadn't contacted her, and she chalked up the exterior protection as his overcautious quirk.

Knox squeaked out a yawn, causing Dani's chain reaction response. She stretched her back, then offered him a scratch between the ears. "You're tired too."

Unaware of Tessa's normal schedule, she couldn't tell if the baby regularly slept in short three-hour increments. Maybe the unfamiliar bed affected her. Each time Tessa fussed, Dani and Knox awoke with her. She'd not complain, at least not to Walsh. He'd made his intention of putting Tessa in Child Protective Services clear and Dani refused to encourage that notion. She'd survived on less rest during her undercover ops. Of course, that was ten years prior.

Once more, respect for Jayne's life as a single mom had Dani praying for her friend. How had she worked full-time with regular intervals of limited sleep? She'd never heard Jayne whine. "Please heal her, Lord," Dani prayed aloud. She'd called the hospital several times, but Jayne's condition hadn't changed.

Dani feared the worst.

Knox glanced up from the bed as though in agreement with the petition.

Tessa let out a howl, and Dani lifted her from the playpen. "Good morning, darling." She rubbed the infant's back. "I know, you're missing your mama."

Dani walked to the kitchen and completed

mixing Tessa's formula, then sat to feed her. The doorbell rang, and she readjusted, cradling the infant in one arm, and hurried to open the door.

"Morning." Walsh extended a drink carrier containing two cardboard cups. His gaze bounced from her to Tessa, then at the drinks, before he retracted the offer.

"Sorry, I'm short a hand," Dani joked. "Come in."

She turned and walked back to the chair she'd previously abandoned. He followed, pulled out a seat opposite her and withdrew the coffee. "I wasn't sure what you'd like. I have one plain black brew and a vanilla latte."

"Oh, the latte, please." She reconsidered. "Unless you wanted that."

"Not a chance." He passed her the cup marked with a big V on the side.

Dani glimpsed her reflection in the decorative mirror over the couch and winced. "I'm running behind." She still needed to shower and dress. She'd pinned her hair in a messy bun, and she wore the sweats and an oversize T-shirt Eliana had provided.

"It's okay. I'm early, so I'll make calls while you're getting ready." Walsh's cell phone rang.

"Case in point." He smiled, revealing the handsomeness Dani had tried to ignore before.

She blinked and averted her eyes. Sleep deprivation made her wonky.

"Morning, Skyler," Walsh answered on speakerphone. "I'm here with Dani."

"Hola," the chipper ATF agent responded. "I'm visiting my *abuela* this month and need to practice my Spanish to impress her."

Walsh chuckled. "Whatever works to bring us her amazing tamales."

"Definitely. I've got news."

"Hopefully good?" Dani asked.

"Not exactly. My NIBIN contact called this morning. The ballistics evidence recovered from the warehouse shooting came back as a match already logged in the system."

"How's that possible?" Dani asked. Then it hit her. The gun had been used in a previous investigation. She sat straighter. "You have my full attention."

Tessa wriggled, frustrated, and a small wail escaped as she readjusted the bottle.

"Hola, Tessa," Skyler said.

"Sorry, we're multitasking here," Dani explained.

"No worries."

"Go ahead," Walsh prompted.

"The casings matched a Smith & Wesson 9 mm collected in the Enrique Prachank case."

"The missing firearm our team logged into the GIPD evidence locker with the rest of the weapons cache after the takedown. Prachank's compelling, literally smoking, gun," Walsh concluded.

"*Sí jefe,*" Skyler said.

"What?" Walsh asked.

"Yes, boss," Skyler translated.

Dani blinked, staring at the phone, thoughts racing. "But that makes no sense."

"Trust me, it's legit. Ran it three times," Skyler replied. "I don't have to tell you the mess this opens."

"It's the first connection we've had on Prachank since he escaped custody," Walsh said. "Notify the rest of the team."

"Okay. That gun tied him to several homicides," Skyler added, as though Dani needed the reminder. "Without it, Prachank's lawyer has a chance of getting his case thrown out for insufficient evidence."

The same weapon Jayne was responsible to secure as part of her job.

"We'll be in the office shortly," Walsh said.

"Roger that."

They disconnected.

Dani excused herself to finish feeding Tessa in the bedroom, while Walsh made phone calls.

"Help me out, kiddo." The baby grunted her disagreement, melting into tears as Dani settled her in the carrier. "You asked for it." Dani belted out an '80s song, and Tessa quieted. Poor kid probably wanted her to stop, but it worked.

She got ready faster than she had during her academy days as her mind raced with the implications of Skyler's call.

Within ten minutes, she finished, whipping her hair into a ponytail. She hauled Tessa in her carrier—occupied with a stuffed elephant—to the living room and placed her beside Walsh. His expression shifted between amusement and intimidation as he looked at the baby. Had something happened? Was he debating Prachank's situation against Jayne's involvement... or did infants make him uncomfortable?

She stifled a giggle. "Babies not your thing?" She retrieved Tessa.

"Uh, haven't been around them much." She'd never seen Walsh appear anything other than confident in any circumstance. But when he beheld Tessa, his forehead creased, and he appeared conflicted.

"Ready?" Walsh seemed eager to leave as he hurried to the door.

"As I'll ever be," she responded, picking up the carrier.

"What can I haul out for you?"

"Grab that," Dani said, gesturing with her free hand toward the purple diaper bag by the door.

"Want the playpen too?"

She considered the request. "Probably not a bad idea."

Walsh walked to the Pack 'n Play and stood looking down at it. "Do I need a degree in engineering to fold it?"

She smiled. "No worries, I've got it." Dani put Tessa down, then with a few quick movements, she'd folded the playpen.

"It's a giant origami project," Walsh teased.

Dani laughed a little too hard. She gave herself a mental slap upside the head. "Lack of sleep is affecting me." Why had she confessed that?

"Did she keep you up?" Walsh glanced at Tessa.

"No problem," Dani insisted, hoisting the carrier. "C'mon, Knox, time to work."

The Dobie mix stretched out his lanky legs and slowly got to his feet, and they trailed Walsh to his SUV.

"If I hauled her around every day, I could eliminate some of my upper body workouts," she quipped. "After the meeting, would you mind driving me to GI later today to pick up my vehicle?" She used the initials for Grand Island, as most Nebraskans did.

"Sure, but I don't have a problem chauffeuring you," Walsh assured her. "It's nice to have the company."

Dani doubted he felt that way, but she didn't comment.

"In fact—" he glanced at his watch "—let's get on the road now. I'll update the team on our plans." They finished loading Tessa and Knox. The dog leaned closer to the infant, guarding her. "Good boy, Knox."

Once they were moving, she said, "We need to talk about the newest elephant between us."

As though in response to her words, Tessa let out a wail of disapproval. His gaze flicked to the rearview mirror as he dialed his team using his hands-free device and updated them of his plan to take Dani to GI. Rather than take Tessa on the four-hour roundtrip and to the station,

Eliana agreed to watch her at the Rock. Dani hated leaving her, but headquarters would be the safest place for her while they continued investigating—starting with the evidence room.

After a few moments of silence, Dani said, "I can guess what you're thinking." She shifted uncomfortably in the seat.

"I've got no doubt."

"There's a reasonable explanation and we'll find it," she told him confidently.

"Jayne is the GIPD evidence technician responsible for Prachank's gun," Walsh replied. "There's no coincidence here."

"He's a fugitive," Dani contended. "We've got no proof Jayne stole it from the locker."

"That's the likeliest scenario," Walsh argued.

She hesitated. Her internal cop self agreed with Walsh. The implications against Jayne were strong. But Dani refused to believe her friend would risk her career and her baby to help a criminal. Still, she needed a justifiable argument with validity, not feelings, to persuade Walsh.

"Prachank has connections. There's a reason he's eluded capture all this time. It's conceivable he paid someone on the inside to get the gun for him. Without it, the state will have trouble prosecuting. It's crucial proof against him. His freedom is his strongest motive for getting that weapon back."

"True. And his scumbag lawyer could've suggested or even helped Prachank line up the theft, since he's harped most on the fact that the weapon is the only evidence against Prachank. Eliminate it, and the rest teeters off balance," Walsh stated. "He could be mocking us. Not only was he able to get it out of the evidence locker, but he plans to keep using it."

"Yeah." Dani sighed. "Except why do something as foolish as shooting at us with the gun he stole? It practically advertises he has it."

"Desperation," Walsh replied. "It has the power to convince even the smartest people to make poor decisions."

Dani couldn't agree more. And she was determined to prove Jayne hadn't stolen the firearm.

Finally, on the road after transferring Tessa into the team's care at the Rock, Walsh and Dani were on the highway. He'd silently considered the situation with Prachank's weapons, and concluded they had to first question the fugitive's attorney.

Walsh slid on his sunglasses, shielding his

eyes against the late-morning sun that pierced the windshield.

"It's going to be a hot one today," he said.

"Supposed to be record highs all week," Dani replied.

They were discussing the weather? How pathetic was that? But he struggled to talk with her. She'd not come out and argued with him regarding the implications of Jayne stealing evidence. However, Walsh understood the depth of Dani's devotions. They'd fought this battle once before and it had ended their relationship. Now they were in a similar position. He didn't want to repeat the same mistakes this time. But he'd been correct all those years ago about her boss, Varmose, and the corruption he'd dragged into Cortez PD that Walsh had unveiled.

And he felt certain he was on target about Jayne.

Dani's reason for withholding her defense argument was more than the words. He again debated removing her from the investigation. She was too invested. They couldn't jeopardize the case, for Dani's sake.

In Walsh's experience, he'd learned the best people could still make the wrong choices for the right reasons.

He agreed with her on some points, though. What had made Jayne desperate enough to risk prison, her livelihood, and losing custody of her daughter? Those questions remained his focus regardless of Jayne's relationship with Dani. He was the commander of the Heartland Fugitive Task Force. If necessary, he'd pull rank and remove Dani from the investigation, prepared for the battle that he'd face with her.

"Aren't we going to GI?" Dani asked, interrupting his thoughts.

He winced, merged onto Highway 81 and headed north, realizing he'd not shared his intentions with her. "I apologize. I'm working through everything in my mind and neglected to share."

"Regarding what, exactly?"

"Change of plans. It's a reasonable assumption someone with insider knowledge and capability stole the gun from Grand Island PD's evidence room. Regardless of the motive, I want to talk to Prachank's lawyer first."

"You think he's behind this?"

"If anyone knows Prachank, it's his attorney," Walsh replied.

Dani withdrew her cell phone. "Should I call and demand he meet with us?"

"Nope. I prefer the advantage of surprise."

"Works for me." She settled back in her seat. "So, who is this illustrious lawyer, and where does the bottom dweller work?"

He chuckled at her silliness. "Raymond Strauss resides outside of Humphrey, under a different name. Though his office address is in Omaha, even he doesn't want his clients to know where he lives. If that tells you the type of clientele he services."

"Wow, no kidding."

Walsh flipped on the air conditioner, and Knox peered through the divider, soaking it up. Walsh used one hand to pet him.

He turned off the highway onto the county road. They traversed the rolling hills, typical of northeastern Nebraska, toward the small town of Humphrey.

They rounded a pivot corner, spotting a house and barn. The loud whirring of a bright red motorcycle gained his attention. The driver and passenger were both clad completely in black-leather gear, with full helmets and darkened face shields.

"They have to be baking in those clothes," Walsh said.

Dani twisted around.

The motorcyclist revved the engine and Walsh got a better glimpse of the newer model Kawasaki Ninja. "Fast ride."

Emphasizing Walsh's evaluation, the bike screeched and did a slingshot to the left. The red blur zipped past Walsh on the driver's side.

"What an idiot," he muttered.

"Yeah. I'd charge him with excessive display of acceleration," Dani confirmed.

"And reckless driving." Walsh shook his head.

"I'm calling him into the state patrol." Dani withdrew her cell phone, and he listened as she reported the bike.

The Kawasaki disappeared by the time she'd finished.

"They'll be watching for him."

"Doubt they'll catch him, though," Walsh argued. "Those guys know how to dodge the authorities, and there are plenty of side roads for them to disappear."

"Well, aren't you Mr. Negative today," Dani quipped.

He frowned. "I'm pessimistic. There's a difference."

"If you say so." She chuckled.

The landscape transitioned into deeper rolling hills, surrounding them in acres of corn and soybean fields. The SUV crested the rising peaks of the road before plunging down into the valleys. "Being out here makes me want to get back to the ranch."

Dani quirked a brow. "Is that code for something?"

"No." Walsh guffawed. "Marissa and I own a rescue horse ranch near Ponca State Park."

"I haven't seen her in forever," Dani said, smiling. "How's she doing?"

Memories of the fire that nearly killed his sister only a short time ago assaulted him, instantly sobering Walsh. Strangely, it also reminded him how close danger had come to his family. He flicked a glance at Dani, empathizing with her worries for Jayne. "She was involved in a horrible attack when we were working a case. But she's fully recovered and back to her normal ornery self."

Dani grinned. "Don't you dare talk bad about her. I've always loved your baby sister. Does she still call you Becky?"

Walsh grimaced. "Yes. And don't try it."

"No guarantees." Dani laughed.

Walsh and Dani had met at the academy, becoming quick friends. It had taken him two years after they'd parted and started working in their respective departments to ask Dani out. Mainly thanks to Marissa's help. He'd forgotten the many dinners the trio had spent together before Walsh had exposed Varmose's drug dealing corruption in Dani's department. Sadness hovered with the bittersweet memories. "She's exactly as you remember her. Rescued another mare last week."

"You buy the horses, then resell them?" Dani asked.

"Nope. We provide forever homes at the ranch. Many were abused or neglected by their previous owners. Marissa and I give them a home where they're loved and cared for."

"That's cool. I'd love to see it sometime." The sincerity in her tone made him want to tell her more.

He wanted to prove to Dani that he wasn't the cold-hearted robot she'd once accused him of being. "We'll have to make it happen."

They settled into a comfortable silence.

How was it that decades had separated them, yet being around Dani still felt natural? As though they'd picked up right where they'd left off all those years ago?

The road narrowed as they approached a semi-truck hauling a massive load of hay bales.

"Well, we *were* making good time." Walsh decreased his speed. "Is it my imagination, or is that bale not secured up there?" He gestured toward the humungous, yellow roll of hay teetering ahead of them.

"They always look like that," Dani assured him. "Really, they're tightened down."

"Hmm," Walsh murmured, unconvinced. He prepared to pass the semi but was restricted by the No Passing road sign. "Makes me nervous watching a two-thousand-pound roll of hay rocking in front of me."

Ahead, the truck crept at a snail's pace up the steep hill with its weighted load. Walsh's gaze flicked forward where a shadowed figure inched atop the bales. "Is that—" His question was cut off by the distinct sound of a revving motorcycle engine screaming behind them.

"What's going on?" Dani twisted in her seat once again.

"Is that the same guy from earlier?" Walsh glanced in the side mirror, watching as the dark-clad figure drew closer, this time without a passenger.

Dani seemed to study the rider. "I'm not sure, but it doesn't look good."

Walsh unclipped his holster and withdrew his Glock, placing it beside him on the seat.

Dani also retrieved her gun and ordered, "Knox, down!" The dog immediately dove into the rear kennel.

The semi continued its painfully slow climb up the hill.

Blocked by the truck on the narrow uphill country road, where visibility was hindered by the semi's load, and the motorcycle behind them, they had nowhere to go.

Trapped.

The Kawasaki drew closer, and the driver hoisted an automatic rifle. He slung it across his chest, repositioned and aimed at the SUV.

Walsh's gaze flicked to the truck in front of them. There, he spotted the motorcycle's leather-clad passenger perched atop the bales, aiming an identical weapon at them.

"Get down!" he hollered, slamming into Park, then ducking in his seat as a barrage of bullets was unleashed upon them.

Chapter Four

Glass rained in the SUV from the relentless gunfire. Dani and Walsh remained low while bullets pierced the seat cushions and interior just above Dani's head.

Then, as suddenly as it began, the shooting stopped. The motorcycle's engine revved as the bike sped away, leaving its screaming tires fading in the distance.

"Are you okay?" Walsh rose slowly, checking his surroundings.

"Yeah." Dani scooted up in her seat. "Knox, stay down!"

Still on the hill, the semi in front of them had come to a complete stop, its hazard lights flashing.

Walsh twisted around to see Knox. "Is he hurt?"

Dani leaned over the headrest, spotting her Dobie mix flat against the floorboards, thankfully unharmed. "No, he's fine." She reached out a hand to him. "Good job, Knox," she praised. "Stay." Dani didn't want her dog to cut his paws on the broken glass.

She turned, prepared to open her door, when a thud caught her attention. The massive two-thousand-pound bale of hay rocked.

As if in slow motion, the enormous bundle tumbled off the stack, barreling straight for Walsh's SUV.

"Down!" Walsh yelled.

Dani again slid to the floorboard as the bale crashed onto the hood of the SUV. The impact lifted the vehicle's back end, which remained suspended for a horribly long second before slamming down.

Dani's teeth rattled. Dirt, dust, and shards of hay filled the atmosphere. For several seconds, neither moved. She held her breath as the cloud of debris hindered her vision. Finally, she found her voice. "Walsh!"

"I'm here," he answered with a cough. "Are you okay?"

"Yes, I think so."

Walsh snagged his Glock from where it had fallen to the floorboard and Dani did the same. Both grunted with the effort of shoving open the vehicle doors, which were damaged but not demolished, and escaped the SUV.

Dani unlocked the kennel and the dog inched out of the rear passenger door, thankfully protected by the steel structure. He hopped down and gave a thorough shaking of his fur. She knelt beside Knox, running her hands over his short black coat. "Not a scratch." As though confirming her words, Knox lapped at her face. Dani chuckled. "I love you too." She snapped on his leash, keeping him close.

Dani took in the unbelievable sight of the supersize bale of hay caving the vehicle's hood.The semi remained still.

"Why did he stop?"

"I don't know." Walsh waved her to follow.

"Knox. Stay." The dog sat and Dani dropped the leash. "Stay," she reiterated.

With guns at the ready, they parted, each moving forward to approach the semi's cab.

The bales were wider than the vehicle, hiding the driver from view. Dani stayed with her back flat against the hay and inched closer. When she reached the front of the trailer, a wide grin crossed her face at the sight of the herd of cows meandering in the middle of the road.

Walsh rounded the semi too.

Her surprise at the bovines shifted when Walsh whispered, "Dani."

Her gaze roved to a section of plaid fabric fluttering in the breeze, apparently snagged on a break in the wire fence surrounding the pasture. Acres of cornstalks on the opposite side of the road beckoned the animals.

Dani raised her gun, prepared.

She glanced at Walsh, who brandished his Glock and stared ahead.

"Come out with your hands up!" Dani ordered, aiming her weapon at the field. "If you run, I will send my dog after you."

"Don't shoot!" a man wearing a red baseball cap called, emerging from the stalks.

A second man followed. He wore cowboy boots and a plaid shirt with a rip. Dani surmised it was the same fabric torn on the fence. He approached with his hands raised. "Please! Don't shoot."

"Come toward us. Slowly! Keep your hands above your head," Walsh ordered.

"Are you police?" the first asked.

"Yes," Dani replied, realizing she wore jeans and a blouse while Walsh had on BDU pants and his uniform shirt. At least one of them looked professional.

Relief seemed to pour over the men's faces.

"Am I imagining that?" Dani asked under her breath.

"Nope, they're glad to see us," Walsh said before directing the men. "Stop where you are."

They halted in place, two feet from Dani and Walsh.

"Are you carrying any weapons?" Walsh questioned.

"No, sir," both replied in chorus.

"We need to check for our safety," Dani said.

The men turned, hands still above their heads, allowing Dani and Walsh to search them. Satisfied, they stepped back, holstering their weapons.

"You may lower your hands," Walsh said. They did as instructed, but apprehension covered their faces.

Dani whistled for Knox and the dog raced to her side, leash trailing. "Good boy."

He sat beside her, focused on the strangers.

She addressed the ball-cap-wearing man as he was closest to her. "Do you have identification?"

Both men warily gawked at Knox while reaching to retrieve their wallets from their back pockets. Walsh collected and studied the IDs before passing them to Dani.

"Vinson Jessup," Dani spoke to the ball cap wearer.

"Yes, ma'am. Are you all right?" Jessup replied.

She blinked, confused by the question.

"Were you hurt by the bale or the shooters?"

the second, whose driver's license read Timothy Bartle, reiterated.

"No. What happened to your shirt?" Dani asked Timothy.

He glanced down. "I don't know."

"We heard the gunshots and bolted out of the truck," Jessup explained.

"Then we saw the trailer rock and realized a bale had rolled off," Timothy added.

"Why did you stop?" Walsh asked.

"The cows," Jessup said.

"Were you aware a person was on the hay bales?"

Both men gaped in confusion. "Is that who was shooting?"

"Yes, along with an individual on a Kawasaki," Walsh replied.

Timothy swatted at Jessup. "Told you it was that dude!" He faced Dani. "We got to the hill and saw the cows strolling across the road. It's not easy to stop a vehicle with a heavy load."

"Did you know the people on the motorcycle?" Walsh asked.

"No, sir!" Timothy shook his head emphatically. "We were a ways back when a red Kawasaki flew around us."

"The passenger must've disembarked the bike and climbed onto the bales," Dani surmised.

"Like those awesome action movies!" Jessup exclaimed.

"We figured it was one of those kids with the body or helmet cams doing stunts," Timothy said.

"Did the motorcycle shooters also release the cows to trap us?" Dani asked Walsh.

"Possibly. I'll call this in," Walsh said, reaching for his phone.

Dani half-heartedly listened to Walsh as the two men spoke excitedly about the incident. "Please stay here," she said, moving closer to inspect the ground. The thick tire tread revealed the motorcycle had gone into the pasture at the break in the fence, confirming the presumption the biker had forced the cows onto the road.

Walsh approached. "State patrol is on the way. I also requested a hauler to help with the hay bale," he informed the men.

They walked with the drivers to survey the damage. Jessup took off his baseball cap and swiped at his head. "I'm really sorry about this."

"Yeah, that's not good," Timothy replied.

Sirens sounded in the distance, announcing the state troopers.

"I'll talk with NSP." Walsh turned toward the strobing lights.

"Knox and I can help with the cows," Dani offered. She glanced down. "Ready to work, Knox?"

The K-9's entire back end wagged with excitement.

She pointed to the closest animals. "Go!"

The Dobie mix darted past her, starting at the rear of the herd and yelped sharply. Irritated at the canine, a cow mooed annoyance, but with a few more probing yelps, Knox got the animal moving. The group watched in amusement as the dog herded the remaining loiterers into the pasture.

The troopers secured the gate, ensuring they didn't have a repeat escape. Dani surveyed the landscape, listening as the semi drivers spoke with the officers processing the scene.

"They appear genuine," Walsh said, sidling up next to her and nodding at Timothy and Jessup.

"Yeah, but it played out conveniently, right? The cows, the truck, the shooting," Dani said.

"You think they were working with the shooter?"

"I don't know."

"If the motorcyclist broke the fence to release and push the animals through, the rest was easy," Walsh said.

★ ★ ★

Two hours later, riding in the SUV Skyler and Graham had dropped off for them, Walsh pulled off the country road outside Humphrey. He drove up a curved lane to a ridiculously prodigious estate set amid a burbling fountain and stone pillars.

"This is Raymond Strauss's home?" Dani asked, disgust in her tone.

"Yep."

"How do you know he'll be there?"

"Eliana checked his online calendar, and it shows he's teleworking today."

"Nice," Dani replied. "Think he'll have an issue with me bringing Knox?" She jerked her chin toward the rear kennel where the dog sat.

"Knox is an officer as far as the law is concerned." Walsh shut off the engine. "He goes where we go."

She gave him an appreciative smile as they exited the vehicle. Dani leashed Knox, and they walked up the short sidewalk to the double glass doors.

"Talk about overbuilding for a neighborhood," Dani mumbled.

"Right?" Walsh strode beside her. "Defending criminals is apparently lucrative." He knocked on the door, then pressed the doorbell and casually positioned himself in front of the camera sensor to block the view.

"You're bad." Dani chuckled.

He offered her an innocent shrug. "What?"

Several seconds ticked by without a response. Walsh rang the bell again and, finally, footsteps sounded before a voice asked, "Who is it?"

"Deputy US Marshal."

A long pause and the locks clicked. Raymond Strauss, looking as Walsh remembered, stood on the opposite side. He wore shorts and a loose-fitting, button-up shirt, clearly dressed in casual attire. "What's this about, Marshal?" The man was easily a foot shorter than Walsh and his thick dark hair still bore the shaping of a 1980s feathered cut.

"Just need a moment to talk with you about one of your clients," Walsh said.

Strauss hesitated.

Would he demand a warrant?

"We won't be long," Dani declared, holding Knox's leash. "We have a few questions."

Strauss, ever the charmer, glanced up at her. "Sure, come in." He gave Knox a double-take before stepping aside.

Walsh stifled a grin as he entered behind Dani.

"My office is straight to the back," Strauss said, closing the door.

They strolled through the elaborate main level, complete with marble floors and pillars. Strauss's office, with floor-to-ceiling cathedral windows, was at the furthest end of the building.

Walsh and Dani took opposite seats at the octagon conference table centered in the room. Both he and Dani had chosen chairs that provided them a full visual of the doorway and the windows. Knox dropped to a sit beside Dani.

"Officers, how can I help you?" Strauss meandered to the chair at the far end of the table. His light tone didn't match the perspiration already soaking the armpits of his shirt and shining on his forehead. He spoke to Dani, keeping a reasonable distance, no doubt because of Knox.

"This is my colleague, Chief Danielle Fontaine," Walsh introduced.

Dani kept her palm on Knox's head in a silent warning. Walsh surmised her body language was also an avoidance to shake Strauss's outstretched hand.

"Pleased to meet you," Strauss said, taking the hint and settling into his seat. Walsh didn't miss the effort to show dominance.

"Has Enrique Prachank contacted you recently?" Walsh asked.

Strauss leaned forward, feigning interest. "Enrique is incarcerated, awaiting trial."

The man was a horrible liar. "I'm sure you're aware he is a fugitive who escaped custody some time ago," Walsh replied.

The attorney furrowed his brows and tapped at his temple as though in deep thought. "Oh, that's right. Sorry, I confused him with another Enrique I'm currently representing. It's a common name." He flashed a toothy grin. "I remember now. No, I haven't spoken with Mr. Prachank since his hearing. I'm certain he understands there's not much I can do for him since he's a fugitive."

Dani shot Walsh a glower. "He's not tried contacting you?"

"Officer—" Strauss began.

"Chief," Dani corrected him.

"My apologies." Strauss placed a hand to his chest in an exaggerated effort. *"Chief—"* he emphasized the word "—my job is to protect my clients to the full extent of the law. I take that responsibility seriously. Especially because law enforcement has falsely accused several." He held up both hands in surrender. "Not that you fine folks would do that."

"We need to talk with Prachank directly," Walsh added. "You're certainly welcome to be present during that questioning. However, the matter is of utmost importance."

"As I've stated, Marshal, Mr. Prachank hasn't contacted me," Strauss said coolly. "I am curious what this is in regard to?"

"An ongoing investigation that includes attempted murder charges," Dani replied.

"Prachank was already charged with multiple counts of homicide," Strauss explained. "All of which were loosely tied to him by a single weapon. When we have our day in court, we'll disprove that accusation."

"Or it will seal his fate." Walsh gritted his teeth. Was the man serious? "He puts illegal weapons on the streets for criminals to use. He's most definitely no law-abiding citizen."

"Let's save our arguments for the courtroom, Marshal." Strauss exhaled. "Again, I haven't heard from him. But should that change, I'll be in touch with you both at the earliest possible convenience."

Clearly, Strauss was attempting to dismiss them, but Walsh refused to give up. "There's been a recent development in Prachank's case. Should he contact you, there might be an opportunity for him to contribute to the investigation." He paused for effect. "I'm sure I don't need to remind you how cooperation could bode well for him with the authorities."

Strauss opened his mouth, then closed it again.

Walsh pushed away from the table, and Dani mimicked him.

"Thank you for your time." She slid a business card toward the attorney.

Together they exited the house, not speaking until they were inside the safety of the SUV.

"Is he telling the truth?" Dani asked, snapping on her seat belt.

"That's debatable, but based on his responses, he's not communicating with Prachank." Walsh donned his sunglasses. "If he has, maybe the lure of a deal will bring the fugitive out from under his slimy hidey-hole."

"Now where to?" Dani asked.

"The Rock to touch base with the team. I'm hoping they'll have an update for us."

"First, let me check on Jayne," Dani said, withdrawing her phone.

Walsh listened in on the call. By her downcast expression and tone inflection, he surmised it wasn't good news. When she disconnected, he asked, "Any change?"

"None. She's still in critical condition and hasn't regained consciousness." Dani leaned back in her seat with a sigh. "How did I get here?"

"Over the past few years, I've asked that question a lot," Walsh confessed.

Dani faced him. "Tell me about Prachank's case. I'm only familiar with the media's reports."

"He's a skilled manipulator and has outstanding sales skills. He also has connections deep in militia groups and cartels. We worked hard to bring him down. Getting his last cache of weapons was a monumental victory. Solid evidence against him. A pistol registered to him—"

"Wait, let me get this straight. He legally owned a gun?"

"On paper, but we discovered he was running weapons in an underground trafficking effort. We tied the one pistol registered to him to the triple homicide."

"That's the missing gun?" Dani asked.

"Yes. We didn't have strong enough evidence against him for arms trafficking, but the murder charges carry more time behind bars. We want to ensure Prachank isn't on the streets anymore."

"Strauss said there was only a loose connection to Prachank."

Walsh snorted. "That's been their defense from the start. Prachank claimed someone stole the gun before the murders, and it happened to appear at his home prior to the takedown. He insisted the same person planted it there to frame him."

"Prachank stuck around Nebraska and stole his weapon only to use it on us? That's ridiculous."

"I agree. A lot of this is bizarre." Walsh inhaled. "Except the connective dots lead to Jayne. She had access. Whether she gave it to Prachank willingly or under coercion is the bigger question."

"She wouldn't do that," Dani argued. Her jaw set tight and stubborn.

"I understand you care about her, like you did Chief Varmose."

Anger flashed in Dani's blue eyes, and she averted her gaze. "Don't bring up ancient history. It's not helpful."

Walsh considered the words, disagreeing. He remained silent.

Just as she'd initially refused to acknowledge the corrupt practices of her old chief, she was unwilling to see the obvious signs in front of her face. He had to prove Jayne's involvement, and that would come when he uncovered the connection between the evidence technician and Prachank. And he needed to do it before anyone else got hurt.

Chapter Five

Dani fought the urge to defend herself in another battle with Walsh. How dare he bring up their painful past.

Recollections of the incident with Varmose returned. She'd trusted her then boyfriend, Beckham Walsh, who had gone behind her back, secretly collecting evidence against her chief. His investigation had set her up with the other Cortez PD officers. Of course, they'd believed she was in on the takedown and that she'd worked with Walsh to gain Varmose's trust. Surely, Walsh remembered that little detail.

He had unfairly blindsided her by arresting Varmose. She had caught the aftermath of the investigation, bearing the disdain of the other officers until she'd surrendered and transferred to a different station to escape the hatred. If Walsh wasn't aware of that, she'd not give him the satisfaction of sharing her pain. Especially not when he was throwing her naïveté in her face again.

"I'm just saying…" Walsh interrupted her thoughts. "You're too close to the problem."

Unable to hold her tongue any longer, she blurted, "I was wrong about Varmose then, but that's not the situation with Jayne."

Walsh glanced at her. "Dani, I'm not blaming you. We must remain objective."

Right. Like she believed that. "I am, and that includes consideration of the verifiable facts that I can provide. Jayne has proved herself trustworthy over the years."

He sighed, clearly annoyed with her, and despite her brain's demand to stop defending Jayne, Dani added, "I was young and trusted my commander. You can't hold that against me."

"Varmose's behavior is totally on him."

"But you think I'm naïve, like I was back then, and I don't see the truth about Jayne. This isn't the same scenario."

"Whoa. First, I never said you were naïve. Second, if you're unwilling to be honest about Jayne's involvement, either with yourself or my team, recuse yourself from this investigation."

Dani opened her mouth to defend her position, but Walsh went on. "If that's not an issue, then don't worry about it." Something in his tone told Dani that he'd made up his mind.

Frustrated, she turned away, and they rode in silence to the HFTF headquarters. Recusing herself wasn't an option. Jayne needed an advocate. Dani owed her that. She hoped to remain unbiased, but the weight of Tessa's future, and Jayne's life, hung heavy on her. Separating her emotions from the case evidence was a difficult but not impossible request.

The team had assembled in the Rock, actively working as Dani and Walsh entered. While he addressed them, Dani moved to check on Tessa where she slept peacefully in the Pack 'n Play near Eliana.

"She's a sweetheart," Eliana said, rolling to face Dani.

Dani slid into the chair beside her. "Thank you for babysitting. I realize this can't happen regularly."

Eliana tilted her head, compassion written in her expression. "It's hard to see an innocent child caught in the middle of such a difficult situation."

Emotion tightened Dani's throat. "Exactly." She leaned over Tessa, restraining the urge to stroke the infant's feathery-soft hair.

The room filled with chatter and discussion pertinent to the case, and Dani listened as the group bounced ideas and details off one another.

"People, assemble and update," Walsh commanded.

Dani marveled at how the task force cooperated effortlessly, like a perfectly oiled law enforcement machine. They sat around the table, joining Dani and Eliana, with Walsh at the head, furthest from Dani. As usual.

Was she reading too much into his actions, or was he deliberately keeping his distance from her?

"Skyler, any word from NIBIN?" Walsh asked.

"*Sí*." She scooted closer, holding a folder. "We dug into all the inventory that our team had logged at GIPD, and discovered there were several weapons stolen from other cases."

Walsh leaned forward. "Besides the Prachank case?"

"Yes," Tiandra replied.

Dani gaped. "How?"

"That is the ultimate question," Riker said.

"Our most worrisome is the compromised illegal munitions we seized four years ago," Skyler said.

"The militia investigation?" Eliana clarified.

"Yep." Skyler shook her head. "That was significant firepower that has no place on the streets."

"As in military-grade artillery?" Dani asked. The group remained quiet, answering with their silence.

"It was one of our first cases," Tiandra explained. "We seized it all from a mountain militia in South Dakota."

Dani studied each member, feeling the weight of their scrutinizing stares on her. This was more than a few missing pieces of evidence. Not that it wasn't significant, but military munitions raised the stakes. "How did this happen?" Dani whispered.

"Are there specific arms that create a pattern or are they random items?" Walsh asked.

"Random, as far as we can tell," Chance said.

"Tiandra, Elijah and I will conduct a thorough inventory at the GIPD offices," Graham advised. "We'll know more once that's completed."

"Did someone send their grocery list of weapons and have Jayne steal them?" Walsh asked.

Dani glared at him. "There's no proof Jayne's

responsible." Even as she spoke the defense, she doubted herself.

"That's a viable possibility," Graham replied.

"Identifying who stole the artillery and/or who ordered them is crucial," Tiandra added.

"Yes," Elijah responded, touching her hand.

Dani did a double-take. They were together too?

Tiandra's cheeks blushed a rosy hue. "Elijah and I are engaged."

Dani blinked. "So, Riker and Eliana." She pointed to the couple, then shifted, pointing at Tiandra. "And you and Elijah?"

"It's bonkers, right?" Skyler rolled her eyes.

"Wow." Dani's mind reeled with the information. Here they were, personally connected, while Walsh raked her over the coals for her and Jayne's friendship. She'd deal with him in private.

As though reading her thoughts, Skyler said, "Dani knows Jayne best. She's our closest connection to Jayne and offers that personal insight we won't gain by digging through evidence."

Gratitude for the comment softened Dani's bitter viewpoint and reminded her that without HFTF conducting the inventory, another agency would perform an internal affairs investigation on her department. That would openly expose the incompetency, and Jayne might face criminal charges based on the circumstantial evidence. Not to mention, Dani being recused from her position as chief. She glanced at Walsh. Her life and that of her friend depended on a man she'd never fully trust. Yet, where else did she have to go?

They were letting her contribute to the case. She had to stop defending Jayne and find proof to exonerate her.

"Dani, would Jayne have any reason to betray you?" Tiandra asked.

Defensiveness raged through Dani, but she fought the urge to lash out at the FBI agent who'd posed a valid question. "None that I can think of. For her to do so jeopardizes her career and custody of her child. Why would she take such enormous risks?"

"You said the baby's father is deceased?" Eliana asked.

"Yes." Dani sighed.

Tessa grunted and rolled over, facing Dani. She rose to gather a bottle just as the baby erupted into loud wails. Dani hurried to prepare the formula, quickly appeasing the infant. Though the team made no protests to having her there, she caught Walsh's gaze. They weren't a babysitting service. She had to find care for Tessa if she had any hope of clearing Jayne's name before an outside agency took over the investigation.

Dani inhaled a fortifying breath and sat with Tessa in her arms while she greedily devoured the bottle. The team's attention rotated to the evidence board already in progress. They'd linked pictures of the criminals and weapons from their prior cases with red lines. Interestingly, none of them intersected.

Tessa finished, and Dani repositioned the infant to burp her. She cooed contentedly over Dani's shoulder. "Is it possible the stolen artillery isn't about Jayne at all? The common denominator is HFTF."

As though she'd revealed a huge epiphany, the team faced the evidence board.

"She's correct," Tiandra agreed.

"Beyond the compromised GIPD evidence locker location, all were linked to cases you worked," Dani said, confidence building.

"Can't disagree," Graham replied. "Great job, Dani."

"I'll make some calls. You all keep working," Walsh said, and the group stood for dismissal.

"Elijah and I will head back to the evidence locker," Graham said.

"I could go with you," Dani replied, gazing down at Tessa. How was she supposed to care for the baby and work simultaneously?

"Actually, with all due respect…" Graham shot a look at Walsh. Dani glanced between the men.

"Walsh hates that phrase," Elijah chuckled.

"Hmm. Well, it annoys me when he answers the phone without so much as a 'hello' before he launches into a discussion," Dani teased.

Stifled chuckles confirmed their agreement.

"Are you finished?" Walsh grunted.

"Anyway, Dani," Graham cut in, "it might be better if you're not there."

"Right." She nodded. "Keeps the investigation unbiased."

"Exactly," Elijah concluded.

Thankful they'd given her the out, Dani said, "Holler if you need anything."

"Roger that," the twins replied in unison.

"Eliana, track down the criminals, besides Prachank, linked to the missing weapons," Walsh ordered.

Dani gazed into Tessa's sweet face. Parting with the baby broke her heart, but the best way to care for her was to help exonerate Jayne. For that, she needed to focus on the case.

The group dispersed. Resolved, Dani carried Tessa and followed Walsh to his office. She dropped into a seat opposite him.

He slid into his desk chair and faced her. "You have something on your mind."

"You're right. I need to devote my attention to the case, and I can't do that while providing the care that Tessa needs." Her mother had spent her life demonstrating the impossible task, which had solidified Dani's notions that marriage and family didn't mix with work. "My devotion is to uphold the law to the best of my abilities. That must come first."

Walsh leaned back in his seat. Dani expected to see satisfaction in his expression. Instead, he said, "I can't imagine the difficulty you're facing. Torn between keeping Tessa safe with you and handing her over to Child Protective Services is no simple choice."

His compassion nearly undid her. She could deal with their contentious relationship, but Walsh's gentle and understanding tone proved more difficult. Dani's heart recalled the reasons she'd first fallen for him. His kindness and the way she felt safe with him combined with his rugged handsomeness. Her gaze traveled the contours of his face. Remembering his touch and their shared tender kisses. Dani looked down. *Get a hold of yourself.* "I've never had the responsibility for a child before."

Walsh nodded.

"One request." Dani met his gaze. "I have to meet the person caring for her first."

"That's totally reasonable. Would you like me to make the call and set things up?"

"Yes, please."

Walsh lifted the receiver of his desk phone.

Tessa squirmed, and Dani got to her feet, slipping out of his office.

Was it a betrayal to Jayne if Dani wasn't the one personally providing Tessa's care? Caught between an impassable mountain and a wall of fire, Dani didn't know which was worse.

By the time Walsh and Dani had evaluated the foster home options available for Tessa, the sun was fading on the horizon. They pulled up to the large ranch-style house set on an acreage north of Lincoln in Valparaiso.

"Such a beautiful property," Dani whispered. "Not what I pictured."

"Me either," Walsh replied.

The expansive house stretched out with the double front door centering the structure. A four-car attached garage to the left side permitted them space to park in the driveway.

Children's outdoor toys were scattered around the pristine lawn. Flowers in a variety of bright colors created a boundary along the sidewalk. Perfectly trimmed bushes lined the white banister rails of the wraparound front porch. A picturesque scene.

Walsh shut off the engine, and Dani threw open her door wordlessly. Was she second-guessing her decision to leave Tessa with the foster family?

They'd left Knox at the Rock, unsure how the transition would go. Now Walsh wondered if that had been a mistake. The dog would no doubt offer Dani the emotional support she'd need to do this.

Dani released Tessa's carrier and the base from the backseat, and he followed her to the sidewalk and up the front porch steps. The aroma of something delicious wafted to them from the open windows. Walsh's stomach grumbled, and he realized they'd not taken the time to eat that day. Dani shot him a confused look, and his neck warmed. "Guess missing breakfast and lunch wasn't a great idea," he confessed, rapping softly on the door.

"I haven't had an appetite since this all started." Dani turned to face him. "I feel like I'm abandoning her."

"You're not," Walsh assured her. Then he posed the question he didn't want to hear the answer to. "Are you having doubts about leaving her here?"

"Can't say until after we've sat and talked to them. If I don't have any red flags as far as the house or their behavior, then no regrets. Otherwise, I may change my mind and take her with us."

"My contact, Mrs. Terrote, at CPS confided she highly recommends them and calls the Ibarras her best family," he said. Walsh didn't add that he'd requested the most trustworthy vetted parents CPS had on file. Mrs. Terrote hadn't taken the request lightly, knowing Walsh wouldn't make an appeal flippantly.

Footsteps drew closer, and they stepped back as the front door opened. A thirtysomething woman dressed in athletic shorts and a T-shirt with flowery letters that read Ask Me About My Kids, smiled at them. She'd pulled her auburn hair into a loose ponytail, and she wore no makeup.

"Mrs. Ibarra?" Walsh asked, since Dani seemed unable to speak.

"Sadie, please." She extended a hand. "You must be Chief Fontaine and Commander Walsh."

"Call me Dani." She shook Sadie's hand, regaining her professional composure. "Yes, thank you for seeing us on such short notice."

"Beckham," Walsh said.

Sadie stepped aside, waving them in. "Perry is putting down the kids. He'll join us in a few minutes."

They entered the spacious living room where a massive U-shaped couch centered the space. Shelves with children's toys neatly filled one side, and nothing appeared out of place.

"Have a seat." Sadie dropped onto the sofa.

Dani and Walsh took seats at the opposite end. "And this must be sweet Tessa." Sadie leaned with her elbows on her knees, smiling at the baby.

Dani shifted Tessa to sit facing forward. The infant held on to Dani's fingers and cooed happily. "How many children do you have?"

"Depends on the day. We offer emergency care, so sometimes we have little ones with us for a few days before CPS places them in permanent housing," Sadie explained. "Currently, we have four. Ages eighteen months, six years old, and eight-year-old twins."

Dani nodded, and a frown crossed her face. "Will you have time for Tessa without compromising on the care of the other children?"

Sadie appeared nonplussed by the direct question. "Absolutely. She'll have all the attention and love possible while she's with us. Perry telecommutes, providing him the availability to help with the children's daily needs."

"One of the significant advantages of working from home," a tall, lanky man added, entering the room. He sported a spiky haircut with his shock of red hair. "Sorry for the delay. I'm Perry." He extended a hand, addressing Walsh before moving to Dani.

"We try to keep their lives as normal as possible," Sadie said as her husband sat beside her.

He smiled kindly. "We've fostered children from many types of situations," he replied. "The goal is to reunite them as long as it's in the best interest of the child."

"Good," Dani said, lifting her chin. "Just to be clear, as soon as Jayne's recovered, they'll be reunited."

"Mrs. Terrote from CPS filled us in a bit on the situation," Sadie said. "We're praying for Ms. Bardot's total recovery."

Dani interrogated the couple, and Walsh listened, feeling like an intruder to a personal conversation. She withheld nothing, pointedly making her queries. But he understood she needed reassurance that Tessa was in the best possible care. Her posture softened slightly, and the Ibarras seemed nonplussed by the inquisition.

They offered a tour of the home, which appeared clean and welcoming. Children's drawings plastered the large refrigerator in the kitchen. And Sadie showed them the room where Tessa would stay before they peeked in on the other sleeping children.

When they returned to the main floor, Dani still cuddled Tessa close, rubbing the baby's back with one hand. "I'll try to visit as often as possible until Jayne recovers," she pledged. She gingerly passed Tessa to Sadie, and the baby giggled as the woman tickled her arm and spoke in a soft voice.

"Thank you again, and please don't hesitate to contact either of us if you have any concerns or questions," Walsh said, handing Perry his business card.

"I'll call for daily updates," Dani said.

"Absolutely," Sadie replied, and Tessa turned, smiling at Dani as though reassuring her everything would be all right.

Walsh moved toward the door, and Dani stayed close beside him. They exited the house after another rendition of goodbyes and walked to the SUV. The wind had picked up in heavy gusts.

After they'd both climbed inside the vehicle, Dani said, "I hate this."

"I know." Walsh inserted his key and turned it to start the engine. The car dinged with a message light warning the trunk was open. "That's weird."

"What's wrong?" Dani leaned closer.

Walsh thought back. Had they put any of Tessa's things in the trunk? He didn't recall opening it and removing items before walking into the Ibarras' home.

The hairs on his arms rose in a visceral response. He scanned the surroundings, but night had settled.

"Dani, get out of the vehicle. Now!" He kept his tone calm and firm.

"Why?" Her eyes widened as she threw open her door simultaneously with him.

They leapt from the SUV, scurrying as far as possible and taking shelter near the house.

Several long seconds passed.

Images of his tours in the Middle East where IEDs exploded his unit's military vehicles, and the desperate shouts of innocent civilians invaded his mind. Walsh shook off the painful memories. Had he overreacted, transferring his past into the present?

Dani quirked a brow at him.

"Guess I—"

An explosion rocked the ground, and the SUV went up in flames.

Chapter Six

Dani stepped back, gasping for breath.

Night had descended, which enhanced the orange-and-red blaze that devoured Walsh's SUV. The flames danced with the increasingly strong wind, stretching high into the sky. A gust whistled eerily through the trees, and toys skipped across the yard.

Dani turned to Walsh. "What just—"

A loud pop sent them diving to the ground. They scurried for cover, hiding on the side of the porch. Shots pinged around them, impaling the railing. They scoured the inky landscape for the shooter's location.

Together, she and Walsh hurried up the steps, pelted by chips of spraying wood from the rapid gunfire. "It's coming from the tree line," Walsh advised.

From their protected positions, they returned fire in the direction of the shooter.

Dani briefly twisted to look at the windows of the Ibarra home behind her. "We have to warn them!" She prayed the Ibarras wouldn't open the door at the wrong time.

At last, the shooting ceased.

The air became too still, thrusting Dani and Walsh into a creepy silence.

They surveyed the area, unsure where the shooter had gone or if he continued to watch them. The vast copse of trees offered their assailant many places to hide while they remained exposed on the front porch.

When several seconds passed without further incident, Dani beat on the door. "Mr. Ibarra! Let us in!"

Walsh hollered into his cell phone for backup and rescue personnel.

Crouched low, Dani prepared to tackle whoever answered. At last, the door cracked open, and she met Sadie—also in a squatted position.

"We heard the gunshots."

Dani and Walsh scurried inside, closing the door behind them.

"Was anyone hurt?" Dani asked.

"No," Sadie said, no quiver in her voice. "Everyone is safe."

"I've contacted rescue and fire personnel."

Walsh stepped up to the windows, tugging the blinds and curtains closed. "Keep the lights off. We don't want to give away our location to the shooter."

Perry and Sadie stayed clear of the entrance. She held Tessa.

"Did someone blow up your vehicle?" Perry asked.

"Yes," Walsh replied.

"Get the children," Dani ordered, rushing toward them.

As though snapping to the present, Perry made eye contact with her before he spun on his heel and scurried down the hallway.

"Please give me Tessa," Dani said, reaching for the baby.

Sadie didn't argue, gently passing the infant to her. "What just happened?"

Dani considered her next words. She didn't want to frighten the Ibarras, however, she had to convey the severity of the situation. "Gather the children. Grab any essentials, prescriptions, et cetera, and meet us back here ASAP!"

"Steer clear of the windows and stay low," Walsh added.

Sadie nodded and turned, following her husband down the hallway to the bedrooms.

Walsh glanced out a corner of the curtains. "I think the shooter fled."

"Could you estimate the gunman's position?"

"No. He was a lousy shot or it wasn't a scoped rifle," Walsh said. "Thankfully, he missed. A lot."

"Yeah. The wind certainly helped," Dani added.

Once they'd gathered Tessa's belongings, they sat in the dining room shielded by the interior walls.

"Are the Ibarras in danger after we leave?" Dani whispered, holding Tessa close to her chest.

"I hope not, but let's not take any chances. They need to find a place to stay tonight. I'll have the team sweep the house before they return."

The familiar shriek of sirens promised assistance.

"How did someone get a bomb into your SUV?"

"It was unattended while we were inside." Walsh shook his head. "I should've stayed outside on guard."

"I can't believe this." Dani shivered. She ducked low and peered out the corner of the dining room curtain. The land stretched far into the expansive darkness, leaving her feeling vulnerable. "Is he still watching us?"

Never one to mince words, Walsh stated the obvious. "It's possible, but with responders on the way, I don't think he'll shoot at us again."

"I'd be surprised if he set the bomb and left."

"Agreed."

"But why here?"

Walsh leaned back in the chair. "Nobody but my contact at CPS was aware we were coming to the Ibarras'."

"Is that person involved?"

"Doubtful," Walsh said. "My guess is he followed us here."

"None of your acquaintances have the propensity to be corrupt?" The comment was out of line, and Dani bit her lip. "Sorry, that was uncalled for."

"We won't rule anybody out until we have evidence to support it," Walsh assured her.

"What if he put the bomb in the SUV at the Rock?"

"Negative. There are too many surveillance cameras there," Walsh's tone was unconvincing.

"Why not attack us on the road? Why wait until we're here with Tessa?" Even as she spoke, the thought assailed her. "Unless…am I in danger or is Tessa?"

Walsh studied her. "I want to believe nobody is malicious enough to target an innocent baby, but unfortunately, it's not out of the realm of possibility."

How could she leave Tessa if she was in danger? But if the threat was to Dani, how could she keep Tessa close?

Rescue personnel pulled onto the property, and Walsh took the escape, hurrying out the door to greet them. Dani got to her feet and walked into the Ibarras' bedroom. "It's safe for us to go now."

Sadie held a frail toddler in her arms. Perry carried a six-year-old on his hip while he gently ushered twin girls from the room.

In a mute march, the group exited the house and paused. Destruction from the bullets scarred the beautiful wraparound porch. Sadie appeared to take in the damage and her lip quivered, but she said nothing.

"Please wait here. I'll find out what the next steps are," Dani said.

She hurried to Walsh, who stood beside a Valparaiso police cruiser.

Firefighters worked to extinguish the flames, and the strobing lights filled the night sky.

Dani paused at a distance, not wanting to interrupt Walsh's conversation. "I'd appreciate that," he said to the officer before turning and walking to her.

A chill snaked up her spine with the sensation that the bomber was watching them. Surely, he'd wonder if he'd completed his task.

"Let's have the kids move toward the fire engines," Walsh said. "It'll lessen their fear if we make it fun."

"Okay." She glanced over her shoulder to where the Ibarras sat on the porch.

Perry held the toddler on his lap, and the child rubbed his eyes.

Sadie draped her arms protectively over the six-year-old girl and the twins.

"Hey, guys, I'm Commander Walsh." He approached slowly, his tone light. "Have you ever seen a fire engine up close before?"

The twins shook their heads in synchronicity and the six-year-old sucked her thumb.

"Great! Let me show you." Walsh tenderly led the group down the stairs. "This is my friend, Dani. She's going to walk over with you, so baby Tessa can also see the truck."

Dani took her cue and plastered a smile on her face. "Come on." She waved with one hand.

Sadie gave her a confused look, then seemed to understand and joined the discussion. "We don't get many chances to do this. What an adventure."

The group moved toward the largest rig, where firefighters unrolled hoses and shouted orders. Two paramedics stepped out of the ambulance. Parked behind the fire truck sat an SUV with Battalion Chief printed across the side. Walsh offered a wave to the man climbing out of the SUV. He wore a white uniform shirt and dark pants. Based on the way he smiled at them, Dani assumed Walsh must've already told him about the situation.

"Let's start with stickers!" the chief said, passing out small plastic badges with the fire department emblem printed on them.

The kids cautiously approached him, their apprehension slowly lessening in the officer's presence. He chatted easily with them, even getting a couple of grins. He rattled off the names of the equipment and engaged the children in the discussion.

The adults stayed back, giving him room.

"Thank you," Sadie whispered.

"You all will need to find some place to stay tonight," Walsh said, joining the conversation. "My team is on the way, and they'll ensure there are no additional detonation devices, but it would be best to keep the kids away for the night."

Perry stepped closer, slowly lowering the wriggling toddler to the ground. The baby waddled toward the fire chief and the other children. "Not a problem," Perry said, glancing over his shoulder.

Sadie nodded. "We have family not far from here. We'll stay with them."

"I'm sorry," Dani said. How had she not considered the horrific possibility that the attacker might come after them here?

The fire chief reached into his vehicle and handed the kids tattoos and plastic fire hats, eliciting cheers.

Dani smiled at his efforts.

"Do you need any help collecting supplies before you go?" Walsh asked.

"No, we're ready," Sadie replied.

Two black SUVs drove up on the property. "That's my team," Walsh said. "I'll be right back."

Sadie reached out and patted Tessa's back.

"She's a sweet baby. I know you'll take good care of her."

Dani glanced up, meeting Sadie's soft brown eyes. Words eluded her. She'd never cared for another human being, certainly not one this tiny. She wanted to tell Sadie that standing here with Tessa she felt more inadequate than ever.

Sadie squeezed her shoulder, then hurried to meet Perry and corral the children.

Walsh approached with Tiandra, K-9 Bosco, and Skyler trailing. Dani spun to face them, and they stood at a distance from the SUV, which sat in a dripping mess from the fire extinguishers.

"Tiandra and Bosco will search the Ibarras' house for any other explosives," Walsh explained.

"We'll maintain perimeter watch and conduct evidence collection," Skyler said.

"Meet at the Rock at 0800. If you're still working the scene here, connect via video conference once we're there," Walsh said.

"Thank you," Dani replied.

She longed to say more, but the current situation overwhelmed her. The bomber's motive and intentions had endangered too many lives. If the target was on her or Tessa, they had to be wiser.

The garage door opened, revealing Perry and Sadie as they loaded the children into a large minivan. Any of them could've died in the gunfire and explosion. Her stomach roiled. How far would this person go to kill her? Tessa cooed, and she looked down at the baby. Or was Tessa his target, and if so, why?

The next morning, Walsh leaned back in his office chair, still exhausted from days of no sleep. The team would arrive soon, and he had no clue where to steer the investigation.

He spotted Dani and Tessa in the conference room, where the glass wall offered him a clear view. They needed a better solution for Tessa's care. Whoever had targeted Dani and/or Tessa was relentless. Only his team could handle their protective detail. It was too risky to put the infant in a foster home.

Or perhaps that was his own bias. He had to protect them.

For a single moment, Walsh allowed his mind to consider what it would've been like to father his own child. Now that retirement hovered like a vulture waiting to consume its prey, those dreams had faded into the impossible. But in the years when life was good with Gwen, and they'd talked about having a family of their own, he'd dared to hope.

He glanced down at his desk and lifted the expensive Montblanc pen Gwen had given him for their first Christmas. Why he kept it, Walsh couldn't explain. It didn't even write anymore. He'd eliminated all other remnants of her memory from his home and office, but the Montblanc pen always accompanied him. It also reminded him of his failures to protect Gwen and to be there when she'd needed him most. It served as a penance for his selfishness that had cost Gwen's life and their future together.

Yet, spending time with Dani had awakened his heart again, resuscitating his dreams and the feelings he'd buried for Dani even before Gwen came into his life. Prior to the Varmose case, he'd felt certain he'd marry Dani. They'd shared the most wonderful romance. A vulnerability he'd never known consumed Walsh. The swirling emotions made him wonder if God would give him a second chance to love.

No. He'd failed Gwen, and now he was doing the same with Tessa and Dani. Walsh shook off the thoughts. He didn't deserve happiness. Gwen's parents had reminded him of that unmercifully, reinforcing his personal vow to remain a bachelor. *A man needs to protect his wife.* He hadn't done that. Gwen's father's accusations replayed in his mind.

How was it possible that he'd come full circle again? Frustration as his ineptitude to safeguard Dani and Tessa, not to mention the entire Ibarra family weighed on Walsh. Perhaps it was time he retired.

No. Not until he finished this case.

He would get his head in the game and find the bomber/shooter.

Renewed by his mission, Walsh stood and snagged his files off the desk. He exited his office just as Skyler and Tiandra entered the Rock with K-9 Bosco, Elijah, and Graham behind them.

Riker, K-9 Ammo, and Eliana trailed with Chance and K-9 Destiny. The team had arrived, and it was time to get to work. Chance carried a long flat box of what Walsh hoped held breakfast.

He joined the group as everyone settled around the table. Chance slid the box into the center.

"Thanks," Eliana said, passing out napkins.

"He's still trying to earn favor," Elijah teased.

"Just for that, you don't get any." Tiandra

swatted playfully at her fiancé, and he leaned over, kissing her forehead.

Walsh's heart swelled for his team—no, his family. As he encroached to the mandatory retirement age of 57, driving him from his career, Walsh's purpose for living would vanish too. What was he without his title? Being a commander was his entire identity. What would he do when they stripped him of it in a few years?

"May I?" Graham approached Dani and reached for Tessa.

"Sure?" Her reply came out as more of a question than a statement. She passed the child to him, but her tentative gaze remained on Tessa.

Graham, being the self-absorbed and completely confident man he was, didn't appear to notice or care. He dropped onto the seat, sitting the infant on the tabletop in front of him. He cooed and made silly faces, gaining baby giggles.

Walsh gawked. "How did we not know this about you, Graham?"

"Is that not normal behavior for him?" Dani asked.

"Of course it is," Skyler teased. "He's a charmer."

"No, the accident softened him," Tiandra said.

"You're all wrong," Graham replied, glancing

over Tessa's head. "I have always had a gift for communicating with babies. Ask Elijah."

Elijah sat with a donut stuffed in his mouth and shrugged.

"All right, settle in and recap where we are." Walsh surveyed his team.

God had brought him an incredible group of skilled and capable people. He considered himself blessed to work with them. A twinge of sadness lingered as he debated how soon that would end. Exactly why he was developing his successor.

"Skyler, take the lead." He'd already begun working with the talented AFT agent, prepared to pass down the title of commander to her when the time came. Though he'd not shared that with her yet.

"Tiandra and I—" Bosco sidled up to Skyler with a whine. "My apologies. *Bosco*, Tiandra, and I," she corrected, earning a hearty laugh from the team, "conducted the surveillance and perimeter search. We found no other explosives on the property and released the house to the Ibarras first thing this morning."

"The assailant placed the bomb at the rear of your SUV," Tiandra added. "It appears he failed to notice the strap that interfered with the trunk lid closing completely. That's what saved your lives."

"He followed us there and then put the explosive inside?" Dani asked.

"I locked the vehicle," Walsh said, then second-guessed himself.

"It's easy enough to break into with an electronic decoder," Graham said, never taking his eyes off Tessa's head before resuming his baby talk and silly faces.

"Is your brother all right?" Tiandra whispered to Elijah.

He chuckled, biting into another chocolate-frosted donut. "Yeah, he's a sucker for babies."

"Was that attack intended for Dani or Tessa?" Skyler asked.

"Or both," Chance added.

"But why Tessa? She's an innocent," Dani interjected.

"That's an important clue for us to unravel," Skyler replied. "If Tessa is a threat to the attacker, was she the planned target instead of Jayne?"

"Surely all this goes toward proving Jayne's innocence, too," Dani said.

"It definitely moves in her favor," Walsh agreed. "I think it's safe to deduce Jayne had essential information that the assailant wants. Her relationship or connection to that person is key."

Chance tilted his head, studying the evidence board. "What threat is an innocent baby to the bomber?"

They all glanced at Tessa, still enthralled with Graham's silly antics to entertain the infant.

Dani picked at a donut. "Unless the shooter was using Tessa as a way to control Jayne. Threatening to hurt her?"

"Unfortunately, that adds up," Eliana agreed. "I'd do anything to protect my child."

"If that's the case, then the assailant knows Jayne is still alive." Walsh grabbed a second donut. "I've got 24/7 protection detail on her." He considered whether that maneuver was sufficient.

"I'll also connect to the hospital's live feed and monitor through the security cameras," Eliana added.

"I need to call for an update," Dani said. "Wait, maybe I should go see her instead?"

"Negative," Walsh replied, already dialing. "I'll request they move Jayne under an assumed name to another room for now." Then to the team, "Take five while we get this handled."

Walsh called Jim Bonn, a Nebraska State

Patrol captain assigned to Omaha and a close friend. When Bonn answered, Walsh blurted, "Need a favor."

"Someday, try starting conversations with 'hello,'" Bonn teased.

Walsh chuckled. "Sorry. I keep hearing that." After explaining the situation, Bonn assured he'd handle the request.

They disconnected, and Walsh returned to the table. Dani sat, posture deflated.

"I take it there's no change in Jayne's status?"

"Her condition has worsened. The next twenty-four hours are crucial."

The group stilled for a moment, weighing the seriousness of the news.

Walsh desperately fought against the urge to comfort Dani and to reassure her that everything would be fine. He couldn't do that. Not from a command position standpoint, since he wasn't sure what would happen to Jayne. Her injuries were serious.

Conversely, from a personal view, getting that close to Dani wasn't an option for him. He'd succeeded in his career by maintaining a clear and professional distance from all women. Dani was no different. They were coworkers on a case. Nothing more, regardless of their past or the way she'd chipped at his heart's defenses. His gaze flitted to Tessa, smiling at Graham, and patting him on the head with giggles. He swallowed hard. This precious child who had nearly died on his watch.

Dani glanced over at him with a look of desperation and pain. It practically undid him.

Walsh got to his feet. "I need to make some calls," he said, excusing himself. He needed distance from Dani before he did something stupid.

Chapter Seven

Two days without leads and no further attacks had stalled the team's progress until Skyler announced, "We've got an update!"

The Rock buzzed with excitement as they assembled to hear Skyler's report. Dani stood, rocking Tessa. Again, Walsh positioned himself on the furthest side of the room, away from her. Could he make his avoidance any more obvious if he tried?

"The casings we found near the edge of the Ibarras' property came back as a match in NIBIN for a shooting five years ago," Skyler said. "And it was from a gun we'd logged into a cache from one of our cases."

"A pending investigation?" Chance asked.

Skyler shook her head. "No. Closed and marked for destruction."

"What?" Eliana's confusion was obvious. "I thought we kept evidence forever."

"After the case is closed, they're sent to a munitions destruction contractor," Tiandra clarified.

That was news to Dani, but she remained quiet and listened.

"Fantastic. Our criminal is taking old and new weapons?" Chance exhaled. "Why not steal those marked for destruction? We'd have never noticed."

"Until they used the guns on the street again," Elijah put in.

"Exactly." Riker rose and wrote the notes on the evidence board.

"That seems really strange," Graham murmured.

"Yeah, his motive is evolving, or we've overlooked something," Riker agreed.

"Worse, it shows we have a serious leak in the entire system," Walsh said. "Were those weapons initially housed at GIPD?"

Dani glared. Why was he determined to make her department the scapegoat for this?

"Yes," Skyler said.

Dani stifled the groan. Jayne and HFTF remained common denominators in the case. "The weapons destruction contractor is also a viable suspect."

"He has means and opportunity." Riker updated the evidence board. "Instead of eliminating suspects, we're adding to our list."

"But we have no solid motive for any of them," Walsh added.

Grateful that Walsh considered Jayne's lack of motive, Dani said, "Unfortunately, greed is always a viable reason. Maybe the consultant was manipulating the system?"

"It's feasible," Eliana said.

"I've never heard of this person," Dani said. "Jayne didn't mention him either."

The implications were increasingly serious and getting the munitions back remained a huge priority. And her department was on the line while the evidence mounted against Jayne. For the first time, doubt about her friend's involvement crept into her mind. How would Dani prove Jayne's innocence with what they'd discovered? Was that even possible? She glanced down at sleeping Tessa and crossed the room, transferring the infant to the playpen.

The group's discussion continued while Dani fought to shove aside her personal bias and shift into investigator mode. Nothing would help Jayne or Tessa if she got stuck in the loop of useless worry and fear while trying to prove Jayne's innocence.

"Where was the cache sent for destruction?" Dani inserted her question into the conversation. "Since that's before my appointment to GI, I'm not sure."

Eliana typed away on her computer. "I'll find it."

"Chief, if you trust us to babysit Tessa, my wife, Ayla, has offered her time for a short while," Chance said. "She's on a break from her office." A buzzing interrupted him, and he glanced down at his cell phone. "Speaking of, she's here."

Dani paused midstride.

"We didn't mean to overstep, just figured you had a lot to deal with," Riker explained.

"I appreciate your thoughtfulness," Dani said. "Thank you."

"We will work together to make sure she's taken care of," Skyler said.

Chance hurried out, returning a few moments later accompanying a petite woman with long auburn hair. She smiled at Dani.

"Hey, Ayla. Great to see you." Tiandra crossed the room to hug the newcomer.

SHAREE STOVER

Dani approached with an outstretched hand. "Dani Fontaine."

"Nice to meet you," Ayla said, her expression softening as she glanced at the playpen.

The sounds of cooing had Dani hurrying to retrieve Tessa. She held her up and turned to face Ayla.

"And this must be darling Tessa."

In response, the infant blew spit bubbles, entertaining herself.

"May I?" Ayla asked.

"You don't mind?"

"Are you kidding?" Ayla chuckled. "This is a great break from dealing with criminal cases."

Dani gently passed off Tessa.

"Ayla understands the trauma of being a witness in need of protection." Chance smiled at his spouse. The adoration written on his face spoke of love.

"Right? I'm happy to help after all this team did for me," Ayla said.

Dani wondered at their story, but with all that was happening, she put a pin in the question. "You guys are amazing." She forced back the tears threatening to erupt. She couldn't deny the bond she already felt with HFTF. This incredible group led by the one man who had stolen her heart so many years before.

"It's what family does." Tiandra gave her a wink.

Family. The small word held power. Hadn't Jayne referenced their friendship that way, too?

Walsh moved near Ayla, then pivoted before exiting the conference room.

Had the others noticed how he avoided Tessa? For the first time, Dani considered the possibility that he didn't like kids.

Eliana gasped and jumped to her feet without saying a word. She hurried from the Rock.

"What was that about?" Elijah asked.

Through the walled glass, they watched as she rushed into Walsh's office. The two quickly returned to the Rock.

"The weapons destruction consultant is Aiden DeLuca," Eliana announced to the group.

"Should that mean something to us?" Chance asked.

"It does to me," Walsh replied. "Is his name familiar to any of you?"

"Vaguely." Skyler placed a finger against her lips, in thought.

"Aiden DeLuca is a former Omaha PD officer," Walsh advised. "He sustained permanent damage to his shoulder after a suspect shot him during a call. He took an early retirement."

"Wow, that's harsh," Chance said.

"I wouldn't wish that on anybody," Graham agreed.

"Aiden's got a solid reputation in the law enforcement community," Walsh explained.

"He started a new career as a weapons destruction expert?" Riker surmised.

"Yes," Walsh replied. "I haven't talked with him in a long time." Something flashed over his expression, then disappeared just as quickly, leaving Dani curious.

"Regardless if Aiden was a stand-up guy, a life-changing injury could provide a catalyst for behavior transformation," Eliana said.

"It would destroy his entire identity without warning," Walsh replied.

"Let's not venture down this road yet," Elijah said.

"True." Skyler nodded. "We'll take the information into consideration."

"Eliana, run a background on Aiden DeLuca and update us," Walsh instructed. "Dani and I will interview him."

"Roger that." Eliana's fingers danced over the keyboard.

Dani stepped toward Ayla. "Tessa's diaper bag has whatever you'll need." She glanced over her shoulder at Eliana. "Thanks to Eliana's quick and generous thinking."

The tech smiled at her. "My pleasure."

Ayla got Tessa settled with some toys in the playpen, talking to her while Eliana collected data on the weapons consultant. Within minutes, she announced, "Sent his LKA to your phones."

Dani's phone pinged with the Last Known Address for Aiden DeLuca and his driver's license picture. He didn't look familiar to her, but that wasn't unexpected. "Knox, ready?"

The Dobie mix looked up from his position next to Destiny, then got to his feet and strolled to Dani.

She snapped on his leash. "After the bombing at the Ibarras' home, I'm not leaving Knox behind."

"Agreed. We could've used his nose the other night," Walsh responded. "We'll also search Jayne's residence."

Dani debated asking for a delay, considering nothing thus far had fallen in Jayne's favor. Secretly, she feared what else they'd find. But they'd put off the inevitable too long. It was time for them to go. An idea bounded to mind. "We need a warrant."

"Already secured," Riker said.

Dani whipped her head in Walsh's direction in a silent demand for an explanation. "It's a normal part of the investigation." He shrugged.

Everything within her wanted to argue, but he was right. Still, she didn't like the thought of strangers going through Jayne's possessions. "Could we conduct the search after we visit De-Luca? I'd like to swing by my place again, too. I'd like to pick up a few more things." She'd been in a hurry when they'd gone the first time and neglected to grab her running shoes and workout clothes.

"Absolutely," Walsh replied.

Relieved to have some control over the situation, Dani focused her attention on her canine. "C'mon, Knox, road trip." The Dobie mix wagged his stubby tail, conveying his eagerness to work.

The other dogs rose with him, barking and tails wagging. All watching expectantly for their handlers to leash them.

"Not yet, Bosco," Tiandra cooed, stroking the Malinois' head.

Ammo sauntered toward Riker, nudging his hand. "You started a dog riot," Riker teased.

Dani winced. "Sorry about that."

"I'll assist Elijah and Graham at GIPD, too, and work on the missing evidence search," Chance said.

"Good." Walsh exited the conference room.

Dani would need Jayne's keys to enter her apartment. If the team broke down the door, they'd attract the neighbors' unwanted attention. She called Nancy, the nurse she'd spoken to several times since Jayne's admission. "The medics secured Jayne's purse with her belongings when you admitted her. I'd like to pick that up for safekeeping."

"Of course, when you get here, ask for me," Nancy replied. "I'll ensure it's released into your custody."

"Thank you." They disconnected, and Dani looked up, meeting everyone's compassionate stares.

"We'll continue praying," Eliana promised.

Skyler touched Dani's arm. "Don't give up hope."

"No time like the present." Walsh returned to the room.

The group surrounded Dani, lifting their

voices. Petitions for wisdom over Dani and Walsh, the team's safety, Jayne's healing, and justice in the case, humbled Dani. She blinked back tears at the collective amens that filled the Rock and their genuine concern.

"The hospital is first on the route, so let's start there," Walsh said. He understood Dani's desire to stall the search in Jayne's apartment, and he'd done his best to give her time to come to terms with the inevitable.

He'd acquiesced, but the mounting evidence forced his hand. He expected Dani to unleash on him about obtaining the warrant without her approval, but it seemed she realized they couldn't avoid protocol. Perhaps her experience working in command had taught her the difficulties of following rules, regardless of the cost to one's personal relationships. Maybe they'd both learned a lot since Walsh's investigation of Chief Varmose. Him to be more understanding and her to put the job ahead of her feelings.

Once they reached the hospital, Dani secured Knox's department-issued halter. With the identification, there wouldn't be issues taking him inside. The intense summer heat was too much for him to be left in the vehicle.

They rode the elevator in silence. Knox seemed to sense Dani's stress. He nudged her hand and offered a compassionate gaze from his dark eyes. Walsh envied the quiet understanding that passed between them without words.

"He gets you."

She nodded. "Yeah, truthfully, Knox is more comfort dog than K-9," Dani replied, absently stroking the animal's short coat. "He's such a softie at heart."

When they reached the floor where Jayne had been transferred and admitted, they strolled to the nurses' station. A short woman with Nancy on her name badge was waiting for them. "Chief, it's nice to meet you in person."

"This is Commander Beckham Walsh," Dani introduced him as he shook the nurse's hand.

"The state troopers guarding your friend are very kind," Nancy led them down the hallway.

Walsh noted the nurse didn't speak Jayne's name aloud. Captain Bonn had advised that aside from the security detail, only Nancy—as the head nurse—would be aware of Jayne's real identity. As they approached the trooper on duty, he rose from the chair positioned in front of the door.

"Commander Walsh and Chief Fontaine." Walsh extended a hand.

"Trooper Nguyen."

"We won't be long," Walsh assured him.

Nancy released the lock with her badge, allowing them to enter. "I'll give you privacy and bring the items you requested." The door shut softly behind them.

Tubes and wires streamed from the unconscious woman. Her pale skin and dark hair contrasted the white pillowcase.

Walsh stepped back, giving Dani space. She slowly eased around the bed, passing him Knox's leash. The dog dropped to sit beside him.

Dani gently swept loose strands from Jayne's face. She placed her hands on the railing and closed her eyes. Walsh felt like an intruder on a private moment, but unsure where else to be, he remained silent, watching. Dani never spoke, but slowly swiped at a stray tear streaming down her cheek.

Nancy returned and handed Dani a plastic bag with the hospital's logo on the front.

"Thank you," Dani said. "We should go." She led the way out.

Walsh addressed Nguyen, and he and Dani exited the hospital, not speaking to one another.

After loading Knox into Walsh's temporary replacement pickup, Dani slid into the passenger seat. "I appreciate you staying with me."

Stunned and humbled, Walsh passed her a pair of latex gloves. He'd expected Dani to admonish him for the lack of privacy. Instead, she'd thanked him for accompanying her.

She opened the bag and withdrew Jayne's purse, examining the contents. "I'll do a thorough inventory when we get to my office." Finding nothing of consequence, Dani replaced the items into the bag. "At least we have her keys. I don't want to ignite nosy neighbor rumors."

"I understand this is hard…" Walsh began.

Dani shook her head. "Let's focus on the case, okay?" She withdrew her phone, starting the GPS for Aiden's address. "DeLuca's place isn't far from here."

Walsh eyed the directions, started the engine, and headed westbound on Interstate 80.

Aiden's home sat on the edge of Gretna, a suburb west of Omaha. They pulled up to the modest, two-story building with a single garage, which sat in an older but well-maintained neighborhood. Walsh surveyed the structure, noticing the drapes were closed, prohibiting them from seeing inside.

He parked, and they exited the vehicle. Dani leashed Knox, then trailed Walsh up the sidewalk to the front door.

He rapped twice.

Silence.

Walsh pressed the doorbell.

Again, no response.

"Mr. DeLuca?" Walsh called.

Dani tried the number Eliana had provided for Aiden. "The line rang several times before transferring to an automated voicemail."

"Few people have landlines anymore. It's possible a cell phone is his only mode of communication."

"Something seems off," Dani said.

"Let's check around back."

They walked the perimeter of the house to a six-foot privacy fence that portioned off the yard. A gate to the right of the driveway stood ajar. Walsh pushed it open, and they entered the backyard. An older model grill sat on the square concrete porch where several lawn chairs were positioned next to a table with a dilapidated umbrella, leaning precariously to one side.

Walsh watched as Knox sniffed the area. "What's he doing?" The hairs rose on Walsh's neck.

"He's showing interest, but not alerting."

"Interpretation, please?" Walsh scanned the windows facing them.

"We're not in danger. At least not by explosives."

"Thanks for that clarification," Walsh grumbled.

An old gas mower was pushed against the shed. Overgrown sections of grass and weeds in the unkempt yard said someone had started landscaping work and never finished.

A screen door at the rear side of the house also stood ajar.

"Mr. DeLuca?" Walsh glanced at Dani and gestured toward the entrance. She gave a curt nod.

Both armed, they moved into a stack position.

Walsh pointed to a rust-colored smear on the doorframe. Blood.

"Mr. DeLuca," he called again, inching the door wider with the toe of his boot.

"Police," Dani added, tugging Knox closer to her right leg.

They stepped into the kitchen, where a mound of dirty dishes covered the countertop and overflowed into the sink. Flies buzzed overhead.

Someone had pulled out the drawers, and the

cabinet doors stood wide open. All the contents were tossed haplessly onto the floor. Indication of a search.

They made their way to the living room adjacent to the dining area. The disorder continued. The intruder had ripped cushions off the sofa, scattered pictures and sports memorabilia across the carpet.

Walsh shifted closer to the coffee table, which was broken in the center. "Clear signs of a struggle."

"Mr. DeLuca, police!"

She and Walsh turned their backs to one another as they inched through the hallway, clearing the bedrooms and bathrooms on both sides. Every room was in shambles. When they'd cleared the house, they holstered their guns.

"I'll call it in." Dani reached for her phone.

Walsh scanned the living room. Pictures of Aiden, with whom he assumed were friends and family, lay on the floor. He squatted to gain a better look. A younger version of the Aiden DeLuca he'd remembered stood proudly while an older woman with similar features pinned his badge.

Dark stains on the gray carpet got his attention. "Hey, Dani?"

She walked over and knelt beside him. Walsh pointed to blood droplets that led to the front door.

"Well, this changes things."

"And as of right now, we're classifying De-Luca as a missing person."

"He's a suspect," Dani corrected. "I checked the garage and there's no vehicle there."

"Yes, he's a person of interest, just like Jayne," he said. "I'll request an APB for him and his last registered vehicle," Walsh said, referencing the all-points bulletin. The sound of screeching tires carried to them.

Knox lunged, barking at the entrance.

An eerie silence fell. Then rapid gunfire shattered the front window. Walsh dove, tackling Dani and Knox simultaneously to the floor. They rolled toward the hallway as rounds pelted the drywall, shattering pictures, and glass around them.

Walsh gripped his phone and called 9-1-1, shouting into the receiver, "Shots fired, shots fired!"

Chapter Eight

The firestorm seemed to come from every direction in an unending cacophony of blasts. Walsh stayed in a crouch, Dani beside him. He dropped his phone into his breast pocket, unable to hear the dispatcher's response. He prayed help was on the way.

Both prepared to return fire, but the relentless attack offered no opening. Glass and drywall exploded around them, filling the space in a cloud of debris. Dani hovered over Knox, protecting him.

Then, as quickly as it began, the firefight ceased abruptly, followed by squealing tires. Walsh moved to the window and peered out. Thankfully, the shooter hadn't destroyed the temporary SUV he'd driven. One minute advantage.

He helped Dani to her feet, and they visually assessed the damage.

"Someone doesn't want us to find the connection," she said.

"Yeah." Walsh's instincts told him there was a lot more to the case than missing weapons. With three suspects in the mix, things had grown increasingly complicated.

At last local PD arrived. Walsh and Dani exited through the back door, not wanting to disturb any potential evidence.

They approached the two patrol units, and Walsh offered a rundown of the events and requested crime scene processing.

The officers took the report and once they'd assumed command, Walsh, Dani, and Knox headed out.

Walsh called the tech. "Eliana, please provide a group update to the team." Again, he provided a synopsis of what had occurred.

"Got it," she said.

"Look for details on Aiden DeLuca's registered vehicle."

"Will do. I'll be in touch."

They disconnected, and Walsh merged onto Highway 80 eastbound.

Within minutes, Eliana texted him with the information.

Using his speakerphone feature, Walsh called

Captain Bonn. "Need your help," he blurted before Bonn said hello. "Could you please issue an APB for Aiden DeLuca and an older model Ford F-150. Tan with Nebraska license plates." He rattled off the plate number.

"I'll get it handled," Bonn replied, hanging up.

Walsh's phone rang, and he again answered on speakerphone. "Chance, are you in GI?"

"Yes, sir," Chance replied. "We found something interesting and need you to come here ASAP."

"We're on our way," Walsh advised.

"See you soon." He disconnected.

"The evidence at Aiden's doesn't prove he was in cahoots with Jayne," Dani said, "but whoever shot at us is most likely the same person who has him."

"True. However, Aiden's reputation in the law enforcement community is solid. I suspect foul play."

"I'm not disagreeing with you, but I believe there's more to the story than Jayne dishing out evidence," Dani countered.

Walsh considered his words. "I get the need to be loyal to your team. You've met mine. I'd lay my life on the line for any of them without a second thought."

Her eyes drilled through him.

Walsh braced for her argument of his next statement. "Perhaps you'll want to recuse yourself. Focus on taking care of Tessa."

Dani crossed her arms. "I knew you'd say that."

"I'm not implying you're incapable of handling this investigation. I'm simply saying I'm aware that eliminating your personal feelings isn't always achievable."

"Beckham Walsh, you might have issues with that, but I do not. I'm a professional. First and foremost, a cop."

"As am I."

"Then you understand that partiality isn't allowable. Yes, I believe in Jayne's innocence, but not because I'm ignoring the evidence. I've seen her day-to-day work ethics. There is nothing substantial linking Jayne to the missing weapons."

"There is plenty of evidence," Walsh contended.

"All circumstantial," Dani corrected. "And we cannot arrest or charge her purely based upon that. If, and/or when, we find proof of her involvement, we will handle it at that time, and not assume it beforehand."

Walsh sighed. A twinge of guilt pricked at him. Not so long ago, he'd faced a similar situation with Riker. Additionally, he'd told Dani they'd not jump to conclusions about Aiden's involvement. He had to extend that same courtesy to Jayne. Admittedly, he'd not questioned Riker's innocence, regardless of the evidence stacked against him. "Maybe it has nothing to do with her personally. Could be a group targeting smaller agencies or enemies of HFTF seeking revenge," Walsh said.

The remainder of the drive was quiet until they pulled into the GIPD parking lot and exited the vehicle.

If he wasn't imagining it, Dani appeared on edge with him. He fought the urge to reach over and squeeze her hand, reminding her they were on the same side, allies, not enemies. He sighed, hating the contention that lingered between them like an unwanted guest.

They walked into the building, greeted professionally by officers and personnel. However, Walsh didn't miss the aloofness they all exhibited. Understandably so.

"Might as well talk with Chance first." Dani led him to the evidence storage area.

Chance stood beside a worktable, wearing a somber expression.

"Your face tells me we won't like what you have to say," Walsh said.

"Yeah…we've sorted through the records for our stored evidence and there's an issue." He passed a paper to Walsh and Dani. They both leaned forward to read.

Walsh immediately spotted the color difference in the ink. Similar, but different, and not authentic to the original writing. The same person had changed the inventory numbers too. "Someone falsified the records," he said.

"Yes, sir, and the numbers do not match the inventory. Furthermore, someone compromised the evidence tape that sealed the containers, then tried covering their tracks." Chance pointed to a box on the side counter. "At first glance, it wasn't obvious. Upon closer inspection, we confirmed the sections were tampered with." He stepped back, stroking Destiny, who panted softly beside him.

"Jayne would've secured the tape after logging the items into the evidence locker," Dani explained. "If someone requested to get into the sealed box, they'd have to sign the log and the original binding to establish the chain of custody."

"Right," Walsh agreed. "But this document shows those steps weren't followed."

"This isn't the only one." Chance passed his cell phone to Walsh.

The device showed a box that HFTF had logged into evidence several months prior. Walsh expanded the picture and spotted the severed tape. He handed the device to Dani.

"That's impossible." Dani zoomed in on the screen and her cheeks reddened. She opened her mouth, then clamped it shut again. "I'm speechless." She lowered her arm, setting Chance's phone on the table.

"Chance, thank you for the update. Please continue the work," Walsh said. "Dani and I will be in her office before heading to Jayne's apartment."

The younger marshal gave a curt nod as they exited the room.

Once they were in Dani's office with her door closed, she perched on the edge of her desk. "Don't say it."

"Evidence speaks for itself."

At her glower, he lifted his hands in surrender. "It's time we went through Jayne's things." He'd not pushed the issue with the chain of events, but he couldn't delay any longer.

Dani nodded consent. "Before we go, let's check Jayne's locker."

They moved to the main office where a husky man sat behind a desk with a sign on the door that read HR Manager. She didn't introduce Walsh, so he hesitated, listening.

"I need Jayne Bardot's personnel file and the key to her locker," Dani said.

The manager shot a look at Walsh but didn't question the order. He got to his feet, returning with a manila folder. "Chief."

"Thank you," she said curtly before walking out.

Walsh followed Dani to her office and settled at the small conference table. She placed the folder between them, and they sorted through the documents. Nothing seemed out of the ordinary. There were no disciplinary actions. Her file proclaimed the opposite. Jayne was an exemplary evidence technician.

"Unless you see something here that I don't," Dani said, "I'd say the information confirms what I've said from the start."

"She appears to be a stellar employee. On paper."

"She is." Dani rose. "Let's check her locker."

They walked through the building to an ajar door marked by a sign that read Women's Locker Room. Women's voices carried out to the hallway.

"They should be out shortly. It's close to shift change." Dani leaned against the wall.

The voices grew louder, as the speakers neared where Walsh and Dani waited.

"Heard that task force is here doing an IA," a woman said, referencing an internal affairs investigation.

A second added, "Rumor is Jayne Bardot's somehow involved."

Dani cringed, saddened by her personnel discussing the situation. Yet, what did she expect? That was human nature.

She didn't recognize the speakers, but then she was still new to the agency.

"I never trusted Jayne. She's too close to the chief. Figure she's a plant spying for Fontaine," the first woman replied.

Dani's ears warmed, disheartened at their opinions of her. The moment triggered emotions from the years after Walsh arrested Chief Varmose. Her fellow officers had shunned her then too.

She lingered, hating herself for eavesdropping, then reasoned this was a fact-finding mission. Would they say anything to help with the case, since they were unaware she and Walsh were listening in?

Walsh worked his jaw, apparently unimpressed with the chatter.

"Yeah, wonder what this means for the chief?" the second woman asked. "Can't be good for that kind of accusation this early on her watch."

Dani's stomach plummeted straight to her boots. She glanced down. Losing the confidence of her officers would be a detrimental obstacle to overcome. All this time, she'd worried about Jayne's involvement in the case, completely ignoring how the situation affected her own job.

"That K-9 officer from the Heartland Fugitive Task Force is easy on the eyes," the first commented, changing topics.

Dani met Walsh's gaze, and he gave a slight shake of his head, realizing the speaker meant Chance Tavalla. She thought of his kind wife, Ayla, who was taking care of Tessa, and sent up a prayer of gratitude.

The door swung open, revealing the speakers. Olga, the receptionist, stepped back startled, colliding with GIPD officer, Yessinia Zarick, who blurted, "Hi, Chief." The young officer's wide eyes spoke surprise, resembling a teenager caught sneaking in after curfew. "Oh hi, Knox." Her joyful tone didn't match her embarrassed expression.

Knox harrumphed, moving closer to Dani. She recognized Yessinia as the speaker beaming about Chance.

"Good morning, Chief," Olga parroted, leaning against the doorframe in an attempt at a casual response, while her countenance mirrored the same guilt as Yessinia's.

"Ladies," Dani replied. "How was your workout?" She glanced at her watch pointedly, reminding them they needed to get to work.

"Excellent." Olga's face was so red she looked like she might spontaneously combust in place.

Yessinia swallowed hard. "Well, I gotta get ready for shift change."

"Have a great day!" Olga bounced behind her, and the women quickly exited the locker room.

"Shall we?" Dani peered inside the room, avoiding Walsh's eyes. Once she'd confirmed it was empty, they entered, propping the door open.

"Are you okay?" Walsh asked.

"Guess their candid comments shouldn't shock me," Dani said, leading the way to Jayne's personal locker. Knox remained at her side.

As the new chief, she should expect her personnel to pretend to be kind to her face while talking behind her back about the issues of command staff. The overwhelming evidence against Jayne weighed on Dani. Though she longed to argue plausible reasons in her friend's favor, truthfully, her own assurances quavered.

She'd never admit that to Walsh.

Not yet anyway.

Dani exhaled, then inserted the key into Jayne's assigned locker. She tugged open the door and stepped to the side, allowing Walsh to see the contents: workout shorts and a tank top sat atop a pair of running shoes. She remembered Jayne often came in early, taking advantage of the exercise facilities.

Donning gloves Walsh handed her, Dani removed the evidence bag she'd stuffed into her pocket. She lifted the items carefully to check deeper inside the space. A makeup pouch filled with toiletries was hidden beneath the clothes. Dani sorted through, feeling like the worst kind of intruder.

Would it matter if she had to arrest her friend?

Dani paused and withdrew a piece of paper sticking out of a compact mirror case. It was a picture of Jayne with Aiden DeLuca. Dani's heart raced, and she lifted the photo higher up to the light. It was a photo-booth shot, like those taken at a mall kiosk. Jayne smiled for the camera, while Aiden planted a kiss on her cheek.

Nausea overwhelmed Dani. Jayne not only knew Aiden but was also in a relationship with him. On the back was written *Love you, babe.*

Dani's stomach twisted with hurt and anger. She leaned hard against the locker, passing the incriminating evidence. How had she been so wrong about Jayne?

Her mind raced with the implications. Had Jayne used Dani, gaining her trust and her position to obtain access to the weapons, then conspired with Aiden to steal them? If so, why was he missing? Had they gotten wrapped up with Enrique Prachank? Dani wanted to believe there was a reasonable explanation. But she couldn't deny the proof in front of her.

Even if both were casualties of a poor decision, they were romantically involved. That wouldn't bode well with HFTF.

Conviction rose within Dani. Ridiculous as it might sound, she believed there was more to the story. Jayne wouldn't risk custody of Tessa without a valid explanation. Jayne's participation could've been involuntary.

"Let's move to your office for privacy," Walsh suggested, breaking the silence.

Dani nodded, secured the locker, and trailed him out of the room.

Lord, what do I do?

Walsh closed the door, and they settled at her conference table. Knox sat beside her, laying his head in her lap. "Hey buddy." She stroked his soft coat.

The task force already believed Jayne was guilty. The picture would solidify their assumptions. They'd pursue the path to charge her with the missing evidence. Yet she'd called Dani to meet with her, asking for help. She'd even gone as far as to hide Tessa in the closet and ask Dani to care for the infant if necessary.

People made mistakes and simple things got out of hand. She'd seen it all the time in law enforcement. She had to believe the best about Jayne. If she'd deceived Dani, and Jayne had used her, then their entire friendship was fake.

And that meant Dani was a fool. Just like when she'd ignored the signs of her husband's shifting priorities though he claimed he didn't need more than a career-seeking wife. Mark had promised a life without kids was enough for him. Then he'd left her for another woman and had the family he'd claimed he never wanted from her.

Before that, she'd ignored the truth about her commanding chief—a horrible, conniving criminal. She'd defended Varmose to the end, destroying her relationship with Walsh and enduring the hatred of her fellow officers.

Dani couldn't be that naïve ever again.

She sighed.

"Let's talk it out." Walsh's even tone and tender expression tore at Dani's heart.

"What if Aiden used Jayne to get the munitions? Perhaps he'd convinced her to help him steal them? After all, your team found guns that were logged in his possession—weapons he was supposed to have destroyed."

"Plausible." Walsh leaned back.

Encouraged, Dani added. "What if he threatened or betrayed Jayne? She might've played a part in the crimes, but if it was under coercion or fear for her life or Tessa's, that explains a lot."

And that sounded much more like the Jayne Dani knew.

"Okay, let's follow up on DeLuca and notify the team of the finding," Walsh replied. "Trust the system and the process to reveal the truth."

Dani nodded mutely. More so, she had to trust God to handle it all because it was far beyond her abilities. "You make the calls. I need to give Knox a break outside."

She rose and hurried from the room.

Dani took a side exit. She needed a second to gather her thoughts and pray. The photo weighed like a fifty-pound cannon ball on her heart.

Standing on the front lawn of her department, Dani contemplated the totality of events. For the first time, she got honest with herself. Walsh had hurt her by hiding Varmose's investigation, but she understood why he'd done it. The pain of betrayal remained, though she might never confess that to Walsh. Just as Jayne had to understand Dani's responsibility to investigate this case, regardless of their friendship. Funny how history had repeated itself. She'd walked out of a situation where she'd trusted someone immensely, only to have egg on her face.

Worse, Beckham Walsh was there to witness her mistakes.

Again.

Chapter Nine

"Got any updates on Aiden DeLuca?" Walsh asked when Captain Bonn answered his call.

"Negative on DeLuca. Crime scene techs completed a thorough workup on the house. They found nothing beyond the blood droplets and smear you reported." Bonn continued, "We're waiting on DNA to confirm whether the sample is DeLuca's."

"There wasn't a significant amount."

"Correct. Most likely a minor wound. Forced entry into the house. No missing valuables, so we ruled out robbery."

Walsh recalled seeing electronics and cash on the nightstand at Aiden's place. "I appreciate it."

Bonn disconnected. A glance at his watch had Walsh concerned. He'd already called in HFTF, and Dani hadn't yet returned. After all she'd endured, she probably wanted alone time. Away from him.

A rap on the door got his attention.

"Come in."

Chance entered, Destiny at his side. The K-9 strode to Walsh for a quick petting before curling up on Knox's bed.

"Eliana updated me on the picture." Chance dropped onto the chair opposite him. "Does the word 'Decorah' mean anything to you?"

"No. Never heard of it."

"It's a small town in the northeastern part of Iowa."

Dani entered with Knox and the Dobie mix rushed to Destiny. The German shepherd glanced up lazily and offered a few thumps of her tail. Knox settled beside her, and both emitted contented sighs.

"Guess those two bonded." Dani smiled but it never reached her eyes. She sat next to Chance. "Why do you ask?"

Chance flashed Walsh a look, the silent request for permission to continue talking in front of her.

Fleeting annoyance shadowed Dani's face and Walsh gave an imperceptible nod.

"A receipt for a Decorah coffeehouse was in Jayne's desk." Chance passed the slip sealed in a plastic zipper bag to Dani. "Did she have family or friends there?"

"I don't think so." Dani tilted her head, studying the paper.

"Hmm. Seems strange." Chance reached for the bag.

"Hold on." Dani snapped a picture with her cell phone. "Maybe she had a weekend away."

The verbal dismissal didn't match the deceit Walsh detected in her response. Had he imagined it?

"Consider everything," Walsh said.

"Agreed." Dani sighed, steepling her fingers.

"It was the only out-of-place part of her workspace that we've found so far. Jayne's meticulous."

The anomaly stood out. Accidental? Or had Jayne left it on purpose?

"We'll check her schedule for any recent travels," Chance said.

"I don't deal with her daily assignments, so I'm unaware when she comes and goes." Dani's posture conveyed defensiveness, though her tone remained light.

"Eliana will dig into Jayne's financials and see if she can tap into her phone's GPS as well." Chance pushed away from the table. "We'll keep you updated." He walked to the door, gesturing for Destiny. The shepherd opened an eye but stayed curled beside Knox.

"She's welcome to stay here," Dani said.

"Thanks." Chance put his hands into his pockets, hesitating. "Um, one last thing."

Dani and Walsh shared a look before offering him their full attention. Chance had become more secure in their discussions, but he lacked the confidence Walsh wanted him to exude when on duty.

Did he intimidate the marshal? If so, why? He'd offered support and encouragement. Walsh recognized his rough edges sometimes came off harshly.

"The county attorney's office called..." Chance began, referencing Ayla's employer. "Eliana is at the Rock with Tessa, but Ayla has to go back to work overtime on a case."

"She's a paralegal," Walsh explained to Dani.

Understanding swept over her expression. "Oh, sure! I appreciate all you've done." She smiled and started to rise.

Walsh gestured for her to relax.

"I'm missing Tessa. We'll return to Omaha immediately."

"No rush." Relief covered Chance's face. "Eliana said not to worry. It's all good."

"That sounds like her." Walsh chuckled. "I'll advise our ETA after we search Jayne's residence."

Dani frowned. Was she hoping to postpone it?

Chance squatted in front of Destiny and whispered, "Be back soon. Relax here." She thumped her feathery tail in reply. "Holler if you want me to get her," Chance added.

"No problem," Dani replied with a smile.

Chance left the office, closing the door behind him.

Before Walsh could speak, Dani blurted, "I'm sorry for the extra work Tessa has put on your team. They're not babysitters. I don't expect them to behave as such. Perhaps we could call in protective detail from another agency?"

"That's a great idea." Before she changed her mind, Walsh called Nebraska State Patrol Captain Bonn.

The line rang twice before he answered. "We've never talked this much in such a short amount of time."

"Seriously." Walsh smirked. "I have a request." He provided a brief explanation and asked for troopers to assist with Tessa's protection at headquarters. "If possible, have them meet us at the Rock first thing in the morning."

"Expect them," Bonn replied.

"I owe you."

"Happy to help." They disconnected.

Dani looked up, a light shimmer in her eyes. "Thank you." She glanced at the photo of Jayne and Aiden DeLuca.

Walsh scooted closer. "You walked in here looking like you'd witnessed a train wreck."

"That's not too far off as analogies go."

He lifted the photo and fought to maintain a stoic expression. "I must admit, I didn't expect to find this."

"There's a reasonable explanation." Dani reiterated her belief that Jayne had been coerced somehow.

Walsh stifled his irritation and impatience, quirking an eyebrow in silent protest.

Dani rambled on, undeterred by his obvious skepticism. "Until we're certain, we have to keep an open mind."

Walsh weighed his next words. "No argument there, but this is totally reaching."

"I resent that." Dani sat back, crossing her arms. Several seconds passed and her defensive posture faded. "No, I don't. You're right. Just please don't give up on Jayne until we uncover the truth."

"You have my word." Walsh leaned forward. "What else has you rattled?"

She averted her eyes. "I debated taking the chief position here. I didn't have a history with the department and wasn't sure they'd receive me since I hadn't risen through their ranks."

"I get that."

"Earning my personnel's trust is huge."

"Unquestionably." Walsh thought of his group. They'd worked together, creating the solid bond.

"You haven't had that issue with your task force. They're amazing."

"Every new commander contends with challenges," Walsh corrected her. "The trust and confidence team members have with one another doesn't happen overnight. It takes time to build up to the level HFTF has now. I'm grateful for the incredible privilege God has offered to me in leading them."

"Your faith bonds you."

"Yes. It doesn't fix all our problems, but it provides a solid cornerstone. That's why we call our conference room the Rock and start every case in prayer." Walsh glanced down. "You're the one who inspired my faith."

Dani blinked. "Me?"

"Absolutely. It has always been one of your most attractive traits." Realizing his confession, he quickly reversed topics. "Your personnel will come around."

"For this to happen early in my career as a chief is rough. I cannot believe their insinuation that I sent Jayne in as a spy for me." Dani rolled her eyes. "As though I have the time to orchestrate nefarious plans."

Walsh crossed one ankle over his knee.

"Although Olga and Yissinia were complimentary of Chance." Dani leaned back and he acknowledged her efforts to divert the discussion.

"They'd never drag him away from Ayla." Walsh stifled a grin. "He's as loyal as they come."

She smiled. "She's a blessed woman. Men like him are a rare and precious find."

Walsh wondered at her comment, realizing he knew little of her personal life after their falling out. But now wasn't the time to ask. "Does Jayne have friends here?"

The team had questioned the personnel. So far, no one had claimed to be close to the evidence tech.

"She confessed I was her only friend," Dani

said. "Painful, considering she never mentioned Aiden DeLuca."

"That puts you in an awkward situation as her boss," Walsh surmised.

"I thought I was handling it well. Apparently, I was wrong."

Walsh tamped down his anger, recalling the women's locker room conversation. The urge to deal with their hateful comments warred within him. Dani was perfectly capable of defending herself, but he longed to assume that role for her.

"Not only are they questioning my authority and competency, but I don't blame them."

Shocked by the heartfelt confession, Walsh assured her, "This isn't your fault."

He hated that Jayne had put Dani in the difficult position. And in typical Dani fashion, she'd willingly fall on her sword to protect her friend.

Walsh added, "Jayne made her own choices."

"What if they were ultimatums?"

The woman's relentless hope, though inspiring, wore on Walsh. He pointed to the picture. "This proves they were in a relationship. Regardless of the hows and whys, why not come to you if she'd gotten in too deep?"

"That's exactly why she asked me to meet her. She might've had evidence to give us then,"

Dani contended. "That paints Aiden as the warehouse shooter. He tried to stop her from ratting him out."

"Okay, suppose that's true. Where is he now?"

"Simple. He took off when his plan didn't work. He's afraid of being caught."

"Why was his house ransacked? He could've skipped town without adding that detail. And they found blood evidence."

Dani waved him off. "That's an easy plant."

"If Aiden's a victim, Jayne might've played him."

Her jaw hardened, but she didn't argue. "I suppose there's probability in your scenario," she conceded. "If she doesn't recover, we'll never know."

Walsh reached out a hand to comfort her but stopped before making contact. He needed to keep his professional distance. "On that note, have you considered the next steps with Tessa should Jayne's condition continue to decline?"

"Yes, sort of." Dani blew out a long breath. "I can't go there yet. The tiny thread of hope I'm clinging to is the only thing keeping me from completely unraveling."

Walsh understood her point of view far better than he dared to share.

★ ★ ★

Dani stood in Jayne's living room. They'd entered the residence without drawing the attention of Jayne's nosy neighbors, but they might not leave with the same results.

"Divide and conquer?" Walsh asked.

"Yeah." She faced Knox. "Stay."

The dog dropped into a regal sphinx position at the door.

Dani paused in the familiar space, surveying it through an investigator's eyes. The love seat sat opposite a console table holding a TV and framed pictures of Tessa. Dani fingered the delicate threads of the hand-embroidered pillows placed on the sofa. Dani agreed Jayne had a talent for the hobby. Tessa's baby swing stood beside the window and a carousel toy lay on the floor. Everything in the house attested to a devoted mother who doted on her only child. She strolled to Jayne's bedroom.

Walsh was digging through the dresser's contents.

Taking his lead, she tugged open the nightstand drawer. Inside lay a Bible, a piece of paper peeking out from the center, beside a women's devotional. Dani extracted it. The same name of the Decorah coffee shop Chance had found on a receipt earlier was printed at the top. Centered was a hand drawn sketch of a cube and half-rounded triangle.

Walsh approached her, and she passed it to him. "Looks like doodling."

"Doubtful."

Dani captured a photo, then bagged the item for evidence.

They perused the rest of the apartment, finding nothing incriminating, to her relief. Dani said, "We should scoot to Omaha. C'mon Knox." Dani ushered Walsh out the door and locked it.

Dani drifting to sleep on the return trip, waking as Walsh pulled into HFTF's underground garage. Eliana met them with Tessa, allowing them to get to the condo faster.

Dani studied the picture on her phone of the drawing from Jayne's apartment. "I thought it was a triangle, but it's round." She opened her internet browser and searched Decorah attractions. Immediately, one got her attention. "It's the ice caves in Palisades Park!"

"Great work!" Walsh commended.

Knox pushed his head between the seats, joining the discussion. Tessa cooed from the backseat, happily swatting at a hanging toy from her carrier. Grateful they'd taken out the seat at the Ibarras' before the explosion, Dani sent up a prayer of thanks.

"Why sketch it instead of writing the words?" Dani asked.

"What's an ice cave hundreds of miles from Grand Island, Nebraska, got to do with Jayne?"

"We must check it out," Dani said.

"It's late. Let's make the drive first thing in the morning after we meet with the troopers handling Tessa's protection detail."

"Okay. Thank you again for handling that."

Walsh didn't look her way. He most likely feared she'd explode. "You're a fantastic investigator. Jayne needs your skills now."

She exhaled. "This is all new to me."

"Did you want the husband, children, house with a picket fence, and a dog?" Walsh's tone held a teasing element.

Dani met his unwavering gaze for several seconds.

"You don't have to—"

"I married my career. Balancing a family and a high-intensity job isn't a viable option. You can't serve two masters."

"Actually, if you're referencing the Bible verse, I think Jesus meant money," Walsh replied lightly.

"It's true. Something will take precedent." Against her mind warning her to stop talking, she blurted, "I never told you this when we were dating, but my father abandoned my mom and me. He chose another woman and then had a family with her. Mom instantly became a single parent. She did her best to balance her surgical career and me, but I felt like an inconvenience. I vowed to never put a child in that position."

Walsh gaped at her. "That must've been awful."

"It was a life lesson for me." She glanced down. "I'm grateful I learned it early on."

She'd fought a male-dominated vocation. Always having to be twice as good, competent, and skilled. No criminal would take that away.

Walsh pulled into the condo's parking lot and Dani threw open her door. "Let's finish this. It's cost me too much to get this far."

Chapter Ten

Orange and purple splashed the sky with the sunrise the following day. Dani and Knox trailed Walsh through the HFTF building to the elevators.

"Captain Bonn notified me this morning that the personnel I requested are already here," he said, pushing the up button for the elevator.

"Okay." Dani shifted Tessa, pressing a kiss to the infant's head.

The elevator doors opened, and they stepped out, Walsh leading into the Rock. Two men sat at the table with Skyler and Chance. Both wore black BDUs and navy blue short-sleeved T-shirts printed with the Nebraska State Patrol logo.

Knox trotted to Destiny. The shepherd glanced up from her place in the corner and they shared a customary sniffing. Graham, Elijah, Tiandra, and K-9 Bosco joined. The Malinois moved to join the other dogs. Walsh greeted the troopers then conducted introductions with his team.

The troopers got to their feet. The shorter of them, a husky man with a kind face and smiling eyes, stepped forward first. "Good morning. I'm Vernon Ulrich and this is John Nguyen."

"We met at the hospital, though not formally," Walsh replied with a glance at Nguyen. He offered handshakes to both. "I'm Commander Beckham Walsh. Thank you for agreeing to help us with the protection detail."

"Glad to be of service," Trooper Nguyen said.

Dani introduced herself to the troopers as Walsh circled the room, sidling to the far side. Today, the action didn't appear as standoffish. Rather, he took the seat at the head of the table, as a leader should. She blinked, realizing how her biased perception had skewed her reality.

Eliana, K-9 Ammo, and Riker entered, quickly introducing themselves. Eliana sat beside her. The tension evaporated from Dani's body at the team's inclusion.

"I'm guessing this is our protection asset?" Trooper Ulrich said, making a silly face at the infant that earned him a giggle.

"This is Tessa," Dani said.

"Pleased to meet you, Ms. Tessa." Ulrich held

out both hands, and she eagerly reached for him. Dani gently passed the infant to him. "I have three littles of my own at home," he told her.

"We're expecting our first," Nguyen said. "This will be great on-the-job training." He smiled.

"We plan to keep Tessa here, as it seems to be the most central and secure place for her," Walsh explained.

"We've set up an area," Eliana added. "There's a locker room, bunks and shower facilities as well."

"Follow me, and I'll show you around," Riker said.

They stepped out, with Ulrich entertaining Tessa with his silliness.

Walsh smiled, calling the group to order. "Troopers Ulrich and Nguyen will board here, taking shifts until we have a better handle on things."

"How long are you thinking?" Chance asked.

"Not sure." Walsh shot a glance at Dani. After a short debrief, Walsh advised the team of he and Dani's plans to visit Decorah and they departed from the group.

Dani contemplated stopping to see Tessa once

more, then decided against it. The delay would only make it harder to leave the baby.

Dani and Walsh loaded into his SUV and got on the road. The drive was quiet and pleasant through Nebraska. When they reached the northeastern part of Iowa, acres of rolling hills surrounded them on the way to Decorah.

"We're about fifteen minutes out," Walsh advised.

"I'm not sure what I expect to find at the ice caves, but if Jayne kept that note, it has to mean something, right?" Dani asked.

"I agree. And as of now, we don't have any other leads, so I'd say we leave no ice cave unturned."

Dani chuckled at his combination of clichés, an endearing trait she'd forgotten that she loved about him. Loved? She studied him. Walsh's muscular form and handsome exterior hadn't faded with age.

But loved?

It was just a figure of speech. She shoved away the thought. It wasn't as though she had those feelings for Walsh. At least, not anymore.

Or did she? The days they'd spent together had revealed the degrees that Walsh had matured since their younger romance. His steadfastness and support when she'd felt out of her depth only added to his handsome exterior features. She also couldn't deny that her heart did a triple beat and warmth radiated up her neck whenever he glanced at her.

"I appreciate everything you and your team have done to help Tessa and I." Dani deliberately left out Jayne's name to avoid ruining the peaceful moment. She didn't want to debate with Walsh today.

"As Tiandra said, it's what family does." Walsh never took his eyes off the road while simultaneously sipping his coffee.

"I'm sure the troopers will do a great job with her, though. We don't want to overstay our babysitting welcome."

"I don't think that's an issue."

Still, it was a temporary solution to a larger problem. Dani's responsibility for Tessa was becoming clearer by the minute. Jayne's condition continued to decline. They were on borrowed time before Dani would face the hardest decision of her life. Whether to establish permanent guardianship for Tessa.

Unwilling to deal with those thoughts today, she shoved them aside.

"Baby protection duty is highly unusual," Dani replied.

"I'd say most of our cases end up taking on that classification in one form or another."

"How so?"

"We've accumulated assets like Eliana's computer technical skills and her DNA phenotyping program. Chance and Destiny are a force to be reckoned with as manhunt experts, and Elijah brings a wealth of street experience to our unit. Not to mention a shared face with Graham, so it works great for undercover ops."

Dani tried absorbing the information. "Yeah, I suppose you all are used to handling unique situations."

"Couldn't make this up if I wanted to." Walsh chuckled.

Dani relished the sound, enjoying the laugh lines that appeared around his brown eyes. "Your team also resembles the law enforcement version of *Love Connection*."

"Tell me about it." He grinned, flicking a glance at her.

Their gazes held for several long seconds, transitioning into an awkward moment. Dani swallowed hard.

Walsh cleared his throat, then sipped his coffee. She averted her eyes, then shuffled with the contents of her purse. Dani couldn't deny the attraction building between them. She'd caught herself inhaling deeper to breathe in his after-shave.

When they'd driven a few miles, Dani said, "The task force's reputation precedes you. Even at Lincoln PD, I heard wonderful things about HFTF." She didn't add how the talk around the law enforcement community about Beckham Walsh's achievements poured salt in their estrangement wound. She'd struggled after Chief Varmose's debacle, while Walsh had soared in his career, promoting up the ranks. He'd fallen off her radar for a period, then reappeared when she learned of his return to the Marshals and subsequently advancing as the commander of HFTF.

Signposts advertised Palisades Park ahead, but construction signs near the entrance advised the area was closed to tourists.

"Why aren't there roadblocks restricting access?" Walsh asked, slowing to a stop.

"We might not be able to drive through, but can we walk in?" Dani offered. "Or perhaps what I should say is they won't see us sneaking through." She snickered.

"I'd say it's worth a try." Walsh parked the SUV as close as he could get to the entrance.

They unloaded and Dani leashed Knox. "Once more, Eliana to the rescue. She provided a backpack of hiking supplies."

"Remind me to give her a raise for her thoughtfulness," Walsh quipped.

Dani double-checked the items, and her heart swelled with appreciation for the tech's kindness. "No, you really need to. Eliana thought of everything down to bottled water." She zipped the pack closed and hoisted it onto her back.

"Ready?"

"Yep." They started up the trail. "For all the K-9s you have on the team, I'm surprised you're not a handler," she said. "You're a natural with them. Knox already adores you, and that's saying a lot. He doesn't take well to men in particular."

Walsh gave the dog a quick pat. "I wouldn't have thought that at all. He seems super at ease with me."

"That's what I mean. He's usually standoffish until he's decided whether the person has passed muster with him. But he acts like he's known you and your team members forever."

"I just extended the proverbial trust branch, and he accepted," Walsh agreed.

Dani grinned at his misuse of the cliché. "Guess animals sense when someone is safe." She considered the comment, realizing she truly believed it. If Knox trusted Walsh, then maybe she could as well. Except emotionally distancing herself by holding onto the past was the only thing that kept Dani from falling for Walsh.

Again. Once had cost her enough. She couldn't afford a second.

If only her heart agreed.

The brisk morning air had Dani tugging her jacket tighter.

Though it was a weekday, Dani expected other tourists hiking in the area. "Is it just me, or are we all alone out here?"

"I'd say you assessed it correctly."

Knox stopped to sniff at a tree before continuing.

They hiked through the woods to an ice cave sign that marked the tourist attraction further up the path.

Knox paused again, this time with his snout lifted.

"What's he saying?" Walsh asked.

"I'm not sure." Dani hesitated and studied her canine. "Knox, seek."

The dog stood still, actively sniffing the air.

"He's explosive detection trained, correct?" Walsh asked.

"This isn't his alert response." A chill passed over Dani as she surveyed their surroundings.

The path stretched out before them, bordered by trees heavily laden with leaves shadowing the dirt floor. A breeze fluttered, wafting the earthy, fresh scent of rain in the air. "Do you smell that?"

"It's called petrichor. Yeah, we'd better hurry this along if there's a storm headed our way."

Knox paused and barked, focused on a shadowed area. Walsh removed his gun. "Get to the side. I'll check it out."

They hadn't seen another driver the entire trip to the park. Had someone followed them? If so, how had the person gotten in without them noticing? She shifted away from the path, taking shelter behind a massive boulder.

Walsh and Knox disappeared around a bend. Only the chirrups of the birds overhead carried to her.

The snap of a twig to her right set Dani on edge and she froze. *Please Lord, help me to be silent and not make a sound.*

Her heart drummed hard against her chest

in what felt like the longest minute of her life. *Where are you, Walsh?*

Finally, a dog's familiar paw clicking and boots stepping closer preceded Walsh and Knox's return. Dani exited her hiding spot and spotted Walsh's wide grin.

"Just a herd of deer," he announced.

"Knox doesn't get much exposure to those." Dani chuckled. "At the end of the day, he's still a dog." She gave the canine a good scratch behind the ears.

"The animals enthralled Knox, but to my surprise, he never barked at them," Walsh commended, kneeling to praise the canine.

They continued the ascent to the ice cave high above the town of Decorah. Stone steps and a majestic rock formation towered overhead, revealing the entrance. The floor disappeared into the cavernous core.

The temperature dropped dramatically as they ventured further into the cavern. Walsh removed a flashlight from his cargo pants' pocket and swept the beam into the dark depths.

"What exactly are we looking for?" Dani's voice reverberated in the confined space. She tugged Knox closer beside her.

"Wish I knew," Walsh said.

The path grew narrower.

"Good thing I'm not claustrophobic," Dani half joked.

Knox stuck his snout into a crevice, backed up, then gently descended into a sphinx pose.

Dani froze. "Don't move."

"What's wrong?" Walsh turned, illuminating Knox with the flashlight beam.

"Knox, seek," Dani commanded.

The K–9 rose slowly, again nudged his nose into the fissure and backed up, returning to the sphinx pose.

Dani spun to look at the path from where they'd come. A thin stream of sunlight illuminated the entrance behind them.

Too far away.

"Knox is alerting to explosives."

"We have to get out of here!"

Dani took the lead, and they started to retrace their steps toward the exit.

An earsplitting explosion showered them with falling rocks.

Dani squatted, Walsh ducked beside her, shielding Dani and Knox with his massive frame.

Before she caught her breath, a second blast in front of them collapsed the cave entrance, thrusting them into darkness.

★ ★ ★

Walsh's ears rang, and the piercing sound dragged him into the depths of his memories. He returned to the Middle East, surrounded by gunfire and IEDs blasting in every direction. The desperate shouts of his comrades screaming orders and warnings.

Walsh gasped, hands stretched outward to ground himself. Anticipating the familiar grit of sand, he startled at the soft fur in his grasp.

Like a lifeline, he clung to the dog and allowed the sensation to stabilize him. The warmth of his coat under Walsh's fingers and the animal's rhythmic panting calmed him. His mind worked to sort between the past and present, filtering the atmosphere and smells. Memories of the endless days in the desert during his deployments overseas.

"Walsh."

Dani.

This wasn't Afghanistan.

He was in Iowa.

Sitting in a cave.

Be present. The silent command soothed him, and muscle memory kicked in. Walsh began combat breathing. *Inhale. Hold. Count to four. Exhale. Hold. Count to four.*

"Walsh! Are you hurt? Where are you?" Dani's voice reached to him like a beacon.

He blinked, realizing his eyes were wide open yet the darkness encroached on him in all directions. "Dani."

"Yes! Are you and Knox okay?" she repeated.

"We're fine. I think." Walsh tasted the dirt and grit. A wet swipe across his cheek made Walsh laugh. "Thanks, Knox."

"What did he do?" Dani asked, voice trembling.

"Offered reassurance." Walsh shifted. Pain radiated from his thigh, and he sucked in a breath. He winced, gently probing the area. Blood. He'd may have spoken too soon. "I'm guessing we found some of those missing military explosives," he said dryly, cringing at the badly timed joke.

"Unfortunately, I think you're right," Dani said.

Walsh slapped at the ground, grasping the flashlight beside his leg and pressed the button. Nothing happened. His fingers brushed the shattered lens. "Great."

"What's wrong?"

"I dropped the flashlight in the blast and broke it."

"Use your cell phone app," Dani suggested.

Impressed by her calmness, Walsh withdrew the device and activated the app, casting a soft glow into the space. Dust clouds filled the air as the rocks settled. At first glance, the area to the entrance was blocked by avalanched stone. Panic seized his chest, and he shoved it down, shifting into command mode. He got to his feet, gritting his teeth against the pain searing his thigh.

"Whoa! What happened?" Dani exclaimed, hurrying toward the light.

He glanced down at the shale piercing his leg. She leaned over, inspecting the injury. "Hold on. It's a puncture, but nowhere near the femoral artery. I'll pull it out." Dani eased off the backpack and withdrew an extra T-shirt Eliana must've packed. She really thought of everything.

"All right. Don't tell me when—"

Dani yanked out the piece and Walsh howled, biting back words his mother wouldn't have approved. She pressed the fabric hard against the wound. "Hold that."

Walsh did as she instructed, and within seconds, she'd fashioned a tourniquet and bandage. Her touch was strong and exhilarating.

The bulletproof vest he wore did nothing to protect his heart from the radical arrhythmia being around Dani inflicted. Walsh returned to combat breathing while focusing on the plan of escape. Anything to stop the dangerous thoughts his mind wanted him to venture into.

"Are you in a lot of pain?" Dani asked, her face too close to his. The floral scent of her hair wafted to him above the dusty air.

"I'm fine," he replied, avoiding the real question. He pushed back and, using the stone wall, got to his feet. "Stay here. I'll look for a way out of here."

Unable to see Dani in the ambient glow, Walsh moved to the crumbled rocks and spotted a sliver of sunlight. With all his strength, he pushed at the boulder. His leg raged in pain, draining his energy, but Walsh refused to surrender. He'd faced worse in prior missions. He repositioned, and after several unsuccessful attempts, shoved the massive rock aside, creating a gap. "It's a tight space, but big enough to wiggle through." At least Dani and Knox would. And they could bring back help if Walsh couldn't get through.

Dani approached. "That won't be large enough for us."

"Not for me, but you and Knox will fit," he replied.

"Negative." Dani motioned for him to hand her the phone.

He smirked, passing her the device. Using the flashlight beam, she inspected the area.

"Here, if you can move this rock, too, it'll give us space to get out."

Walsh did as she instructed, and the stack shifted. His heart stuttered. Would it collapse and trap them permanently? Finally, the shaking subsided. True to Dani's assessment, the change created a wide opening for them to squeeze through.

"Ladies first," Walsh said.

Dani eased through and Knox followed, making the escape look easy. Walsh sucked in his breath and partially inched into the tight fit. Then he stopped.

"What's wrong?" Dani asked.

"Nothing beyond a good diet and no more donuts," he grunted, pressing all his weight back against the stones. At last, he freed himself from the collapsed section.

But the getaway wasn't over.

Fallen rock and cave formations littered the ground, creating an obstacle course in the confined space. Aiming for the splintering sunlight, they exited in a rush, but remained within the tall stone walls surrounding it.

Walsh surveyed the area. Remnants of the explosives the bomber had used fluttered near the entrance.

"Was this an accidental explosion of the stolen/hidden munitions we happened upon at the right time and place, or was it a deliberate attempt to kill us?" Dani asked.

"No clue," Walsh grumbled. "Neither is acceptable." Except they'd either discovered the stash of missing evidence, now destroyed...or the other option meant they remained in danger.

Dani voiced his next thoughts. "If it was an attacker, do you think he stuck around?"

"Let me check first," Walsh said.

Once they stepped away from the cave, they were exposed to whoever waited for them. He inched from the stone formations, peering into the park. "I don't see anyone." Walsh took the lead, with Dani following.

They retraced their way on the hiking path. His leg throbbed, but he didn't complain.

The birds chirping cheerfully overhead were oblivious to the nearly devastating demise Walsh and Dani had just endured.

Both remained silent, with only their footfalls on the gravel as background noise.

The sight of the SUV brought immense relief until they drew closer.

Fury fueled Walsh's steps. The pain in his leg forgotten considering the vehicle's slashed tires. "You have got to be kidding me!"

He started to storm forward, instantly restricted by Dani's arm holding him back. "Let Knox check just in case there's an unwanted explosive in this SUV too."

"Good idea."

Dani knelt beside the K-9 and removed his leash. "Knox. Search."

His stumpy tail wagged in response, and Dani repeated the order. "Knox. Search!"

The Dobie mix went into work mode, sniffing the vehicle's perimeter. He made no indications before returning to Dani's side.

"He says it's clear," she interpreted.

A short measure of relief coursed through Walsh. "At least the bomber spared this SUV," he mumbled sarcastically. After calling 9-1-1 to report the incident, he said, "Help is on the way, but we're stuck until they arrive."

He popped the trunk, and they sat on the deck while he called the task force. Walsh set his phone between them, activating the speakerphone so Dani could interact as well.

Eliana answered the office line. "Heartland Fugitive—"

"We found some of the missing evidence and almost died. Again," Walsh barked.

"Sir?" Eliana inquired.

"Someone blew up the ice cave or we happened upon live munitions that accidentally went off while we were searching," Walsh said. "Either way, it nearly killed us."

Eliana gasped. "Are you okay?"

"Yes, we're fine."

"Walsh has a laceration on his left leg," Dani reported.

Why did she have to go telling them that? "No big deal."

Thankfully, Eliana didn't press the issue. "If it was an attack, how did the person know you were out there?"

"My question exactly," Walsh grumbled. "We'll be in touch after we've spoken with the responders. In the meantime, advise the team it's probable the bomber used part of the missing evidence in the cave. If it was coincidental, there could be more live munitions in there."

"Will do," Eliana said, disconnecting.

"You gotta learn to say 'hello' before starting a conversation," Dani said. Her tone was half teasing and though she tried to smile, it never fully reached her eyes.

"I keep hearing that. I focus on the goal and forget to be polite. Comes from years of barking orders." Again, his mind drifted back to his military service.

"To cops?"

"Yes, but first in the marines."

"You served? I never knew that."

"Joined after the Varmose investigation. I was the OIC Marine in the Middle East. Pleasantries aren't an option when you're constantly dodging danger."

"You were an officer in charge." Dani's expression sobered. "Wow. You're right. My bad."

And this wasn't the time to have this conversation. It would inevitably lead to other personal discussions like that of his widower status. Thankfully, his phone chimed with a text. He glanced down and read Eliana's message aloud for Dani. "'BOLO for Aiden DeLuca revealed a burned-up truck in the middle of a cornfield outside of Fremont.'"

"That's concerning."

"Yeah."

"Were there indicators of victims inside the vehicle?" Dani asked.

"No, it was empty," Walsh confirmed as he continued to read. He shook his head, responding to the message with a thumbs-up emoji, then pocketing the phone.

"Attempt to hide evidence?"

"Possibly." Walsh slid off the tailgate and leaned against the SUV.

Dani removed the backpack and withdrew two bottled waters, passing one to Walsh. "We could've died back there."

"But we didn't," Walsh reminded her.

"I cannot make careless decisions like that. If something happens to me, and Jayne doesn't recover..." Dani's voice cracked on the last word. She paused, then continued, "Who would take care of Tessa?" Her soft tone carried self-condemnation.

Walsh looked down, kicking at the dirt. "Dani, this isn't on you. I should've brought in reinforcements."

"You can't send a ten-person team to follow every lead," Dani argued. "A mother's intuition would've probably kicked in before entering the cave. Jayne wouldn't have acted that foolishly."

She was hard on herself. "But you're not Tessa's mother," Walsh replied. At the hurt that flashed over Dani's expression, he instantly regretted his comment. What had he said wrong? He'd meant to comfort her and instead he'd alienated her.

Attempting to right the offense, he said, "Tessa is safe at the Rock, which proves you were looking out for her best interest. She's with caregivers who have the time and capability for a consistent schedule too," Walsh said, trying to make the situation better.

"Understood." Dani's flattened lips and posture implied his efforts had made things worse. "Our jobs are high risk."

"Yes. So, let's take down this criminal for good." *Stop talking!* He was shoveling the hole deeper for himself.

"Right. Parenting belongs to those designed for it, which is why I've never become one," Dani snapped. "Taking down criminals is what I'm built for." Her declaration didn't match her stance. "Rather than drive back to Grand Island, I'd like to stay at the task force condo, if that's acceptable."

"Sure."

But a plan bloomed in Walsh's mind, and he grinned.

Sirens wailed, growing louder and interrupting the discussion.

He turned as strobing lights approached. "I'll handle the report."

They were going somewhere safe. Together.

Chapter Eleven

By the time they were finally on the road again, heading west to Nebraska, exhaustion overwhelmed Dani. Walsh's comment at the cave annoyed her with the itch of a mosquito bite. Consistency? How was she supposed to do that with a maniac determined to kill her? More so, she hated that she completely agreed with him.

She wasn't mom material, not in her current role. Sure, she could care for Tessa and provide for her basic necessities, but mothers had to have more than that ability. A mother needed to be available for her child. Dani's responsibilities and work hours interfered with that. She couldn't guarantee when she'd be home. She hesitated, her emotions whirling. Was she selfish to consider balancing her career and parenting?

The words tumbled in her brain, tormenting her. They'd nearly died.

And it confirmed the truth that she'd always

believed. The challenges of child-rearing and giving one hundred percent to her high-intensity job didn't mix. She'd experienced that growing up with a constantly worn-out single mother. She'd tried to be enough for everyone and never met the mark. Too often Dani suffered as her mother's career took precedence over their schedule. She'd never complained. If she'd been less of a burden, her father wouldn't have traded Dani and Mom in for another family. She'd never do anything to make her mom abandon her too.

But her child heart had missed her mother. The all-too-often times Dani had spent with a sitter or by herself had erected protective walls mortared by vows to never put anyone through that sorrow.

"In light of the attempts on our lives," Walsh said, interrupting her contemplations, "it's imperative we find a safe place to reevaluate this case. If the attacker is pursuing us, returning to the Rock draws attention to where Tessa is."

"I agree."

"Great. What're your views on staying with Marissa?"

"Your sister?" she asked incredulously. "Would she want that?"

"I took the liberty of asking her before proposing the idea to you." He lifted a hand in surrender. "Just in case. Marissa readily agreed on the assignment."

Dani contemplated the option. They had been friends years ago, but they'd lost touch. She knew nothing about Marissa's current life. As though sensing her hesitation, Walsh said, "If you're not comfortable with it, we'll come up with something else."

"No, it's not that." Dani measured her next words, not wanting to offend him. "It's just... We've had multiple attempts on our lives. You'd never forgive me if your only sister was hurt."

Walsh flicked a glance at her, meeting her eyes for several seconds before returning his attention to the road. "Marissa's tougher than you think. She was a marine before her recent retirement."

"Are we talking about the same person?" Dani asked, picturing the petite, soft-spoken woman who didn't fit the criteria of a hard-core military officer.

"Yep," he replied. "She's one tough brownie."

Dani grinned again at his misuse of the idiom. "Well, that puts a whole different spin on things."

"While assisting HFTF on another investigation, Marissa was almost killed," Walsh said.

"What?" Dani gasped. "When? How?"

"Long story. Suffice it to say, she came out stronger than ever and she's undeterred by fear."

Dani swallowed hard, humbled by the information. "Then, yes, I'd love to visit with Marissa and work on the case."

"Excellent."

She glanced at the backseat where Tessa's car seat would've been and sighed. "Are we meeting Marissa in Omaha?"

"Actually, I figured we'd go to our horse ranch in Ponca and set up a temporary BOO there."

"You want to make your place the base of operations for this case?" Dani clarified.

"Won't be the first time."

"Fine with me." She shrugged. "But we're covering serious miles."

"Get some rest," Walsh said. "I'll wake you when we arrive."

"No need to ask me twice." Dani leaned back and closed her eyes, dreaming of Tessa's sweet face and laughter.

Before she realized it, Walsh's voice drew her out of her peaceful sleep. "Dani."

She inched upward in her seat, stunned the sun was setting low in the sky. "How long was I out?"

"The remaining three hours of the drive." He smiled kindly. "But you needed it, besides Knox kept me company with his snoring as entertainment." He jerked his chin slightly toward the back.

Dani twisted around, spotting her dog stretched out on the seat. He sighed and yawned. "Good boy, Knox."

She surveyed the landscape as Walsh pulled onto a private lane surrounded by lush green rolling hills. Thick cottonwoods canopied overhead, and a split-rail fence bordered the acreage. He drove under an archway, suspended by log posts, sporting a sign that read Meadowlark Lane Ranch in black wrought-iron letters.

"This is yours?" Dani didn't bother disguising her awe.

"Well, me and Marissa. We share the property, though she maintains it full-time while working with our horses." Pride filled Walsh's tone.

He pulled up to a ranch-style house constructed of gray siding, stone accents and white trim. An inviting wraparound porch overshadowed the barn doors in front of the walkout basement. A variety of horses meandered behind the fence.

Walsh shut off the engine and Dani released Knox.

"Becky! You made it!"

Dani turned to see Marissa hurrying down the house steps toward them. She threw herself into Walsh's arms for a bear hug.

"I love that you still call him Becky." Dani circled the vehicle.

"Yeah, it's a treat," he groaned with a smile.

Marissa chuckled. "My favorite nickname for him because he hates it. It's great to see you!" She rushed to Dani and pulled her into a tight embrace. "You haven't aged a single day! Tell me how."

Dani felt her cheeks warm. "Flattery will get you everywhere. You look amazing!"

"It's the good life, living in bliss with them." Marissa gestured at the majestic horses. The animals had strolled closer to the fence, curious about the newcomers.

Dani smiled. "I can't wait to meet them all."

Marissa leaned down. "Come on in. Let's get you settled. I made dinner too."

"Best. Sister. Ever," Walsh replied.

"Tell me something I don't already know," Marissa teased. "Hey, Becky, maybe put your vehicle in the Morton building?"

"Good idea."

Dani reached for Knox's leash while Walsh slid behind the wheel and backed away from the house. She trailed Marissa up the steps and into the home. If the exterior had awed Dani, the interior dumbfounded her.

The welcoming open concept home had a stone fireplace centered in the living room, opposite a kitchen and dining area. Delicious aromas wafted to them, and hunger assailed Dani for the first time since the nightmare had begun.

Marissa led her down a hallway and gestured to a large bedroom with a queen bed.

Touched by her thoughtfulness, Dani settled onto the bed, realizing she had no clothes or personal supplies. She'd not intended for the Decorah trip to extend to overnights in Ponca. As though sensing her worry, Marissa said, "I stocked the bathroom with essentials, and there are clothes in the closet and dresser drawers."

"You thought of everything."

"Hopefully. Sounds like you all have been through the wringer." Marissa paused. "C'mon, Zink, out from under the bed."

Dani tilted her head, unsure what she was talking about. An orange flash of fur darted past Knox and out to the hallway. Knox turned and barked. "No!" Dani ordered. The dog whined but stayed in place. "Sorry, he's not used to being around cats. He won't hurt the kitty though."

"No worries. Zink can handle himself." Marissa winked. The sound of a door closed, and Knox woofed again. "Guess Becky's back. Let's go eat."

"Smells delicious." Dani stood. "I just need a minute to wash up, and I'll be right there."

"Sounds good. Make yourself at home." Marissa exited the room.

Thoughts of Tessa made Dani's heart squeeze. She missed the baby. "Take care of her, Lord," she prayed aloud.

As much as Dani had justified to Walsh why she couldn't or shouldn't be a mother to Tessa, she wondered if parenting was still a possibility. But if that happened, how would she explain to Tessa that her mother was dead because of Dani's failure to protect her?

Tessa would hate her.

Dani wouldn't blame her.

Morning arrived too soon, but Walsh didn't want to waste time sleeping when he needed to be working on the case. He and Marissa were both up before sunrise, and she'd already gone outside to work with the horses. He sat at the dining table, watching through the window, and sipping her thick–as–oil coffee.

Dani hadn't emerged from her bedroom. She was probably still asleep, and that brought great relief to him. At least they'd rested without further attacks. He pushed back from the table and strolled closer to the window. In the pasture, Marissa rode Royal. The beautiful thoroughbred galloped with incredible grace. He was their first rescue. His previous owners had abandoned him in a kill pen after they'd gotten all they wanted from him. Clueless idiots who'd failed to see the majestic creature had so much life left in him. Fond memories of their dad's gentle but strong instruction on equine care returned to Walsh. Their parents had been deceased a long time, but he'd never stopped missing them.

Royal's pedigreed status hadn't changed, regardless of his age. His identity remained the same. Walsh paused, considering the similarities. Had he placed too much on his role as a marshal and not on his value as a person?

Walsh walked outside and leaned on the fence, watching his sister ride. Her thick auburn hair bounced around her shoulders. A grin spread across her lips when she saw him, and she trotted in his direction. Royal's hoofs pounded a staccato rhythm against the soft ground. When they reached him, Marissa pulled back on the reins and slid off the animal. She rubbed his neck. "Good job, Royal!"

The horse whinnied his appreciation.

"Feel like riding?" Marissa approached him.

"I would, but my mind is all over the place."

"That's when processing your musings is most productive." Marissa climbed up the fence and perched on the top rail.

"You only do that so you can look down on me," Walsh teased.

"So." She stuck out her tongue playfully. At six-foot-four-inches tall, Walsh towered over his five-foot-two baby sister. "How're you doing with the unexpected reunion?" Walsh flicked his gaze to Marissa, and she waved him off. "Don't even deny it. I can always read you, big brother."

"It's weird." He sighed. "At times, the guilt over Varmose's case hits me with terrible force. But when I look at Dani, I can't help wondering what could've been." His confession brought a release he'd not expected. Telling Marissa about his confusing feelings helped. That was something he could never do with his team as their commander.

"I figured Tessa might also trigger some of those old emotions."

"It does. Reminds me how I failed Gwen and lost any chance of having a family. I try to keep a distance, but she's a sweet baby." He frowned, kicking at a rock. "We're dodging a bomber, and I'm doing a lousy job of protecting Tessa and Dani."

"Are you sure Dani wants your protection?" Marissa asked. "Seems to me she's more than capable."

"Except whenever I enter the picture, I ruin everything for her." He shoved his hands into his jeans' pockets. "I've got a propensity to sweep the carpet out from underneath her."

Marissa chuckled. "First, it's a rug, not a carpet."

"Whatever." He swatted playfully at her.

"Second, Becky, you did your job taking down Varmose. He was corrupt. Telling Dani you were conducting an internal affairs investigation would've compromised your career and your case. She understands that. Especially now as a police chief."

"Does she?"

Marissa tilted her head. "Did she say otherwise?"

"Not specifically." Walsh reconsidered their conversations regarding Varmose. "I don't regret arresting that jerk. I can't stand anyone who abuses the badge. But I should've warned her. To protect Dani."

"You were a young detective. You made decisions with the information you had at that time. But I concur one hundred percent about Varmose abusing his position." Marissa sighed. "That's ancient history. Is that what's really bugging you?"

"Yes and no. It's playing into this whole mess. I can't stand that someone is trying to hurt her, and I can't stop it." *It adds to my inadequacies as a protector.* "I messed up and didn't shield her then, and I'm doing the same thing now," he confessed. "Multiple attacks from an assassin, her department's declining view of her, and the fallout from this case is too much." Walsh glanced down, remembering the way the GIPD personnel had spoken about Dani. "Not to mention, her stubbornness about Jayne is a replay of Varmose. She's got no one else, just like Tessa. I want to make all the bad go away for them both." And his heart's cry for a second chance with Dani beckoned for his attention.

"And…"

"Being around the baby with the retirement clock ticking is giving me a cruel reminder of what I never had. Remembering dreams Gwen and I lost."

"That's understandable." Marissa glanced past him at Royal, still trotting happily nearby. "But Gwen's situation was out of your hands."

"Was it? I didn't have to stay gone. I was busy chasing my ambitions, climbing the military ladder. Just like my goal in taking down Varmose clouded my judgment." He leaned with his back against the fence, facing the pond in the distance. "Seems my aspirations have done more damage than good. I should've come home when I knew Gwen was struggling."

"And if you had, would your presence alone have given her the will to live?"

At his sister's words, he turned.

Marissa's cerulean eyes bore into him. "Gwen ended her life. You didn't do it to her, nor were you the reason."

He snorted. "Right, tell that to her family."

"You're not responsible for their reactions, either," Marissa replied. "They were hurting, and people lash out when their emotions are super raw. You're allowed to keep living."

"I don't blame them." He paced a path in front of her. "Even if I could move on, how would I get past the memories of Gwen and the emotional tsunami attack her family brought down on me? Honestly, they're probably right that it's a good thing I never got to be a father. I was a lousy husband."

"You were serving your country, Becky." Marissa hopped down, standing in his way. "You cannot be on the battlefield facing real enemies with your mind on your troubled wife. There's no shame in that."

"Except I wasn't there for Gwen when she needed me, and then it was too late. And now my career is ending soon, and what do I have to show for it?" Walsh shook his head. "I'll be living out here talking to horses in my old age."

Marissa laughed. "Well, you won't be alone. I'll be right here with you."

"No way, you're still young and will have a life beyond this." He gestured toward the open spaces.

"So could you."

"Nope, it's too late."

"Wow, are you also stressing about world peace and global warming?" Marissa's eyes twinkled.

"Whatever." He swatted at her again.

"You're a powerful man, Beckham Walsh, but you are not in control of the universe. Past, present, or future. You certainly aren't the regulator of Gwen, Dani, or Tessa's futures. You can't keep trying to protect them right out of the Will of God."

His head whipped up. "What's that supposed to mean?"

"You're no one's savior. That responsibility belongs to God alone. You didn't kill Gwen. As awful and tragic as her death was for all of us, it's not yours to bear."

Walsh looked down.

"In respect to Dani, sometimes God uses the pain and hardships in our lives to mold us," Marissa said. "You want to keep running interference, so Dani and Tessa have no problems. Have you considered that God is using those things to strengthen them and build their character?"

He gaped at her. "You're suggesting I leave them exposed to a killer?"

"Of course not." She cuffed his shoulder. "Protection detail is part of your job. The only way to truly do that is to identify this mysterious shooter/bomber/assassin after you all. But that's not the protection you're talking about."

"Ugh, I hate that you know me so well." Walsh scrubbed a hand over his head. "Dani hates me for not telling her about Varmose."

"Talk to her about it. She's not just a cop, Becky! Dani's the chief of police. She'll understand the position you faced." Marissa tugged at his sleeve. "And while you're at it, tell her how you've never stopped loving her."

Walsh blinked. "What? When did I ever say that?"

Marissa grinned conspiratorially. "She's standing at the window. Let's eat breakfast."

"Go on." Walsh's heart drummed hard against his chest. "I gotta ponder all this."

"Chicken." Marissa strolled past him toward the house.

He wandered the lane to the pond. Had he brought Dani here to cocoon her? If he had, was that wrong? It was his job to protect others.

But Marissa's comments lingered.

He walked to the small dock, studying the mirror-still water. Gwen had died twenty-two years ago. He didn't deserve to be happy. Wasn't that what her family had said to him at the funeral? And he'd accepted those words as his fate.

Yet Dani's return, looking more beautiful than she had when they'd dated thirty years ago, had awakened his heart. Marissa was dead on, Dani had demonstrated how much stronger she was now than when she'd worked for Varmose.

He'd heard rumors that she'd left the department after the chief's arrest and had figured she hadn't wanted to be tied to the corrupt behavior. Who could blame her? Dani exuded fortitude and confidence far beyond what he'd imagined she would. They'd faced a bomber/assassin while caring for Tessa. No effortless task. And she'd done it well. Had those earlier trials helped her to deal with today?

Walsh bowed his head, offering a prayer for wisdom and confessing his doubts and fears. He concluded it with the most terrifying words he'd ever spoken.

"Lord, use me how You deem fit. Regardless of the outcome."

Chapter Twelve

Dani settled into a chair.

"Hope you're hungry." Marissa placed plates of fruit, eggs, bacon, and potatoes in the center of the dining table. "I never have the privilege of cooking for others, so I might've overdone it a bit."

Dani laughed. "As long as you promise not to tell anyone when I stuff myself."

Marissa smirked. "No problem. Coffee?"

"I'll get it." Dani walked to the brewer, snagging a mug on the way. "Is Walsh joining us?"

"When he's done wandering the grounds."

Dani stifled her disappointment, baffled why she cared. That wasn't true. She'd looked forward to seeing him first thing this morning. Being around him was comfortable, and it all felt right.

Marissa sat opposite her. "How're you holding up?"

"Last night was a reprieve. I feel like a new person." She spooned food onto her plate.

"I hear that."

Dani hadn't missed the way Walsh had averted his gaze when he'd caught her looking out the window before walking away from the house. Biting into the bacon, she teased, "Is it bad if there's nothing left for him?"

"Nope. You snooze, you lose."

"I'm glad to see you didn't get your brother's cliché confusion problem."

Marissa laughed. "He's a hoot." She leaned back in her seat, both hands cradling her coffee mug. "Becky's pouting because I scolded him."

"Really, about what?" At Marissa's pause, Dani said, "Sorry. I'm nosy."

"I reminded him his macho save-the-world complex was unnecessary."

"Comes with the job, I suppose."

"Partially. Mostly, it's guilt for not being the ultimate protector." Marissa sipped her coffee. "Becky keeps that grudge alive by nursing it."

A twinge of conscience nudged Dani. "We stopped talking after he arrested my Cortez PD chief. You already know that."

"Some."

Dani longed to avoid the conversation. Out

of respect for Marissa, she forced herself to remain seated. "Varmose's corruption tanked his career and landed him in jail. Imagine my surprise when I learned the person I trusted was a criminal behind a badge."

"No kidding."

"That wasn't the worst. When my coworkers discovered Walsh and I were dating, they turned their hatred at me, assuming I was involved in the sting."

"No." Marissa leaned forward. "Dani! What did you do?"

"They made my life miserable. When I couldn't take any more, I quit." She grabbed a grape. "The Cortez PD hate squad tried badmouthing me to other agencies as a backstabber. Thankfully, their tactics didn't work. News spreads fast among law enforcement, and Varmose's nefarious activities didn't involve me, which helped my situation. I worked in smaller towns before Lincoln PD hired me."

"Is Becky aware of this?"

Dani shrugged, absently pushing food around her plate. "Anyone within a forty-mile radius would've heard."

"That explains it. Becky joined the military

after the takedown. He blamed himself for not telling you in advance."

Dani sat straighter. "Why didn't he warn me?"

"He understood your position and propensity to be loyal—"

"To a fault."

"Exactly. If he'd told you, you'd notify Varmose, jeopardize the case, and Walsh's career." Marissa sipped her coffee. "Ironically, he resigned from the agency, anyway."

"Wow." Dani sighed. "He's right. I would've told Varmose, because I stupidly believed in his innocence…until I saw the evidence and he openly confessed." She shook her head. "If I was in Walsh's shoes, I would've done the same."

"That introduction into IAs took a toll on him." Marissa referenced internal affairs investigations. "That was his first and last one. You're nobody's friend when you're the cop working cases involving other cops."

Dani hadn't considered Walsh's sacrifice. Ultimately, doing the right thing at an extreme price.

"He relocated to North Carolina, met and married Gwen, then deployed overseas soon after."

That got Dani's attention. "Walsh was married?" Did the comment sound as jealous as the words tasted?

"He's never told you about Gwen?"

"No." Dani's chest tightened at the woman's name and accompanying unfamiliar emotion. Jealousy.

Marissa sighed. "Their relationship was tough from the start. Gwen hated the marines kept him gone for long stretches of time. She constantly pleaded for him to return stateside. He used up his leave trying to appease her, but it's the military. You can't turn in a sick day request in the middle of a war." Marissa forked potatoes, and Dani eagerly waited for her to continue. "Gwen struggled with mental illness and refused to seek help. She took her own life while Becky was deployed."

Dani gasped, putting a hand over her mouth. Her throat tightened. She'd put her anger and disdain on Walsh when he'd already suffered so much. Her heart ached for him. "Poor Walsh!"

"Yep. Then her family tore after Becky with a vengeance. Tried making his life miserable. They blamed him and said a better husband would've helped his wife. Which, of course, is a lie. Walsh did all he could."

Dani sat dumbfounded. She'd misjudged

Walsh. As though sensing her shift in emotions, Knox nudged her hand and laid his head in her lap. "Hey, sweetie."

"He's in tune with you."

"Honestly, Knox is a great comfort dog." She stroked his short fur.

"Nothing wrong with that," Marissa said.

"Maybe someday I'll train those types of dogs." Dani paused. Where had that thought come from? "I didn't mean to interrupt what you were saying. Please, go on."

Marissa finished swallowing. "Gwen's family tormented Becky. Contacting him with reminders of her and dishing out guilt. They said he didn't deserve happiness."

"That's ludicrous. It wasn't his fault!"

"Becky accepted the lies." Marissa shrugged. "He never dated again. That's why he's a hopeless workaholic."

"I never knew." Dani picked at a strawberry on her plate. "He processed his grief by avoidance."

"Basically."

"Anybody would understand his position. Besides, a man's emotional wounds endears him to women," Dani thought aloud. "A woman's repels men." Thus, why she'd maintained her relationship paralysis.

"Not sure I agree," Marissa contended. "Careers like the military and law enforcement encourage the façade of impenetrable strength. Nobody goes through life unscathed by pain or disappointment. There's nothing wrong with admitting where we are, but sometimes people assume vulnerability and humility are synonymous."

"One feeds the other?"

"No." Marissa shook her head. "Humility isn't weakness, it's recognizing our deepest need for God."

Dani considered the words. "How long ago did all this happen with Gwen?"

"Over twenty years," Marissa said. "There's a lot Becky should've shared with you."

"Maybe if I'd given him a safe place to talk, he would've."

"Been hard on him?" Marissa asked with the confidence of someone already familiar with the answer.

"Yeah. I owe him an apology." Dani looked up.

Walsh leaned against the kitchen entrance.

"Perfect opportunity," Marissa whispered. "I

need to check on the horses." She rushed out of the room.

"You overheard us?" Dani asked.

"Yes." Walsh crossed to the sink and washed his hands before sliding into a chair beside her. "She shouldn't have told you all that."

"I'm glad she did." Dani met his gaze. Compassion swelled for the man who'd tried to do the right thing many times, only to be hurt. "I'm sorry for the pain you've endured."

Defeat seemed to press on his shoulders. "I brought it on myself."

"No, you didn't." The condemnation she'd held against him vanished. There was so much more to Beckham Walsh than she'd realized. Before Dani realized it, she blurted, "My ex-husband claimed he didn't want children. He pretended to support my career pursuits, then later walked out on me for another woman with whom he built a family." Dani stared at her fork.

"Wow." Walsh touched her hand, quickly withdrawing. "Did you want children?"

Dani shrugged. "I suppose some women do. I saw the way my mom struggled as a working parent and didn't think I could do it."

Walsh didn't comment as he piled a plate high with eggs and bacon. A piece of meat landed on the floor, and he leaned down to grab it. Knox rushed over, snatching the treat. "Beat me to it." He laughed and sat up.

"Sorry about that. He's well-trained, but he's still a dog." Dani met his gaze, grateful for the interruption. She caught a glimpse of yellow stuck to his forehead and stifled a grin.

"What?"

"You must've brushed your head on your plate." She leaned closer, and using a napkin, wiped away the scrambled egg. "You had a little egg on your face."

He grinned. "That seems to happen a lot lately."

Dani smiled, not moving. She'd forgotten how handsome he was when she wasn't looking at him through eyes of disdain and blame. "Thank you for sharing your past with me."

He tilted his head. "In all fairness, my sister did that."

Their gaze lingered. Her breath quickened and Dani inched closer, inhaling his aftershave. She lifted her chin.

The doorbell rang, and Knox barked and hurried to the door. The combination had Walsh and Dani flinging backward in their seats.

Her focus reverted to her dog. Had he saved

her from making a huge mistake or interrupted something wonderful?

"I'll be right back." Walsh excused himself.

Dani fixed her gaze on her breakfast. "I need to remind myself where I am," she mumbled.

In the middle of a case where her friend might die, orphan her daughter, or end up incarcerated. The outlandishness of the moment hit Dani. She'd become the one Jayne would blame.

Just as Dani had done to Walsh.

Ironic.

Knox waited for Walsh. The dog had saved him from making a huge mistake. Dani knew about Gwen. No woman wanted a man who'd failed to protect his ill wife. With a sigh, he tugged open the door.

Riker and his Dutch shepherd, Ammo, stood on the other side.

A perfectly timed visual reminder of his responsibilities.

"Dani's in danger," Riker whispered.

Walsh stepped outside, closing the door. They sat in the chairs on the front porch.

"That's already established," Walsh grunted, stretching out his legs.

"No, more so. Eliana located intel on the dark web that someone put a hit out on Dani."

"What?" Walsh bellowed and then lowered his voice. "Drill deeper and find out who!"

"She's trying, but it's difficult. The creep covered his tracks." Riker leaned against the railing. Ammo laid down with a sigh.

Walsh sat forward, elbows on his knees.

"Are you holding up okay, boss?"

He appreciated the concern, but a leader didn't have the luxury of falling apart in front of his team. "As well as expected." He scrubbed his palm over his face. "We need a lead, and fast."

Riker, like the rest of the task force, understood that once a case went cold, it took substantial reviving to keep it active.

"We're working nonstop."

Walsh exhaled a deep breath. "HFTF is the best. We'll solve this. I just abhor the in-between time."

A cardinal sang overhead, and the crisp morning air held a scent of lilacs, reminding Walsh how he loved this place. In the distance, several horses meandered in the east pasture.

"Sir, all due respect—"

"I hate that phrase," Walsh grumbled good-naturedly.

Riker chuckled, sitting in the chair beside him. "Jayne Bardot's guilty for the missing evidence. Only her motive is questionable. With or without Aiden, she's the strongest connection. We're wasting time looking for something that's right in front of our faces. Dani's trying to defend her, but everything points to Jayne and Aiden as cohorts. Why aren't we pressing charges instead of stalling based on her surmised innocence?"

"I hope your team didn't assume that about you when someone framed you for murder," Dani said.

Walsh and Riker twisted around to see Dani standing beside the open window. She shifted, opening the door. "All I've asked is that we don't make assumptions without fully investigating this case."

Riker looked down, and Walsh's neck warmed. "Riker, Marissa's out in the barn. Would you update her and ask her to join us?"

Like a shot, Riker and Ammo hurried down the steps, eager to escape the uncomfortable situation.

Walsh stood, ushering Dani into the house. "Riker means no disrespect or harm. He speaks what's on his mind."

"I appreciate candidness, but if your team has Jayne charged and convicted, I'm not sure they're the best to handle her case."

Walsh clamped his jaw tight to keep from re-taliating. He knew she didn't mean that. "What did you overhear?"

"Enough. Someone's willing to pay for my death?"

"Yes."

Marissa, Riker, and Ammo returned to the house, interrupting the conversation.

Dani moved toward the porch rail, gazing out with her back to him. "Are we safe here?"

"It's best if you and Walsh go elsewhere," Riker replied. "I'll provide protection detail for Marissa."

"Negative." Marissa shook her head. "I'm not going anywhere."

"Did the assassination order mention Tessa?" Dani asked.

"No. Based on our intel, you're the mark," Riker explained.

Dani exhaled relief. She could bear the danger if Tessa wasn't the target. Walsh paced the kitchen.

"Eliana's working on the source of the hit," Riker said. "Honestly, it's not looking good. The person used the dark web, bouncing their IP address across Russia."

"Great," Dani groaned.

"We still have no leads on Aiden DeLuca. The dude vanished."

"Nobody disappears. Find him," Walsh said, realizing he sounded like a movie villain. "We'll head to the Rock."

"Roger that."

Walsh pulled his sister into a hug. "If there's any sign of danger, please don't be stubborn. Get out of here."

"I'll be fine," Marissa contested. "Finish this case. I can take care of myself."

"Humor me." He embraced her. "Do you need anything before we leave?"

"Nope. We're good."

Dani hugged Marissa goodbye, and they loaded Knox into the SUV.

Once they'd driven several miles from the ranch, Dani said, "I won't run from an invisible assassin. Tessa's the priority. Are you certain she's safe?"

"We're praying so."

"I hope it's enough." *Lord, I need You.*

They'd driven several miles from the ranch when Walsh spotted a car billowing smoke on the shoulder of the road. The raised hood concealed the person before it.

"We should offer to assist."

"Armed." This could be a trap. Walsh holstered his gun, and Dani mimicked him.

He parked behind the sedan, activating the hazard lights, though the road was void of travelers. They exited the vehicle.

"Knox, stay," Dani said.

They cautiously approached. "Need help?" Walsh hollered.

A man stepped to the side, revealing himself and brandishing a pistol.

He aimed and shot at them.

Walsh and Dani dove for cover. They returned fire before bolting for the SUV. A second sedan screeched to a halt, blocking the SUV's driver's door. Two more assailants tumbled out of the vehicle.

Someone had set them up for an ambush!

Chapter Thirteen

Knox clawed at the window, whining and barking.

Walsh and Dani returned shots again, shifting between the vehicles, trapping them.

Dani fired at the assailant beside the car in front of them. He yelled obscenities, confirming her bullet had made contact.

"I got him!" she hollered. "He's getting away!"

The sedan in front of Walsh's SUV sped from the scene in the opposite direction, tires squealing.

Walsh fired, shattering the driver's-door window of the vehicle behind them. Dani hit the grill, emitting steam.

"Go!" the driver of the second sedan yelled.

Both men dove into their car and reversed at high speed before swinging into a J-turn, racing from the scene. A wake of dust plumed in their path.

Walsh and Dani stood watching for a couple of seconds.

"Those guys orchestrated that ambush!"

"Was the hit a way to get us away from the ranch?" Dani asked.

"I'd say that's probable." He ushered Dani and Knox back into the SUV. "If they couldn't find where we were staying, they waited us out."

"Still, how did they know we'd be out here?"

Walsh didn't reply.

Knox leaned toward her, whining. "It's okay." Dani tried calming the frenzied animal, stroking his fur.

"Please call this into local PD while I get the team on the line."

Dani nodded, dialing 9-1-1. When she finished, Walsh was already in discussion with the task force on speakerphone.

"That's seriously disconcerting," Elijah replied.

"We're stuck here until LEOs arrive to take our report," Walsh advised.

"I'll stay here with Marissa, and we'll amp up the watch here at the ranch," Riker said.

"I'm also remote-monitoring the ranch cameras," Eliana noted.

"You have surveillance equipment on your property?" Dani asked aloud, regretting the interruption.

"Yes, after Marissa's attack, we added several, along with other safety features," Walsh replied.

"I've confirmed Meadowlark Lane's location and address are untraceable to you or Marissa's names," Eliana reported.

Dani would love to know how the computer tech had managed that move.

"Good job. My guess is our ambush was part of the paid hit on Dani," Walsh said. "Please continue digging."

"Roger that," Eliana replied. "Dani?"

"Yes?" Dani leaned closer.

"I have an update for you too. Were you aware that Jayne named you as Tessa's guardian in her living will?"

Dani gaped. "What?" She closed her eyes, absorbing the weight of the information. With Jayne's prognosis growing worse, she had to face the possibility that her friend might not live. "I... I'm not sure what to say." Her phone chimed with a text, and the team's voices faded into the background as she read the words.

Aiden DeLuca dies if you don't give me back the guns Jayne stole from me.

The screen displayed No Caller ID, and the number comprised only five digits. She snapped a screenshot and sent it to Eliana.

"Eliana, are you seeing this?" Dani asked.

A gasp came over the line. "Yes."

"Care to fill us in?" Walsh leaned closer.

Dani passed him the cell, and the color drained from his face.

"Why is there no real phone number?" she asked.

"The person is using a messaging program to conceal it," Eliana replied.

The team rapid-fired questions.

"Is it a trap?" Walsh asked.

"Did Aiden take the guns and run?" Tiandra asked.

"That makes sense," Chance replied.

"It stands to reason the text is from Enrique Prachank," Skyler said.

What did that mean for Jayne? Dani withheld the question.

"I think Sky is right," Elijah said. "He's got the most to lose here, and we've already connected him to some of the missing evidence."

"The message says Jayne stole the weapons," Graham pointed out. "Is he implicating her or throwing her under the bus after she helped him?"

"We don't know that she was working with Prachank," Dani snapped, instantly regretting her emotional response. Riker's words bounced to the forefront of her mind, and she couldn't deny he was correct. She had lost focus for the sake of loyalty.

A second message pinged.

Come alone or he dies.

"Aiden is the only link we have," Dani said.

"But we don't have the guns," Elijah interjected. "You can't show up there empty-handed."

"We'll figure it out. We need Prachank," Dani replied.

"We could meet you and establish our own ambush," Riker said.

"Negative," Walsh said. "Riker, stay with Marissa until I release you. If this is a trap, we're not taking any chances."

"I concur," Dani said, reading her response aloud as she typed it.

Fine. Jayne told me everything. If you harm Aiden, no deal.

"Well done," Walsh said.

Drive to Iowa. Will send directions along the way. Share your location via your phone app.

"He's having us follow breadcrumbs," Dani said.

"He's ensuring we can't get there ahead of him." Walsh slammed his hand on the dashboard.

Knox poked his head through the divider.

"Sorry, buddy." Walsh stroked the dog's fur.

"We have Knox for help, too," Dani replied. "I'm going."

"*We're* going," Walsh said emphatically.

"But how will you show up without being seen?" Elijah asked.

"I'll figure it out on the way," Walsh quipped.

"Keep your phones on so we have GPS tracking," Eliana said.

"Roger that. We'll be in touch," Dani said.

Walsh straightened. "First, we pray."

The group's voices rose in prayer for safety, protection, wisdom and resolution. At the collective amen, Dani felt empowered. They disconnected just as local law enforcement arrived to take their report of the shooting.

"I'll handle this and get us on the road," Walsh said, exiting the vehicle.

Dani twisted around, facing Knox. "Did Jayne really do this?" she wondered aloud. "And how am I supposed to be a mother for Tessa if Jayne doesn't survive?"

Knox offered his tender, compassionate gaze.

What choice did she have? Jayne had listed Dani as Tessa's guardian, transferring the complete responsibility of her only child to Dani. Had she updated her will before their most recent conversation? The promise Dani had made to her friend to care for Tessa suddenly fell into place. Jayne's trust in Dani spoke of the love and friendship between the women. Tessa was the most precious part of Jayne's heart. If she died, Dani owed it to her to ensure Tessa's happiness and health.

Yet, the insecurity creeped into her mind again, reminding Dani of her failures in marriage with Mark. She wasn't mother material.

Instead, she'd make the ultimate sacrifice and find the best home in the world for Tessa, with proper parents who'd devote their lives to caring for her. That was the only correct option.

Her job was to ensure justice for Jayne, regardless of the outcome. She refused to believe Jayne had willingly gotten involved with a known fugitive criminal for the sake of weapons trafficking. Jayne was innocent in this, or at the very least, her involvement was based on coercion or threats. She wouldn't endanger Tessa.

Still, Jayne had thought ahead, naming Dani in her living will. Had Jayne feared for her life? Did twentysomething women make wills? She'd never considered that when she was Jayne's age. *Lord, please heal her.*

Years of working in law enforcement had worn on her. She was tired of dealing with the dregs of society. Maybe being a full-time mother to Tessa was possible. She could take an early retirement.

She glanced up, catching her reflection in the visor mirror. Hope, dread, and fears mingled in her mind. Husbands left, but just as she'd stayed faithfully by her mother's side, Tessa might do the same. Her adopted daughter wouldn't abandon her.

Resolved, Dani closed her eyes and prayed for the courage to walk through her biggest fear. If she faced that hurdle, she'd take care of the innocent baby who had stolen her heart.

★ ★ ★

Dread consumed Walsh. For the hundredth time since Dani received the kidnapper's text, he debated turning around. "We should reevaluate. Let's slow down and develop a solid plan rather than cower to this maniac's demands."

"What other options are there?" Dani argued. "If we don't comply, Aiden DeLuca dies. Worse, Tessa, Jayne, and I ultimately remain in danger. We've got one shot at taking this guy down. It's the first time he's crawled out from under his rock. Our phones have GPS capabilities and Knox has an AirTag on his collar. Your team's tracking our location."

At the mention of his name, the Dobie mix popped his head between the divider doors.

Walsh couldn't dispute Dani's reasoning. "This is probably a trick. When Prachank discovers we don't have what he wants, things will get ugly."

"We'll convince him we took precautions as our insurance. We haven't got the weapons, but we'll lead him to them. Then HFTF does the takedown." Dani's phone chimed again. "Turn on Highway 20 eastbound."

Walsh complied with the instructions randomly forcing them on and off county roads and highways. "He's playing games."

"He's using the share location app to trace us. The ridiculous zigzagging ensures we're not being followed and that we don't call ahead for backup."

Again, Dani's logical reasoning made sense.

"Should I worry that you think like a criminal?" Walsh teased.

"Maybe." She joked and glanced down at a new text message. "Turn into Boone and drive to Ledges State Park," she instructed Walsh.

"He's taking us to an open space?"

"Ledges has trails and bluffs."

"High ground to oversee his prey. Great." He didn't hide his sarcasm.

She read the next text aloud. "'Park at the Ledges' lower lot until I give you further instructions.'"

Walsh pulled into the empty parking area. Not surprising, considering it was a weekday morning, but disconcerting, nonetheless.

Dani texted, advising they'd arrived.

"I don't like this."

"You've made that clear," she quipped. Her phone chimed again.

Hike Lost Lake Trail and wait under the shelter.

They exited the SUV and Walsh leashed Knox while Dani snagged a portable bowl and bottled water from the team's supply box. She tucked the items into her purse and they trekked the path. Humidity hung thick and their boots crunched on the dirt. At the divide in the trail, they paused. Stone steps led upward while the other direction offered a descent around the lake.

"Any preference?" Dani asked.

"Higher ground always," Walsh said.

Ascending the narrow steps surrounded by thick foliage, neither spoke, listening for danger. Birds trilled happily from the copse of trees.

Signs depicting Lost Lake Trail guided them, taking them on a shift in direction as they made the descent around a small body of water.

"Resembles a big pond." Dani swatted at a swarm of assaulting mosquitos.

Soft green moss blanketed the lake and low-hanging tree limbs hovered over the calm water. "That's too generous. It's swamplike," Walsh said.

A metal shelter with a table stood on the opposite side.

"Let's do a little recon before we move under that," Walsh suggested. "Have Knox search for explosives."

"Good idea."

They parted, scooting into the foliage. Knox cleared the area without issue, concluding their mission, and they entered the shelter.

"The silence is unnerving." Dani tugged Knox closer.

A dragonfly buzzed past Walsh's face. Frogs croaked in the distance, filling the atmosphere with their calls.

Dani filled the collapsible travel bowl from her purse with water. "I'm grateful your team stores canine supplies in all the vehicles."

Walsh smiled.

A message dinged on Dani's phone. She passed the device to Walsh.

Where are the guns?

He was watching them. Not that Walsh expected anything less.

Dani replied.

Will take you to them.

Again, the cell pinged with a text and her eyes widened as she read it. She turned it to Walsh. "We need to get out of here."

The message—You lied!—included a picture of Walsh and Dani standing beside the lake.

The angle implied Prachank stood on the same level as they did.

"Get to higher ground," Walsh said.

Gunshots exploded, rupturing tree bark next to them.

Walsh pulled Knox closer, and the trio dashed behind a large boulder.

They bolted up the narrow passage bordering the lake to the stone steps. Bullets flew around them from what seemed like random directions.

Dani cried out.

Walsh turned to see her splayed out on the path.

"Are you hit?"

"I tripped, I'm fine! Go!"

He helped Dani to her feet, and they resumed their escape.

"Wait!" Dani withdrew her phone and deactivated the location sharing app. "Okay."

Walsh spotted a lesser traveled trail, descending to the Des Moines River. Stone walls and crevices offered hiding places.

They hiked down the steep embankment to a large opening in the rock. Ducking inside, they repositioned to peek out.

"Is he gone?" Dani kept Knox beside her.

The stillness lingered around them.

"I think so." Walsh withdrew his phone and frowned. "Of course, I have no reception here."

"How long do we wait?"

"If he's watching for us to materialize, let him believe he lost us."

Birds resumed their nature calls and, after twenty minutes, they emerged from their hiding place.

"Use the river to trace back to the parking area," Walsh suggested. "If he's waiting on the path, he'll trap us."

"Agreed."

They trekked the gravelly embankment, searching for purchase on the sandy shore. Frothy scum plagued the water, and the cliffs concealed them if the assailant stalked from overhead.

They reached an opening between the bank and river. Climbing through the thick foliage to the path, they paused. Knox sniffed a leafy bush.

Walsh leaned closer, detecting what had captured the dog's attention. "It's a casing!"

He used a stick to collect and pocket the evidence.

They cautiously trekked to the main road and finally reached the parking lot. Someone had shattered the windows and broken into the SUV.

"Thanks for not slashing these tires," Walsh mumbled sarcastically.

"I'd call this in, but I have no cell phone reception."

"Take pictures to document the scene."

They worked together, capturing images on their phones.

Walsh started the engine, voicing aloud a prayer of thanks that the attacker hadn't messed with the vehicle's mechanics. He cleaned a place for Knox while Dani did the same, brushing off the glass from the seats.

"Hey, Walsh?"

"Yeah?"

Knox sniffed at the section between the door and the floorboard. Walsh used his cell's flashlight app, illuminating a small piece of yellowed paper. Snapping a picture first, he donned a latex glove from the equipment stash and withdrew the sheet. "It's ten digits." He held it up for her to see.

"I recognize the 202-area code. It's a Washington, DC, number. Good job, Knox," Dani cooed. "Let's get out of here and call it."

They loaded into the SUV and drove out of the park.

Once Walsh's cell showed service, he said, "Please dial the team on speakerphone."

"We lost track of you!" Eliana exclaimed when she answered.

"We had no reception in the area." Walsh offered a quick explanation of events.

"That's why he chose the location," Elijah observed. "He planned to trap you and steal the weapons."

"He made them hike, allowing time to break into the SUV," Riker replied.

"If he intended to kill us, he had the opportunity," Dani said.

"Shooting is Prachank's MO," Walsh said. "Breaking into the SUV is not."

"Prachank is more in-your-face," Tiandra agreed. "He's likely to attack you on the road, as those creeps did earlier."

"Nothing registers with this case," Dani grunted.

"We're returning with the casing," Walsh replied. "Skyler, you'll need to run it ASAP."

"Roger that," she responded.

Walsh continued, "Riker, try to convince Marissa to go with you to the Rock. If she refuses—"

"Actually, sir," Riker interrupted, "Marissa already booted me off the ranch. I'm at the Rock."

"I wish that surprised me," Walsh groused.

Dani smirked.

"We're monitoring the ranch's video feed," Eliana assured.

"Thank you," Walsh said.

"Before we end this call, Dani's texting a picture of a piece of paper Prachank or whoever broke into the SUV left. Whether on purpose or accidentally, we're not sure."

"You think it was intentional? As in the reason for the break-in?" Riker asked.

"Possibly." Dani swiped at the screen and forwarded the text. "Eliana, can you reverse trace the number?"

"Absolutely," she answered.

"That's the ATF headquarters office!" Skyler blurted.

Dani and Walsh exchanged a confused look.

"You're certain?" Walsh asked.

"Yes!" Skyler said.

"Why would Prachank leave that?" Graham asked.

"Dig into it," Walsh ordered.

"We're on it!" Chance assured him.

They disconnected, and Walsh faced Dani. "Where do we go from here?"

"This will tell us everything." She used a latex glove, lifting the casing to study it. "It's different. I've not seen this before."

"The whole investigation feels that way."

They drove in silence for several miles.

"We're covered."

"For now," Dani said. "But at some point, I have to face the fact that Jayne might not make it out of this alive or free from prison."

Surprised by her admission, Walsh listened, not daring to speak.

"Am I delusional to be Tessa's guardian?" The whisper resembled a rhetorical question.

Walsh was unsure whether to answer. At her probing look, he took the cue. "You're capable of doing anything you set your mind to."

Their gazes held for several seconds. "Thank you," she said, giving his arm a gentle squeeze.

Walsh didn't move, though her touch sent electric shocks through him. The image of the two of them caring for Tessa as a family flashed before him.

And it scared him speechless.

Chapter Fourteen

Dani's knee ached from the fall she'd taken at Lost Lake the day before, but she wouldn't complain. Eager to check on Tessa, she hurried into the HFTF building, Knox at her side.

"Where's the fire?" Walsh teased.

"Sorry." She held the door open for him.

Refreshed from a full night of exhausted sleep at the condo, she couldn't wait to hold Tessa.

They stopped to see the baby first, greeted with smiles from Troopers Ulrich and Nguyen.

"Hello sweet girl!" Dani pulled Tessa close.

"She's so much fun," Trooper Nguyen said.

"Thank you both. I'd like to take her upstairs for a little while," Dani said.

"We'll give you both a short break." Walsh smiled.

"Roger that," Ulrich replied with a yawn. "She was up early this morning."

Walsh and Dani hurried to the Rock. The

team hadn't arrived yet. Dani dropped into the closest chair, surprised when Walsh sat beside her and reached for Tessa. "May I?"

Dani hesitantly passed the infant to him.

Tessa seemed tiny in his massive arms. He gently patted her back, laughing as she poked at his short hair.

"This is the first I've seen you interact with Tessa," Dani said.

He made funny sounds, eliciting the child's laughter. "Couldn't tell you she's my kryptonite."

Dani blinked. "You like kids?" She'd assumed the opposite.

"Of course. Once dreamed of having a huge family." He glanced at her over Tessa's head. "Losing that hope left me hesitant to connect with any child. But after talking with my bossy sister," he paused with a grin, "I realized keeping a distance is ridiculous."

"I had you all wrong."

"Hopefully, that's a good thing," he said.

Dani smiled. "It is." Even though the glimpse into his heart added to her growing attraction, his comment reactivated her self-protection shield. Walsh had wanted a family, something they wouldn't have in common. Mark had claimed he didn't want children. Then he'd divorced Dani, married another woman, and fathered several kids. Just like her father had done to her mother. She shoved away the unpleasant thoughts.

"Those days are gone with retirement knocking," Walsh interrupted.

"What's the mandatory age for the marshals?"

"Fifty-seven. I've got four years left." He snorted. "They'll take my badge and my identity. In my mind, I'm still twenty-five. Although my body claims a much older version of me." He laughed and made another silly face at Tessa.

"I'm right behind you with no idea what to do when I'm not employed anymore."

"Me either. Sometimes that scares me more than the danger I've faced." Walsh's heartfelt confession touched Dani.

The team arrived, interrupting their discussion. Once they'd assembled around the table, Walsh called the meeting to order. "We need a lead to move forward. The attacks don't coincide with one kidnapper."

Chance added, "If Prachank has Aiden, who bombed the cave in Decorah?"

"Someone had access to the missing cache of munitions, and he's used some of them on us," Walsh noted. "Additionally, he's kept up with our locations, and that concerns me." He faced Eliana.

She took the cue, jumping into the discussion. "Dani's department-issued cell was most likely how the bomber traced you."

"No way. It's gotta be Walsh's?" Dani said, cringing inwardly at her defensiveness.

"His is a possibility," Eliana conceded. "However, we encrypt our devices. For safety reasons, it's best we move you both to burner phones."

"I don't know…" Dani argued. Having her phone taken away was like having an appendage removed. She needed it to do her job at GIPD, and it was also her link to Jayne. She hated being reliant on a device, but she didn't want to surrender it.

"Not a problem," Walsh said, sliding his cell across the table to Eliana.

Dani considered the request. "Can't we deactivate the GPS tracking or something?"

"Negative," Eliana said. "The alternative is to keep it powered off unless you're actively using it. However, as soon as you turn it on, the signal will ping the closest cell tower. If that's how the bomber is tracing you, you've provided him a map to your location."

Dani withdrew her phone and glanced down.

"What about transferring calls from my line to the new burner?"

"I can do that." Eliana frowned. "It's still a risk."

"I'd prefer that for now. The hospital has this number and if Jayne's condition changes, I don't want there to be a delay in getting ahold of me. I also have responsibilities at Grand Island and can't be unavailable should someone need to reach me."

"Understandable." Eliana nodded. "I'll get to work on that right away."

"I have updates from my ATF contact," Skyler said. The team gave her their full attention. "They've analyzed the material collected from the explosion in Decorah, and the casing you provided yesterday from Ledges State Park. They confirmed the munitions used at the ice cave were military grade."

"The same ones from the missing cache?" Dani asked.

"Yes," Skyler said. "And get this, the casing from Ledges is from a scoped rifle. Here's the kicker. The gun is a special design, unique to one gunsmith in Winterset, Iowa."

"Outstanding work!" Walsh commended. "Sounds like we're making a trip to Winterset?"

"Actually, I've got the gunsmith's contact information if you'd rather call him," Eliana said.

"Yes, please." Walsh chuckled.

Skyler smirked. "You won't believe this. Floyd Arming."

Dani grinned. "Is that a real name?"

"Yep. Mr. Arming makes guns," Skyler replied.

Eliana quickly patched the number through the conference call system. The line rang three times before a man answered.

"Good morning. May I speak with Floyd Arming?" Walsh asked.

"You already are," Floyd replied.

"Sir, this is deputy US marshal, Commander Beckham Walsh, with the Heartland Fugitive Task Force. I'm calling regarding a scoped rifle you constructed. I'd like to send you a picture, if that's okay?"

"Absolutely. This is my cell phone."

Walsh gave Eliana a jerk of his chin, and within seconds, her message pinged.

"Got it," Floyd said. "Yep, that was a special order."

Walsh's gaze traveled around the room, meeting the team's surprised expressions. "How many did you make?"

"Just that one."

"Do you remember the buyer?" Walsh asked.

"Gimme a second to pull up my records," Floyd said. "I never forget a face, but names don't stick as well in my mind."

While they waited, Walsh whispered to Eliana, "Have Prachank's picture ready."

She nodded.

Floyd returned. "Yep, John Smith."

Walsh groaned. "I don't suppose you asked for his identification."

"Marshal, I always ask for ID. I run a reputable business."

Dani flicked a glance at Walsh and gave a slight shake of her head.

"My apologies," Walsh blurted. "With such a common name, I wonder if you'd recognize him if we sent a photo?"

"Never forget a face," Floyd replied.

Walsh nodded at Eliana, and she texted the picture.

"Hmm, nope. That's not the guy," Floyd said.

Dani gaped. If not Prachank, then…

"May I show you another possibility?" Walsh asked then mouthed *Aiden* to Eliana. A second ping.

"Yep, that's him," Floyd confirmed.

Dani met Walsh's gaze. A small measure of satisfaction welling inside her.

"Sir, you've been very helpful," Walsh said. "Thank you."

"Happy to help. You want the contact information he gave me?" Floyd asked.

"That would be great." Walsh jotted down the data Floyd provided. He thanked the gunsmith again, and they disconnected. "Looks like Aiden DeLuca has an address in Council Bluffs, Iowa."

"That answers part of the mystery," Graham said.

Dani noticed how he didn't mention Jayne, but she bit her lip from commenting. Instead, she said, "Stands to reason that Aiden DeLuca played everyone. Weapons contractor turned arms dealer under the assumed name John Smith?"

"He had the connections and understood the law well enough to stay below the radar," Riker said.

"Hold on. The gun Aiden ordered and purchased doesn't prove who shot it. His kidnapper might've stolen it. Aiden's still missing." Walsh tapped the paper with Aiden's secondary address. "Unless we find him there." He rose and walked to the evidence board. "Any other leads? Other than the thief using his stash to try and kill me and Dani?"

The group shook their heads.

"Talk to Aiden's associates," Walsh suggested.

"We spoke with Omaha PD," Tiandra reported. "Everyone's complimentary of him."

"But they also said they've lost touch with him over the years. He wasn't a golfer, had no hobbies, and didn't have many friends," Graham added.

"On the other hand, if Aiden's a victim caught up in this mess, he's in danger," Walsh inserted. "When we didn't produce the weapons to his kidnapper, he might've grown desperate."

"You mean we might've got Aiden Deluca killed," Dani concluded.

"Dani and I will drive to Aiden's address in Council Bluffs," Walsh said. "If he's there, that'll tell us a lot."

"Yes." She offered an affirming nod. "Perfect. He won't expect us."

"Another thing," Skyler said. "The number you found is the ATF main line."

"If Aiden was the shooter at Ledges State

Park, why would he have the ATF's contact info on him?" Graham inquired.

"I think he's busy making connections," Elijah added.

"Keep digging, people. We'll be in touch." Walsh got to his feet and Dani joined him, leashing Knox. They dropped off Tessa with the troopers before heading out of the building.

Once they were on the road, Walsh said, "Talk it out."

"What?"

"Your tumbling thoughts."

She sighed. "Aiden influenced and took advantage of Jayne. It's clear he's a liar and a manipulator."

"That's possible."

They bounced ideas around until they arrived at the address: a mobile home park. Walsh parked the SUV several homes from John Smith's—aka Aiden DeLuca's—unit. They exited the vehicle, and with Knox leashed, approached.

"Is Knox trained in apprehension?" Walsh asked.

Dani cringed. "We tried multiple disciplines as part of his repertoire. As you've witnessed, Knox is more about the comfort than the attack."

Walsh chuckled. "Aiden doesn't know that." He winked.

"Roger that. We'll take the back door."

They flanked the single-wide trailer, Dani and Knox moved to the rear entrance. Walsh approached the front door and knocked.

Aiden answered, wearing shorts and a button-up shirt, surprise written on his face. He'd aged since Walsh had last seen him. More silver streaked the man's dark wavy hair, but Walsh had no doubt it was Aiden.

"Been a long time!" Walsh said.

The man blinked.

"Aiden DeLuca, right? From Omaha PD?" Walsh kept his tone light.

Aiden cleared his throat. "Yes." He glanced around, taking a small step backward, posture stiffening slightly.

"Not sure if you remember me. We only met twice."

Aiden paused for several seconds, then placed a hand over his mouth as though in thought before saying, "You're familiar, but I don't recall your name."

Walsh could tell Aiden was lying based on his telltale body language.

"Beckham Walsh." Walsh aimed for a casual

lean on the metal porch railing. "Mind if I talk with you? I'm hoping you can help me with a case I'm working."

Another long pause. "Uh, sure. Come on in." Aiden stepped aside.

"Chief, we're clear," Walsh called out.

Dani and Knox rounded the house and walked to the steps, joining Walsh and Aiden. The man visibly swallowed again, offering a wary glance at Knox.

They entered the dated dwelling, decorated with lawn chairs leaning against the wall and a box television. Aiden gestured to the only proper furniture, a run-down recliner.

"We're fine here," Dani said, taking her position beside the door. Walsh moved toward the kitchen area, blocking the only other exit.

Aiden nodded. "So, what do you need my help with?"

"Heard you're doing weapons destruction for several agencies now..." Walsh began.

That seemed to calm Aiden, and he dropped onto the recliner. "Yeah. Would you like a bid for your department?"

"Actually..." Walsh stood feet shoulder-width apart, hands on his hips, drawing attention to his duty weapon. "Chief Fontaine and I are working on a case of missing munitions from the Grand Island PD."

Aiden remained silent, probably waiting on what they already had on him.

"You knew the evidence technician, Jayne Bardot?" Dani asked.

"Yes, I did." Aiden looked down. "We were involved."

"I'm curious why you're here under an assumed name," Walsh asked.

Aiden exhaled a breath, an indicator he was ready to confess. "Look, I know I messed up, but the thing is, they're trying to kill me."

"Who is?" Dani clarified.

"Jayne and Prachank."

Dani's posture stiffened, revealing her rising defenses. "Jayne is working with Prachank?"

"As in Enrique Prachank?" Walsh added.

Aiden nodded emphatically. "Yes. They cooked up this plan to steal the weapons and resell them on the black market. Jayne pretended to care for me, then threatened my life if I didn't give them the munitions in my possession for destruction."

"How did she threaten you?" Disbelief etched Dani's expression and was clearly discernible in her tone.

"With a gun and intimidation," Aiden said. "As I explained, we were in a relationship. Initially, I was oblivious that Jayne was using me to get to the firearms. If it hadn't been for Tessa, I would've turned her in to the authorities, but I didn't want to see little Tessa become an orphan because of her mother's bad choices."

Dani glared at Aiden but said nothing more.

"Is she okay?" Aiden met Walsh's gaze. His eyebrows creased in concern.

"Jayne?" Walsh responded.

"Tessa. That poor sweet baby. I adore her."

If Jayne and DeLuca were in a relationship, wouldn't she have told Dani? Though Walsh wanted to ask, he refrained. A twinge of doubt lingered. If Aiden was telling the truth, it explained Jayne's deception.

"I'd love to see Tessa. I've been worried sick since learning about Jayne's injuries," Aiden continued.

That got Walsh's attention. "Where did you hear that?"

Aiden frowned. "You've been in law enforcement long enough. Officers talk. It's an active grapevine. I have a solid reputation in the community, even after my forced retirement." A bitterness hung in Aiden's words.

Walsh couldn't dispute the comment. Cops talked, and it wasn't as if the shooting was a secret. Aiden seemed sincere. Walsh noticed the way Dani had cringed at Aiden's asking about Tessa.

"So, you're hiding out here because you fear for your life?" Walsh clarified.

"I should've gone to the police, but after Jayne was shot, I got scared. Prachank's coming for me. Once word gets out about the missing munitions I was supposed to destroy, that will cost me my job. I need your help!" Aiden straightened in the recliner. "And I'll do whatever you want for the investigation. Just please get those weapons back before I lose everything. Criminals stole my career from me with this stupid permanent disability. I've had to rebuild my life once. I cannot face doing that again." Aiden's eyes shimmered.

"Why did you use an assumed name to purchase a gun from Floyd Arming?" Walsh asked, determined to take Aiden off guard.

The man's head shot up so fast, Walsh wondered if he'd get whiplash. "You know about the rifle?" Something in his demeanor spoke of deceit.

They had him cornered. What would he confess?

"Yes." Dani stepped closer. "Now's a good time to tell us the truth."

"I didn't want it traced back to me."

"You understand using fake identification to purchase a firearm is punishable under the law?" Dani asked.

"It was a gift for Jayne."

Dani used one hand to rub her eyebrow. The guy couldn't possibly be serious. "Why would you buy Jayne a gun under an assumed name?"

"Because I love her, and she asked me to. She didn't want it traced to either of us. I used some of my contacts, called in favors…" He shrugged, letting his voice trail off.

Walsh flicked a glance at her. It was plausible but, based on her frown and the contempt covering her expression, Dani wasn't buying it.

"Why wouldn't Jayne tell anyone about your relationship?" Dani asked.

Aiden appeared hurt. "Maybe she was ashamed of me? Especially since I'm not a cop anymore. Thanks to a forced early *retirement*—" he spat the word as though it burned his tongue

"—for medical issues I sustained working a case." He looked down, intertwining his hands. "Can't blame her."

Pity filled Walsh for the guy. More than one officer had talked to him about the hardship of losing their identity after handing over the badge. Wasn't that his own fear?

"Seriously, though, is Tessa okay?" Aiden's gaze bounced between them.

"Yes, she's in protective custody," Walsh replied.

Aiden nodded. "That's good."

"I'll have to charge you with providing false statements to acquire a firearm, at a minimum," Walsh advised. "That gun was also used in the commission of a crime, namely, to shoot at police officers."

Aiden gaped. "No! Was anyone hurt?"

"That's irrelevant," Dani snapped.

"I'm guilty of buying the weapon for Jayne, but I gave it to her. I did it under duress and coercion."

"You'll have to work that out with your defense attorney," Walsh informed him.

Aiden hung his head. "I understand. Are you arresting me?"

Walsh and Dani exchanged looks. "Yes."

Unable to take Aiden in his patrol unit, Walsh

lifted his phone and called the local authorities.
Once they'd assured him they were on the way,
he addressed Aiden, "You'll be charged and de-
tained at the Council Bluff PD."

Chapter Fifteen

Walsh focused on the road and inhaled deeply while Dani ranted about Aiden. She needed time, space and freedom to vent, but like a bulldog with a fresh bone, she wasn't letting it go.

"He's lying!" Dani exclaimed in the SUV as they drove back to Omaha. "Aiden is a dirtbag criminal! He's got every reason in the world to pin all of this on Jayne. Especially since she's unable to defend herself against his allegations." She harrumphed and crossed her arms.

Walsh counted to three before saying, "We have no evidence to refute what he told us. His account has credence." He maintained external calmness. Inwardly, he stifled annoyance at Dani's infuriatingly stubborn belief about Jayne's innocence.

If anything, Walsh was more inclined to believe Aiden. He'd seen more than one person travel that slippery slope in the name of love.

What would it take for Dani to see that her friend was involved in all of this?

They entered the Omaha city limits without further discussion. By the time he turned onto Harney Street, entering the Old Market neighborhood, Dani's posture had softened. He activated his turn signal and prepared to pull into the headquarters' underground parking garage.

"Let's update the task force and—" An explosion cut off Walsh.

As though someone pressed the slow-motion button, a dust cloud swirled from the upper floors of the HFTF building.

The resounding boom lingered.

Concrete debris landed on Walsh's vehicle, coinciding with the volatile thud.

The SUV rocked, and smoke emitted from the hot engine.

Walsh blinked, trying to focus against the mess and to process the unbelievable devastation before his eyes. He turned to face Dani.

She sat, mouth agape, staring at the building. "Tessa!"

Walsh wasted no time grabbing his phone and reporting the incident. "Send fire and rescue now!" he hollered, not waiting for the 9-1-1 dispatcher to respond, and tossed the cell into his shirt pocket.

He shifted into Park, and then processed the SUV wasn't going anywhere. Thrusting open his door, Walsh jumped out, leaving the impaled vehicle in the center of the road. Dani exited on her side and leashed Knox.

They rushed toward the building and entered the foyer.

Dust and smoke assailed them, making breathing difficult.

Fire alarms blared and the overhead sprinklers sprayed water to extinguish a blaze that didn't exist.

"There's a north and south stairwell," Walsh announced. The troopers were on the second floor, and the Rock was located on the fourth. They couldn't be in two places at once.

"Check on the team. I need to find Tessa! I'll take the north." Dani spun on her heel and sprinted for the door.

Walsh hurried up the south stairwell, taking three steps at a time. When he reached the fourth level, he shoved open the doors and entered the Rock. Smoke billowed, blurring his vision and laboring his breathing. He covered his mouth using the neck of his undershirt.

"Team!" Walsh hollered at the top of his lungs, unable to see his hand in front of his face.

"Here!" Eliana called. She limped toward him, supported by Riker with Ammo at their side.

When they reached Walsh, he saw the dark stain that marred her right cheek. Black dust stained her pale blue blouse. His heart lurched. "Are you okay?"

"Yes. I'm fine. Ammo alerted. We didn't—" Eliana's voice trailed off and tears filled her eyes.

"Get out of here," Walsh ordered Riker, then paused. "Where is everyone else?"

Eliana turned to look at the space. "I'm not sure. We were all working in the office. Tiandra and—" Just as she spoke their names, Tiandra, K-9s Bosco and Destiny, and Chance, hurried up to them.

"Are you injured?" Walsh's inquiry came out more as a bark than a question.

"No," Chance said. "The wall collapsed beside us."

"Skyler and the Kenyon twins left a while ago to deal with Aiden," Tiandra reported.

"Get out of here." Walsh repeated the order. "Use the south stairwell. I'm heading to the second floor to check on Dani and the troopers."

He rushed down the steps with his teammates trailing behind and bolted through the stairwell door. He sprinted along the hallway, checking all the rooms. "Dani!"

No response. Had they already evacuated the building?

Fallen drywall had crushed Tessa's playpen.

Walsh sprinted forward, crying out for the baby and terrified of what he'd find. He skidded to a halt in front of it and glanced down.

Empty except for debris.

Walsh sent up a prayer of gratitude and exhaled relief.

He continued through the hallway, searching the gradually worsening destruction. Crushed walls and concave sections of the floor consumed the area. He stepped carefully around the holes where the first level was visible below.

Fire devoured a section of the east side, filling the atmosphere with more smoke.

Grateful to find no one injured, and confused at where they'd gone, he completed clearing the floor and hurried down the stairwell to the foyer.

He bolted outside, colliding with an entering firefighter. "Sorry, man. We cleared the second and fourth levels," Walsh instructed.

He nodded behind his SCBA mask and several more responders joined him, moving into the building.

Walsh sprinted to find Dani and his team members. They'd assembled outside at a safe distance. All stared at the burning, destroyed structure. Relieved to see Dani was okay, but sickened that she wasn't holding Tessa, Walsh sped up his approach.

"Walsh!" Anguish hung in Dani's voice as she rushed to him, arms outstretched. "She's gone! Someone kidnapped Tessa!"

"Where are Nguyen and Ulrich?" Walsh asked, trying to process what Dani had just told him.

"I found them unconscious in the hallway!" She pointed to the building. "We have to get them out."

"There's no one left," Walsh replied, confused. How had he missed the men?

Against the protests of the firefighters, Dani, Tiandra, and Walsh hurried back inside and up to the second level.

Dani gestured to the empty space. "They were right here!"

"I cleared the floor and never saw them," Walsh attested.

"Walsh! We found them," Tiandra shouted.

Walsh and Dani ran to meet Tiandra in the stairwell door. They followed her outside, spotting the two troopers sitting on the sidewalk beside Walsh's SUV. Both held their heads in their hands.

"They came down the south stairwell and rounded the building," Tiandra explained. "Ya'll must've missed each other in the chaos."

Nguyen covered his mouth. "What seemed like a smoke bomb exploded and then everything went black," he was relating to Riker between hacking coughs. "The bomber must've laced it with some kind of chemical agent to knock us out."

"Where is Tessa?" Walsh demanded.

Ulrich blinked. "We couldn't find her when we came to. We thought you had her!"

Walsh withdrew his cell phone and ordered an Amber Alert for Tessa. Dani sank to the sidewalk, her head in her hands, and melted into inconsolable sobs.

Walsh stared, unable to reassure her or to fix the problem. He struggled with the worst case of helplessness he'd ever known.

Tiandra rushed to Dani's side to offer support. Riker spoke to him, but Walsh's ears were ring-

ing and his mind whirled. He couldn't comprehend anything the man was saying. He looked
at the building, baffled that someone had kid-
napped baby Tessa and nearly killed his team
while destroying their headquarters.

Questions plagued Walsh. How had the
bomber gotten inside? Security cameras and
electronic doors requiring badge entry secured
the building.

Rescue personnel covered the area, rushing in
and out, and working to extinguish the flames.

Walsh shifted into command mode, putting
aside his fears and worries for Tessa. He approached the fire chief on scene and provided an
account of the events. Once he'd established the
necessity for them to contact him immediately
should anything change, he turned to Dani.

"Team, we'll relocate to the condo as our
temporary headquarters." Walsh glanced at
Dani, and she nodded. "Our entire focus is on
finding Tessa."

The HFTF members assembled in the living room of the condo. They created a base of
operations with the remnants of their evidence
board and collected documents.

The firefighters had cleared the scene, confirming multiple ignition devices had destroyed the HFTF headquarters. The source was still under investigation. Though she was a newcomer to the group, Dani felt the pain at seeing their devastation. She couldn't imagine how it affected the incredible team that had worked so hard to establish their space.

Her heart refused to linger on those thoughts when Tessa remained missing. Even with the Amber Alert, the chances of them finding the infant declined with every passing minute.

Dani clutched a stuffed raccoon Eliana had bought for the baby and paced beside the dining room table. Thankfully, Eliana and Riker had salvaged Eliana's laptop before leaving the office. It hadn't been damaged, unlike the rest of the reports and documents destroyed in the explosion. Still, Dani was grateful no lives were lost.

Skyler and the Kenyon twins arrived, bringing food and supplies, while the team ran through the latest updates, catching them up on the situation.

"Where do we start?" Dani paced a path in the space.

"Based on what you and Walsh learned about Aiden DeLuca, do we believe Prachank is responsible for our headquarters bombing?" Riker asked.

"Aiden was in custody," Walsh said.

"Negative," Skyler said. "He bonded out before we got there."

"How's that possible?" Walsh's voice thundered.

"Dunno, but Council Bluffs PD released him," Graham said.

Convinced Aiden was involved, Dani blurted, "He had a connection at the PD." She didn't say it, but the implication was that the brotherhood had protected him. She'd seen it happen before when she'd worked for the Cortez PD. Part of the reason Chief Varmose had gotten away with his crimes for so long. "He's responsible for this."

"How?" Walsh barked. "There's no way they'd just let Aiden go."

Dani met his eyes, challenging him. "I disagree, and we can't exclude the possibility."

"That's ridiculous," Walsh snapped. "Your focus on Aiden is unreasonable."

"Excuse me?" Dani lifted her chin in defiance. "He bought the gun, using a fake ID, and stole weapons that were supposed to be destroyed."

"And he implicated Jayne in all of that as well," Walsh reminded her. "The man couldn't have gotten out of custody, rushed to the Rock ahead of us, blown up the building, and kid-napped Tessa. He's no supervillain."

"The bomb provided the distraction so he could kidnap her!" Dani retorted.

Aware the group was witnessing the exchange, Dani inhaled.

"No argument there," Eliana said softly. "I'm pulling our camera footage to see if there are any leads."

Dani and Walsh held each other in a silent standoff. The team quieted and worked the case in hushed tones.

"I need air." Walsh exited the condo, shutting the door a little harder than necessary.

Dani stared after him, then sheepishly faced the group. Did they think she was ridiculous? Her gaze flicked to Riker. He'd already voiced his opinion. Did the others feel the same way?

"Excuse me." Dani hurried to the bathroom, needing privacy to deal with the flood of emotions threatening to overtake her.

She closed the door and slid down the wall, cradling her head in her hands. Desperation and fear assailed her from every side. "Lord, I can't fix this, and I don't know where to look or who to blame. Please protect Tessa and somehow help us find her." She didn't try to stop the flood of tears. Her throat hurt from stifling the sobs so the others wouldn't hear her.

A rapping interrupted Dani's breakdown and she got to her feet. "Be right out." She washed her face and opened the door.

Walsh stood on the other side. A part of Dani wanted to slam the door, while the other sought to launch herself into his arms, seeking comfort.

He handed her a glass of water. "I thought you might want this."

Dani took the proffered drink. "Thank you." Stalling for time, she sipped at it and stepped out of the bathroom.

Walsh tucked his hands into his pockets, looking more like a teenager than a grown man nearing retirement. "Dani, I—"

She lifted her hand. "We're stressed. Let's just find Tessa."

His expression softened. They returned to the main room, where the team continued working.

"All right, where are we?" Walsh asked.

"We'll have to divide and conquer," Skyler said, taking the lead.

"We've got facial recognition sightings of Prachank all up and down the I-80 corridor," Eliana said.

"Real or staged?" Graham asked.

"Not sure," Eliana said. "Still searching for Aiden DeLuca."

"Then we need to follow up on all of them," Skyler said.

"Graham and I can start tracking those down," Elijah said.

"We've also received another report of evidence unaccounted for from Fremont PD," Eliana reported.

"Tiandra and I will tackle that," Riker said.

Dani remained silent.

"Good. You've got a great handle on this," Walsh commended.

Dani's cell phone rang with an unfamiliar number. She quickly answered, placing the call on speakerphone. Silence hung thick.

"Hello?"

"You will bring me the missing guns, or you'll never see this brat again," a mechanical voice ordered.

Dani's heart froze in her chest. The room spun, and she teetered. Walsh reached out a hand to ground her. Each member shifted closer, the group intently focused on the kidnapper's demand.

"I did that earlier, and you tried to kill me," Dani replied, forcing calmness into her tone.

Walsh waved wildly, trying to get her attention, but Dani ignored him. She would handle this her way and rescue Tessa. Dani refused to avert her gaze from the phone in front of her, as though Tessa's life hung in the balance of her cell's reception.

"You're playing games with me!" the kidnapper snarled.

"No, I'm not," Dani assured him. "I want Tessa back. I'll do whatever you ask."

"You said that before."

"You're right. I'm sorry for not bringing the guns, but I will make sure that you get them this time."

She glanced up, meeting Walsh's wide eyes.

Dani shook her head, reminding him she was bluffing. What other choice did she have?

"Good, I'm glad we're in agreement," the kidnapper said. "And if you come with that stupid mutt or the marshal, I will kill the baby."

Dani cringed at the horrible threat. "Understood. There's no need for that." She hated the quivering in her voice. "I'll bring you the guns. Tell me where."

"Drive to the location I text you and pick up the phone I'll provide for you. You'll get further directions then. Don't try pulling anything funny, or you'll be sorry. I'm watching you." The line disconnected.

"Hello? Hello?" Dani cried.

"Not happening." Walsh pinned her with a stare.

"I don't need your permission," Dani replied.

"What are you doing?"

"I'm getting Tessa. I'll do whatever it takes to make that happen."

"She's right," Tiandra proclaimed. "He has the upper hand. We must play along."

"He said he's watching." Eliana added, "We have no way to identify where he is."

"Correct. But we'll leave as a group and disperse. He can't follow us all," Walsh said.

"We need to distract him and trick him into thinking Dani is one of us and vice versa," Graham said. "A switcheroo. Then we'll have backup in the vehicle with her."

"No." Dani argued, "If he suspects we're trying something fishy, he'll kill Tessa. We can't risk that."

"We're not even sure what munitions he's talking about," Riker said.

"So we'll have to wing it," Elijah replied.

"Right!" Skyler confirmed. "Where's the list of missing weapons?"

Eliana jumped into the discussion. "That's part of the problem. We're finding more are unaccounted for from agencies around the state. There are reports coming in from North Platte, Norfolk, even as far as Scottsbluff."

Dani blinked, processing the information. All at once, the team blurted questions.

"What?"

"How?"

"When did it start?"

Walsh held up a hand to silence them.

"It's like an epidemic," Graham said. "Where do we start?"

"We'll borrow cases and bags from NSP. Make him think we have the munitions." Walsh fixated his glance on Dani. "You do what you've suggested already," he said to Skyler, "disperse and tackle all of them. We need to know exactly what's missing. My guess is that he wants the military stuff most, so let's focus on that for now."

"There was no more found at the ice cave.

Whoever stole them hid the rest somewhere else," Tiandra said.

"What about Dani going alone?" Skyler asked.

"That's not happening," Walsh replied.

Though Dani wanted to argue with him, she was relieved he'd accompany her. Instinct said the kidnapper wouldn't hesitate to kill her.

"Let's go," Walsh ordered. "Eliana, please stay here and continue working on the missing evidence reports and camera footage from the Rock."

"Roger that."

"I'll ride with Riker. We'll drive to the underpass near Fremont, and I'll get in with Dani at that point," Walsh advised. "We have the burner phones."

"Negative. If he has an electronic finder, you'll be made. We won't be able to track you beyond Dani's cell once she's forced to trade it out for the kidnapper's device," Eliana said.

"You want me to go in dark?" Walsh asked.

"You'll have to," Eliana responded.

Great. They were going in without backup or a way to call for help. "No. I'll go alone," Dani said. "You'll just have to trust me."

"It's not on you," Walsh replied.

"No!" Dani fixed her jaw. "I'm getting Tessa back." She grabbed the keys for one of the SUVs and stormed out the door.

Chapter Sixteen

"We're running out of daylight," Walsh said. "You got eyes on Dani?" Knox panted from the passenger seat of Trooper Ulrich's beater sedan.

"Yep, the location is coming through clearly," Eliana replied over speakerphone. "She's headed westbound toward Central City."

It had taken a lot of coercing, but Dani had finally relented to slipping a GPS tracker into her boot for them to trace. Eliana's brilliant suggestion had proved beneficial since Dani had traded her vehicle and cell phone two towns and sixty miles ago, presumably based on the kidnapper's instructions.

Walsh and Knox maintained a healthy distance, following Eliana's verbal directions, grateful for the flat landscape that allowed him to see far into the horizon. Unsure if Dani was alone or had been forced to ride with the criminal, they relied on the transmitting GPS for her location.

"They're still moving eastbound," Eliana advised.

"I'll stay out of sight." No way was he leaving Dani without backup and vulnerable to the criminal's ridiculous demands.

Knox whined.

"I agree, pal." Walsh patted the dog. "Don't worry, we'll catch up to her. I hate not having visual on her."

"You're about a quarter mile behind her," Riker replied.

Keystrokes preceded Eliana's voice. "Go north another mile and turn south. That will allow you to approach from the opposite end of the road."

"Looks like she stopped at an abandoned farm set on the next pivot corner. You'll have to hike in the rest of the way." Eliana referenced the section of land not covered by irrigation pivots.

"There's a wooded area about a half mile on the north side of the fields. The cornstalks will cover you too."

"Excellent." Walsh fought the urge to speed to the location, not wanting to attract attention to himself. He pulled in between the thick foliage as the last rays of sunlight faded into darkness. "I'm signing off. We're in the woods."

He disconnected from the team call and withdrew binoculars from the console.

Knox sat upright, anxious. "Stay here." Walsh pushed open his door and surveyed the surroundings.

True to Eliana's assessment, in the distance, he spotted the caving roof of a dilapidated house. Dani had assured him that Knox understood commands for silent approach, and he prayed the dog cooperated with him.

He shut off his phone, leaving it behind. Eliana had warned if the kidnapper had any electronic detection devices, he'd trace Walsh.

He had to go in dark.

Opening the passenger door, he released Knox and snapped on his vest and leash. They trekked over the uneven ground and ducked into the maturing cornfields. The chest-tall stalks forced Walsh to approach in a crouched position.

Walsh and Knox zigzagged between the thick rows of crops. The field bordered the house's property with its wide dirt driveway.

He spotted an old car, most likely what Dani

had driven based on the kidnapper's orders, parked near a barn. She was nowhere in sight. Fear had his heart triple beating against his rib cage. Where had she gone?

He paused behind the last complete row of corn and offered Knox the hand signal Dani provided for silence. Even the dog's panting had quieted.

No movement or lights anywhere on the property. At the far side stood a large barn. In the distance, he spotted a gardening shed with stacks of wood leaning against it.

Walsh inhaled deeply. With Knox close to him, he exited the safety of the foliage. They advanced in measured steps, keeping within the shadows of the two-story farmhouse. Its crumbling wraparound porch held a rotting bench and the front door stood ajar.

Had she gone inside? Why?

With a last glance over his shoulder, Walsh clung to Knox's leash and lunged into the open area, crossing to the house.

He neared the porch steps.

A whizzing and slight *pfft* rang out behind him.

Knox barked and Walsh turned just as something pierced his back. His fingers went numb, and he dropped the leash. "Find Dani!"

Knox woofed again and bolted through the door.

In a flash, Walsh's knees weakened.

He reached around to his right hip, withdrawing the brightly colored tranquilizer dart. The world spun.

He struggled to maintain consciousness against the thick lure dragging him down. His arms and legs went numb, unwilling to obey his mind's command to run for his life.

From the depths of the darkness, the pitiful, desperate wails of a baby reached him. Tessa!

Then Knox barking.

All of it too far away.

Walsh opened his mouth to speak, but nothing came out. He laid down, arm outstretched, and closed his eyes, surrendering to the chemical.

A piercing headache thrust Walsh awake. He struggled to drag himself from the intoxication still swirling in his system, unsure how long he'd been unconscious. His eyelids were tight, almost glued shut, and he had to work to open them. He squinted, allowing time for his vision to adjust.

Walsh replayed the last few moments, recalling that he'd fallen on the porch steps thanks to a tranquilizer dart.

Dani's empty car.

Knox barking and Tessa's cries.

Suddenly wide awake, Walsh sat up and winced, surveying his surroundings. Only a fragment of light cut through the inky room, revealing the wooden floor. He twisted to see the splintering workbench behind him. Both his wrists were bound tightly behind his back and flexi-cuffs strapped his ankles in front of him.

"Knox," he rasped against the dryness in his throat.

Nothing.

In the distance, the familiar barks reached him. "Knox!" Would the dog hear him? Where was he?

His hip ached where the tranquilizer dart had hit him, leaving the lingering wooziness. "Knox!"

Walsh scooted forward, using both boots planted firmly on the floor. A tiny rectangular window on the opposite side explained the dim light cast across the wooden planks. He scanned for a door. Plastic bags of soil and other tools consumed the room. He surmised he was inside the gardening shed he'd seen earlier.

"Dani! Knox!" Fear and dread warred within Walsh.

The kidnapper had watched in a cat-and-mouse game the entire time. He'd waited for Walsh to emerge, then shot him with the tranquilizer dart. Why not shoot to kill? Because he wasn't the target. Dani was.

Was she alive? Hurt?

Walsh's stomach roiled. Why hadn't he been more careful? Knox had run off, but to where? Was the dog okay?

He'd failed again! Dani was at the mercy of a madman choreographing dangerous games. And when the kidnapper found out the bags and boxes in the car weren't guns, he'd kill her.

If he could do it all over, he'd find a hundred different ways to confess his feelings for Dani. He wouldn't have dodged her. What a coward he'd been! Playing warrior on the other side of the world, yet too afraid to face the woman he'd loved more than half of his life.

"Please God, grant me a second chance." Walsh tugged against his restraints, desperate to escape. He had to help Dani!

Unable to stand, he inched along the shed

floor, searching for a way out. He tried to separate his feet, using body weight to break free. The bindings remained fixed around the base of his ankles, restricting him from even withdrawing his foot from inside the boot.

It occurred to Walsh that he'd not heard Knox barking any more. The silence encroached on him, bringing with it fears of the unknown.

Like his future that sat on that same plain. "Lord, I'm afraid." He'd never confess that. Not during his military deployments or any undercover operation he'd worked in the past.

Lean not unto your own understanding. The words flitted to mind unbidden, providing Walsh the direction he needed. "I've existed in a comfortable place, hiding behind my badge and title. Those things will be stripped away soon. Lord, that scares me. Who am I without them?"

Exhausted, Walsh closed his eyes.

Aiden DeLuca was proof that once Walsh transitioned into a civilian role, he'd eliminate his entire identity and all he'd known for the past three decades. Not that his badge helped him now.

He hadn't guarded Dani or rescued Tessa. His life would end, realizing his worst fears. He'd failed again.

Hopelessness consumed Walsh, and he leaned his head against the hard wooden wall.

Images of Dani played before his eyes. Marissa was right. He'd loved Dani for as long as he could remember.

His ambitions had provided amazing opportunities. The epiphany flashed as bright as a light before him. The accolades and career titles hadn't kept him going. It was the unquenchable need to help others. Hadn't God given Walsh that calling? Then only He could remove it, not some criminal.

No. He wouldn't give up.

Walsh stretched his ankles to the maximum distance, finally hearing the flexi-cuffs snap free. Exhilarated, he scooted against the shed wall. With his hands still bound behind his back, Walsh inched upward until he was standing.

Relieved, he searched for something to cut through the bindings, simultaneously examining the space for the door to escape.

A scream erupted outside, searing his heart. "Dani!"

Knox's familiar bark reached Dani as she climbed the steps of the old farmhouse. She turned, setting the bags with the fake weapons down on the floor.

"Knox?" The Dobie mix rushed to her side.

She dropped beside him, hugging his panting frame. "Where did you come from?" Dani spoke the words aloud for the kidnapper's benefit, fully aware Walsh had followed her.

This wasn't the plan, though.

If the kidnapper saw Knox, he'd assume she'd ignored his rules. Irritation swirled with fear. Had something happened to Walsh? Surely, he wouldn't have released Knox voluntarily.

Her throat constricted.

The criminal's directions had ordered her to ascend the steps to the second floor of the house and leave the bags in the bedroom on the left. In the dark, she scanned the area, wishing she'd grabbed a flashlight before switching vehicles. Another of the ridiculous demands, along with leaving her cell phone.

The cheap burner phone he'd provided was her only method of communication. She prayed the team was still monitoring the GPS tracker in her boot.

Standing alone with Knox, Dani flinched at every creaking board and dangling cobweb.

She'd frozen in fear until the dog had rushed to her side. His presence infused her with courage.

Dani kissed Knox's head. "Thank you," she whispered.

Something was wrong. Walsh wouldn't wait this long. She dared not speak his name aloud, certain the kidnapper was listening in. Knox's powerful nose had brought him to her. But why was he alone?

A chill coursed through her with the sensation of someone watching her.

The kidnapper was here.

Her mouth went bone-dry.

Were there hidden cameras?

The house groaned as if it was tired of standing. Dani reconsidered her position on the steps and paused.

Tessa's desperate wails. She pivoted, searching for where the sound emitted, but the infant's cries echoed inside the cavernous space.

Were they coming from above or below? It was so hard to tell.

"Knox, let's find Tessa," she said, leaving the bags.

Dani gathered his leash, still dragging from his collar, and ascended the last step to the upper level.

The landing extended to the rooms on the opposite sides of the staircase, providing a balcony that looked down to the floor below. In the dim light, Dani struggled to see five feet in front of her. She used the burner phone to illuminate her path, testing the wooden boards before stepping on them.

They reached the first closed door, and she felt for the knob. It offered an ominous groan of protest, though Dani had expected nothing less. She inched it open and glanced inside. Sheet-covered furniture pushed against the wall added to the gothic ambience. Tessa's cries faded, almost muted, confirming the infant wasn't there.

The duo examined the upper floor until they'd exhausted the possibilities. They shifted direction, descending the stairs.

Tessa's wails were inconsistent. They started and stopped as though the kidnapper was trying to console her.

"Keep crying, sweetie," Dani whispered. She needed that audio to trace the baby's location.

With Knox at her side, Dani entered the main hallway. The kitchen stood to the right, and an ajar door to the left, revealing steps to the basement.

Tessa's howls intensified. Louder. More intense. Desperate.

"I'm coming, Tessa," she called.

Dani nudged the basement door open, and the rancid scent of mold and dirt wafted to her.

She aimed the phone flashlight at the concrete steps, but the fading glow wasn't helpful. Dani patted the wall, seeking a light switch, but found nothing.

Tessa's cries erupted from the depths below.

Encouraged, Dani and Knox descended.

They crossed the cement floor, Dani swiping at the cobwebs sticking to her face. "Tessa!"

When they reached the far side of the basement, she spotted a pull string and tugged. A single bulb came to life, illuminating the dank space.

A massive pallet stacked with boxes stood to her right. Dani withdrew her hand from the cord, dragging a sticky mess of spiderwebs at the same time. She flicked them away.

Tessa's cries stopped.

She shivered, scanning the dungeon-like room. "Tessa?"

Silence.

Knox panted beside her.

Again, the baby's ear-piercing wails erupted.

Dani hurried forward, bumping into crates and things.

Tessa's broken whimpers tore at her heart. "I'm coming. Dani's here."

She shoved past her fear, using her desperation to find Tessa, and continued the trek through the dungeon.

Dani pushed aside objects, searching deeper into the mess that threatened to tumble down around her. Mold and mildew assailed her senses. Dampness and adrenaline coursed through her body, making her tremble.

"Where is she?" Dani hollered.

She struggled to comprehend the infant's location amid the surrounding chaos. "Knox, seek!"

She'd never formally trained the K-9 in search and rescue. Asking him to find Tessa wasn't fair, but he was her last hope.

Knox obediently put his nose to the ground, sniffing a path to the opposite corner.

Dani ripped through boxes and trash. As she pulled at the remaining carton, exposing the cold cement floor, the source of the crying became clear. Not the sweet six-month-old infant in need of care, but a speaker wrapped in one of Tessa's blankets.

A lure designed to draw her there.

Dani stared in disbelief at the tiny box before lifting and inspecting the dark screen cover. As the child's incessant wailing continued, Dani's frustration erupted, and she flung the speaker with a scream.

The plastic shattered, silencing Tessa.

"No!" Dani dropped to the floor, Knox immediately at her side. "What have I done?" The only connection she had with the missing baby was gone.

Footsteps echoed above.

Was it Walsh? If she didn't call out, he'd never find her. "Walsh!" Dani hollered, bolting to her feet. She started for the steps. "I'm down here!"

The door above slammed shut.

Dani and Knox sprinted through the rubbish.

Yet the reality settled in before she reached the stairs.

The speaker was a lure to trap her in the basement.

The kidnapper wanted the weapons.

None of this made any sense.

Unless she was the intended target, and he planned to kill her.

Knox whined, always in tune with her emotions.

Rage and fear roiled through her, and Dani used the feelings to fight.

She lunged up the steps, tugging and pounding on the door. "Let us out!" Even as Dani said the words, she felt like a character in a B-rated horror movie. She slammed her hand against the wood, then kicked it for good measure.

Knox barked and growled his agreement.

Silence again.

The walls closed in around Dani.

"What do you want from me?"

Knox settled at her side with a whimper of understanding.

What was happening to them?

The single lightbulb flickered and died, thrusting Dani and Knox into inky darkness.

"God, help us." She reached for Knox, grasping his leash like a lifeline. "We have to find a way out."

They descended into the frigid basement. Dani lifted the cell phone in a last ditch effort at producing light. They stepped cautiously through the trash, seeking any means of escape.

Dani spotted a narrow rectangle of a window.

Hope ignited. Spiderwebs and dust covered the glass. In the days before egress window regulations, the small opening would've been normal. Today, it prevented her from escaping the dungeon. Dead flies peppered the web, testifying to the impossible task of leaving this place.

Dani shivered, forcing down her terror, and assessed the situation. Boxes and bins stacked beneath the sill would help her reach the window, but the minuscule size prohibited her getaway. Knox wouldn't fit through, either.

Dani looked for anything she could use to ram the door above. Junk filled the basement, but she found nothing helpful. Terror cloaked her and, if not for Knox's presence, Dani might've completely lost it.

"Breathe," she reminded herself. "Breathe." Dani pressed her hand over her racing heart. She had to calm down before she hyperventilated.

"Lord, help me!" The prayer was as heartfelt a supplication as she'd ever spoken. She squatted, wrapping her arms around Knox. The dog was all she had to ground her.

She wouldn't cave into fear and let this maniac win at his horrid game. Digging into her criminology training, Dani considered the man's motive.

Had he followed her into the house? He'd wanted to get her away from the vehicle and the task force. If the kidnapper had found the bags filled with Styrofoam and toy guns she'd left on the second floor, he'd locked her in the basement as punishment. She ripped the burner phone from her pocket and glanced down at it. No reception.

No way to call for help.

Panic rose in Dani, and she felt caught between screaming and having a complete breakdown.

"Lord, I can't fix this. I can't take any more!" she shouted at the rafters overhead.

The absurdity of it hit Dani with the force of a hurricane. Was that a threat to God? Would the Almighty throw up His hands and admit, *Okay, okay, you win?*

She froze. "That's how I treat You, isn't it? As though I'm the one in control, and You exist to answer my demands."

Let God be Lord of your life. The comment bounced to mind. It was part of the last Bible study Dani and Jayne had attended together. What did that mean? Weighed down by the circumstances and impossible task of escaping the basement, Dani sunk to the dirty cement floor.

She put her head in her hands. "Lord, people have hurt and disappointed me so many times that I've accepted pain as normal. I protected myself by being alone. Yet here I am. As brokenhearted as I was the day my dad walked out." Knox nudged her hand and Dani hugged him. "Lord, I surrender. I can't save myself. I need You to rescue me from this dungeon and in every way possible."

The plea encompassed her lost and broken dreams, and the ones she'd not allowed herself to hope for.

She swiped away a tear. "But more than that, Lord, I beg You to save Tessa and protect Walsh. I love them both. Please, my life for theirs, if that's what it takes."

Dani rested her head against her knees. An unexplainable peace soothed her aching heart. She loved Walsh. Always had. For the first time, confessing it brought relief.

Knox barked and raced over to the stairs. Dani jumped to her feet and followed.

Her reprieve immediately vanished at the acrid scent of smoke.

The house was on fire!

Chapter Seventeen

Walsh threw himself against the shed door with full force. After two more attempts, the wood splintered and gave way.

He flew through the shed's entry and landed with an oomph, knocking the wind from his lungs. With both wrists still bound behind his back, he couldn't brace for the fall.

Dani's screams reached him.

Walsh got to his feet in an awkward stumble. He inhaled the acrid scent of smoke before he spotted the red and orange flames stretching into the sky.

"Dani!" He bolted away from the outbuilding on wobbly and unstable legs, gaze fixed on the fully engulfed farmhouse. "Dani!"

Loud barking echoed and a black blur rounded the inferno, rushing straight for Walsh.

"Knox!"

Dani jogged with the dog, and Walsh wasted no time closing the distance between them.

"You're alive," he said, uncertain if he was hallucinating.

She smiled. "Here, let me help you." She moved behind him and, within a second, the bindings snapped free. "Learned that trick in hostage training."

Walsh pulled her into his arms. "Thank You, Lord." The heartfelt gratitude emitted easily from his lips.

"I can't find Tessa," Dani said, stepping back, head hung. "He used a speaker to lure then trap me in the basement." She relayed the events leading to their reunion.

Walsh provided a recap of his own experience. "I hoped Knox would get to you before I passed out. How did you escape?"

They staggered away from the inferno.

"Knox." She smiled down at the dog. "He found a coal chute door disguised behind old furniture and we climbed out. He's brilliant." She stopped to hug the Dobie mix.

"But Tessa's gotta be near enough for the speaker to work, right?" Walsh asked.

"No, he probably used a recorder set on a loop

or controlled it remotely with another device." Dani sighed. "It's hopeless."

"Negative, Chief. Nothing is impossible with God."

Knox emitted a low growl, gaining their attention. He stood rigid, staring at the copse of trees where Walsh had parked.

The group sprinted in that direction, and Walsh spotted a figure ducking into the shadows. "We'll never catch him before he escapes."

"We won't, but he will." Dani addressed the K-9, "Knox, hunt!"

The dog took off like a shot, leaving Walsh and Dani trying to catch up. The canine seemed to have ignited an internal turbo boost.

When they neared the man fleeing from Knox, Walsh called, "Stop! Police!"

The man ignored them, attempting to outrun Knox, who was quickly closing in.

He screamed as the Dobie mix launched into the air, tackling him to the ground.

Walsh and Dani finally reached the duo and found the guy flat on his face. Knox's teeth were clamped around his arm.

"Call him off!" the man shouted.

He wore a black long-sleeved shirt and pants,

as well as a balaclava hood that covered his head. But something about his voice was familiar.

"Knox, release!" Dani demanded.

After several seconds and a few more tugs, Knox obeyed. He growled and took two steps back in a stalking stance.

Walsh approached and ripped off the hood, revealing the man's face. "Aiden DeLuca!" Walsh made no effort to hide his amazement.

Aiden cowered on the ground.

"Where is Tessa?" Dani towered over him.

Walsh feared she'd pummel the man. And he might let her.

Aiden raised his hands in surrender. "She's fine. She's fine!"

"Where. Is. She?" Dani stormed.

"She's safe in my car. Over by where Walsh parked," Aiden's voice quivered as he gestured a tentative finger in the direction of the tree line where a dark four-door sedan was partially concealed.

Dani sprinted for the car.

Walsh reached for Aiden. "Try that again, and we won't call Knox off when he gets you," he warned.

"Understood." Aiden nodded vehemently.

"Walk. Slowly." Walsh took his place behind Aiden and they followed Dani.

She ran to them, carrying Tessa.

Walsh exhaled. "Thank You, Lord," he uttered, and the prayer was imbued with more heartfelt gratitude than he'd ever spoken in his life.

"I didn't hurt her," Aiden whined.

"Do not speak," Walsh warned with the minuscule remnants of self-control he could muster.

Dani pinned Aiden with a look that could blast a hole through cement.

Aiden nodded, interpreting the meaning.

Walsh walked to his car and retrieved his cell phone. No service.

"Why doesn't my phone have reception?" he snapped at Aiden.

The man winced. "There's a device in my car that disrupts the signals. Just turn that off."

Dani sprinted to his vehicle and quickly returned with the small handheld gadget. She used the burner phone Aiden had given her to report the incident to 9-1-1 while Walsh notified the team using his cell.

"We've already sent backup," Eliana blurted. "Are you okay?"

"You're picking up my bad habit of skipping the greeting," Walsh teased.

"Sorry, we're worried over here!" Eliana said good-naturedly. "When Dani's tracker didn't move, we called for assistance."

Sirens wailed in the distance, confirming her words.

"We're fine and we have Tessa." Walsh launched into a speedy explanation of all that had happened.

"Outstanding!" Cheers from the team erupted over the line.

Walsh felt lighter than he had in days. "Will advise when we're en route."

"We'll be waiting at the condo," Riker promised. "We're so glad you're okay."

"God is faithful!" Tiandra called out.

Walsh laughed and disconnected before facing Aiden. He shook his head. "I really wanted to give you the benefit of the doubt."

"Why?" Aiden snorted. "Because we were once brothers?"

"Once a blue blood always a blue blood," Walsh contended.

"Right. Until the department retires you," Aiden muttered. "Then you fade to black, and nobody remembers you."

"Is that what happened to you?" Dani asked, joining them.

"Oh sure, at first coworkers, even old commanders, keep in touch. They bring you a few casseroles or desserts when you get home from the hospital." He grunted. "But then you're forgotten. As though you never existed. They go on with their lives, and you find out who your real friends are." Aiden averted his eyes. "And there aren't many."

Walsh's gaze flickered between Dani and Aiden.

Hadn't he been as guilty of forgetting those he worked with once they'd retired? And that's exactly what they would do to him when his day came too.

But he had time to deal with the upcoming change. Aiden's injury had forced him into the unwanted role without allowing him the time for an emotional transition. The department had thrown Aiden into the fire and abandoned him.

"I did my job, and it nearly cost me my life!" Aiden bellowed. "And for what? They handed me a check and took my career!"

"I'm truly sorry," Walsh said.

The softly spoken words seemed to stop Aiden in the middle of his rage. He blinked.

"I'm guilty of everything you said," Walsh replied.

"You didn't work with me," Aiden disputed.

"I'm at fault for doing those things. Got busy and forgot about you."

Aiden looked down. "My life was the badge I wore. When they stole that, I became a nobody."

"I sympathize with you, but it doesn't explain why you did this," Dani said. "Was it all you? Are there others working with you?"

Something flickered across Aiden's face.

"How do you plunge from being a decorated officer to a murderer?" Walsh asked.

"It wasn't supposed to go down like that," Aiden said.

"You tried to kill us both! Multiple times!" Walsh boomed, suddenly angry again at the man's flippant attitude. "That's not a mistake or an accident."

"Figured Jayne confessed everything at the warehouse."

"You shot at us that night?" Dani clarified. "It wasn't Prachank?"

Aiden hesitated, as though trying to decide whether to work that angle. At Walsh's unwavering glare, he replied, "It was me. I meant to hit you, not Jayne."

Dani sucked in a breath and Walsh fisted his hands to keep from punching Aiden.

"I used Prachank's gun to throw you off the trail."

Walsh inhaled, digesting the information. "Wasn't Prachank involved?"

Aiden didn't respond, he continued rambling. "I couldn't find the missing munitions. You put Jayne in protective custody at the hospital. I re-evaluated. I searched her place and found a few smaller pieces."

"Like the explosives you used at the cave?"

"I left the clues for the Decorah ice caves at Jayne's apartment and in her desk to lure you there. Away from your team." Aiden exhaled. "If you'd brought the firearms tonight, I never would've set the house on fire."

As if that was their fault?

"And when your bomb failed?" Walsh asked.

"I'll tell you who set the explosions at your headquarters," Aiden blurted as though Walsh hadn't spoken.

"What about the men who shot at us from the Kawasaki?" Walsh asked.

"What was Jayne's connection with you?" Dani said at the same time.

Aiden hesitated. "That's a lot more complicated. And they're not the only ones involved."

Dani inhaled, rubbing Tessa's back, and prayed before speaking. "You understand you're in deep here, Aiden. If you don't start talking, you will go down for all of it."

Knox shifted to her side, staring down Aiden. The man audibly swallowed. "I really cared for her. At first."

Dani bit her lip to keep from slapping him. He'd used Jayne.

"It's a long story."

"Then speak fast," Walsh growled.

"Jayne didn't have to steal the guns. Everything was working fine, until she ruined it," Aiden said. "I had to recover them. Thought she placed clues to where she'd hidden them."

Jayne's knowledge of Aiden's crimes, coerced or not, crushed Dani. All they had was his questionable word, unless she recovered.

Sirens grew closer, gaining Aiden's attention. "Look, I'll talk. I know how this works. But I need a deal. I'll give up Prachank and the others involved, including my customers that I've sold weapons to," Aiden said. "But first, we deal. The criminals I've worked with will kill me in prison. Not to mention, I was a cop. That's like a double whammy!"

Dani didn't disagree.

"No way. We've got enough with you alone," Walsh said. "And if Jayne doesn't recover, we'll add murder to your charges."

"Wait!" Aiden pleaded. "There's a huge player. If you believe I pulled this all off on my own, you're giving me more credit than I deserve. Trust me, you want the big dog I work for."

At the word *dog*, Knox growled.

Aiden flinched.

"Speak first, then we'll consider bargaining," Dani said.

"Deal first or I'm not saying anything," Aiden challenged.

Police cruisers arrived on scene and the fire trucks pulled onto the farmhouse property.

"You're running out of time before I contact my lawyer," Aiden said, crossing his arms over his chest. "And once I do that, I'm not talking."

"Fine," Walsh said. "I'll request a deal with the DA if you offer the truth."

Aiden's gaze bounced between them.

"Be glad Walsh is a man of his word," Dani said. "I'd have thrown you to the criminals in jail and let them sort it out."

"Keep watch on him." Walsh said, "I'll be right back."

"He won't move, will you?" Dani replied.

"Nope."

Officers exited their vehicles, and Walsh hurried to talk to them, returning within seconds carrying handcuffs.

After reading Aiden his rights, he pulled the man to the side, cuffed him, then called the team. Eliana set things up to video-record the discussion, so they'd have Aiden's confession.

"Okay, go," Walsh ordered.

Aiden started. "I'm working with ATF commander Chuck Lewis. I assumed Jayne had told Chief Fontaine the truth, so I had to eliminate Chief Fontaine before she identified me. When you and Walsh came to my house, I realized you didn't know the details."

"So why the continued attempts?" Dani asked.

"Lewis ordered your deaths and set up the hits on your lives, including the HQ bombing. I didn't tell him the burner phone Jayne and I used to communicate with him was missing. It contained all the evidence of our conversations with Lewis. I figured Jayne hid it with Tessa. Except, I couldn't find it after I kidnapped her."

"That's why you were interested in Tessa's location and well-being?" Dani asked.

"Exactly." Aiden sighed. "The only way to get her stuff was to kidnap Tessa. But, honest, I didn't hurt her. I'd never harm a child."

Dani gaped at him. Was he serious?

"Tell me more about the burner," Walsh pressed.

"That phone will prove I'm telling the truth. Lewis provided us the details regarding which firearms to take and the buyers for each of them. He coordinated everything remotely from Washington, DC. He's got a lot of pull. Jayne and I were boots on the ground. Jayne had the connections with the other evidence technicians, giving her access to the munitions." Aiden shook his head. "Do you understand why I need protective custody? Once you confront Lewis, he'll have me killed. He abandoned Prachank to the authorities! I'll be next."

"Is that why you dropped the phone number?" Dani asked.

Aiden's confused expression conveyed the information was a surprise to him. "What?"

"You left it in the SUV when you broke into it at Ledges."

Aiden cursed. "I'm such an idiot!"

"Is that all you need from him?" Dani asked.

"For now." Walsh led Aiden to the waiting officer. "He's under arrest. I'll be right back."

Walsh returned to Dani and Tessa, still video conferencing.

"This is far beyond anything we imagined," Tiandra said.

"Do you know Chuck Lewis?" Walsh asked Skyler.

"Not personally, but this isn't a shock. Rumors about his corruption have bounced around inner circles for years," she replied. "And the number that you found for the ATF headquarters would give Aiden access to contact Lewis."

"We can't go breaking down doors and demand Lewis confess," Chance arguably noted.

"Aiden's word won't hold much believability without that burner phone," Elijah said.

"He might just be trying to save himself." Graham contended.

"True, Aiden's lied more than once," Tiandra added. "He's got every reason to weave a wild tale."

"But throwing Chuck Lewis under the bus?"

Skyler asked. "That's a massive leap from inventing stories to cover himself."

"Lewis has the ability to orchestrate an operation like this," Riker said. "To take them down, we have to cut the head off this corruption beast."

"So, we look for the burner phone," Dani said.

"I'll accompany the officer transporting Aiden and ensure he's delivered to the marshals," Walsh said. "They'll keep him in protective custody. We'll meet you at the condo."

The team disconnected.

Walsh faced Dani, leaning in to kiss Tessa on the head. The move surprised Dani.

"I thought we were going to die in there," she confessed. "I really need to tell you something."

"Okay." He quirked a brow.

"All the things I once held dear disappeared, and it's hardened my heart." Dani paused, then continued. "Started when my dad abandoned us when I was a kid. You know that part."

Walsh nodded.

"When Aiden trapped me in that awful basement, I realized I've never trusted God to be in control of my life. I didn't want to get hurt again, so I protected myself right into loneliness. I released my fears to God and asked Him to take care of me."

"That's wonderful." Walsh's face softened. "I sort of had an epiphany too. That can wait, this can't." He inhaled and said, "I'm in love with you."

Dani gaped, unsure how to respond. She'd longed to hear those words from Walsh. The courage to tell him that she also cared for him stuck in her throat. Terrified, she held her tongue. Once she spoke her feelings to him, there'd be no going back.

What if she wasn't good enough for him? Caring for Tessa was one thing. Loving a man like Beckham Walsh was another.

Marissa's explanation regarding Walsh's painful past left her hesitant. She couldn't bear the thought of breaking his heart.

After hearing Aiden's confession, Dani realized she'd misjudged Jayne. If she failed to see that deception in a friendship, how did she possess the skills to choose a healthy relationship?

Walsh might be the best person in the world, and he'd more than proved himself trustworthy. But Dani didn't trust her own judgment. If she was wrong, or he changed his mind about her, he'd destroy her heart.

She'd fallen hard for the man, decreasing her defenses and clouding her vision.

The hurt on his face warned that her silence had lasted a moment too long.

"We'd better get going," he said, disrupting the awkwardness. He turned on his heel, and she followed, feeling like she'd just made a huge mistake.

Chapter Eighteen

Sunshine poured through the condo's living room window. Dani cradled Tessa, gleefully consuming her morning bottle. Tiandra and Skyler had provided the overnight protection detail. The rest of the team had arrived before dawn, developing their plan. Only Walsh was absent due to a meeting with the marshal's office regarding Aiden DeLuca.

A mix of emotions washed over Dani. Grateful Walsh wasn't present and disappointed at the same time. She'd grown comfortable with him. Worse, she hated the way they'd left their relationship conversation in limbo.

Get over it. Once they completed this case and arrested Lewis, she and Walsh would return to their worlds, apart from each other. Wasn't that what she wanted? Yet, doubt lingered.

Dani sat Tessa upright and rubbed the infant's back to burp her.

The investigation had uncovered issues regarding the security and handling of evidence in her department's custody. And the first thing she'd rectify was a regular inventory with two-person accountability.

After Jayne recovered, her legal situation and whether she'd face a jail sentence remained an unknown. Dani planned to help with Tessa. Perhaps if Jayne had had that support earlier, she wouldn't have fallen prey to Aiden DeLuca's schemes. Regardless of what the man claimed, and Jayne's obvious mistakes, Dani wouldn't abandon her friend in her time of need.

Her new strategies ensured Dani wouldn't have the opportunity to bemoan the romance that couldn't happen between her and Walsh.

Riker paced a path between the kitchen and dining room. "Aiden's accusations against Lewis have our takedown on a timer."

Dani faced the group. "We must strike hard, fast, and without warning."

"Right," Chance agreed.

"How long will the marshals conceal Aiden's identity and location from Lewis?" Elijah asked.

"Only until we make our move," Skyler answered. "DeLuca's not officially under WITSEC protection." She reached for Tessa.

"Great." Dani passed the infant to her and stood. "Our timetable just accelerated."

"If Lewis learns about Aiden, his nefarious operation comes to a screeching halt," Graham noted. "We've got one shot at charging him. Any weak spots in the case and he'll escape conviction."

"Absolutely." Tiandra tapped the evidence board. "If only Jayne corroborated or refuted Aiden's claims, it would help."

"Jayne's involvement is undisputed. We just don't know to what degree," Dani replied, hating the way the words tasted like betrayal. "We need that burner phone."

Walsh entered, and Dani sucked in a breath. Her pulse quickened, and she averted her eyes.

"Morning. I brought breakfast burritos." Walsh held up the bag, wafting the delicious aroma to her and standing too close.

Dani plastered on a smile. "They smell wonderful."

"You're my hero." Eliana and Graham hurried to distribute the proffered food while Walsh perused the evidence board.

"Good work capturing the information we lost in the explosion." With his back to her, Dani surveyed Walsh's muscular frame and military-neat appearance. The group rallied around him, offering the minimal updates they'd discovered since the night before. Their respect for him impressed Dani. His handsome exterior matched his kind, thoughtful, and compassionate interior. The years hadn't diminished her attraction for him. As though sensing her perusal, Walsh glanced over his shoulder, making eye contact with Dani.

Skyler settled Tessa in her swing and moved to Walsh's side, discussing options.

Had Dani made a mistake ignoring his romantic interest?

Tessa's grunts gained her attention and offered an excuse to leave the room. Hoisting the infant, Dani carried her to the bedroom. She reminded herself that looking at Walsh in any context other than as a coworker was unacceptable.

Yet, her emotions pleaded with her to reexamine her stance.

"Where is your paci?" Dani asked Tessa, spotting the pacifier connected by a clip on her car seat.

Dani retrieved it, detecting a lump in the seat fabric corner. Setting Tessa beside her,

Dani removed the padded cushion, revealing a burner phone.

"Walsh!" She used Tessa's blanket to withdraw it.

He was immediately at her side. "What's wrong?"

"Check this out." Dani passed the device to him.

Walsh inspected the phone, careful not to contaminate the evidence. She leaned closer, smelling his cologne and pretending not to.

Her olfactory senses again had her second-guessing. Everything with Walsh felt right. Could they work through her insecurities together? She lifted Tessa who gripped a section of Dani's long hair and tugged. She chuckled, prying away the infant's steel hold, reminded that Tessa was her priority. With Jayne's condition and legal complications, a romantic distraction was out of the question. "Is it the device Aiden mentioned?"

Walsh frowned. "There are a series of numbers saved in the notes."

"Messages?"

"Only one." He held it up for her to see.

Dani sucked in a breath. "That's the original anonymous text I received at the start of this case!"

"Why would Jayne hide a cell phone with nothing on it?" Walsh asked, heading for the living room. He placed the device into a clear plastic bag, then each member examined it. "Dani found this hidden in Tessa's car seat."

"Is it the burner Aiden used to communicate with Lewis?" Elijah asked.

"There's no call history," Eliana said.

Graham quirked his brow. "What're the series of numbers saved in the notes section?"

"Evidence logs for other weapons?" Tiandra guessed.

Elijah shrugged. "Account numbers for money drops?"

Walsh added the suggestions onto the evidence board. "All good ideas—keep them coming." He paused and hurried to look at the phone again. "Wait." A slow grin spread over his lips.

The group stilled. The clock on the wall ticked away the seconds.

"You're killing us, Walsh," Dani urged.

He winked at her. The simple notion made Dani weak in the knees.

"Type in the first number as a GPS coordinate," Walsh instructed Eliana.

Eliana tapped rapidly on her keyboard. "Yes! Winterset, Iowa, is coming up." She continued searching. "The others aren't working."

"We've got a place to start," Walsh said.

"Is it the location of the missing munitions?" Excitement encompassed Graham's tone.

"Road trip!" Riker stuffed the rest of his burrito into his mouth. "Ready to work, Ammo?" The Dutch shepherd trotted to his side.

"Maybe the other numbers are a ruse?" Skyler asked.

"Riker and Chance, follow Dani and I," Walsh said. "We're not going in without backup."

"Hey." Skyler put her fists on her hips. "That's marshal discrimination," she teased.

"Sorry." Chance laughed, leashing Destiny.

"Take my SUV." Skyler passed Chance her keys.

"Skyler and Tiandra, you work the Fed angle." Walsh leashed Knox. "Uncover Lewis's activities, involvement, and travel schedule."

Dani glanced down at Tessa.

"Leave her with us." Tiandra reached for the baby. "We'll take good care of her."

Dani relinquished hold of the infant. Though she feared leaving her again after what had happened, she trusted God was in control.

The group loaded into two SUVs, driving eastbound on Interstate 80 toward Iowa.

Dani could barely contain her eagerness on the two-hour drive. Always in tune with her, Knox sat perched with his head poking through the divider. Dani stroked his velvety ears, easing her anxiety. When they entered the driveway for the neglected green clapboard house amid a copse of dead trees and ugly yellowed grass, she was practically crawling out of her skin.

"There?" Dani leaned forward.

Walsh parked at a distance from the structure and dialed Riker on speakerphone.

"Yeah, boss."

"Recon before we head in. We'll keep watch outside."

"Roger that." Riker pulled up behind him.

Thin boards braced the weathered awning over the door. The connecting fields reflected abandonment. On the opposite side of the road, acres of soybeans and open pastures flourished.

The two marshals with their K-9s approached the house, returning a few minutes later.

"All clear."

Dani and Walsh holstered their guns and exited the SUV with Knox.

The wind kicked up around them, whistling through the trees. Dirt clouded the scene. "Where'd that come from?" Dani shielded her eyes with her hand.

Riker and Chance investigated the interior of the house. Dani and Knox took one side of the perimeter, Walsh the other, and they met on the backside. Knox strained against his leash, moved to the far end of the property, then backed up and dropped to a sphinx position.

"Walsh. Be still." Dani inched closer. "Knox, seek."

The dog rose and repeated the alert. They investigated, spotting blue barrels hidden within a grove of overgrown lilac bushes. "Good job, Knox!"

He wagged his back end enthusiastically.

"Bombs?" Walsh asked warily. "Riker and Chance!"

The men hurried up to them.

"Knox alerted," Dani said.

"Hold on! Skyler had us bring her SUV because she has something for just such an occasion." Chance ran toward the vehicle, returning with a crowbar and a little robotic gadget in hand. "ATF uses these to check for bombs," he explained, setting the device on the ground.

The group stepped backward while Chance

piloted the robot with a remote control, circling the barrels. A series of long beeps preceded his announcement. "It's not a bomb."

Riker and Walsh used the crowbar to remove the tops of the barrels. "Bingo!" Walsh exclaimed.

Dani scurried closer, spotting the firearms that filled each drum. Chance and Riker documented the discovery while Dani removed the cell phone taped to the inside of the last barrel. "It's dead."

"Knox. Down." Dani gave him the accompanying hand command. Riker and Chance repeated the order for Ammo and Destiny. The dogs dropped to sit, panting softly and waiting for their next assignment.

"I've got a universal charger in the SUV," Walsh said.

They rushed to his vehicle and plugged in the device, bringing it to life. A litany of threatening texts and voicemails from Lewis to Jayne provided the evidence they needed.

"Aiden wanted us to find this, but I bet he didn't realize Jayne had saved this message," Dani said, pointing to Aiden's text dated several months prior.

Tell the authorities, and Tessa pays with her life.

Walsh's eyes narrowed. "He thought he'd put everything on Lewis and get away."

"We've got them!" Dani lunged into his arms, whooping joyfully. They embraced for a few minutes, and she relished the moment. "I wasn't wrong about Jayne."

"No. You weren't." Walsh's breath was warm on her cheek, sending a shiver up her back.

Dani eased herself onto her feet, creating distance. "This proves they forced her participation."

A ringing interrupted them.

"It's the hospital." A lump lodged in her throat. Walsh kept his arm on her shoulders as she answered, "Hello?"

"Chief Fontaine, this is Nancy. Jayne is awake and doing great!"

That afternoon, ATF commander Chuck Lewis looked down his pointed nose at Walsh, Dani, and Skyler. "You'd better have a stellar reason for storming into my office." Haughtiness rolled off the man in waves.

Walsh smiled. They had the evidence to apprehend him. This personal interview was icing on the arresting donut. "I'm sure you're aware that a significant quantity of stored munitions were reported missing from several Nebraska law enforcement agencies."

Lewis steepled his fingers. "Yes, such a disgrace to the chiefs responsible for those departments." He pinned Dani with a glower.

"Great news, though," she replied. "We've recovered them."

A flash of something akin to panic passed over Lewis's face. "Superb."

"Better yet, we traced all of it to a conspiracy within the ATF," Walsh said.

"That's why you're here?" Lewis's attempt at nonchalance flopped. "Write it in a report."

"You'll want to hear this in person," Skyler assured him.

"Jayne Bardot regained consciousness and is recovering," Dani said.

"Aiden DeLuca is in custody, and both will testify against you," Walsh added.

"That's preposterous!" Lewis's eye twitched.

Walsh passed the ATF commander a printed listed of the messages from the condemning phone.

"I have no idea what this is? What am I supposed to do with it?"

"Check out the texts and voicemails," Walsh replied.

The color drained from the man's pale face as he scrolled through the contents. Lewis audibly swallowed.

"We've already linked you to the crimes," Walsh replied. "Your only hope of any leniency is handing over Prachank."

"You're mistaken!" Lewis bellowed. "I'll have your badges for this vile accusation."

Skyler added, "Our technical expert obtained the electronic trail you left."

Lewis pushed away from his desk. "I see." Several silent seconds passed before he said, "I'll give you Prachank, but I want a deal."

"You'd be amazed how fast people talk when they're trying to save themselves," Walsh said. "With or without your help, you're facing a lifetime behind bars."

"Where's Prachank?" Dani pressed.

Lewis exhaled, pausing as though considering his options. He scribbled on a piece of paper. "He's hiding at this address."

Walsh glanced at the information. Prachank was in Omaha, blocks from the decimated HFTF headquarters office. They'd been so close! He bit his lip from saying a word his mother would throttle him for and passed the document to Skyler. She offered a nod, then texted the team, already staging for the takedown.

"You and the AUSA," Walsh said, referring to the assistant United States attorney, "can work out your 'deal.' Although, he's seen the messages."

"Especially those to Jayne, threatening her innocent six-month-old baby if she failed to comply with your nefarious deeds." Dani crossed her arms. "You'll need to do some fast talking."

Lewis gawked and hung his head. At Walsh's signal, the arresting officers entered the room and took Lewis into custody.

Walsh had one more piece of unfinished business to handle.

An hour later, he and Dani stood at the airport gate, waiting for their flight.

"Are you going straight to the hospital when we arrive in Omaha?"

"Yes. Jayne's doing well, and I want to take Tessa to visit her." Dani smiled. "Thank you again for the offer to help her find good legal representation."

"She got caught in something way bigger than her."

"With her confession, maybe the AG will

have mercy regarding the charges," Dani said. "If not, Jayne is prepared to accept full responsibility for her involvement. She was relieved to admit everything about Aiden after living under his constant threats and intimidation."

"I'm still fuming that he lied and threatened Tessa's life if Jayne didn't comply with his orders," Walsh growled.

"Jayne was smart to compile and hide the evidence the whole time," Dani said. "When she realized Aiden had taken the illegal guns, she called me the night she was shot to confess and ask for help."

Walsh squeezed her shoulder. "Are you feeling better about taking on the role of guardian for Tessa?" He quickly added, "Just until she and Jayne are reunited?"

"Yes."

Walsh paused, working up the courage he needed. "I have to tell you something before we board our plane."

"Okay."

"I'm grateful for this case. God used it to teach me a lot about myself." He inhaled a fortifying breath. "I assumed my identity was in the badge I wore, or the title I held. And I was terrified to surrender them."

Dani nodded. "I understand."

"I realized who I really am isn't tied to those things." He exhaled. "I guess that sounds dumb to you."

"Not at all. I'm glad you see the amazing man I've come to know you are." She offered him a side hug.

"Thank you."

"My turn." Dani's eyes shimmered. "You asked me a question I never answered."

Walsh blinked. He had more to say, but his throat went dry.

"I've always been in love with you, but the timing was never right. And after the Varmose investigation, I held my bitterness against you. That was wrong of me."

"No, it wasn't. I failed to be there for you and protect you from the aftermath." Walsh sighed. "I seem to have that MO."

"Come again?"

This was what he'd waited for. He had to let her off the hook. "I don't blame you for not wanting a relationship with a guy who's inept at caring for those in his charge."

"Marriage isn't about one person assuming complete responsibility for another's life and safety. It's about a partnership, helping each other."

Walsh stared at his boots. If only that were true.

Dani touched his arm, and he met her gaze. "You needed love and support too."

He swallowed hard.

"What happened with Gwen was tragic. Mental health issues are complicated. You did the best you could at the time. It wasn't your fault."

At the release, Walsh's chest constricted, and his eyes stung.

"How about if we both lay down our pasts and stop nursing old grudges?" Dani asked. "I think God's big enough to handle those and still give us a bright future. Together."

Had he heard her correctly? "I would love that."

"Remind me to thank Marissa," Dani said.

"For what?"

"She's wise."

Walsh chuckled, his emotions overflowing. "Yes, she is." He pulled Dani close, brushing her lips in an overdue and heart-awakening kiss.

The speaker overhead announced their boarding call, and they reluctantly parted.

Walsh glanced over Dani's head, spotting the group of strangers smiling at them. "I think we're a hit," he whispered.

Dani laughed. "We've waited too long for a lifetime together." She slipped her hand into his. "Let's go home."

Epilogue

Two months later...

HFTF assembled at the Walsh horse ranch with the blueprints for the renovated headquarters building spread out on the table.

"It's going to be better than ever." Eliana grinned.

"We'll have the option to add in necessary additions as the team grows," Walsh said.

"Enough talk about that," Marissa injected. "Celebration time!"

"Agreed. I'm drooling over that cake." Tiandra rolled up the prints while Elijah placed the massive dessert in the center of the table.

"Let's pray and dive into this!" Walsh said.

The team circled and lifted their voices in gratitude for closing the case, for Prachank's arrest and return to prison, and for Jayne's continued healing.

A knock instigated Knox's bark. "Thank you for the warning." Dani laughed, walking to the door.

Captain Bonn and Troopers Ulrich and Nguyen entered.

"Are we late?" Bonn asked.

"Nope, right on time." Skyler waved them in.

As Tiandra and Elijah passed hefty slices of the dark chocolate cake around, Dani said, "The one thing I can't shake is Aiden's claims that the law enforcement community abandoned him after his retirement."

"I need to make more of an effort to keep in contact with the retirees," Walsh said. "Especially since I'll be joining them soon."

"No way." Graham stabbed a hunk of cake. "You'll remain on staff as part of the newly developed HFTF board of directors."

Walsh chuckled. "We'll see." Dani inched closer to him. "You look like you're cooking up an idea."

"Two months of dating, and you already know me too well," she replied.

"I've had thirty years of studying you." He winked, and she leaned in for a kiss.

"Come on, you two, we want to hear the plan," Skyler probed.

They parted, and Dani grinned. "Actually, it's all Marissa's fault."

Marissa flopped onto the seat beside her. "Now that sounds negative. Reword it to say, 'It was Marissa's brilliant idea' instead."

"What? My soft-spoken, keep-to-herself, mind-her-own-business sister offered her opinion?" Walsh teased, earning him a swat from Marissa.

Dani chuckled. "Meadowlark Lane Ranch solidified a secret dream I've been praying about."

Marissa shot Walsh a wink. What did his sister know?

The group quieted, listening.

"Retirement is around the corner for me..." Dani began. Knox strolled to her side and dropped into his sphinx pose at her feet. "Ever feel like your dog can read your mind?" She laughed.

"All the time," Riker and Chance chorused.

"Bosco's aware of what I'll say before I say it," Tiandra joked.

"Exactly. They're amazing," Dani said. "Which brings me to my plan. I'm retiring from GIPD. I'll train comfort dogs like Knox to bridge the gap between retired and injured law enforcement personnel. It would provide them a connection to their blue brothers and sisters. The canines would offer mental and emotional support toward healing."

"I love that idea!" Skyler jumped to her feet.

"We'll help train them as handlers and assist with the canines too," Tiandra added.

"You'd do that?" Dani asked, eyes wide in surprise.

"I want in on this team," Ulrich quipped.

"Get in line," Bonn replied with a grin.

"Of course," Eliana said. "It's what family does."

Dani wiped at the moisture on her face. "You all are amazing."

"Since we expect to hear wedding bells soon, it's a natural progression," Marissa said.

Walsh's cheeks burned with heat.

"What?" Dani whipped around.

"Thanks, sis," Walsh growled playfully.

Marissa shrugged. "Sorry, I'm terrible at keeping great secrets."

"Excuse me." Walsh exited the room and collected the ring he'd bought for Dani.

He returned, feeling the weight of the team's stares. Clearing his throat, Walsh approached Dani. He'd not intended to do this publicly, but his heart, and his sister, nudged him forward.

"It's taken me thirty years to reconnect with the love of my life."

Dani gaped.

"Dani, if you'll take me, I'll spend the rest of our days loving you to the best of my ability."

She swallowed, eyes shimmering with tears.

Had he scared her?

"Give her the ring," Marissa whisper-yelled.

Walsh shot her a good-natured glare and opened the box. "Dani, will you marry me?"

Dani nodded then blurted, "Yes!" She flung her arms around his neck.

The group hollered their approval and the K-9s barked and bounced.

Walsh beamed at the joy of second chances and the incredible gift of family.

Then he captured Dani's promise with a kiss.

★ ★ ★ ★ ★

A NOTE TO ALL READERS

From October releases Mills & Boon will be making some changes to the series formats and pricing.

What will be different about the series books?

In response to recent reader feedback, we are increasing the size of our paperbacks to bigger books with better quality paper, making for a better reading experience.

What will be the new price of Mills & Boon?

Over the past four years we have seen significant increases in the cost of producing our books. As a result, in order to continue to provide customers with a quality reading experience, the price of our books will increase to RRP $10.99 for Modern singles and RRP $19.99 for 2-in-1s from Medical, Intrigue, Romantic Suspense, Historical and Western.

For futher information regarding format changes and pricing, please visit our website millsandboon.com.au.

MILLS & BOON
millsandboon.com.au

Romantic Suspense

Danger. Passion. Drama.

Available Next Month

Colton Undercover Jennifer D. Bokal
Second-Chance Bodyguard Patricia Sargeant

···

Cold Case Kidnapping Kimberly Van Meter
Escape To The Bayou Amber Leigh Williams

···

LOVE INSPIRED

Search And Detect Terri Reed
Sniffing Out Justice Carol J. Post

Larger Print

···

LOVE INSPIRED

Undercover Escape Valerie Hansen
Hunted For The Holidays Deena Alexander

Larger Print

···

LOVE INSPIRED

Witness Protection Ambush Jenna Night
A Lethal Truth Alexis Morgan

Larger Print